THE LENIN PROJECT

by Paul Templeman

*"Remembrance of the past kills all present energy
and deadens all hope for the future."*
- Maxim Gorky

TABLE OF CONTENTS

Prologue

October 1998 - Moscow

DOGS AND GANGSTERS make lousy timekeepers, reflected Grigor Malenkov. He watched the doors of his nightclub for signs of the arrival of Olensky, a hood from Moscow's Solntsevo District. Leaning back against the door to his office he sighed, facing a barrage of noise and light. He was used to it. Tobacco smoke drifted in the air like dry ice, presided over by the ghoulish features of a nightmarish Politburo of the dead and the damned. Above him the busts of Lenin and Felix Dzherzinsky presided with grim disapproval. The air trembled with the boom of the bass and the scream of a guitar. Searchlights danced upon the faces of revellers. A lone girl peeled off her clothing on stage in a pool of white light as, lapping at her feet, men jostled swilling beer and vodka shots, their pallid faces cast in shadows beneath the low lights.

Grigor carved a path through the mass of shuffling dancers and voyeurs towards the bar, meeting little resistance, like a Soviet ice-breaker oblivious to spilled drinks and shattered egos. He was a bear of a man, leaving a trail of cigar smoke in his wake. A porcelain limbed girl stood aside with a fragile smile and murmured a greeting that he didn't hear. He nodded at her, and her eyes sparkled, reaching out a hand that didn't touch him. Her male companion glared.

A gaunt barman in a stained white jacket signalled Grigor with a wiggle of a glass and he nodded, bouldering his way to the front of the crowded bar. It was a busy night at Red Nights, and for that he ought to be grateful. The barman poured a shot then slammed the glass and a bottle of Stolichnaya vodka on the copper counter in front of him. He settled on a bar stool and knocked back the vodka, savouring its icy passage as it slid down his throat. It was just past eleven and Olensky was a half hour late.

A small clearing had formed around Grigor's place at the corner of the bar, and he sat there with bloodshot eyes watching Fyodr work the doors, drawing on a thick Cuban Cohiba. Fyodr was on face control duty: they could afford to be selective about their clientele these days. No riff-raff. They should put a sign on the door, thought Grigor.

He glanced at his watch the instant Olensky appeared at the doors. Twenty-past-eleven, and Fyodr raised both hands in a forlorn shrug, looking across the room at Grigor as Olensky pushed past with a phalanx of heavies packed around him like extras from 'On the Waterfront'. A crowd eddied and thrust behind Fyodr and he turned back to admit two men and block another who remonstrated loudly for effect but left in a hurry. Grigor waited for Olensky and his bodyguard to make their way to the bar, without standing up.

Olensky had a twisted, equine face with a long nose and nascent beard and was half a head smaller than Grigor. He wore a long overcoat. His men were larger and wore short leather jackets that must have been stylish in America at the time of Elvis Presley. Olensky gave a curt nod but said nothing. Tina Turner sang 'Private Dancer' and in another dimension a girl performed a naked cartwheel. Grigor stepped down from his stool making a casual gesture as he led the way through to his office at the rear of the club.

Grigor's office was insulated from the noise of the club, but even so when he closed the heavy oak door the thump of the music was all-pervasive. Olensky seemed about to seat himself behind Grigor's desk but he caught Grigor's warning look and changed his mind. There were deep leather couches around the room and a Soviet era steel filing cabinet that looked as though it had been rescued from a war zone whilst an ochre Afghan rug that really had been, covered the bare boards. On the desk a pile of bills was anchored by an army issue pistol. Grigor sat down and glared at Olensky who remained standing. The other men lowered themselves into couches, looking bored.

'So what do you want, Arkady Ivanovich?' said Grigor at last, addressing Olensky.

'I like what you did to the place,' said Olensky. 'Nice. And you attract a good crowd.' He perched on the side of Grigor's desk. 'Peaceful too,' he added with a pointed note.

'Peacefulness is what I'm paying you for,' said Grigor. From a drawer he extracted a bottle of vodka and a single glass. 'So what do you want?'

'Thirsty work,' said Olensky, looking at the bottle with undisguised longing.

'Your money's good at the bar,' said Grigor pouring himself a shot and nodding at the door.

'You've made something quite special here, Grigor Vassilyich,' pursued Olensky, choosing to ignore the snub. He seemed to be chewing something. An idea, or a wasp, thought Grigor. Olensky stood up and began pacing the room, looking at objects in a proprietary way: He patted a bust of Andropov on the head. 'Looks like nostalgia sells—even Soviet nostalgia.'

'It's worked out so far.'

'I'll be honest with you, Grigor. I'm seriously thinking about taking it off your hands.'

'It's not for sale.'

'Who said I was offering to buy it?'

'It's my place.'

'Lenin said 'The land belongs to those who will till it.' I want to till it.'

'Lenin was full of shit.'

'We can reach an understanding. You can manage it if you want. On a profit share.'

'Get the fuck out of my nightclub,' said Grigor, reaching for the gun on the desk.

Olensky nodded at the gun, 'Does that antique work?'

'You don't want to find out,' said Grigor, pointing the barrel. The men in the couches tensed and leaned but didn't reach for their weapons. Olensky looked unperturbed.

'Our protection fees just went up,' said Olensky heading for the door. 'You'll be hearing from us.'

'It's been nice chatting,' said Grigor.

Chapter One

October 1998, London

SHE TOOK HER seat, felt the carriage lurch and rock, and tried to make up her mind who was following her.

A lesson she had learned from her inner, other life: How to watch without watching. The train ground its teeth and the lights wavered, jumping and jarring so she rocked with the motion. She reassured herself: it didn't happen here. Not in London, and not to her. There was nobody following her. But the paranoia lingered all the same, and the thought of it made her skin prickle.

A shabby, grey jowled man in the seat opposite was staring at her. She crossed her legs and he blinked, coloured, then looked away. When he touched elbows with a woman in a bear-like coat she flashed him a savage glance and he mouthed an apology. Not him. They never apologise; never explain.

The woman opposite pulled her string bag closer to her for security: inside it a copy of Vogue and two tangerines was visible. What they used to call a '*perhaps bag*' in another world. A bag for impromptu bargains. For the queues that were so problematic for her watchers, she had once welcomed them as a way to smoke them out. Her mind drifted.

'What are they selling?' She remembered asking a woman at the end of one such queue that stretched and shimmied for 100 metres along an ashen faced block of offices then dribbled around the corner. Snowflakes like scraps of tissue floated in the air, and her stalker had faltered, some steps behind.

The woman shrugged. She had mottled, crimson cheeks and a baked-in grimace. 'Who cares? Must be something good. A queue this long. You're last in line, you know?'

'Yes.'

Her stalker had been wearing a shiny black coat that fitted around him like the wings of a cockroach. He seemed to be debating something with himself. A moment later he walked up and joined the line. Soles slapped against the crystallised pavement for warmth:

shoes, not boots, she noticed, like he had a car parked nearby. She wished him a good day, which he acknowledged with a nod. His jaw was rigid, eyes front, looking past her. 'You're following me,' she said to the side of his head. He fixed her for an instant, then looked into the middle distance, saying nothing. 'I'd like to ask you: Is it for my protection?' she said. 'Or something else? It would be nice to know… that I'm *safe*.'

'You're mistaken, Comrade.' he said, 'Nobody's following you.'

But they were. They had been her constant companions. You were meant not to notice: to pretend at least that you didn't notice. It was their game. They made themselves instantly forgettable with the clothes they wore; their blank expressions. She used to pick them out in the streets and in the supermarkets. Never quite pursuing but accompanying. Not following but rejoining. Reappearing as faces in a shop window or at a table in a cafe. The same faces, over and over. Was she mad to think like this, even now? People at the Club where she worked thought so. They talked about her behind her back. Maybe, in truth, she *was* a bit odd. Different. They called her crazy - and not in a nice way.

So, was she safe? It didn't make much sense, but she imagined herself older in her memories than today: more capable than now and familiar with the routine. Safer perhaps for that reason. She breathed in sips and kept watch on the passengers out of the corner of an eye. A bespectacled type, pinstriped and buttoned-up, sloped from a grab handle: respectable on the surface – but aren't they all? At the Club, for instance? *I know you look at me when you think I can't see you.* Tugging at the hem of her skirt, she willed herself to return his stare and when he looked away she felt a quiver of triumph.

The train emerged into London Bridge, brakes squealing, carriages banging. A gaussian blur smeared the line of travellers at the platform's edge. She sought something in the carriage that seemed always just out of sight: a gesture; a look. Evidence.

In the reflection of her window, bulked up against the cold, they boarded and alighted limp-limbed, briefcases, handbags. A chill swept in. She shuddered, half closed her eyes, absenting herself, abandoning all hope.

But there was no escape, because all at once there he was, distilled in the reflection in the window. A sullen-faced man in a corner seat who sank into the upturned collar of his overcoat. A glance that she was meant not to notice.

She caught sight of her reflection. Did she look crazy? Paranoid?

There was no mistake this time: he was looking at her.

They assessed each other in turn without pretence, he with a secret glint she felt sure was meant just for her. There was a message for her in his look. A message she didn't want to acknowledge.

He was over fifty. Plump, which was unusual—but she guessed he had once been lean because he had sunken eyes like a reptile. Close-cropped dark hair, receding. And when he glanced at an expensive watch that seemed out of place she observed that he moved with economy, wary of attention. A trait they all shared, she was sure. Almost sure, at least. Those memories were at once flawed and conflicted. She looked again and he didn't shift his gaze. An inflated feeling in her chest made her realise she had been holding her breath. She exhaled. Her whole life she had fought what her mother had christened her 'misrememberings'. They were imagined. False. And yet, they seemed no different to her recollections of just a moment ago. An hour ago. They were her shadow memories and they lied.

The doors slid shut with a rubbery bump and her neighbour's shoulder nudged against her as the train pulled away. Pale light allowed a glimpse of the sooty cables in the tunnel. Grim, swaying passengers, hooded eyes in the glass. Surveillance on all sides, but mostly in his eyes. She was scared.

How to leave the train without him following? He had positioned himself in a seat by the door, and she watched him move with the rhythm of the train, staring at the floor. But she was careless. He looked up and held her gaze for an instant too long. Long enough for her to be doubly sure. Pulse racing. Nowhere to hide. Like on stage at the Club. Gawky. Trapped in the spotlight. On stage she had trained herself to look away. At the lights; the ceiling. So she read the advertisements: 'Yellow Pages. Let Your Fingers Do the Walking'. A picture of a girl with a broken smile pointing to an open directory. And: 'Become What You Want to Be. London South Bank University.' But every time her eyes strayed from the ads, there he was lying in wait, and he smiled. A crocodile smile that stirred an uneasy recognition.

But surely *they* didn't smile. They never smiled. Maybe it was her imagination? *Get real*, she scolded. Nothing to be afraid of. Not here. Not anywhere. She clenched her fists until her nails left indents in her palms. She had lived with this for so long: anticipating the moment when her false memories would blend with the real; when the containment of her other past would fracture. She made an effort to return to her magazine, but her mind was blurred with dark and light and traces of words she half read and instantly forgot. *'Become What You Want to Be.'* Urged the advertisement. Out of the train she would be safe. Out of sight. She grasped the handle of her sports bag. '*Let your fingers do the walking.*'

Next station was Borough: Not her stop, but close enough. She stood, pushed her way through winter-coats, stepped with care on her high heels around briefcases and bags. Muttered apologies. Then the train jerked to a halt, doors juddered, and she had to steady herself with a hand on the door as she stepped down. It wasn't too much out of her way: A twenty-minute walk to her apartment.

But as she stepped off the train with a heavy breath, hurried along the platform, she imagined she caught a glimpse of the man over her shoulder, a hulking silhouette of all her fears.

She stopped, searched around for the 'Exit' signs, then walked with purpose, urging herself not to look back, heels tapping on the concrete. A draught tangled her hair, flapped the tails of her coat. Like a child she held her breath against the sour air as the approaching train pummelled out of the tunnel. Quickening her pace she turned off the platform, listening hard for his footsteps. A sign defaced with graffiti said the lifts were broken. She didn't look back, walked faster, heading for the stairs behind a man with a stainless steel briefcase and the acrid smell of cigars. Only once, she couldn't stop herself from looking – and there he was. Angular. Purposeful. Long strides. Tipping his head back as if about to shout something, but if he did his words were swallowed by the noise of the train.

Mutterings and footfalls echoed in the stairwell. She clanged up the steps almost tripping. Somewhere in the distance she heard an accordion braying half familiar chords. She always knew they would find her one day. Whoever they were. Pungent smell of sweat from the man above made her want to retch. His heels were splintered and worn, the expensive briefcase a facade. He was slow and she couldn't pass him. Almost collided with his back when she reached the top. He paused, fumbled, thrust his card into the barrier. Ticket in hand, she reached out. Then a hand restrained her.

He was taller than she had expected. A hint of garlic on his breath. He said:

'Katya?'

A name straight out of her misrememberings. 'No, no.' Trying to shake off his hand. 'I'm not...' But his grip didn't falter.

'It's you, isn't it, Ekaterina Ivanovna? I'd know you from anyone.'

There was something strange about the way he spoke. Something ill-formed. Awkward. Drunk?

'I'm sorry. Bit of a hurry... You've got me mixed up with

somebody. Please…' she panted, trying to find a way around his wide body, avoiding his eyes, but he laughed and side-stepped into her path.

'Still, you understand me pretty well! You speak Russian? Some coincidence, yes?'

She froze. The twisted, sibilant consonants and long vowels of her dreams. Felt herself turned around somehow, his hand taking her other arm.

'Let me see you properly, Katya.' He stopped short. 'But how can you look so young? It's impossible.' When she steeled herself to look at him there was a mystified look in his eyes. Not a complement but something else. 'It's incredible … But look, Katya, you have to believe me—I was overcome when I heard. Overcome with worry. I didn't sleep at night. When they said you'd been taken. Imagine how surprised … and now here you are! Just exactly like before. *Exactly* like before. *Younger* even, if it's possible!'

She felt her mouth open but no sound came. She stumbled. Recovered, righted her heel and cast around for assistance. A ticket collector regarded them with casual interest. She should call him over. Enquire about something. Envelop herself in his reality. 'I.. I don't know what you mean.' But she had betrayed herself already.

'There's no need to be frightened. Not of me—of all people. It's

Dmitry. *Old* Dmitry. You don't recognise me? But of course you don't. I'm fat and bald.' He passed a fleshy hand over his head. 'And old. Whereas you.. How did you?' He trailed off and looked at her. And she felt like she was emerging from underwater. Dmitry Yevdokimov. A name buoyant with recollections from a past she had never lived. Some kind of doctor… flash of a white coat. She thought she remembered other things too: a grim-faced eighth-floor apartment, plumbing that banged and grunted in the night. She said:

'You can't be him.' It was the first time the other, parallel memories had left the tracks, crossed the line into what she had been taught was reality. Could she be dreaming after all? She was peculiar. Crazy. Everybody said so. Bordering on what? Schizophrenia? Was that what she had?

Dmitry's laugh bounced off the tiles. The ticket barriers buzzed and clicked as commuters ticked past, jostling for position in their winter bulk. 'So what? I'm mistaken?' He leaned into her and she flinched when their eyes met. Long lashes, like those of a child. Like those she now recalled as Dmitry's eyelashes. 'What did they do to you Katya? I always wondered. But of course there was the child too. The birth I mean. All that pain. How you must have felt. Then when you disappeared I was sure you were done for. We all were sure.' A collective she could not bring herself to contemplate. 'I even thought there might be some repercussions. For me, you see? You know what they were like ... How it was?' He glanced around him as if nursing a paranoia of his own, then made an expansive gesture with his free hand. 'Now - here we are in London. Here *you* are in particular, more lovely than even I remember. Old scores forgotten, yes?'

'I really don't know who you are—what you mean. I'm not who you think |I am,' willing herself to maintain the protest, but she realised she had stopped struggling. He saw it too, and released her, fished inside his jacket. Expensive, well-tailored. Not like in those misremembered days…

'Take this.' He produced a business card and gave it to her. 'I'm at the embassy. You know which one. Give me a call. You *should*, you know. There's a lot to talk about.' He hitched up a sleeve, consulted the wristwatch that had seemed so incongruous before. Blue bezel. 'Shit. I'm late. I must run. But you'll call me, won't you? You *must* call me.' He was leaving already, making parting motions as he backed away. 'I have new masters these days. Maybe you didn't read about it, but we *all* have new masters. Everything's changed. Exciting times. You don't need to hide anymore.'

With a final wave he disappeared down the staircase. 'Call me,

OK?' she heard him shout.

She thumbed the embossed surface of the card. 'Dmitry Andreyevich Yevdokimov. Vice Consul.' When she flipped it over, there were Cyrillic letters on the reverse. As if observing herself in a mirror, she noticed her hand was quivering.

Chapter Two

THE PRIVATELY AIRED consensus in the smarter cafés of the eclectic, imperial-inspired vicinity of Kitai Gorod in Moscow was that General Borilynko was a kingmaker without a prince. Soviet, old Russian, but he could be a New Russian if you wanted, plying his influence with intelligentsia and bureaucrats alike - red or white affiliations made little difference to him. Certainly corrupt some believed, but then who in his position could resist the incentives that must have passed his way? Of course this private consensus was known to Borilyenko, and even the whispered dissent that travelled on careless tongues through the corridors of the Kremlin, for the eyes and ears of the *Bureau,* the security services, were everywhere and they were his organs.

'To the Soviet Union!' The General lifted his glass once more to a dozen sombre-faced veterans of lengthy campaigns of war and of peace and drank a contrived toast to lost empires and a revolution staged by fathers they could scarcely recall.

A meeting of the Feliks Group had passed with nothing new, and little of substance debated. Geriatric revolutionaries, he thought—himself included. His deputy, Major Kvitsinsky the exception in a roomful of old men.

They stood around a magnificent, burnished table thinly effaced with the scratches of generations of resolutions, and scattered with the debris of notebooks, pens and water jugs.

'Comrades, tomorrow is the anniversary of the Great October Socialist Revolution. We've finished our business. Let's take some time to remember the heroes of those days. A toast.' General Borilyenko raised his glass in a challenge to each of them in turn, and watched them drink. 'It didn't turn out the way most of us expected. The way our ancestors planned. But they lived in different times. Now it seems the wolves are already sniffing around the new man.' Yeltsin still the new man to Borilyenko, even after five years as President. 'The President is a sick man, and the wolves are scenting blood.'

Gavrilenko said, 'Aren't we the wolves? The silent opposition? Shouldn't we leverage one of our own? Otherwise, what's the point of us? I'm sick and tired of this talking shop.' A petulant man in a sharply cut black suit, prickles of sweat on his forehead, Gavrilenko was of a certain generation that prefaced any nostalgic reflection with: 'In Soviet times…' A deputy of the Russian parliament, the Duma. He wore a party pin in his lapel like a badge of honour, but it seemed more like a badge of antiquity these days - like a 'sell-by' label. Borilyenko thought he found something glamorous about belonging to some kind of underground movement. A frustrated revolutionary. Across the room, Vrublevsky leant his fists on the table and said:

'Just what kind of candidate should we put forward, Comrade Gavrilenko? What kind of *silent* candidate for the silent opposition, if there can be such a thing?' General Vrublevsky wore his officer's tunic unbuttoned, famously refused to wear medal ribbons or decorations. A grizzly war hero with a demeanour that seethed with rage in any circumstance. 'A silent opposition is no opposition at all,' he grumbled.

A lieutenant-colonel with yellow nicotine-stained eyebrows said: 'There's a man I heard of in Uglich owns four of only 18 water utility contracts in the country.'

Somebody said: 'So what?'

'So how did he get them? I ask myself. Some kind of minor

procurement bureaucrat. That's what he was. What does he know about water?'

' What are you trying to say, Colonel?'

'They say he's worth a billion dollars. Has his own helicopter. I don't know much about that. But it's that kind of thing. That kind of thing the Feliks Group should be opposing.'

Ignoring the Colonel, Borilyenko said: 'Maybe you're right, Comrade Gavrilenko. What's the point of the Feliks Group nowadays? What are we doing here? Why don't we have that debate?'

'Many times we've had that debate.' The weary-eyed Justice Minister passed a hand through his silver hair and and settled in his seat. He flicked at a glass, and it left a wet trail on the veneer as it slid in the direction of a half empty vodka bottle. Kvitinsky moved to top up the glass. 'You invited me to be a part of this group so the justice we dispense can carry a measure of legitimacy. And I still believe. I still believe *somebody* needs to make a stand against the corruption we see everywhere. People think we make summary assassinations. Compare us to terrorists. It's even in Pravda. But we know it's not like that. We consider the facts. The risks to our country. Even the risks to the current administration. We make public a few sordid revelations in the guise of 'research documents' from our fictitious intelligence officer. Ivan Ivanov. A public service. That's what we're providing. So we kill a few gangsters. Justice, as I see it. Setting off some fireworks to show we mean business.'

Gavrilenko said: 'So what are we, then? Revolutionaries or policemen? Was Feliks Dzherzhinsky a revolutionary or a policeman when he founded the secret police?'

'There's no place for revolutionaries in modern Russia.' Grumbled Vrublevsky. 'What are we? A group of the party faithful, clinging to the coat-tails of Lenin and hoping for another chance of power? I don't think so.'

'I suppose this was always my project.' Said Borilyenko. 'The Feliks Group. Not much more than an extension of my official duty as head of the President's security, when you come to think of it. Except our mandate is the security of the State, not the President. Especially not the President. What we're opposed to above all is the erosion of order. The criminality. The high levels corruption. The kind of thing we see every day. The kind of thing this Government condones.'

'Guardians of the State.' Said Gavrilenko, and Borilyenko couldn't make up his mind whether he was being ironic. He looked at him with suspicion. Gavrilenko dabbed his forehead with a handkerchief, looked at the Minister for Justice for support but received only a stare.

'If that's what you want to call it. But I want us to be clear: There must be no more bombs in apartment buildings. The Minister for Justice is right - in the press the Feliks Group has been compared to terrorists. Mafia. We don't want that.'

'If he's so sick, the President,' said Gavrilenko, 'why not put him out of his misery? You're in the perfect position. We've talked about removing the Prime-minister before. Why not the President? I'm speaking amongst friends, or so I hope.'

'Now is not the right time. We need to consider who would fill that void, now that the Communists are strong again in the Duma. Do you see the current leader of the Communist Party leading Russia?'

'I can think of worse leaders than Gennady Andreyevich.'

Vrublevsky said: 'I can't believe we're even having this conversation. There would be a civil war. And Gennady Andreyevich is no Lenin.'

The Minister for Justice said: 'I hope this is not a serious proposition, Comrades? It's not something I would put my name to.'

'Shall we put it to the vote?' said Borilyenko.

Vrublevsky looked around the room. 'I wouldn't want to dignify it with a vote.'

'I agree. Then the meeting is over.' He nodded to Kvitsinsky who was now standing in a corner of the room at the side of an ancient Korvet record turntable that had a distinctive tonearm shaped like a globe. Kvitsinsky lowered the needle and the bars of 'Hymn to the Soviet Union' began. Cracked and tuneless voices took up the refrain:

'Sing to the Motherland, home of the free,

Bulwark of peoples in brotherhood strong.

O Party of Lenin, the strength of the people,

To Communism's triumph lead us on!'

The General watched the faces.

'Be true to the people, thus Stalin has reared us

Inspire us to labour and valorous deed..'

The old version, of course, before Stalin's name had been expunged by the liberals. He felt invigorated as he sang, lifting his chin and recalling the stature of the man he had once met. A powerful man. Fearless. And - 'The Boss' - not that he, Borilyenko, would have presumed. But in those days it's what *they* would have called him. The Politburo. The man who decorated him 45 years ago. Was it so long? He sang, and sang well.

After the anthem and the toasts and the grim calls to action. After pledges of allegiance, and more. After all of these things, the men filtered out of the room, with a desultory handshake here and there.

All except Kvitsinsky and the General.

Once the heavy oak door was shut the General poured two large vodkas and slid one across the table to Kvitsinsky. Like the great man would have done, he reflected to himself with satisfaction. Like the Boss. Then he moved to stand at the window, framed between the heavy drapes that, for all he knew, dated from the time of the Tsars. He looked out over Prospekt Marksa. Watched the Mercedes and BMWs cutting through the streets far below. Fewer Russian cars than ever. Volgas - mostly yellow taxis; the ubiquitous Zhigulis. He breathed heavily. Almost to himself he said: 'Do you remember something called Project Simbirsk?'

Kvitsinsky sat at the foot of the table, a reflection of the light from the windows shimmered on the tabletop. He inhaled the mellow odour of beeswax, sawdust and leather. Examined his glass. 'I heard about it. I thought it was just a story.'

The General nodded to himself. 'A story. Is that what they are saying now?' He glanced over his shoulder. 'A story?' The sudden emphasis made Kvitinsky twitch. The General returned to the sparring traffic below. 'It was more than a story, Comrade. Much more. It's been on my mind. Sometimes I ask myself what would have happened if we'd been successful.'

'I didn't hear… I mean I don't know much. ' Kvitsinsky said.

'Of course you don't, Comrade. Project Simbirsk was a state secret. There was a silence. 'But we were successful in some ways. More than anyone would have believed possible. So tell me what you heard. About Simbirsk.'

'Just rumours. That they were trying to… well, to bring Lenin back from the dead.' He looked at the General as if for validation: It sounded ridiculous. Hare brained. But in the Soviet Union everything had been possible, even when it wasn't, and he had learned not to be openly cynical. 'To bring him back to life.'

'Not quite.' The General said without turning round. 'But I'll share a secret with you, Comrade. Simbirsk was real. Not some kind of Frankenstein experiment like it sounds. What we were doing…' He glanced over his shoulder. '…what *they* were doing, I should say. It's no exaggeration to say it would have rivalled the space programme in scientific achievement. Our scientists were the best. The very best.'

'So what happened?'

'Treachery. Sabotage. The usual suspects. Still there might be a way…'

Muffled sirens from the street. The traffic backed up. Some incident out of sight. He sighed.

'We've got to face facts.' said the General. 'We're not revolutionaries any more. Most of us never were. You think Russia needs men like us? Old men plotting implausible conspiracies? You think Russia *wants* another revolution? After '91 and '93. I was there, remember, standing alongside the President on that tank in '93. In spirit, I mean.' He waved a hand then reached for his glass, emptied it. The vodka numbed his throat. 'Look at our flag, and what d'you see?' The scarlet banner of the former Soviet Union still hung in a corner of the room. 'A relic! How many hammers do you see in industry these days? How many sickles in the fields? The sole purpose of our flag is to intimidate the uninitiated. We need to be looking forwards, not backwards at the fields and factories of the past. What good are we? We're as much relics as our symbols. I think Gavrilenko was right to question what the Feliks Group is about.'

'Comrade General?'

The General swept up the bottle and refilled both their glasses.

'I'm sorry, Yevgeny Vassillov,' The sudden use of Kvitsinsky's patronymic made him start. The General saw his surprise. 'Don't worry, I don't place you in the category of a relic. I'm talking about my generation. But it's time, I think, to dispense with the Feliks Group.'

A knock at the door and a uniformed FSB officer took a tentative step inside, wary of the weight of rank and power.

'The President, Comrade General. He'd like you to call him.'

Vrublevsky was leaning in the corridor talking to another Duma deputy. When he saw Borilyenko he fell into step with him, placing a confiding hand on his shoulder. He bowed his head so close that he couldn't help but notice stray hairs on his chin that had escaped the razor.

'Don't be too troubled by what was said in there. In the heat of the moment. We face difficult decisions in the service of our country.' Borilyenko knew all about the burden of difficult decisions, and he was still visited by phantoms from Soviet times, when his only thoughts had been the security of the state.

'What we're doing,' said Vrublevsky, 'is necessary and worthwhile. Some day it's sure to be recognised. If not, we hold our heads high.'

In his office Borilyenko made the call to Yeltsin, who was, it seemed, barely lucid. Nervous about the plans for the parade tomorrow. Much the same each year. He strained to hear the rambling voice at the other end. Threat levels. TV broadcasts. Borilyenko issued platitudes and reassurances. The parade would pass without incident as it had every year.

He laid down the phone and looked up at the black and white photograph on the opposite wall. He and the geriatric president. He was holding Borilyenko's hand and grinning. Yeltsin was so drunk on that occasion he could barely stand. That's why he was gripping his hand so firmly it hurt.

It was ironic that as head of the Presidential Security Service, Borilyenko presided over the security of a government that he privately regarded as illegal, and a president he despised.

Once he ran the 9th department of the KGB, responsible for government security. One of the few senior officials to make the transition to the senior ranks of the new services after the traitor Bakatin under Gorbachev disbanded the KGB. Borilyenko had made all the necessary political allies. Pulled some strings. He made himself the obvious choice to head the new Presidential Security Service, spawned from the old KGB. Promoting himself as a new liberal, he had carefully severed his public links with the Communist Party, and had been quick to forge new alliances in Yeltsin's circle. For the past three years, alongside the head of the FSB, which replaced most of the functions of the old KGB, they had virtually run the country.

To overthrow the government, he first had to infiltrate it, and that was the secret task that he had once set himself.

That was in the days when he had fostered political ambitions of his own. Andropov had risen to power from the ranks of the KGB. Why not him? But he was old now, in his declining years. Older even than Andropov had been, he speculated. He wanted to leave some legacy.

Anyway, he was no longer sure he had the energy for leadership. And the resurgent communists had become a dangerous and suddenly realistic threat as the State began to disintegrate. Russia needed a strong man to take control, like Stalin, white or red. But there were no more Stalins.

So he bred his quiet brand of insurgency through the medium of the Feliks Group, a collection of disenchanted former and current KGB and GRU officers, like a band of brothers, and waited for a leader to attach himself to. A term had been invented for such people: The *siloviki*. The Hard Men. He thought it set the right tone.

The phone rang.

'Yes?'

'There's a call for you, Comrade General. Dmitry Andreyevich Yevdokimov. He said you would know him.'

A tingle of foreboding. A name from a past that he thought had been sealed shut. 'I know him.' He said.

'I'll put him through, shall I?'

Dmitry Andreyevich: a political officer, in the days they'd thought such things necessary. He had worked for the General in the days of Project Simbirsk over 20 years ago. Probably reported on him.

'Hello, Comrade General. It's been a long time. Not since Soviet times… How are you? I read great things.'

'Dmitry Andreyevich. Sounds like they are Westernising you with their pleasantries. My health is fine if that's what you mean. Next thing you'll be asking about the weather. Where are you? What do you want?'

'London. I work at the Embassy. And if you want to know about the weather here it's *Pizdec*. Fucked up.. Always raining. You never have to ask about how it is. Just assume it's *pizdec* raining. But everyone asks here, all the time. Platitudes. The English have a name for such things: 'political correctness.' Dancing around things. Never saying what they mean.'

'I don't want to know about the weather.'

'Of course not, General. I'm phoning because I have interesting news for you. It was difficult to get through to you…'

'Dmitry, I'm a busy man. What do you want?'

'I'm sorry, Comrade General.' And Borilyenko imagined a smirk. 'You remember in the old days we had a scientist who worked at the facility? Comrade Borodina? Pretty girl.'

'Of course.'

'The one that escaped.'

'Disappeared, Comrade, if that's what you mean.'

'Disappeared, yes. That's what I heard. But she must have escaped to the West because I saw her in London yesterday. Difficult to believe, after all this time.'

'Impossible.'

'Pure chance. I saw her on a train.'

'When was this?'

'Yesterday afternoon. Up close she's unmistakable. But here's the thing - young! Like she hasn't aged since the old days. 25 years - they never touched her. Whereas me, whereas I.. All of us.. Regardless - it's beyond question it's her. You know we… well we had some kind of thing. So I knew her better than most.'

Unable to resist the opportunity to censure, The General said. 'We knew about your indiscretions.' He drummed his fingers on the desk, impatient to get the full story. 'You spoke to her?'

'In Russian.'

'In Russian? And she said she was Ekaterina Borodina?'

'Denied it. Said I was mistaken. But I swear it's her!'

'Young you say? Unchanged? She knew who you were?'

'Of course she knew. She recognised me on the train. Tried to get away but I followed her.'

The General thought for a moment. 'You know where you can find her?'

'No. But she promised to call me. I was caught unawares.'

'Some kind of intelligence officer you are. Wait for her to call. You just allow her to walk away…' He felt a tightness in his chest. He worried sometimes about his heart. Placed his palms flat on the table. 'Never mind. Let me know if she gets in touch. As *soon* as she gets in touch. Find out where she lives. Find out everything you can. Thank you for calling me, Comrade. It's very interesting. And we must meet.. When you're next in Moscow. To chat about old times.'

Afterwards he sat in silence tracing the implications. He'd imagined they'd taken care of her. They got as much out of her as they could, but her work had proven almost impossible to replicate. She'd been thorough. Everything destroyed. All those records. Years of research. Could it really be that with the help of some insider she'd managed to get away? He couldn't be everywhere. Hadn't been present when they executed her. Didn't like to be present on those occasions, if he was truthful. He presented his squeamishness to himself as some kind of humanitarian weakness.

Then he poured himself a generous vodka and drank a silent toast to Lenin. A master he wished he could have served. The architect of his youth—a happy time for him.

Chapter Three

OUT OF HABIT she checked off the models and registration numbers of the cars parked along her street. *White Fiat. Broken wing mirror. Ford Sierra. Miniature of Chelsea football kit hanging in the rear window. Red Citroen hugging the kerb, gashed driver's door.* Familiar cars. She didn't know what drove her to do this. Some instinct. *G364 XPP. K960 CNH.* Like a compulsive urge to cover her tracks.

She thought about the man on the train. A Russian: but how would she have known? His language had brushed against her parallel memories. Ignited them. She experimented in her head: A mangy dog that started at her in a shop doorway translated to *sobaka* in Russian. The familiar line of cars along the street became *mashini*. She shuddered. *Po Ruski. Ja govorju po ruski,* I speak Russian, she told herself. And she was uneasy because something wild and tethered inside her had broken free. And it felt like a violation to have this other voice in her head.

She walked unhurriedly, lost in memories of corridors she was sure she had never walked, cement-floored lobbies where she could never have waited for arthritic elevators. A reluctant tourist in a land of the false memories that her parents had warned her to hide away, she tried now to fit herself inside them to put them into context; she wondered why her parents would never talk about her 'misrememberings'. Tried to figure it all out on her own. How she hated that her mind was so cluttered: she craved clarity. Certitude. But it wasn't normal to have these memories. *Nenormalnaya*. She tried to block out the Russian, but the words kept coming, like some kind of Tourettes affliction, shouting in her head.

Her earliest childhood memory was gazing up at a tall brass object with intricate curves. The pinnacle was a spike, and in the middle it stretched dome-like and shining in the light. The distorted reflection of a young child returned her stare: bloated cheeks and impossibly round eyes. She used to like to move and watch the image alter. High above her, an old lady with a very straight back and a slender neck drained liquid from a tap. She felt a great affection for this person, but she had no idea why. The old woman's shoulders were draped in lace, and she wore flowery skirts that brushed the floor when she moved, as though she was gliding across the room. But it was almost *beyond* childhood, she thought. Further back. Like she could reach beyond birth. Sometimes the memories were involuntary. At other times they came to her only with a supreme effort. Memories or dreams? Real or imagined? *Pravda ili lozh?* shouted her new companion in translation.

This event had no place in Kate's real childhood: It was a jigsaw piece from a different box. She was ordinary. Grew up in an ordinary English village with unremarkable parents. Early memories of birthday tea parties and scuffed school shoes that pinched her feet. And yet all of her life she had harboured vivid memories of other places, places she knew she could never have been. Ragged, sooty cities; ranks of ashen apartment blocks pitted with blank windows and beyond them frosted plains that stretched as far as she could dream. Incongruous palaces, more exotic than in fairy tales with gleaming minarets and swathes of pastel colours. As a child, she had supposed that everyone had memories like these. She even wrote about them in English essays.

Her best friend in Junior School was Laura Parker. They used to hide from the other children in the stairwell of a classroom block during break times and tell each other stories. Laura had a parallel life too: but hers was full of castle keeps and rescues and dashing princes. It was a made up world. She wanted so much to be like Kate. Followed her like a puppy dog, and listened to Kate's stories, slack-mouthed rapture, as they sat on the stairs side by side. Between them they invented an acronym for the episodes in these parallel lives: TIKINDs - Things I Know I Never Did.

'I remembered a new TIKIND today.' And Laura would sit on a stair with her knees together and shining eyes.

'Tell me. What happened?'

'Well, the city was gripped by a big snow storm…' she would begin in her narrative voice. 'Everything was twinkling and there were no footprints in the snow. It was smooth like ice cream.'

'Where were you?'

'In the park near our house. We lived in a very big house but lots of families lived there too. That day, Mummy told me not to touch the climbing frame with my nose because of the frost, because it would stick. I don't really know why she thought I would do that. But afterwards I was *drawn* to it. I wanted to put my nose on the frozen climbing frame just to see what it was like. It made me scared.'

'So did you do it?'

'No. But I always think of it when I see a climbing frame.'

'Is that all?'

She shook her head. The story didn't stand up on its own so she embellished it. The problem was that embellishments sometimes got mixed up with the real thing. If it could ever be called the real thing. 'There was a big brown bear. Dead in the snow. The snow was pink around the body. I touched him…'

'You didn't!'

'Yes. And the fur was all matted and rough.'

'Oh Katie, that's horrible! What could it mean?'

'I wish I'd put my nose on the climbing frame. To see what happened.'

She told her father about the climbing frame TIKIND, including the made up part about the bear, and he had laughed and told her what a vivid imagination she had. That it never got that cold in England. But as she grew older he had become frustrated with her stories, and there had grown a side to his moods that was half anger and half touched with anxiety. What could have troubled him so much?

Mr Travers once made her stand in a corner for two entire periods of geography because her essay had been a pack of lies. Mr Ogden (they called him ('Ogden the Ogre') gave her a beating for a flawless maths paper once. She had copied. Cheated! Where did she get the answers? Who was helping her? An emphatic glare at the class. Who dared? Nobody dared. Not for Kate. Her classmates thought she was strange. Always in a world of her own. Which some of the time she was.

It wasn't exactly an aptitude that she had for mathematics. It was more a kind of learned competence - even to the point that she was aware of using techniques that were different to the way they taught her in school. Techniques that seemed to work just as well if not better. After that she got into the habit of making deliberate mistakes so that her coursework accurately reflected everyone's perception of her. She was a grade 'D' student. Anything else was too much heartache.

'So this is your real work then, is it?' said her chemistry teacher once with apparent satisfaction, awarding her a 'D' at the foot of her red-lined exercise. 'At least we know what we're dealing with now, Kate. We have a starting point – something to work with. Well done for effort, Kate, well done.'

It made her feel good. Made her feel proud to have failed so spectacularly, and to be praised. She felt normal. It was good to be normal.

Looking back, she found that so much of her growing up was

pre-empted by fully formed conclusions and recollections. She experienced her first memories of sex when she was only eight, which tainted her transition to adulthood. At eight she recalled the stifling weight of a man who panted with hot uneven breath, and a feeling of damp rimmed constipation. She woke up crying when these visions stole her dreams, but some instinctive shame prevented her from revealing them to her mother. As a teenager she wondered if she had been abused: but by whom? And when?

She had to learn to partition her life, in particular the jumbled, accumulated misrememberings that formed a kind of parallel universe in her mind. But often the fiction became muddled with fact. There were times when she would submerse herself in her other life, so that it became difficult to distinguish between her 'false' memory, as she came to know it, and the stories she had started to invent about it. But her false memory had the same reality as her everyday memory. It was like being able to dip into two separate books and make sense of them.

There was moisture in the air, and the sky was bilious and grey. She felt the icy pinprick of rain on her bare legs as she walked. Her pace lengthened. Passing the familiar blocks of terraced houses now, with soot-stained plaster, dark windows already stippled with rain. She could see at the end of the street the angular, sepia block where she lived. She hated the way it loomed up like a penal block. The very sight of her building awakened in her the smell of boiled cabbage.

Unwanted associations seemed to attach themselves to buildings and everyday things. The smell of chocolate, for example, conveyed to her the image of a view from a bridge across a wide and puddle coloured river. It was a memory she coveted, as though from her earliest childhood – but the actual taste of chocolate always left her unfulfilled.

If she spoke Russian, then what else did she know?

Dance, of course. That was another unexpected skill. Her parents had enrolled her at a drama school with some misguided conception that her imagination could turn out to be an asset. She discovered that she could dance: It wasn't that she was rhythmic. Like the maths it was a technical competence that she had - without teaching. Changements and Échappés that made her dance teacher clap her hands in delight. 'Well done Kate. Wherever did you learn to do that?'

At Livingstone House she mounted the steps two at a time, skipping around the fast-food containers and crushed cigarette packets. The staircase was rank. She passed along an open corridor, feeling the cool of the now teeming rain outside. Past the rows of scratched, identically painted red doors with aluminium letterboxes and safety glass windows.

She saw him at once, slouching in the passage outside her door. A man in Nike trainers with a heavy paunch, chin sparkling with silver stubble. He watched her approach with a dour look. She steeled herself. Felt his eyes assess her. In passing had to turn to face him. He didn't make an effort to move. Stale coffee lingered on his breath.

'Excuse me.'

Without turning back she passed her door - Number 29. She could sense him watching the swing of her haunches as she passed out of the other end of the passage. She couldn't go home now.

Clipping down the rancid steps to the next floor, stumbling, suddenly unsteady on her high heels. *What now?* Another passage, identical to the first. Scratched doors. Heady smell of ozone.

At number 17 she stopped and knocked. The wind carried a flurry of rain into the open passage and she shivered. She wasn't dressed for this weather. A net curtain at the window flipped aside, then came the rattle of a door chain and the door swept open to reveal Manda, diminutive in the dark doorway, looking at her with hard round eyes. She was short and trim and her arms were crossed tightly over her chest. Ginger hair slicked back like a twenties moll. She waited.

'Bailiffs,' Kate said at last. 'There's a bailiff on my doorstep.'

Manda snorted. 'He'll go away. They always do.' She didn't move. Kate wondered if she had a man inside. A punter, maybe. She looked past her into the bare hallway. A rusty bicycle was propped up against the scuffed wall.

'It's Thursday.'

Manda's face softened a little. 'Of course,' she said.

'I can't let my daughter see me like this.'

Manda's stare flicked over her. Tiny skirt. Thick make-up. Black stilettos. 'I'd let you have something of mine,' she said at last. 'But I don't have anything that would fit.' Resentful. She stepped aside. 'I'll see what I can do. Probably gone by now, anyway.'

But when after a too-milky cup of tea they returned to the next floor, Kate peeked around the wall and he was still there, kicking the heels of his trainers against the wall. 'He's there!' She hissed at Manda.

'It's all right.' She grabbed a coat from a hook overloaded with drab garments, and edged out of the front door.

Kate watched Manda head towards the man, jangling a set of keys. She stopped at number twenty-nine. Kate saw only her narrow back. Heard her say, 'You want something?'

The man reached inside his jacket and produced some folded

papers. 'You Kate Buckingham?'

'What if I am?'

'I've got a warrant of execution.'

'What's that?'

'Means I can seize your "goods and chattels"', with audible speech marks around 'goods and chattels.'

'Let me see.'

Kate watched as Manda manoeuvred herself to the man's other side, pretending to read the papers.

'Fuck you.' She said suddenly and snatched the papers, ripping them apart in one deft movement. Stuffing her keys in her bag she strode past him.

The bailiff was scooping up the damp sheets. 'You bitch!' then hurried after her, ''Oy!' When they were out of sight Kate splashed through the puddled walkway to her door and let herself in. *Good old Manda.*

Manda was a whore, but she hadn't always been. They had danced together before at White's. Manda was older though, and her appeal hadn't lasted. Then, when the bookings stopped for good she'd started to accept the odd trick - just to get by. Now she was a full time whore, and still she didn't get by because she was cut-price. Had to be, these days. But Manda was also the only real friend Kate had. Who else would steer the bailiffs away from her door?

Everything in its place in her room. Scatter cushions on the bed in autumnal colours, and a red alarm clock that had stopped months ago: She always woke up when she needed to. On the back of the door a flannel nightgown gown that carried the aroma of fabric softener. At the dressing table, where an array of expensive cosmetics stood in a neat row, she pawed the make-up from her face in the mirror, with cotton wool dipped in cleansing lotion. She thought only of Becki now. Tried not to think about Robert because it always made her feel encumbered. Their marriage had been stillborn, but they had a child. Poor Rebecca. Becki.

She leaned back on the bed and dipped out of her skirt, then hauled on a pair of blue jeans. One day, when she had enough money, she planned to take Becki away. She would pick her up from school and magic her some place where the sun always shined and they could be together all the time. She would feel guilty about Robert for a time, because he was a good father. But the guilt would pass, and she supposed that Robert would forget them both in time.

Major Nikolay Sokolov aligned the transparency and flipped on the light of the overhead projector. It buzzed. Ageing technology. Who in these days of PowerPoint presented using transparencies?

'Here's the latest one.'

Projected onto the grubby wall was a press cutting from Pravda, still the main outlet for the allegations. The other two men tried to hide their discomfort. They hadn't asked to be on this investigation and were assessing the implications. It was hot in the room. The iron radiator ticked and there was a smell of singed clothing in the air.

'The following research report was released by the Feliks Group,' read the slide, *'purportedly attributed to the usual source, one Ivan Ivanov, Intelligence Agent:*

'New information has been uncovered by this officer regarding the activities of the usurper Andrey Polivanov, Foreign Minster in the illegal Yeltsin government. This officer has already made revelations in the past about Polivanov's role in the Moscow narco group, and his shameful involvement in large-scale drug trafficking. It can now be confidently reported that Polivanov holds foreign currency accounts in Luxembourg, Gibraltar, Cyprus and Antilles, housing the substantial gains of his criminal activities. It can also be reported that his interests in several major Russian banks have been used to channel large quantities of illegitimate funds out of Russia. This agent has

uncovered detailed evidence of significant numbers of fraudulent transactions totalling many millions of rubles. The information will be transmitted to the proper authorities for their action.

'Why does there continue to be so little initiative from this government to stamp out corruption and organised crime? Is it because every member of this coterie of thieves has his own interest at heart? As a former General in the KGB Polivanov continues to be permitted to use his influence in the intelligence services and the government to feather his own nest. This officer demands that he be arrested and tried for his misdemeanours.'

Sergeant Dikul read it with dismay. 'You don't think there could be any truth in all this?'

Dikul was a truculent officer with a defiant manner that bordered on insolence. But resources were limited, and he and Chernov, the diminutive Georgian, were the only two officers that could be spared. So he would make the best of it, like he always did. With a sigh he perched himself on the edge of a scratched and splintered desk.

'And what if there is?'

'It wouldn't be the first time. I read Pravda. This Ivan Ivanov character is some kind of folk hero, like Stenka Razin.'

'As I said: That's not this department's concern. Our orders come from the very highest authority..'

'From the accused.' Interrupted Dikul with instantly stifled laughter. 'From Polianov?'

'From the Foreign Minister, yes. We need to identify the people behind the Feliks Group. And put an end to these press releases. And the killings.'

'Which means investigating General Borilyenko?' Said Chernov, the other officer.

'If that's where the investigation takes us.'

'Comrade Major, can I ask you something?' Said Dikul, rising to his feet. He had an enormous belly and the buttons of his shirt stretched like vertical wounds.

'If it's relevant.'

'Did you ask for this assignment?' Sokolov switched on the lights, and the projector image faded to grey. 'Because it seems to me we're between a rock and a hard place. Here we've got Polivanov. Didn't he used to be head of the Fifth Chief Directorate?' He knew he did of course. They all knew. The Fifth Chief Directorate of the KGB once had a special mandate for the persecution of dissidents. 'And here,' continued Dikul without waiting for an answer, 'we've got General Borilyneko. Head of the Presidential Security Service!' He threw his hands in the air. 'Yeltsin's personal bodyguard for fuck's sake who, last time I heard, had political ambitions of his own. This is political warfare. Can't the FSB investigate themselves? They're supposed to handle internal security for Christ's sake. We're SVR. I thought we were supposed to deal with all the exotic foreign intelligence? Or did I miss something. I mean I joined up to go to Paris and London. Not to get a death warrant.'

'Ask for this assignment? I'd have to be crazy. But you know full well the FSB can't be trusted to investigate one of their own.' He looked at Dikul. He could sympathise. He had had the identical reaction. 'And the police… well. I don't need to go there. Somebody's got to do it.' He said. 'And we're the only department I suppose Polianov thinks he can trust. It's been going on for months, these so called press releases, as I'm sure you both know. And it's not only that. You've heard the stories. The Feliks Group has been associated with other things, including murder.'

'Let me tell you what I think.' Said Dikul. 'As Foreign Minister Polianov treats the SVR like his own personal army. He gets pissed off by some story in Pravda and decides to mobilise. To take the war to the enemy camp. Never mind that he's a corrupt little shit. Never mind that he's…'

'Careful.' Said Sokolov.

'Never mind careful. I stopped being careful after the wall came down. Whatever happened to glasnost? They wanted openness, now they complain when it opens up things they don't want anybody looking at.'

'Well I've personally got some sympathy with Feliks.' Said Chernov. 'Seems like they're doing a fine job. The police should be doing what they're doing. Whoever they are. Some of this stuff just needs to be told. And some of those people deserve what they get.' Chernov looked around for support but saw none. 'I just thought I had to say that. Sorry sir.'

'Thanks for that perspective.' Said Sokolov. 'But none of this changes anything.'

'I'm just a simple intelligence officer.' Grumbled Dikul. 'I haven't been paid for two months. But still I was hopeful of one day collecting my pension. When I joined the service I thought I'd do some international travel. Spy on some Americans. Instead this.'

Sokolov nodded. 'I know what you mean.'

Chapter Four

ROBERT OPENED THE front door knowing it was Kate and hating that he couldn't look at her after all this time without a a rush of longing.

'Hey,' she said like she always did, looking diffident and cold in the pale light from the hall. Her eyes were a little crazy, and she glanced around, making connections he tried hard to follow.

'Hey,' he echoed, cursing himself for the clot in his voice. He stood aside and breathed her perfume almost guiltily as she stepped past him. The fragrance of another life.

He saw her fleeting look around the hall, and wondered if she noticed the minor changes he had agonised over and for which he harboured an irrational guilt, for he lived here alone now. It was just a hall. A bit grand. Grandfather clock. Chinese ceramics. Probably bigger than the living room of the wretched place she lived in now. He felt he should apologise for something.

She looked at him and hooked her hair behind an ear. Smiled. Politely – not like before. Smiled like she would at a stranger. Frictionless. He smiled back. How do you make a smile warm? Forgiving? How do you make a smile say what you mean?

Becki's stockinged feet rumbled and thudded down the stairs; she almost fell over the last step.

'Mummy! Mummy!'

Then he watched Kate sweep up their daughter and hug her, brushing cheeks. A flash of jealousy made him flinch.

'I've got a new Barbie doll. *And* a new coat.' Becki said with precision.

'I know. You had those last time.'

'Yes. It's a nice coat. Daddy says it will keep me warm as toast, but I like it because it's red.'

'Did you miss me?'

'Yes. Daddy missed you too.'

Robert swallowed hard and Kate flashed him a look. Accusatory, he thought. 'Did you, daddy?'

'That's not fair. You know I miss you very much.' And he was on the point of telling her she should come home, that he loved her, that he wanted her more than anything in the world, when he was reminded of the hopelessness of their relationship. Of the restless nights he had waited for her until 5 and 6 in the morning, still with a day's work ahead of him. Of the credit card bills that slipped through the door with their deadly payloads. What had she bought? Who had she been with? How could he trust her? She chose to leave. It was because of trust. No one could trust her. Still he would beg her to come home, if only she would. And if only she would give up the dancing.

Kate lowered Becki to the floor, who started back up the stairs at once. 'Shall I show you my new Barbie, mummy?'

'I've seen it sweetie.' Bewildered. Then '...Sorry,' with a forlorn look. She knelt and began the usual nonsense game only mother and daughter shared:

'My telephone began to ring

Who's there?

Elephant.

From where?

Camel's place.

What do you want?'

'CHOCOLATE!' Becky interrupted with a squeal

Robert watched them play. 'What *is* that?'

She shrugged. 'Just something I know. A nonsense story.' She seemed to dip inside herself, seeking something. 'It's called Telephone.' She said. 'For whom?' she continued to Becki.

'For my son!'

'You look wonderful.' He said from a distance. It was something he always said of course. Couldn't help himself. Once she had made him promise that he would tell her she was wonderful every day. These meetings were dogged by ritual. She finger combed her long hair that the wind had tangled, and glanced around for the mirror that had once hung in the hall. Mirrors spooked him these days - reminded him of her. She looked neat and homely in a black leather jacket over a blue cashmere sweater and jeans, as though she had just stepped out to the shops. She looked like she always had when they shared a home together. Not this empty place, but a proper home. A year of bliss, so fulsome it seemed longer to him: It seemed to occupy half his memories.

'Thanks.' She glanced up the stairs with a deep seated unease. 'Where's the mirror?'

'I moved it. I didn't like it there.'

'Oh. How's Becki been?'

'The same. It's just a week since you saw her.'

'I know. But I worry. You know I do.'

'She's safe.'

'Of course she is.'

'I didn't mean..'

'I know.'

Becki appeared again at the top of the stairs gripping a doll with tangled hair. Like her mother's hair. 'I've got my new Barbie.'
Robert led her into the living room where they sometimes made love on the sofa. He bit back the thought of it. 'Can I get you something? Coffee?'

'I thought we'd go straight out. Maybe have Sushi. Maybe some bowling. She likes that.'

'Sure.' They always went out, of course. It was Kate's way, he supposed, of maintaining their separateness. 'Can I come?' but he knew the answer.

'You know what they say?' she said. 'Three's a crowd.' Words felt like they had jagged edges: they didn't fit together easily like they once had. And sometimes they injured. She smiled to let him know she was joking, but he knew she meant it all the same. Even so, he tried to read into it some reticence, some trace of sadness. There was none.

Becki tumbled into the room wearing her mother's grin. She held out the doll with both hands.

'Do you like my new Barbie?'

'It's very nice. But you showed me last time. Do you want to eat sushi?'

'Can I have a drink with it?'

'Of course.'

Robert fished in his pocket. 'Take the car if you want. It's still insured for you, you know.'

'It's ok. We can take the bus can't we?' she addressed Becki.

'I like the bus, don't I Mummy?'

'Yes you do. How about you take me bowling?'

'Yay!'

Becki was hustled into her coat and shoes while Robert watched, feeling superfluous. On the doorstep, kissing Becki goodbye he asked as casually as he could, 'Still dancing?' He had a reflexive urge to kiss Kate too, but he knew it was out of the question and the impulse died stillborn.

She shot him a fierce look that said 'back off'.

'You know I am. What else can I do? It's what I did before I met you.'

He wanted to tell her that he always thought she judged him for being at the night club the night they met. He wanted to tell her that it was just the one time, even if it wasn't true. But these were some of the thoughts that were never aired, and the conversations they may once have sparked turned around and round in his head, until he almost persuaded himself that they had taken place after all.

Then in a noisy exodus they were gone. The two people he loved most in all the world.

Chukovsky, she thought. That's where the nonsense poem came from. She'd been scouring her memories ever since they left the house. A children's writer from a long time ago. A rhyme she'd known all her life and now Becki would know it too. The clack and rumble from the bowling lanes and the strident eighties music diverted her. The screens above the lanes flashed improbable scores - improbable to Kate, who was poorly equipped for bowling with her manicure and her skinny jeans. She helped Becki to manoeuvre a metal ramp into position and set her ball on the rails. Becki pushed at the bright orange ball with two hands, and it drifted towards the pins, bouncing off the cushions, then tumbled gently into the pins, which collapsed. She clapped her hands and jumped up and down.

'Strike mummy. Strike!' She held up both hands to do a high five, and Kate touched against her hot palms, laughing.

'Good girl!' she said.

In the next aisle two fat teenagers with round cheeks were pulling on the straws of giant fizzy drinks in paper cups. Their father performed a pointless jig before letting his ball loose with a straight arm, and cursed as it pitched down the gully. Kate watched a waitress in a tight 'T' shirt and a piercing in her nose bring the family a tray of food, piled high with spindly French fries, and the teenagers descended on it at once, before the care-worn mother had time to find her purse.

'Can we have chips, mummy?'

'Let's wait and have Sushi, shall we? You know it's your favourite, and you need to make room.' She lifted her own bowling ball, and let it roll down the lane, collapsing a handful of pins. She didn't look up at the score. 'Are you looking forward to going to school? It's not long now.' she said, waiting for her ball to return.

'Daddy said I'll have lots of friends to play with at school. And I've got to have a special bag for my books.'

'I'm sure daddy's right.' Becky looked so earnest that she

couldn't help laughing. 'I'm sure you'll make lots and lots of friends,' she said through her smile, and stooped to plant a kiss on her forehead. It was as she straightened up that she caught the edge of a look from another aisle that made her start.

' What's wrong mummy?'

Two men were playing a serious competitive game. The scores were littered with strikes and spares when she looked at the monitor. They were sturdy and had crew cuts like soldiers, and took no pleasure in their game. Maybe she was mistaken. She was used to attracting the attention of men, after all.

'Nothing. Nothing to worry about, sweetie.'

But she had seen that look before. She had seen how they watched her, not in the usual way, but in the way of professional watchers - indirectly through reflections in glass or mirrors, or straight through her as though looking beyond her at something else. When they spoke to each other she strained to hear them, but the background noise was too loud. Meat Loaf bawled and curdled *Anything for Love*. Everything was normal, she told herself, and she hustled Becki to finish the game, which made her feel guilty.

When they left, the two men were still slamming out strikes, and made no sign of interest or recognition as they passed their aisle. Kate felt a little ashamed, but as they passed a glass faced wall she saw one of the men look at her, and the paranoia took hold of her again. 'Let's go, sweetie. Let's grab a taxi.'

As they headed towards the door, a loud bang made Kate catch her breath. She looked this way and that, half crouched without knowing why.

'Mummy you're hurting.'

She looked down and realised she was squeezing Becki's hand tightly.

'It was a balloon Mummy,' said Becki with a pained, mystified expression, and she began to cry.

Samantha padded across the bedroom naked, to fetch the cigarettes from the dresser. She had a thick waist, observed Dmitry with sudden repugnance, sitting up in bed. She lit a cigarette and offered the pack to Dmitry, but he shook his head. He felt her cold body rummage and settle beneath the quilt beside him.

'What's the matter with you tonight, darling?' she said, breathing smoke into the stale air. She had the burr of an English dialect that irritated him. He didn't know where it was from and he didn't much care.

'Nothing. Just ghosts.'

'Ghosts?' She propped herself up on her elbow and took another drag.

'I met someone I haven't seen in a long time.'

'A Russian?' She prickled. He had noticed she seemed to resent anything Russian, like she felt excluded by it. Sometimes it amused him to use Russian that she couldn't understand. He savoured her hurt.

'Somebody I knew in Soviet times.'

'A she?'

'Yes, a she.'

'Who was she?'

'Her name was Ekaterina Ivanovna Borodina. Katya. A scientist - where I used to work.'

'And now? Why's she here?'

'That's what I'd like to know. It wasn't a long conversation.'

'Were you lovers?'

'What does it matter?'

'I see.'

'No. You don't see. It was a very long time ago.' He thought of their chance meeting. Almost to himself he murmured, 'Hard to believe. Just the way I remember her. Exactly the same. I don't know how it's possible…'

'Pretty?'

'Not aged at all.' He registered her question: 'Beautiful.' He said, looking at Samantha with a faint smile. 'Prettier than you'll ever be, Suka'

She recoiled. 'What does that mean? *Suka*?'

'It means bitch.'

'Bastard.' She swung her fist at him but he was too quick for her, and he snatched her wrist. She yelped.

'That hurts!'

He squeezed tighter before releasing her with distaste.

She rubbed her wrist on the quilt and said, 'You don't play fair.' He glanced with satisfaction at the rosy imprints of his fingers on her arm. 'Sometimes I hate you,' she said.

'You can always leave.'

'You'd like that.'

He shrugged.

'What happened?' she said, 'With you and her?'

'She did something stupid. Then she had to leave. We could be unforgiving in those days.'

'Like what? What did she do?'

'It doesn't matter anymore.' And he meant it. It didn't matter to him what she had done. 'All ancient history.'

'What kind of scientist was she?'

'A good one.'

'You never tell me about the old days.'

'No.' He could feel her waiting for him to continue. Finally, he said 'It's because you're too stupid to understand.' It was said with humour, but there was an edge to it. There was always an edge.

She ignored the insult. 'Did you talk to her? Will you see her again?'

'What's it to you? You think you own me because we sleep together?'

She grimaced. Folded her arms over her breasts. Over her *glaza*. He felt a strange and overwhelming urge to speak in his native language. To be with Russians again. Not embassy people. Maybe with Katya. A surge of tedium swept over him. 'It's not even good sex.' He added, meaning it.

Samantha thrust herself out of bed, flinging aside the bedclothes. 'Right! So that's it!' She stabbed out her cigarette on the bedside table. 'Forget it. I never want to see you again.' Now she was plucking items of clothing from the carpet and from the chair. He watched her thick stomach crease as she stooped. 'I've had enough Dmitry. How do you think you make me feel? You think I'm made of stone? Well you've done it this time. It's over.'

'Stop it! Just stop it, OK?' Then, more softly, 'You know I don't mean it. Any of it.' And he cursed himself for being so needy. What did he want with this woman? Where was it leading?

She paused, still naked except for her blouse, which parted in front revealing the shadows of her breasts. 'I never know when you're teasing.' She wavered, caught in the question mark that separated staying from leaving.

'No. You don't.' He felt suddenly aroused. 'Come back to bed, *suka*, so I can fuck with you some more.'

She leapt onto the bed with a laugh and sat astride him, but even then his heart wasn't in it, even as he tugged her hair and fondled her breasts. He was pre-occupied.

He needed to decide what to do for the best. About Katya.

Chapter Five

IN THE WINGS of the stage, Gold squared his shoulders and barely glanced at Peaches as she ducked out of her 'G' string, tipping her chin at the audience. She cast away the last of her clothing, flipped the lacy thong into the audience, then performed a naked pirouette and launched herself onto the pole. She revolved there, hair streaming, then descended upon the stage. The bass beat thrummed and stuttered so you could feel the vibration in the back of your teeth. Kate thought Peaches' breasts were uneven. A bad boob job.

Gold was a West Indian with short, tight dreadlocks and a huge, rugged body. Gold was short for something, she guessed, but nobody ever asked what. He attended to the music and the lights as Peaches thrust her torso, splayed her legs, caressed herself, eyes half-closed.

But no matter how hard she tried it wasn't erotic but formulaic.

Was that even a word 'Formulaic'? Nobody would use words like *formulaic* in her world, so she would have to imagine how it would sound. She needed to imagine how a lot of words sounded, words she never heard spoken. Like the Russian vocabulary that now snagged her thoughts. What about Latin? She knew some - for reasons she couldn't begin to guess - and she didn't know how that ought to sound either. Somebody called out, 'Yay!' and Peaches stepped from the stage. A few men clapped but not many. Some shifted stance, or looked abandoned like people do at the end of a performance, when the lights come on.

Gold ruffled through CD cases, dismissing some with a clatter. A mixed crowd at lunchtime in Whites. Some laddish groups of office workers in suits, necking beer and pretending to be oblivious to the stage, and when they were not oblivious sharing sniggers and grins like schoolboys in class. A few older, jaded types separated themselves from the others during the dances and came closer to the stage. An ever present hard core stared like they always did, perched on stools at the edge of the stage, nursing drinks like stage props.

In her tiny skirt and thigh length boots Kate passed around the jar for tips, watching Gold out of the corner of her eye as he glowered over his CDs. She didn't croon over him like some of the others. Why did they do that? For tricks she expected. Favours. She didn't need favours like that. She danced. That was the deal. No contact. Definitely no sex.

She came up to a man with a sprinkle of dandruff on his dark suit, brushed against his sleeve. He didn't look too bad. Expensive suit. 'Maybe a private dance?' She said in his ear 'What d'you think?' She exercised the smile she used for the punters - the same for them all. But it was wasted: he didn't take his eyes off the stage. He inclined his head.

'For what?' He had to shout to make himself heard above the pulse of Sade's *Lovers Rock.*

'A table dance.' She tugged at his sleeve so that she could reach his ear. 'In private. C'mon.' She gave a dispirited twirl.

He glanced at her with indifference. A prospective purchase: comparing, discarding. 'Not now.' Then his attention went back to the dancer on stage. He had that absent look she saw all the time here.

'Okay. But don't forget. For twenty quid you get me all to yourself.' *But you don't get to touch. You keep your hands to yourself.* She patted his cheek with a disheartened smile and went on collecting tips.

She could clear a week's rent on a good day at Whites. Good

money. And no tax, but sometimes 14-hour shifts. She hunted around the men in the bar. Nobody escaped for free. Not on her watch. And she wouldn't let them get away with silver.

'Is that all you think I'm worth?' She said to a small man with a grey moustache who had flipped a fifty-penny coin into the jar. He dipped into his pocket at once and produced a pound.

'Sorry.' He addressed her breasts in a cracked voice. 'You have beautiful eyes.' But he hadn't seen her eyes, and she didn't offer a private dance. Selective. Staying safe. He gave a beery belch as he dropped the coin into the jar.

'Thank you.' She blew him a kiss, turned, and weaved through the bar looking for signs of affluence. This was the hated part of the job. She didn't mind the dancing, because she was on her own up there. Doing it for her. But down here in the bear pit it was different. *There's one. I bet he's a groper.* She could tell them at once. *Keep your distance or I'll set Gold on you.* Because Gold could handle any of them.

At the end of the bar two girls chattered about the merits of bleaching their hair with lemon juice, sipping alcohol free cocktails in the colours of sunset. One of the girls looked at Kate with an appraising, improbably eye-lined eye.

'I like that. Where's it from?' Reaching out a hand to sample the silk of here dress between her fingers.

'From Sally. Eighty quid.' She said, wondering why she felt the need to monetise - but they all did it. Sally's sideline - a tawdry rail of lycra and lace that she peddled around the clubs and bars.

'Nice.'

'Mm. Quite sexy.' Said the other.

Kate shared a look with Jenny, doing her first spot for more than two months. She was edgy, and when she smiled back it didn't touch her eyes. A petite girl who Kate liked. She put her all into the her dances, but the make-up struggled to hide the crow's feet, and Kate was afraid to mention she'd begun to notice the spread of cellulite on her thighs under glare of the spotlights. Jenny had begun her decline to the bottom of the booking list and Kate had heard she was doing the rounds of some of the seedier places where security was arbitrary, and the rules were few. Soon Jenny might start accepting Gold's tricks. If he ever even offered. which was doubtful. Gold had his favourites.

When she had teased and flirted and cajoled enough to make her arches ache in her stilettos, she joined Gold at the corner of the stage just in time for a scrawny girl with an uneven fake tan to finish her act to a desultory round of applause. The jar was so heavy in Kate's fist that her knuckles were white. Gold bared his teeth in a grin.

'Aw right?' His melodious baritone was the kind of voice you wanted to draw out. You wanted to close your eyes and just listen. She leaned on the console.

'Not bad.'

Gold moved the microphone close to his mouth. He barely needed it at all.

'Let's give Leanne a great big hand. One of our lunchtime favourites at White's!' He winked at Kate. 'Next up in a few minutes we'll be having the very lovely Sapphire do a full striptease for you. So don't go away.' Sapphire was Kate's stage name. All the girls had them - not to add mystique but distance. For her it was like another identity to manage, and she tried to segregate the memories. She watched Leanne haul herself off the stage with her knickers in her hand and wondered about her tan. As she passed Kate she rolled her eyes. A tough crowd.

At the push of a button a projector screen lowered behind the stage. In between acts they had Sky Sports on the big screen. Today it was Rugby League. The punters broke into their groups and some peeled off to the bar and away from the stage. Some of the hard core stayed, nursing their beer glasses.

'Y'know I can still get you tricks if you want?'

'I know you can.'

'Not pervs. *Businessmen*. Know what I'm saying?'

As if there were a difference.

'I don't want to get into that. Slippery slope.'

He sniffed, nodded at the curtained booths. 'Not much different from in there, my opinion. More money too.'

'It's different.' Her stomach tightened. 'They can't touch me in there. Strictly no contact - you know the rules.'

Gold threw his head back with a laugh. 'Depends on the girl, innit? Some of 'em... ' and he nodded towards a Polish girl she half knew, working the tables. Somebody had told Kate she did heroin. '*You* know what they get up to back there. Anyway. Your choice. Just don't say I didn't offer, a'right?' He shrugged his meaty shoulders and changed the subject. 'See your kid yesterday?'

She nodded.

'Bet she's a doll.'

'She is.'

'I got a kid.'

Peaches was collecting now, coursing through the punters in a cheap frilly neglige that she might have bought from Ann Summers.

'You never told me that.'

Gold shrugged. He was watching Peaches with a proprietary air. 'Yeah, well. Don't see him much, do I? Lives over in Lambeth with his mum and some ... loser. Must be five now. Is that school age?' He flashed her a brash grin that she saw through at once...

'Gold?' Kate thought he looked sad, but he didn't meet her eye. 'Yes. Should be at school.'

Gold waved a hand. 'Whatever,' and was distracted by a commotion in the bar. Peaches was yelling at a tall man in a dark blue suit. Kate was about to say something to him but the DJ platform was empty. She turned to watch him cut a swathe through the bar. The man in the suit was a head taller than Gold, but Gold had a firm fist around the back of his neck, and had rammed the man's right arm behind his back. Other men made frantic space. Peaches was spitting. Screaming. He'd probably touched her. Sneaked a hand inside her knickers maybe. She shuddered. It happened all the time. Gold propelled the man, twisting and cursing to the doors. It was almost casual the way he did that. She'd seen him do it a hundred times, calmly, almost without a trace of aggression. One of the other girls was soothing Peaches, an arm around her narrow shoulders, leading her to the end of the bar where the girls eddied and fussed, sharing righteous curses.

Then it was over.

Gold swung himself in front of the record deck, unruffled. 'Fucking pervert,' he said. Then: 'You're up next, Kate.'

In the evening, cornered in a booth with a man in a loose-fitting linen suit that was wrong for the time of year, sipping at a glass of sweet sparkling wine that masqueraded as Champagne, Kate found herself confronted with the usual questions. He put his hand on her knee and she let him leave it there because she liked how he looked. He had a clever mouth and a large mole on his cheek like Al Pacino, and she felt safe. But she wasn't kidding herself: There are no white knights in Whites.

'You mean what's a nice girl like me doing in a place like this?'

'Something like that. I suppose you get asked all the time.'

'Yes. It's an old line.' She hooked a lock of her hair behind her ear and took note of her action because she realised it was in danger of becoming an irritating habit, a social tick.

'So?'

'So. Not much to tell. I was a drama student. Not far from here.'

'Guildhall?'

'Maybe. My grant didn't cover the rent on my shitty bedsit. I ate leftover pizza sometimes for breakfast. A friend of mine did this. Called it dancing not stripping. She said it was cool and I could earn good money. I did it once for fun when I was drunk. It wasn't as bad as I thought it would be. Now it's what I do.'

'Ab inconvenienti.' Kate registered the Latin phrase. Trying to be clever.

'Out of hardship?' She translated. 'Not exactly. I got by. I could have gone on benefits.'

'How did you know that? Latin I mean.'

'I didn't know I did until a minute ago. You think because you're a what—?'

'—a lawyer.'

'You think because you're a lawyer you're the only one who knows some posh Latin words?

'I apologise.' And she felt sorry for using the word 'posh' 'But you're not a student any more?'

'I wish. My ambition was to be an actress. Or a dancer. A proper one. That's what I used to tell people if they asked - everyone these days is intent on having a plan, aren't they? Makes me sick. But I don't think I wanted that. Not really. I didn't know what I wanted to do. Did you? When you left uni?'

'I did actually.'

'OK, but a lawyer? Of course, you were studying law so you must have had an idea.'

'So what then?'

'Graduated. Did a few auditions. A *lot* of them, in fact. And answered hundreds of ads in The Stage, but none of them ever came to anything. So, I got to do more and more of this while I played occasional bit parts in Eastenders.'

'Really?'

She laughed. 'Just walk on parts. I made the best of them but you wouldn't have noticed.'

'But you're so....'

'Young and beautiful and I have a great sense of humour.'

He laughed 'I was about to say you have a great body.'

'If you see any girls in here who don't fit that description you better complain to the management. Next you'll be telling me I should be a model.'

'Is that what everyone says?'

'Yes.' And she laughed again to take the edge away. 'The world's so full of young and beautiful girls they should turn the sidewalks into catwalks. There's a glut of prettiness in case you hadn't noticed. I blame cosmetics. That, and cheap breast enhancements.'

'What do your parents think?'

'About breast enhancements?'

'You know what I mean. About what you do for a living.'

'What do your parents think about you hanging out in places like this? Or your wife, for all I know?'

'Touché.'

'Sorry. They don't like us to talk like that to the punters. No offence. I haven't seen my parents for a long time. I'm not proud of what I do, and if there was another way I knew to make a living, then maybe.' But she missed out the fact it was easy money, a few days a week. You needed to learn to compartmentalise, or it would drive you crazy, and not define yourself by what you did. But she thought she managed pretty well. If anything, sometimes she found the job empowering because she had something that men all wanted. She was in control. That's the part they don't warn you about. That's what makes it addictive for a few of the girls. 'Who's in charge here? Who says what goes?' she said.

'You are. You do.'

She lifted her empty glass. 'And who's paying?'

'I'll order another.'

'Exactly. Seems to me like I've got the better end of the deal.' But neither of them believed it, even though he was quick to concede she had a point.

'What's your real name? It can't be your real name. Nobody's called Sapphire.' He summoned one of the waitresses who glared at her. The waitresses hated to see the dancers making money. Every drink he bought earned her another fiver and postponed the prospect of a private dance. Gold announced the next act and the music started up so she had to cup her hand and lean in to his ear:

'What's the difference?'

He shouted, 'I'd like to know what to call you.'

She cupped her hand again, raised her voice. 'Call me Sapphire.'

Chapter Six

'GOOD TO SEE YOU again Katya. So good,' he said, leaning his elbow on the table and bunching up his shoulders. His use of Russian alarmed her. It seemed surreal to be having a conversation in a language she never knew she spoke.

'I'd rather speak English,' said Kate. 'If that's alright. And it's Kate, not Katya.' Even so, the name was familiar. Like discovering a favourite doll she'd played with as a girl but finding the dress was a slightly different tone of pink and the nose was more pointed than she remembered. Familiar, but different.

Dmitry was smug. He leaned back. She noticed now that when he smiled he revealed a gold tooth, and she wondered when he got it. '—whatever you're comfortable with,' he said. 'But I'm glad you called.'

They sat on tall stools. Café customers unfolded newspapers, sipped at oversized china cups, made bland conversation. The menus were plastic and slotted between the salt and pepper. Dmitry lay the menus on the table so they could see each other better. They ordered drinks. Vodka for Dmitry - straight up, no ice, and the waitress pursed her lips because it was before midday. Mineral water for her - with a dash of lime. How could she not have called, she wondered? Here was some clue to this woman she had never known but who squatted in her dreams and her memories. Ekaterina. Who was she, and how did she inhabit the shadowlands of her dreams?

'This feels strange.'

'What does?'

'You. Me.' She picked at the corner of the menu. Still wearing her working clothes. At least, wearing the kind of clothes she wanted to be seen in when she arrived at Whites. She dressed the way she thought a stripper *should* dress, off duty. Still making movies. Into character. People were looking. Men were noticing her, in the way that they did. Like she was naked. A gold iguana dangled in the crease between her breasts, and she watched Dmitry's attention flicker.

'What about you and me? You look amazing by the way.'

'I can honestly say I've never seen you before in my life.' She picked her words carefully. The word 'amazing' grated. Shifted earth. 'That's what's strange. I don't understand how I seem to know so much.. so much about you.' *The apartment block. Olga - stern, but delicate. Dmitry at work, in a white coat. A doctor?* The memories were building, one on one. *Simbirsk. Who or what was Simbirsk?* 'A doctor? Were you some kind of doctor?'

'Not really. I was in the lab. Assigned to your project. Amongst others.' He said with business-like haste, and frowned. Thick, black eyebrows that she wondered if he dyed. Then his face broke into lines and he laughed, so loudly that one or two people turned around. 'You're joking with me?' He leaned across the table and she moved back. 'What we shared.. it's never been the same. Not with Olga. Not with anyone. And look at you. Look at you now. Like you're no more than 25 years old.'

'I'm 32.'

'Sure you are,' he said with a surly look. 'So what's the secret? Surgery? Diet?'

'I'm Kate Buckingham. I'm 32 years old. I dance in a club. I'm wondering why I'm here. That's all.'

He was tapping with his fork on the table. 'I couldn't help it you know. What happened. It wasn't my fault. I had orders. Come on. Let's be frank - we all had orders. For a while I thought it was a set up. You and me. I thought they'd arranged it to spy on me. Boilyenko. He never liked me. He shook his head. 'Who knew who was spying on who? I wouldn't have betrayed you, the way you think I did.'

'Who is Borilyenko?' No answer. Just a dark look. The conversation had taken another oblique turn. 'You couldn't help it,' she repeated. 'But I don't know what *it* is. None of this makes any sense. And what project? Is that what you called it? What project were you assigned to?'

'Where are you living?' The waitress came and hovered with her order pad.. 'You want to eat?'

She shook her head. 'Nothing.'

'Club sandwich,' he ordered, without looking up. 'And another vodka. Large this time.' He watched Kate, waiting for the waitress to leave. 'You work? Dancing, you say?'

'Just tell me - who is this person that you think I am? What did she do?'

He folded his hands on the table. 'Who indeed?' He began to play with his fork again. 'We're not going to get far like this.' He conceded. 'So I tell you how we'll do it, I'll make a deal with you. If you stop denying who you are and answer me some straight questions I'll tell you whatever you want to know?'

Kate thought about this. It was plain he wasn't going to be shifted from his perspective that she was someone she wasn't. She might as well play along.

'Ok,' she nodded. 'I'll be this Ekaterina, if that's what you want.' She gave an ironic wave of greeting. 'Hi. Pleased to meet you.'

He pounced. 'There! I told you so. So how did you escape? Who brought you to England? You led them a dance, you know, back then.' He laughed. 'Well done you, I say. So tell me. Tell me everything.'

The subdued light made the colours vibrant and saturated, like a technicolor movie. Dmitry's face was smudged, like there were two Dmitry's. One younger. Thick hair. Sallow cheeked. And this one. Brash. Plump cheeked.

'This Ekaterina – me if you like - did she do something bad?' she ventured.

Dmitry whistled, shaking his head. 'Oh yes. Yes.' He leaned forward again. 'Yes, yes.' He licked his lips. 'You betrayed your country.' He pushed back against the table. The diners clinked and muttered from their distant planet. *Simbirsk*. That was a name she remembered above everything.

He smiled at last. 'But as the poet said, "That was in another country and besides the wench is dead."' He paused. 'The country you betrayed only exists in the history books. That's why we can be friends again. More than friends if you want. Like before. Carry on where we felt off.' A glint of the gold tooth. After a moment's consideration he asked: 'What did they do to you? Afterwards? You don't have to tell me if it's painful.'

She said: 'I don't think I much like you. Did Ekaterina like you?'

He shrugged. 'Please yourself. Maybe the spark is gone. Maybe it will come back. Who knows? Why did you ask me here if not to resume our game?'

'Our game?'

'I even thought you loved me once.'

'How could I love you? I don't even know you?'

'Here we go again. I thought we had a deal? Who arranged this new Kate Buckingham identity for you? I like it. Suits you. Was it the British? The Americans? What did you give them in return? Tell me, Ekaterina. Remember, I'm your friend. We *were* friends, weren't we? In spite of everything you must think. Lovers, once. Not just friends. TELL me Katya. Please?'

She noticed he seemed to have forgotten to smile, as casually as you might forget to open the curtains or to put out the waste. At length Kate decided she had had enough. She stood up. Robert used to say she had poise. Dignity. Mustering the remnants of her poise and dignity, she said, 'I think I should go.'

Dmitry glanced up at her. 'It's your prerogative.' He said, without looking at her. 'They tell me it's a free country, although really I don't see much in the way of evidence.'

She scooped up her coat from the back of the chair, thrusting her arm into a sleeve.

'Don't go, Katya. There's so much to talk about. I don't know what they did - maybe wiped your memory. Maybe they can do that - I'd believe anything of them.'

'Before I go. One thing....' She looked down at him without much hope. 'What is *Simbirsk*?'

'You see! *Simbirsk* is a secret that only a few people share. How would you know about *Simbirsk* if you're not Katya? Something we share, and that we can never talk about to anyone else.'

'So what is it?'

'Think about it. Think hard and you'll remember.'

She stepped into the darkness of the street, half expecting him to follow. *Because that was the way his moods used to work,* she caught herself thinking. *Controlling.*

Dmitry nodded to the couple sitting a few tables away, and they stood up to leave.

It was the same Katya, he reflected, despite her denials. But suspended in time: so credible he almost doubted himself. But how could it be otherwise? She looked the same. Spoke Russian with a distinct Moscow drawl, just like he remembered. She knew about Simbirsk - or at least the name. It was like she had woken up after a coma, and re-learning everything from the beginning. What had they done to her?

The faltering engine of the Zhiguli and the rasp of the fan were the only sounds. Agents Dikul and Chernov sat in a blast of stale hot air that didn't reach their freezing toes, watching the road. Chernov was sulking. They'd been sitting this way for almost an hour, and Dikul had a low-down ache in the pit of his back that occupied all his thoughts. The seat was drawn back as far as possible, but his stomach still touched the rim of the steering wheel.

Chernov muttered something to himself, probably in Georgian, and Dikul didn't bother to ask what he had said. He wanted to be home and warm.

A black Mercedes swept past, rugged, and heavy as a battle cruiser. Low to the ground, weighted with armour.

'We're off.' Muttered Dikul, letting off the handbrake and revving the engine. Chernov snorted and watched some faraway space, retreating further into his big black rug of a coat.

They followed the Mercedes the short distance from Red Square to Arbat, maintaining a safe distance, letting themselves be overtaken to put some traffic between them. Dikul watched the sudden roll of the limousine as it rounded a corner, and was threading the steering wheel through his hands in pursuit, when a Volga pulled across the turning right ahead of them, tyres scrabbling for grip.. He hauled the wheel and the Zhiguli veered sideways and lurched to a halt parallel with the Volga. Dikul swore. Slammed the steering wheel hard with the heel of his hand. Then he heard Chernov yell.

'What's going on?'

Four men had leapt out of the car in front and were approaching with outstretched hands clasped in front of them. Dikul realised too late that they held guns. He reached inside his coat in an instant, but the closest man was shaking his head at him through the glass, mouthing the word: 'Nyet.'

'*Krysha*, Mafia.' Announced Chernov in a dull tone that lacked emphasis.

The doors were tugged open. Dikul half stumbled out of the car. A stolid man in a military style fur hat yanked at his coat, and he felt the barrel of a gun pressed into his neck as he emerged, bashing his head on the roof of the car.

Two men propelled him by both his arms over the bonnet of the car. His forehead almost collided with Chernov's, whose face was ripped in a stripy red grimace. He caught the sour reek of vodka on his breath. Cars swished past, the traffic compensating for them, unrelenting.

'What do you think you're doing?' Someone was demanding, as heavy hands rifled his pockets. Dikul's arms were pinned behind his back. There was a searing pain in his joints. He glanced at the Volga and noticed the blue license plates. Official license plates.

'You're in big trouble.' Dikul managed to respond with venom. 'You'll see.'

Somebody laughed. Dikul tried to move his face away from Chernov who was gagging or coughing. 'In trouble, he says. You hear that?' a balanced voice continued. A Northerner, remarked Dikul. St Petersburg. Not Chechen, at least. But not a Muscovite either. Official plates. But a Volga - the Mafia drove expensive German cars. Maybe not mafia. The pressure on his arms increased and everything became suffused. A red haze descended. Then he was let loose and he managed to push himself from the bonnet of the car. When he found his feet he found himself confronting two men in long dark overcoats. The traffic dodged around them, giving a wide birth. No one would stop, nothing was more certain. An everyday occurrence in modern day Moscow.

A thick-set man with a bulbous nose was looking at him, pointing a gun. The other man, was inspecting Dikul's papers with casual interest. He was bare headed, grey and lean, with a commanding air. The tails of his coat eddied around his ankles in the icy wind.

'So now you know.' spluttered Dikul as importantly as he could. There was a tightness in his chest that alarmed him. 'You better return those..' he said, nodding without much hope at the two pistols that had been placed side by side on the roof of their car. The man ignored him.

'So now we know.' He returned instead, without looking up. 'We are in the company of Sergeant Yevgeny Nikolayevich Dikul of our renowned Foreign Service.' He seemed to consider this for a moment with a hint of irony. 'And you were following whom?' He paused, then watched Dikul with intent grey eyes. 'General Borilyenko, for example?'

A wave of nausea swept over him. He shot a glance behind him and saw they hadn't released Chernov, who had ceased to struggle and was watching him with swollen features like a stuck pig, eyes red-rimmed. Two thugs stood meanly at his back, their shoulders bunched. Not Mafia, he told himself again.

'So, who the fuck are you?'

The man sighed. He looked past Dikul and spoke quickly to one of the men. From behind he heard Chernov wheeze as he was released. Then he started to swear in a thick Slavic slur. Someone must have hit him then because he stopped swearing and began wheezing again. Dikul steeled himself, refusing to allow himself to turn around. 'It's not important. What *is* important is your interest in General Borilyenko.' The headlamps of the early evening traffic lanced around them like they were a traffic island. Dikul caught the soviet blindness in the eyes of the drivers. Another unseen Moscow heist. Another Russian widow.

The reality, when it came to him was even more unwelcome than Mafia. Borilyenko's men. Not directly, but almost certainly FSB. And there in the grey man's eyes was the yellow reflection of the Lubiyanka.

'You are fat and most probably slothful.' he observed to Dikul in a tone that suggested this conclusion was the result of lengthy study.

'You should be at home with your Russian wife, who is also fat, and your revolting children. I say this without criticism, you understand.' Dikul wondered whether this demonstration of knowledge about his family was intended as a threat. 'I advise you now. Speak with your superiors. Have yourself re-assigned. Tell them you're not cut out for surveillance, which you're not. Sometimes it's necessary to choose your friends carefully.' Dikul felt strangely apologetic, like he'd been caught out. The man looked into his eyes with a mixture of empathy and contempt. Then he pointed first to Chernov's assailants, then to the Zhiguli. Dikul still didn't look around, even when he heard a car door open and shut. 'Remember this advice. It's good advice.' And he collected up the weapons like abandoned toys from the roof of the Volga and ducked into the car, which pulled away at once. The Zhiguli followed close behind, pink in the glow of the Volga's tail lights. Dikul turned to find Chernov sitting cross-legged in the gutter looking miserable and clutching his side.

Chapter Seven

THE PARANOIA HAD descended again as she left the café so she avoided the subway and hailed a cab, and as she bundled herself inside, she felt sickened - a feeling of ant-climax and unspent adrenaline. The meeting with Dmitry she had awaited with so much anticipation had revealed nothing new, except that there was much more to be uncovered than she ever dreamed. Her parallel memories were crystallising, glacier-like in her head. They were gaining in depth too. Toughening up. It would take a bigger effort to deny these new imposing memories.

'All right luv?' The cab driver was looking at her over his shoulder. He had a mad flock of ginger hair and deep-sunk eyes. When he looked at her he looked directly at her breasts.

'I'm fine.'

'Where to?' The driver burbled.

She felt herself colour and gave the driver her address, then she glanced around, as drivers do when they are passengers, looking for a space in the traffic. A blue Volvo flashed its lights to let them pull away from the kerb. She settled back and immersed herself in her diverse memories, looking for clues. She recalled again the reflection from her childhood, sliding over the glossy brass. Then the old lady, sweeping past in her long skirts. *Keep away from there, Ekaterina. You'll scald yourself.* She froze. She never remembered the old lady speaking to her before. And certainly not in Russian. *Keep away from there, Katya.* She replayed the memory like a video in her head, and it was the same each time. The child's reflection. The trophy like object seated above her on a lace covered table. The old lady, stooping to draw some liquid from the tap. Then the imploring voice. *Keep away Katya. Katy:* what Dmitry had called her.

The blue Volvo had drawn alongside at the lights. In the yellow streetlight she glanced at the car and glimpsed two shadowy figures behind rain-spattered glass. Then the cab jerked forward again, and the Volvo slipped into their wake.

They made good time across London. She watched Livingstone

House materialise ahead with a feeling of foreboding. She didn't want to be alone in her bleak apartment, but there was nowhere else to go. It was almost nine when she stepped into the damp night and paid the driver, clutching the front of her coat.

Rushing towards the steps, looking over her shoulder as the cab splashed away. Then she paused just an instant, gripped with an odd sense of anticipation. Two cars passed, before the blue Volvo. It seemed to slow, then sped around the next corner with its taillights ablaze. She couldn't be sure, but she thought there was only a single occupant. Or maybe it was a different car altogether.

She shouldered her way through the swing door and rattled up the steps to her floor. Then she stopped and listened, holding her breath. There was a pulse in her head. A baby wailed in the distance. Otherwise, silence. After a few minutes she turned to go. It was then that she heard it: from the foot of the steps the shudder of the door opening and closing. She wasn't mistaken after all. With sudden electric energy she ran to her door along the passage, scrabbled at the lock with her key. Burst inside. Messed with the chain and the bolts. Then strained to hear any slight sound of movement outside, leaning with her back against the door as if to fortify herself. She must have stood there for half an hour. Her mind was a blank: She found herself repelling the memories, even the safe ones. She didn't want to know any more.

When at last she was satisfied there was no one outside, she wandered from room to room trying to persuade herself that everything was normal. Her limbs were taut, strung out like her nerves. Finally she discarded her coat on the floor in the bedroom, and threw herself on the bed, in a hurry for sleep to consume her...

The children stood in line with wide eyes outside the grey-green double doors with steel handles, trying hard to suppress their excitement. They were each identically dressed in school uniform of dark-blue dress with a white, Edwardian style collar, and white aprons. There was no giggling or chattering because it was explicitly disrespectful. A uniformed guard in a long coat stood at either side of the doors, stony faced and silent. The children's' toes ached from the cold, and their noses and cheeks glowed.

Watching their breath form wintry clouds in front of their faces, they waited shivering at the head of a long and ragged line of people that stretched behind them across the road. It seemed like an hour or more before they were admitted. Finally, they were permitted to file into the yellow lit chamber in a crocodile, their shuffling feet resonating.

There, with his head propped against a pillow, in a glass sided coffin that resembled the elongated head of a giant lantern, its base swathed in silken drapes, was the wax-like doll that was all that remained of the leader of whom they had read and revered so much. Eerily lit: His face seemed to shine. Like an angel, Ekaterina pondered with awe, staring past the reflections of her classmates at the tranquil figure. She tried to hold her breath at first, scared she would breathe in the smell of death. Then, when her lungs could not hold out any longer she breathed out in a rush, panting for breath. The other children milled about, shoulders pressed together, their reflections mingling with her own. She wondered what it would be like to touch Lenin, and she reached out her hand, feeding her imagination. Her belly felt taut, and she felt a little nauseous. She swallowed some bile.

When she lowered her hand to touch her stomach, she noticed it was bloated, swollen up. She felt with both hands in sudden panic and found her abdomen round like a football. No children around her anymore. Only adults with gruff voices. Some wore military uniforms, some white coats. They were all watching as the glass coffin was opened. She knew now, instinctively, that she was pregnant. Her breath became uneven as she struggled for air. There was something obscuring her face. Cloth of some kind. A surgical mask.

Kate awoke in a sweat, pawing the bedclothes from her face.

Chapter Eight

COLONEL LISAKOV PUSHED a padded brown envelope across the desk. The mouth gaped open to reveal the grey barrels of the two confiscated Makharov pistols, emasculated in the bland package.

'I can't apologise enough, Comrade Major, for this misunderstanding. This *incident*. Most regrettable.'

Sokolov thought that Lisakov appeared jubilant.

'I wish to put on record, Comrade Colonel, that my officers were assaulted in the course of their duties. Assaulted by your officers. By the FSB.'

'You wish to put it on the record. Of course you do.' Lisakov repeated. He sniffed. Nodded. 'I agree they may have been over-zealous. But you must appreciate it was only out of well-meaning concern for the security of General Borilyenko.' He folded his hands on the desk and as he did so Sokolov tried to estimate the value of the Rolex that his sleeve exposed. The Colonel had silver hair and wore steel rimmed spectacles that flashed in the light from the window. He gave an impression of being metallic and invincible, from the sheen on his suit to the flash of his watch. 'Sadly, Comrade Major we live in violent times, despite the best efforts of my department. We have to be vigilant at all times.' He made a helpless gesture and smiled without humour. 'We can't be everywhere. We do what we can, when presented with certain *scenarios*. These new *freedoms* we have in modern Russia have brought unexpected challenges to the security services, as I'm sure you know. In many ways we are victims of our new liberties.'

With both hands Nikolay gathered up the envelope, and stood up.

'I understand, Comrade Colonel. But it was clear these men were official. There were engaged in a sensitive operation which your officers may have compromised.'

'If there is any assistance the FSB can offer in your operation, then I would be glad to make amends. In confidence, Comrade Major.' Lisakov proceeded in an affable tone, 'What is this operation? Just why was it that your officers were tailing the official car of the Comrade General?'

It was hot in the Colonel's office, which had a collegiate, academic quality. Leather armchairs. A bookcase lined with legal and political volumes. There was even a copy of '*Das Kapital*', Sokolov noticed. The room seemed out of keeping with the Lubyanka. Under his jacket his shirt felt damp.

'You'll appreciate, Comrade Colonel, I'm not permitted to discuss matters of an operational nature. But you must be mistaken. Nobody was following the General.'

'Oh, I don't think my officers are mistaken.' Sokolov had his hand on the door when in an abstract tone Lisakov added, 'Actually, I feel rather sorry for you. You've been handed an impossible assignment. Everybody says so.'

'With respect, Comrade Colonel, what would people know about confidential assignments of the Foreign Intelligence Service?'
'Only what they would be expected to know, Comrade Major. Nothing more.' Sokolov was already leaving, 'And I wish you luck, Comrade Major. Really I do.' Lisakov called after him in a tone laced with irony.

'Thank you, Comrade Colonel, for your offer of assistance.'

Outside Lisakov's office, Sokolov's rubber soles squeaked on the tiles. There was a pervading smell of carbolic in the corridor and the walls were painted a pale green that cast a sickly glow. He walked briskly, took the stairs, waved a dismissive hand at the two uniformed FSB officers as he stepped through the doorway. The air was crisp but tainted with petroleum. He headed in the direction of Lubyanka Square, past the main building with its yellow façade and rows of black windows. The prison was still there - lines of cells on the sixth floor. He wondered who they incarcerated there these days. Below, the basement. It used to be said that the Lubyanka was the tallest building in Moscow, because from the basement you could see Siberia. In the old days it was the basement where they carried out the executions. For all he knew there were still executions there all the time. He passed the empty plinth that once carried the statue of the intelligence service's founder, Feliks Dzherzhinsy. There were calls from some quarters to restore it. Russians hungered for the strength of past leaders, past glories. Across the Square was Children's World, the largest children's store in Russia. He crossed briskly to the south side of the square, and passed beneath the concrete arches of the Lubyanka metro station, part of the original stage of the Moscow metro, once a triumph of the Soviet Union. People, bulked up against the cold, came and went, flicking through the barriers, with empty eyes. In the vestibule, resonant with the shuffle of boots and coughs, a bust of Felix Dzherzhinsky remained. He would will himself to walk by without a glance. It was no use of course. Each time he passed he caught a glimpse. Hard to believe that within his own lifetime this metro station had carried the name Dzherzhinskaya - a celebration of the life of a murderer and a tyrant. But who was he to think this way? He'd served for long enough in the very organs that Dzherinsky had created. Acronyms had come and gone, but not ultimately the organs were intact. He was still KGB when it came down to it.

He travelled south to Yasenevo, some 20 kilometres across town, changing once at Kitai Gorod and then at Oktabyrskaya.

Yasenevo district was where the headquarters of the Foreign Intelligence Service was situated, an imposing skyscraper out of town. It pained him to be so far from the centre. The SVR was the poor relation now the dust had settled on the cold war, and Yasenevo had become an outpost.

When he reached his office Dikul and Chernov were waiting for him. They didn't get up. He offered the lumpy package to Dikul.

'A misunderstanding.' He said, without much sincerity.

'Don't take off your coat.' Said Chernov.

'You'll never believe who wants to see you.' Dikul took a

shameful peek inside the envelope. He was tapping his heel, his knee bouncing like a nervous tick. Chernov too looked uncomfortable. 'You'll have to go back into town. Right now.'

'Don't tell me that Boris Nikolayevich Yeltsin has requested the pleasure?'

'Not quite the President…'

Chapter Nine

KATE FELT A perverse impetus, but even so she paused with her hand on the wicker gate of the cottage where she grew up. There were symmetrical stripes on the lawn, the rows of miniature shrubs that lined the pathway were precisely spaced. And there was the dreaded black door with its shiny brass fittings. She hadn't been past that door in years. It was just the same as she remembered. A quiet pool of suburban respectability. A tumble of Austrian blinds at the windows. Gleaming black panes like still water. Once as she stood poised outside the gate, she thought she heard a movement behind her, and her heart leapt. But when she turned around there was nothing. Just an empty street and banks of lawns that eddied around tiny cottages just like this one. And what would she say to them, after all? A part of her hoped they might be out. But they never went out. Not since her father had retired in fact. They closeted themselves together in their tiny fortress in Tring and shunned even the neighbours.

A fresh resolution drove her forwards, but then she found herself pondering again, hand poised at the slick, bony doorknocker, marvelling at its gleam. She remembered how her mother, wrapped in a florid apron she wore almost all the time, would polish it with Brasso. Then it was the turn of the letterbox in an invariable sequence, a ritual of cleanliness. She was always busy around the house. 'Cleanliness is next to Godliness' she used to tell her. It was as though she was trying to atone for something every hour of the day. Father would just sit with his long legs crossed, outstretched in defiance of the vacuum cleaner, engrossed in his Times and drawing on 'that filthy thing' as her mother called it when she appealed in vain for him to put out his pipe.

She wondered how the routine had changed in her long absence. How long had it been? Taking a deep breath, she was about to knock when the door opened, and there was her mother in that same florid apron and tight grey curls. She stood at the door unsmiling and without a hint of greeting or surprise. For a moment Kate thought she might ask if she had forgotten her key again. She might point out that it was late. Too late to be coming home at her age. But instead, her mother said nothing. She just waited in silence and judged her without words.

'Hi Mum.' Kate thought her voice sounded forlorn. She hadn't meant it to sound that way. She could scarcely look her in the eye.

'Your father's in the drawing room.' Her mother said, inching aside for her to pass. Kate though she caught a hint of distaste in her look, even though she'd made an effort. No trace of make-up. A simple sweatshirt and blue jeans that were not too tight. A red skiing jacket she had bought one winter when she'd been meaning to take a holiday, but never got around to it.

Her father was sitting in the chair by the window where he always sat, smoking 'that filthy thing'. When she came into the room something strange happened. At first there was almost the flicker of a smile, and then his expression seemed to alter at once, as though he had noticed something in her demeanour. He uncrossed his legs and stiffened, leaning forwards in his chair.

'Kate?' he said, and she could sense an unvoiced question hanging in the air.

'Dad. I know.' She said, watching his eyes. The eyes had aged. There were crevices around them that she didn't remember. Like they'd been sketched in pencil. *What? What did she know?* 'I know about Russia.' She said at last. Hoping it was enough.

He got to his feet in silence and positioned himself in front of the empty fire grate, arms behind his back, with military poise. He seemed to swallow hard before he spoke.

'Then you'll know there's nothing for you here.'

'I need to know the rest. Everything. I want to hear it from you.'

From behind her then her mother's anguished voice. 'Tell her Bob. It can't hurt now. It was all so long ago.'

His face closed up for an instant, and then his eyes misted over and his face became somehow flaccid: it seemed to her that he avoided looking at her. 'If you're sure. If you're really sure you want to know,' he said, as much to himself as to anyone in particular. Then he sighed. 'Sit down.' He gestured at an armchair. 'Please, sit down.' But she stood all the same, waiting, until reconciled, he began: 'Your mother ... we couldn't have children. She ... we were desperate to have a child. Of our own. It seemed the right thing to do. And when they told me about you... well...' He coughed into his hand. There was a long silence before he began. Kate was about to say something, feeling an urgent need to fill the void of silence, but stopped herself in time.

'They smuggled you across the border just after midnight.' He began again, 'Maybe the border guards had been bribed because there were no questions. They didn't search the bags which was also too good to be true. I was waiting, of course. Alone, because it was impossible for your mother to come along, even though she wanted to.. even though she begged me to let her come. It would have been too dangerous. For everyone.'

Kate had no idea what to expect. She was struggling to interpret what he was saying.

'The border..?' It was all she could think of to say.

'They took you through Turkey first of all.' He explained, as if that were the most natural thing in the world. 'It was safer than Germany, in those days. And I had contacts, you understand.' He sucked on his pipe, but it had gone out, and he stooped to bang the ashes into the grate. 'Through the office.'

She knew her father had worked in the Foreign Office for years. A minor bureaucrat, he used to tell her. Nothing very important. 'So..? What happened?' she prompted with a gnawing feeling inside.

'It turned out to be simpler than I thought. Kris came out too of course. He had to. He knew he could never go back. He brought you out in the bottom of a small suitcase with holes punched for air. A tiny bundle wrapped in white, like a doll. A tiny Russian doll.' Her father looked at the ceiling with unseeing eyes. 'I was shocked when I saw your face. All wrinkled. I'd never seen a new-born baby before. Thought you were ill, to start with. Five days old, when Kris brought you out. Sleeping, peacefully. Maybe they'd given you something—'

He was rambling now. 'Getting you out of Turkey was always a concern, but I needn't have worried because Kris had all the right papers. Kris was a professional. Then Heathrow … well that was never going to be a problem. Not with the Job.' He said, looking away. *Something at the Foreign Office. Just paperwork. Nothing important.*

And that was when it dawned upon her what she was hearing. She should have seen it sooner. The strangers that she had known all her life were just that – they were strangers. She was an orphan. She felt giddy but she pressed him. '—and my real mother? My real father?'

'We *are* your real parents.' Came her mother's voice from behind. 'It doesn't matter who conceived you. We clothed you, fed you.' She paused. There was a click in her voice when she added, 'Loved you.' It sounded odd coming from her.

'But who were they? What happened to my parents?'

Her father shook his head. 'They never told us. Russians? Maybe not. Maybe diplomats? But it didn't matter to us who they were. They were gone. We were all there was. We are your parents, Kate. We're all you have.' He opened out his hands, then seemed to notice them and clasped them behind his back. Embarrassed to be caught out.

'When I got you back to the UK we registered the birth as our own. Kris had prepared us for this long in advance.' He nodded at his wife. 'Your mother had to go away during the 'pregnancy' to make it look right.

'Who's this Kris?' she said.

'Kristofer Njevjedovski. He was—well he was a contact of mine. In Russia. Not Russian you understand, but Polish.'

A thought occurred to her for the first time. It seemed ludicrous. She could barely conceal the incredulity in her voice when she said: 'So were you some kind of spy?'

Her father coughed again. Just office work, he seemed about to say. He laughed, but it had a hollow ring. 'Not really a spy. Not really. But I was involved in the *intelligence* business.'

In spite of everything it was hard to believe that her father had been some kind of James Bond. And that she was a Russian girl smuggled at night across some ragged border post. But there was more to it than that. Much more.

'And this..Kris you called him? Is he still alive?'

'He's alive,' said her father. 'So far as I know.'

'Where can I find him?'

'It won't do you any good,' he said.

Chapter Ten

SOKOLOV LEFT THE metro at Tverskaya because he wanted to kill time before his meeting. Crossing under the road, stepping around puddles of muddy water, he passed the usual morose and restless lines outside cut-price kiosks selling anything from cabbages to vodka.

On the way to the Kremlin he ducked into Gazetny Lane where he paid a ridiculous sum for two large vodkas in a tourist café. The bar was empty but the barman ignored him until he slapped the counter with his hand.

'Are you serving, or not?'

'What's the hurry?'

'I just don't want to die here waiting for a drink.'

The barman said something under his breath and pulled him a

grudging shot. He wore a green apron like a waiter in a French Bistro and was bald and surly.

As he delivered each shot, Sokolov threw back the vodka in a single gulp. The vodka failed to enervate him as he'd hoped it would. A summons to the Kremlin was not a common occurrence for him, and he thanked the stars for that. He caught the barman's stare.

'Another?'

'Now it seems you're in a rush to serve me.' He pushed the glass across for a refill. 'This place is empty.'

'So what if it is? It's Tuesday.'

'What days does it get busy?'

'It's usually like this. Until the tourist season.'

'When's the tourist season?'

'How do I know? I've only been here a couple of months.'

He drank his final vodka, unable to put off his meeting any longer.

'Comrade.' He said to the barman with a dark nod, and he turned to leave. The barman returned his nod and watched him go in silence.

The Prime Minister of the Russian Federation, Viktor Chernomyrdin was not alone. A sharp-suited man with slick black hair was sitting at his side, behind a long table. Sokolov noticed that this man's eyes were the same shade of blue as his shirt. He was sure he had seen him somewhere before. A log shifted in a fireplace behind them, spitting out a flurry of sparks.

Chernomyrdin acknowledged him. He was restive. His skin was the colour of parchment, and he didn't look as assured as he did on TV.

'Thank you for joining us, Nikolay Sergeyevich. You probably know already who I am, but to save you any embarrassment, my name is Alexander Ivanovich Lebed.' He had a bass undertone and a lugubrious, studied look. Now he came to think of it Sokolov had never seen Lebed out of uniform, which is why he hadn't recognised him at once. Lebed the hero who had, if his press was to be believed, single handedly brought the Chechen war to an end, only to see it fall into conflict again in recent months. Still Lebed had done what he could, and stepped to one side to watch other politicians scrabble over the mess that could easily be another Afghanistan. Lebed the leader. 'I hear your officers had some difficulties yesterday?'

Sokolov remained standing. 'It was nothing, sir.'

'What happened?'

'They were tailing Borilyenko. Then they were ambushed by the

FSB. There were some bruised egos, that's all.'

'Colonel Lisakov?'

'I saw him earlier. He was apologetic.'

'He's a tricky one. Careful of him.' He turned to Chermonyrdin as if to bring him into the conversation. 'The Prime Minister thought the important nature of your assignment should be made clear to you. He thought it appropriate to see to this personally.' Lebed looked at Chernomyrdin, seeking affirmation, but the Prime Minister looked disinterested. He cleared his throat as if he felt that something was expected of him, and said:

'Listen to what the General has to say.'

Sokolov had a sneaking respect for the Prime Minister. An old communist who had worked hard and seemed so much less burdened after the old regime had fallen away that he spoke out, sometimes unfortunately, leading to a reputation for malapropisms, many of which turned out to be succinct. In 1993 after a disastrous intervention by the Russian Central Bank he had explained in a speech: 'We wanted the best, but it turned out like always.' It was the best-known assessment of Russian Economic Policy and the phrase had become legendary.

Lebed leaned across the desk and offered a soldier's clenched handshake, then gestured towards a cracked leather armchair with bowed cushions. 'Please.'

Sokolov sat down. He could feel the hot breath of the fire. Chermonyrdin spoke again:

'There are people that would love to see Russia return to Communism. People with vested interests. They behave like puppet masters. Some of those people are behind the Feliks Group. Destroying the Feliks Group will help to throw our backward direction into reverse.' Said the Prime Minister.

'What the Prime Minister means…'

'Yes, I get it, sir. But why are they such a threat? Who are they?'

Chernomyrdin was looking out of the window, and Lebed answered. 'Some people think it's a mythical organisation. But it's not that. And it's not a harmless bunch of well-meaning patriots as the occasional press releases would suggest. They kill people. Believe me when I tell you that Feliks is a real threat to Perestroika. To any surviving chance of a Democratic government in Russia. A retrograde movement, made up of renegades and terrorists, mostly from the old KGB. We know this for a fact.' He patted the desk with his palm, stood up and walked to the window, where he looked down on Red Square. 'We're certain that Borilyenko is responsible. Which presents us with a dilemma. ' He turned around and looked at Sokolov. 'You see, without proof we can't do anything. Our President and the General have history. Yeltsin won't hear anything against his chief of security. His bodyguard. I know, because once I was favoured in the same way, until I tainted myself by aligning with the political opposition. So we must have proof—your proof, I should say.

There was a silence. Chernomyrdin was peering at him, forming an assessment, he thought. Sokolov wondered if it was favourable.

'I founded the political party 'Our Home - Russia' to be sure to capitalise on the advances we've made since Communism. It's an attempt to promote the principles of freedom, property, legality. Legality above all. It's not an exaggeration to say that these principles are at risk. Our tragedy in Russia is that whatever organisation we try to create, it ends up looking like the Communist party. My party of course is supportive of the President and his reforms. We need to discourage elements that seek to undermine him. Only then can we build the framework for democracy to hang itself on.'

He saw Lebed smile to himself at Chemonyrdin's turn of phrase.

'I'm not political, sir.'

'Good. Russia needs the apolitical.'

Lebed said: 'You must be asking yourself why you've been

chosen for such an important assignment. Why you?'

'Something like that. I'm not a policeman, and I'm not FSB either.'

'Hah!' Lebed pointed a finger as though this was what he expected to hear. 'Then of course you must wonder. I know all about you, Nikolay Sergeyevich. I've read your file. Your time in London. Washington. An impeccable record. Successes. What's attractive to the Prime Minister and me is that you don't have the wrong kind of allegiances. With the old comrades I mean. Or with the Silioviki. The hard men. We think that you...' He tapped his temple with a finger. '..you're a free thinker, Nikolay Sergeyevich. Not easily fooled. We need men like you in the new Russia. In influential places, if you see where I'm going.

'It's going to be dangerous for you. You recognise this already. Of course, there are powerful men involved. But it won't be without reward when you are successful. It goes without saying your investigation must be conducted in the utmost secrecy. No more clashes with the FSB – and absolutely nobody must be aware that either of us is in any way connected with this enterprise. The stakes are higher than you can possibly imagine. But you're on the winning side. The right side. Trust me, Nikolay Sergeyevich, and you will be rewarded for your loyalty.'

Chapter Eleven

A SHABBY TERRACED house in SW19 with un-curtained windows, inky black like dark pools and impenetrable. The door was rugged and lined with furrows that may have been made by a dog's claws, and there was no sign of a bell or a door-knocker. When she pushed the flap of the letterbox twice to announce herself a stale smell seemed to seep into the cold air. She waited some moments before she tried again, but there was no sound from within. The front path was bordered by a low and shambling white brick wall. Some of the bricks had crumbled away. She hopped over the wall and peered through the window. A sturdy worn couch and an armchair. An electric fire in an iron grate with two bars glowing. And a half-imagined shadow at the door. She stepped back over the wall and gave the letterbox another prod.

The door opened and she was confronted with a tall and gaunt old man who reeked of iron-filings. His eyes were unnerving, glancing around as though they were independent of each other. She took a step backwards.

'So. You.' He said in a sombre tone. 'I knew you would come.' He had a strong Slavic burr. He screwed up his eyes to look at her, then threw a fleeting, haunted glance at the road. 'Come in. Come in.'

Inside the stale smell was stronger. He seemed to sense her distaste. 'I not leave the house so much anymore. No reason. I buy food sometimes. Newspapers.' He shrugged and showed her into the room she had seen through the window. One eye seemed to keep watch on the street, while the other appraised her. 'You look how I thought.' He said after a moment.

'What do you mean?'

'*Nothing*. Nothing. I don't mean nothing.' He waved a hand, then settled himself in the armchair and folded his hands together as though preparing himself for some kind of tedious entertainment. The threadbare carpet was strewn with old newspapers and a plate with the remnants of some meal or other. There was a saucer of salt in the middle of a coffee table. She thought she had read – or dreamed - that it was a Russian custom to keep salt for guests. The light struggled to penetrate the room, despite the un-curtained windows. Perched on a sideboard was a tarnished, vase like object that she thought for an instant that she recognised. She felt a little afraid of this old man who looked at her with hunger and clasped his bony hands together as though in desperate prayer. 'Understand first: I have nothing for you. No comfort. Nothing to offer you,' he said in his cracked voice. 'I can't speak about these matters. I am pledged to secrecy. You must know such before you begin.' He seemed to lose his composure for a moment and when she followed his gaze she saw the photograph and jolted. Unmistakably her. She reached across and in a single movement plucked the fussy bronze frame from the mantelpiece.

'Where did you get this?'

It was a monochrome print. The clothes were unfamiliar – they had never featured in her wardrobe, and she was standing on a bridge she didn't recognise – but there was no doubt it was her. Looking at the print she had the strangest sensation - she imagined she could smell chocolate. The old man grunted.

'Your mother gave she to me. For memories.'

She scrutinised the picture again with a frown. It was an old photograph. The face in the picture was her. But it couldn't be.

'She looks so...' she trailed off. 'And you keep it on your mantelpiece? It looks like me.'

He shrugged.

'But it can't be me. So, who? My mother? Is that who this is? Where was it taken?'

'On a bridge. You can see this.'

She could see that it was pointless to pursue this line of questioning. She replaced the photograph. 'Tell me about Ekaterina.' She demanded. He averted his eyes for the first time, darting towards the window.

'I don't know nothing about Ekaterina.'

'Then tell me about my mother and father.'

'They don't alive. That's all I know.'

'They were from Russia?'

'You are from Russia. From Russia with love,' his throaty laugh at this attempts at humour mutated into a coughing fit. She waited for it to subside.

'And you brought me here?'

'I brought you to border. From there it was your father taking you.'

'You mean Bob?'

'Robert,' he said.

'So, what happened? What happened to my real parents?'

The old man shrugged again. He rose then with a hoarse cough and peered out of the window into the empty street. 'I cross border same time as you. I don't go back. I can't go back to this place.'

'I need to know about Ekaterina.'

He was still at the window. He looked uneasy. 'I told you. I not know her.'

She felt light-headed. Empty. She hoped she wasn't about to cry. 'Please… there are things I just can't explain. Things I need to know. I have these.. *memories*. I don't know who I am. You have to help me.' She entreated.

He shook his head without looking at her.

Then: 'I met a man who mistook me for someone else. This.. Ekaterina.'

He threw her a sharp, attentive look. 'Who?' Both his eyes were pinned on her.

'He works at the Russian embassy.'

'Russian?'

'Yes.'

He abandoned his vigil at the window and stood over her –

reached out to her with his bony hands. 'Leave it alone. There are devils in the past. Sometimes maybe better not to know. Don't speak with this man. Don't speak with *nobody* about what is in past. Past is dead. Keep inside like you did before. I speak like your protector. I help you before, long time ago. Now I protect you again.'

She had a vision of the old lady in her sweeping skirts. *Keep away.* 'But I have dreams…' She began again.

'We all have those.' He said as though from a very long way away. For the first time she experienced a stir of recognition. Something welled up inside her, and she almost shouted in desperation: 'Russian! I speak Russian. How is it possible? If what you say is true, I was just a baby when I left Russia. And I know things too. I know ... places.'

For a brief moment he seemed to lose his composure. 'I never thought would work such like this—' But he swallowed his words. 'What things? What things you know?'

'Things like—' but her second set of memories had abandoned her altogether, leaving her beached and incoherent, and she floundered. 'Just memories. Memories of things that haven't happened. Not to me. Not to anyone I know. Or maybe they only happened in dreams. I can't explain the way they feel. As real as yesterday's memories.'

The old man looked about him, then pursed his lips and sank back into his armchair, staring in his odd, disorientated. She realised that the interview was over.

'Leave me alone. I cannot speak about such things. It does not help. I am glad to see you safe and well.'

'You *must* help me.'

But the old man had retreated into a sullen silence in his chair in the half-light, and seemed to be about to fall asleep.

She was at the door when she flung a final glance at the picture above the grate. She had an unsettling impulse. 'Do I have a sister?' There was no answer. He had closed his eyes, as if to shut her out. His head was nodding.

Chapter Twelve

NIKOLAY WAS ROUSED from a fitful sleep by the sound of the telephone. He sprang out of bed and through the bedroom door in his shorts to rescue the phone on its dying ring from the plastic veneer coffee table by the TV.

'Sokolov,' he answered.

'Did I wake you?'

Nikolay looked at his watch. It was after six in the morning. He was nursing a hangover that had only just begun to assert itself. A vodka bottle lay on the carpet. 'Who is it?'

'It's Lebed. Get dressed.'

Nikolay was already shrugging on a creased white shirt. 'Sir? What's going on?'

'There's been an execution.'

Nikolay paused. 'What do you mean an execution?'

'A Director of the Uvyerenny Bank. Viktor Bukovsky.'

Nikolay was perplexed. His forehead was tight. A litre all alone in his bare apartment last night. He caught sight of himself in the mirror. His eyes looked sore. 'I don't understand…' Was all he could manage, his eyes flitting around the room as though seeking inspiration.

'Do you have a pen?'

Nikolay scrabbled in a drawer for a biro and wrote down the address in Old Arbat that Lebed dictated.

'Respectfully, what does this have to do with me? Like I said before, I'm not a policeman.'

'Just go there.' Said Lebed with a warning note. 'Ask some questions. Make a nuisance of yourself. Make it known that you have an interest.'

'And do I?'

'If we say you do, then you do.' Lebed rang off.

The house in Old Arbat was crumbling but still grand and the grey dawn lent it a monochrome hue. Nikolay parked his car behind a police car with a relentless flashing light at the other side of the empty street. A policeman slouched in the doorway of the house and tapes cordoned off the gate. An ambulance waited at the kerb with its doors spilling open, its exhaust pumping thick white clouds into the air. Nikolay was surprised to see Lisakov presiding at a distance. When he saw him Lisakov beckoned with a cheerful expression.

'What a surprise, Major. That our esteemed Foreign Service should trouble itself with miserable domestic business like this!'

Nikolay joined Lisakov at the side of his parked official Volga. 'Good morning, Colonel.'

Lisakov smiled, but his gaze didn't stray from the house. They were bringing a body out now, swathed in a soiled sheet that flapped in the wind. Two paramedics man-handled the stretcher down the steps with bad grace. Nikolay said: 'Is that Bukovsky?'

'Him or one of his bodyguards.'

'Bodyguards?'

Lisakov threw him an odd glance. 'Bukovsky was mafia. Even if he wasn't he would have needed a 'krysha' himself. A roof. Protection. He was vulnerable.'

The paramedics had deposited the corpse in the ambulance and were returning to the house without urgency, presumably for the next victim. Nikolay cleared his throat and attempted to sound like a policeman. He didn't think he was very convincing. 'What do you think was the motive?' It sounded trite. Like he was playing a TV cop.

Lisakov laughed. 'The usual one.' He put a gentle hand on Nikolay's shoulder. 'And what is your interest in Bukovsky exactly? You think perhaps he may have been a Western spy?' His eyes opened wide with playful intrigue. Nikolay found it difficult to answer, even to himself. 'Or is it,' Lisakov continued in a casual tone, 'is it his patronage?'

Nikolay froze. 'I don't know what you mean.'

Lisakov shrugged and removed his hand. 'It's no secret that Bukovsky was a friend of our Prime Minister.'

Nikolay attempted to change the subject. He felt miserable, and he had no idea what he was doing here. He huddled inside his overcoat and shivered. 'What happened?'

Lisakov seemed to evaluate him for some moments, as though trying to resolve a puzzle. Then he sighed, and replied in a detached voice: 'They sprayed the front facing rooms with automatic fire while two of them broke down the door. Then they worked their way through the house room by room. Household. Bodyguards. They're all in there..' He nodded at the house as the paramedics emerged with another corpse, as if on cue.

Nikolay waved a hand at Lisakov as though he had seen enough. There was nothing for him to do here anyway. What had Lebed been thinking of?

As he walked back to the car, he passed a construction site, with a semblance of building work – a few upright girders holding up a concrete platform that would have no doubt become a ceiling had the builders not run out of money. It was clear that this site had been abandoned for some time. He noticed that a small fire was burning, and he stopped. A man was hunched over the fire.

'Hey!'

The man hauled himself to his feet and lumbered across the rubble. He looked a big man, but he was wearing so many layers of clothes that it was hard to tell. His face was lined and cracked and he wore a shabby fur hat. He could have been seventy, Nikolay supposed, but equally he could have been thirty. A medal was pinned to his shabby coat. Ordinarily Nikolay wouldn't have given it a second glance. There were plenty of vets on the streets these days. 'Where did you get that?'

The man looked down and seemed to notice the medal for the first time. 'Afghanistan.' He replied in a challenging tone.

'What does a man have to do to win a Medal of Honour?'

'Not much,' he said. 'Lose his dignity. Be a Russian.'

Nikolay noticed that the man's left sleeve flapped empty at his side. There was a moment's silence. The man looked hard at the ground, the way people used to in the Soviet era when they were confronted with authority. 'Did you see what happened over there?'

'I saw nothing. I heard nothing.'

'I'm not the police.'

The man raised his head at last and assessed him. 'You dress like a Westerner. Are you a newspaperman?'

Nikolay shook his head.

'A Chekist then.' The man concluded. In some quarters the old term for the secret police had never died. The numerous official manifestations - Vecheka, OGPU, NKVD, KGB, FSB, SVR, FSO - all of these were encompassed neatly in the old word, 'Cheka'. 'I saw you talking to him..' He nodded his head in the direction of the house.

'He asked me some questions.' Nikolay fumbled in his pocket and pulled out the only note he could find, crumpled into a ball. When the man smoothed out the 20 rouble note he cursed himself, and the man seemed about to return it but Nikolay waved it away.

'What do you want?'

'I just want to know what happened. And he's not going to tell me that.'

'For the record, or for something else?' said the man. Then he drew a deep breath, and thrust the note into his pocket. 'I saw the Spetsnaz storm that house.'

Lisakov had a sudden feeling of foreboding. Special forces. 'What makes you think they were Spetznaz?'

'I've seen them often enough.' He said. 'Take it from me, whoever lived in that house must have upset someone special.'

'But what makes you think they were Spetsnaz?' He persisted.

The man cackled. 'I'm an old soldier, see? They had AK47's for instance. Not the usual kind. Short stocks and barrels. The kind they give to Special Forces. If you were Mafia you would maybe use something more.. *modern*. Like an uzi.' He snorted. 'Also they left in an unmarked van. It was a Chekist van. I would swear.'

'Nothing else?'

'Only that they made a clean sweep of the place. Nobody survived in there, you can be sure. They did their job.'

'Thanks.'

The man grinned, exposing gaps in his teeth. 'Good luck, Comrade,' he said, with irony.

Chapter Thirteen

OLD NED SAT in silence for a long time after Kate had left. *Old Ned.* He had learnt to become accustomed to that name. It was the way in this hated country that people hadn't the patience to grapple with foreign names. When he had worked in the factory, turning lathes it had been 'Ned the Pole'. Now, in the fag end of his days, it was just '*Old Ned.*' That was when anybody referred to him at all, which was not often.

He nursed her photograph almost without noticing. The girl had turned out just the way he always imagined, of course. How could it be otherwise? If they could see her now in Moscow … if they knew...

The thought of Moscow seemed to crystallise something, and he sat bolt upright, listening. He could hear the scraping of the second hand of the wall clock from the kitchen. The buzz and vibration of the refrigerator. Now and then a car swept past the window. He settled back into his thoughts.

A single act of heroism illuminated a bleak past. It was true he sometimes yearned to return to Russia. Ironic that when he came to England he had exchanged the white coat of a medical researcher for the almost identical white overall of a factory worker. Every day he dissected the newspapers for news of home. He was a Pole by birth, but his spiritual home was Russia. He had read about the new climate of democracy. Perhaps it wasn't out of the question for him to return? But what would he do there? His scientific knowledge was crusted with time. On the one hand he knew too little. And then, on the other hand he knew too much. He knew too much...

The bang of his front gate made him start and he hurried to the window. One of the men caught his eye at once as he advanced down the path. They looked like policemen, he thought. The man that caught his eye was ruggedly built beneath a light raincoat, with the drawn expression of a late-night card player, his hair raked back in greasy furrows from his forehead. His coat tails flapped in the breeze. The other man was smaller and darker, with sharply defined features that gave an impression of an inquisitive bird.

One of the men hammered on the door. Old Ned paused in the hallway, half inclined not to answer, but the hammering continued without respite. He felt a tightening in his chest as he reached to release the catch, and it was only then, too late, that he thought he heard a curse in Russian. '*Pizdec*'

The door was rent aside, and the men burst inside. One grabbed him by the wrist in an iron grip. The other just barged straight past.

'What did she want?' The big one demanded over his shoulder in a bad accent. 'Where did she go? You better tell us, old man.'

'Who are you?' But he was certain that he knew, as he was hauled down the passage by his forearm like a rag doll.

'It's enough that we know who *you* are.' said the other man in Russian. 'You are the dissident Njevjedovski.'

The big one was in the living room, hurling Kristov's few possessions at the walls after a cursory examination of each. 'We are your worst nightmare, old man. Tell us what we want to know and we might let you live.' His eyes lighted on the photograph and he snatched it from him and flashed it at his colleague. 'This her?'

The other man strained over the picture with his eagle eyes, gripping Old Ned's arm. 'Looks like.'

Then the big one squared up to Kristov with a wide gait. 'What did she want?' he demanded again, this time in Russian.

Old Ned had a vision of the KGB Border Guards that night long ago. He remembered the pale light on the snow. He remembered the shabby cardboard suitcase that felt so fragile in his grasp. He remembered all of this, and he thought it was worth it. He clenched his jaw.

The crash of the fist on his jaw wasn't so painful as he had been expecting. He didn't attempt to resist. Where would be the point? He just folded on the floor and made a silent prayer. A Russian prayer. He felt himself being dragged to his feet, but he made himself a heavy load, and his legs flapped beneath him so that they let him drop back to the ground. His cheek rested against the threadbare carpet, and he inhaled the acrid dust of his long time squalor with a perverse satisfaction. Far above him the ritual played itself out, but already he was oblivious to their questions, which they asked repeatedly in the mother tongue. Perversely it was almost a joy to hear Russian again to this old Pole. And in-between each question they kicked him, and the strange thing was, that even as the kicks became more frenzied they seemed to lose their edge. There was just some all-consuming ache that was like a tiredness in his bones. He remained there curled on the floor and awaited the inevitable onset of unconsciousness. He didn't feel nauseous at this stage. In fact, he was surprised to feel almost exhilarated. Once, he tried to peer up at them, through a single swollen eyelid, but it wasn't worth the effort. There was just some haze of movement and the sounds seemed to get louder, so he closed his eye and allowed himself to drift away.

Late last night she had endured Robert's ritual pleading in a vodka trance, lying on her small pink bed with the phone clamped to her cheek, not really listening, contemplating the ceiling that was smudged in the corners with the effects of the vodka. It was like that now, except that the smudged ceiling had more to do with the welling of tears than alcohol. Her bed was pink because it was intended to remind her of her childhood, but it didn't succeed; small because she didn't intend to share it with anyone. Not anymore. Not for a long time. She couldn't imagine a time when she would sacrifice this solitude. For anyone.

Robert wanted her to come home. What he called home. He wanted them to try again. He was willing to try, why wasn't she? It frustrated her that she couldn't make him understand why it was impossible – she barely knew herself - so his argument exhausted itself as it usually did. 'For Becki' he would plead. 'For our daughter.' She wondered if he was drunk. The irony of being drunk together at either end of the phone made her bite her lip. Robert had emitted a strained note then that ought to have wrung some sympathy from her if she had any to spare. Then he had hung up - or maybe she did, she couldn't recall - but she had kept the receiver against her ear, listening to the tone, followed by the recorded voice instructing her to hang up. She had felt tearful then, like today.

It was the anniversary of something today, although she struggled to remember what. There were anniversaries that she celebrated in the quiet of her mind, not with champagne and streamers but with the instinctive acknowledgement that one day or other was significant for some reason. Today had once been a cause for celebration, she knew. It was 12 September. She frowned and swung the vodka bottle to her lips, but it didn't stir her memory, just dimmed this sensation of special-ness.

Vodka was a habit she had acquired almost without noticing. Perhaps it had started at drama school. It seemed like she had always drunk vodka - neat with no ice. She had taken to keeping the bottle in the freezer. Even so, it never seemed cold enough.

She ought to love Robert. She supposed she once had, although it was difficult to imagine when. He had done his best to make her happy, but in a way it was the wrong kind of happiness. It was to settle for something. She couldn't ever explain that to him - she wouldn't have known where to start. To shore up their crumbling relationship he pressured her into having a child. She tried to believe that she loved Becki, but it seemed to her that even there something was lacking. It was as though she had once known a deeper, more profound love that surpassed everything, and reduced anything less to something trivial.

Her thoughts were erratic. She thought of her visit to the old man's house – except that when she tried to remember the face of the old man it had shed its lines and hollows and it was a much younger man that she remembered: Kris. She felt an odd warmth towards him, like he was someone she had known all her life.

How did it change things now that she knew that she was a Russian orphan, and that Kris had risked his life to smuggle her across the border? What strange passion had driven him to do that, she wondered? She screwed up her eyes, like she was trying to focus on something. A number assembled itself in her head in a rhythmic two-digit sequence. Some impulse made her sit bolt upright and she dialled International directory enquiries for the dialling code for Russia. With a tremulous hand she tapped out the number that by now had crystallised and become urgent and unforgettable.

When she found the number was dead it was with a mixture of relief and disappointment. Who had she hoped would answer?

And then it was as though some inner membrane snapped. Faces and voices filled her mind – people she had not had the time to meet – each accompanied by a rush of associations. Murmured confidences over dinner. A shared litre of vodka. Street names. Relationships. Lives that were filled with trivia and pathos. She clutched at her temples as if to stem the tide. And then one overriding memory seemed to break free and shatter everything. The tarnished object that her eyes had lighted upon amidst the clutter of the old man's house came back to her, and she realised that it was almost identical to the one in her dreams. It used to be commonplace in Russian homes. It was a simple tea urn. A samovar.

She didn't have time to absorb this—didn't recognise the significance—before she remembered that it was time for her to leave. But how could she leave, now that her dreams were beginning to melt into her real life? She glanced at the clock with its teddy bear face. Midday. She needed to be at the club.

It was Kate's turn to dance the graveyard shift—the afternoon shift— but nobody was dancing because of the old man. Nobody was dancing

EXCEPT the old man. He was a minor sensation. The girls and the punters gathered in knots to watch him. He wore a cheap grey suit that had gone baggy at the knees and elbows, and no tie, and his shoes were worn to paper soles. Just outside the door to the club he writhed and kicked in a striptease parody that the girls giggled over. His face was toothless and mischievous, and he jutted his pointed chin out as he danced, grabbing his crotch and rubbing at his concave chest in all the right places to the music that blared out onto the streets.

Vanessa nudged Kate as they stood and watched. 'Could be you in a few years.' Kate thought the old guy must be fit to keep going this long.

Gold had been observing from the pool table with a listless grin, but it had gone on for too long already. As he shambled to the door the girls and punters parted for him and booing went up. He grinned. 'Yeah all right all right. Maybe I'm just gonna book 'im. As an act.' He waved them away and strode out on the pavement towards the old man, who, when he saw Gold coming, stopped dancing and took a few paces backwards. Gold was too quick for him - with a swift movement he had gathered the old man up under his chunky arm. Kate strained to see what was happening over the shoulders of a balding punter in a brown suit who scarcely seemed to notice her bare flesh. She saw Gold laughing with his head thrown back, and patting the man's narrow shoulders with his big paw. She saw him press a note into his eager hands, although she didn't see the colour. Then the old man scuttled down the street shouting something in his mad language and sawing his arms in the air like a windmill, and Gold returned to a minor ripple of applause. His face was a row of white teeth. He nodded at Kate, raised a quieting hand. 'It's you, innit? You got an impersonator.' and he swung himself up to the music deck, murmuring into the microphone with a voice that was holding down a gurgle.

'How much did you give him?' she whispered as she tripped onto stage with her painted punters' smile.

'Something and nothing,' said Gold, still grinning.

'Maybe I should take up pavement dancing.'

He covered the mike with his hand. 'You'd get raped, you would.' And he giggled. Which was meant to be a compliment.

When Kate finished her shift at six 'o' clock she gossiped in the changing room with the other girls for a while, slipping out of her gossamer threads and pulling on her jeans. She felt sticky and dusty at the same time, and she was sure that the occasional hint of body odour that she caught was her own. She wouldn't shower here though - not since one of the punters had rampaged through the changing rooms. It didn't feel safe. Not that she ever felt safe anymore. Paranoia was a moment away. *The samovar... what was that all about?*

When she stepped outside a fine drizzle was falling and the passing cars used dipped headlights. She started to set off in the direction of the tube station with her head down and the muffled music of the club just behind her. A car drew up to the kerbside. As paranoid as she was, she looked up in time to see two men emerging with their eyes on her. One of the men seemed to flap like a vulture in his long coat as he came around the car, trailing a hand on the bonnet. He had a hooded expression and a barrel chest. His hair was as glossy and grey as the wet pavements. She took a step backwards. The other man was closer. He was dark and tightly packaged with lean features and a nose like a beak. Without a word he grabbed for her but just brushed her arm as she drew away. Her heart leapt. She cast around her, still retreating but not daring to turn her back on the men. Images flashed in her mind like she was channel hopping on TV.

'We just want to talk,' said the smaller man in a thick accent, pinning her with his beady eyes and reaching out again for her arm. She backed away. The vulture flapped behind him. 'There's nothing to worry about.' But she could tell there was everything to worry about. The car still murmured at the side of the road, its headlamps painting a pool of yellow on the tarmac, wipers juddering across the glass. The driver's door and the kerbside back door hung open. She wrote tomorrow's headlines in her head. *Stripper abducted.* A hand seized her wrist and her stomach churned.

A voice yelled out behind her 'What's happening? Everything alright, Kate?'

She struggled to turn around and there was Gold. He was standing with his legs apart like a gunfighter. Her wrist hurt. There was a lump of a cash bag hanging from one of Gold's arms. 'Help.' She choked. The vulture lingered a few metres away, watching and waiting.

Gold closed the distance between them in a breath. Her captor tugged her arm. Gold swung high in the air and the cash bag smashed into the side of the man's face with a chink. He let go of her wrist at once and made a sound like air coming out of a balloon, then staggered with his head buried in his hands and Gold took a handful of him and threw him like a mannequin into the gutter where he collapsed in a heap. Weighing the cash bag in his arm Gold was already advancing towards the vulture, who took a faltering step towards the car. Then the vulture seemed to change his mind, and squared up to Gold. He was reaching inside his coat.

The blast, when it came was like the noise of a traffic collision.

Gold met the impact with a grin and then a grimace, then heaved himself to the left with his arms flailing as though he was about to perform a cartwheel. Then he dropped in a lumpy pile on the pavement and didn't move. The cash bag landed with a metallic thump beside him.

Even the traffic seemed to fall silent. Kate was transfixed. The vulture looked at her once, as though trying to fix her location in his mind. The gun had disappeared into his coat. Then he tugged his friend to his feet and bundled him into the rear of the waiting car. He leered at her before he folded himself into the driver's seat.

'*Dos vidanje.*' The door slammed and the blue Volvo sped away with its tyres scrabbling and spray in its wake.

She hadn't noticed before that people had begun to congregate on the pavement. A murmur struck up. A man had crouched at Gold's side with a grey, anxious look. A thick black puddle had accumulated around the wreck of Gold's body. Somebody tried to put a comforting arm around her shoulder but she shrugged it off. Without thinking she hefted the cash bag out of the road, looked fleeting around her, and then ran from the scene as fast as she could, the rain wet and cold against her forehead ... a commotion behind her suggested that she was being chased, but when she looked back all she could see was a huddle of people gathered in the pale light that seeped from the club.

Chapter Fourteen

"IN A LITTLE over a week, two bankers have been killed in Moscow, including one who was the president of one of the largest banks in Russia. A wave of terror is picking up force. Obviously, this is a crime wave. The Feliks Group has evidence that shows that the criminal world is no longer satisfied with its take from legitimate businesses but wants to control them outright. The murder of Uvyerenny Bank president, Viktor Bukovsky, was clearly intended to send a message to all businessmen that the mafia will stop at nothing to take over. Unfortunately, we believe that law enforcement agencies are implicated as well. Their inaction and involvement with the criminal world have created a situation where criminals can kill with the knowledge that they'll never be caught. In 1991, every example of

corruption was a media sensation. Now, there is so much that no one

even comments on it. Cases are announced but never brought to trial.

Senior officials steal and go unpunished. And in

this sense, Yeltsin himself must share some of the guilt for the murder

of Viktor Bukovsky. Immediate and effective responses to crimes are

needed but nowhere to be found. Instead, Yeltsin has appointed a

crony rather than a specialist to head the FSB and names a similar

man as minister of the interior. We can't expect any changes until

there have been elections for the parliament and the president. We

demand action. Ivan Ivanov."

Nikolay read the new 'intelligence report' from the Feliks Group in Izvestia, which was accompanied by a lurid photograph of the aftermath of the killing in Arbat. Who stood to gain from this? He wondered.

It was early in the morning. Layers of fine dust particles danced in the morning sunlight that peered through grimy sash windows. The office had the impression of an evacuation. Desks piled high with case files were silent and abandoned. Telephones went unanswered. Nikolay perched on the edge of an unoccupied desk with a cup of foul liquid masquerading as coffee. A few solitary insomniacs were bowed over their desks in silence.

Could it be, he wondered, that there was a connection between General Borilyenko and the Feliks Group? And were these murders perpetrated by the Feliks Group as some kind of perverse publicity stunt? And why had Lebed instructed him to be on the scene?

Chapter Fifteen

ROBERT WAS CHOOSING a sandwich for lunch without much appetite when his mobile phone rang. He flipped open the Motorola, tugged out the antenna and pressed it to his ear. A woman standing next to him made a disapproving expression and reached across for a cellophane wrapped green salad.

'Robert? Where are you?' said Sally. In an effort to get a better signal he swapped the phone to his other hand, then stepped outside the shop. He stood with his back to a window display of pastries. Across the road was a temporary traffic light. Cars lined up at a red light with idling motors and the boom of muffled radios. One played 'Don't look Back in Anger'. He raised his voice above the traffic:

'Down the road. Grabbing a sandwich. What's up?'

'Are you coming back?'

'Of course. Why?' He waited. The line hissed. The traffic lights changed. A boy in a hot hatchback gunned his engine.

'The police are here.'

'Police? What do they want?'

'They want to talk to you.'

'Did they say what about?' He turned to the window as though to shield the call from any onlookers.

'They didn't say. Well... They don't, do they?' She sounded doubtful. 'But they say there's nothing to worry about.'

'Nothing to worry about? They would say that wouldn't they? Even if there was.' He was now hurrying back towards his office. 'I hope it's nothing to do with Becki,' his first thought. But she was at school. 'I'll be there in five minutes. Tell them five minutes, OK?' He lengthened his pace and ended the call, almost colliding with a woman loaded with shopping bags. 'Sorry.'

When he reached his small estate agency, he could see past the property boards in the window two men sitting in front of his empty desk. They turned as he pushed through the door, and when he looked at them they stood up, one hitching up his trousers.

'Mr Chambers?' Said the other, taking the lead and holding out a hand in anticipation.

'What is it? Not my daughter?'

They exchanged looks. 'No, no. Nothing like that. I don't think there's any need to worry,' said one, without much enthusiasm. 'Is there somewhere we could go?' glancing at Sally. Nobody else in the office.

'Sally, why don't you go to lunch,' said Robert, taking the hint. Sally unhooked her coat from the stand by the door, eager it seemed to be gone.

'You need to phone Mr Henderson about Portland Avenue.' She said, leaving in her wake the peachy aroma of cosmetics as the glass door shut out the road noises. Robert locked it, asking over his shoulder,

'So, are you going to tell me? What's it all about?'

The taller officer produced a warrant card and presented it to him. The other officer had resumed his seat, propping his arm over the back of his chair in an over-casual gesture that irritated Robert somehow. 'I'm detective constable Trent - and that's detective sergeant Morris,' nodding towards the seated man. 'We're here to talk to you about your wife.'

He looked from one to the other. 'Ex, actually. Ex-wife now, that is. What's wrong? What's happened to her?'

'Well, firstly we need to know her whereabouts. We wondered if you might know where she can be found?'

'Found? What's she done?'

Morris picked up the conversation, as though they had reached the crux of the matter. 'There was an incident yesterday in which she may be a key witness. We need to interview her as soon as possible.'

Robert narrowed his eyes. 'What kind of incident?'

'Do you know where she is, Mr Chambers?' he said with an edge.

'No. I don't. What kind of incident?'

'When was the last time you saw your *ex*-wife, Mr Chambers?'

'It must be… I don't know. A few days ago. What day is it today?'

'Tuesday.'

'Then Thursday. Last week.' He said, trying to count the days but the arithmetic refusing to work. 'Please… she's still… I mean she's my daughter's mother. What's happened?'

'Close are you? You and your ex?'

'We have a daughter. So we try to keep... on good terms, if you like. We talk. We're friendly.'

'What is it...? An *exotic* dancer, is she? So we're told.'

Robert flushed. 'So what?'

'So… So, maybe some criminal types might be associated with the type of establishment she works in. What do you think?'

'I've really no idea.'

'Possible she got mixed up in something? Over her head?'

'Like what?'

Morris shrugged. 'You tell me. Know any of her *friends* do you? Anywhere she could be staying? A *boyfriend*?' He added with a tone that Robert resented.

'What exactly happened?'

'That's a no then, is it?'

'Yes. A no. So, are you going to tell me what this is all about?

'A weapon was discharged, Mr Chambers. Somebody with whom we believe your wife to have been *familiar* was critically injured.' He paused to scrutinise Robert's reaction. 'Critically.' He repeated, making sure that Robert had registered its implication. Somebody dead.. But who? Somebody she knew… 'Need money does she? So far as you know?'

'Not more than usually.' He looked from one to the other but their faces were blank.

The constable started to speak but Morris interrupted. 'It was a serious incident, Mr Chambers. Involving loss of life. But we only want to talk to Mrs Chambers as a potential witness.' He stood up. 'At this stage.' He produced a card. 'If and when she gets in touch, please ask her to call us at once. And, let us know. If she does get in touch. It would be very helpful.'

The two policeman went to the door and waited while Robert unlocked it. Morris pointed to one of the properties listed in the window. 'Nice.' He said. A detached five bedroom in Rickmansworth.

'Interested?' Robert replied with what he hoped was irony, holding the door open wide.

'Not on a policeman's salary.' Morris touched his forehead in a mock salute. Trent nodded at Robert with a trace of sympathy. 'Be in touch then?' Said Morris, unlocking a Ford Mondeo parked right outside on a double yellow line.

Chapter Sixteen

THE BARMAN WATCHED her table with lascivious, sunken eyes. A bald, fat man in a stained business shirt open at the collar, he slouched at the corner of the bar challenging anyone to disturb him. There were few enough customers: a scrawny young couple in a corner whispered over their empty glasses, and touched hands. A man in a shiny suit was feeding money without much hope into a fruit machine. To get to this smoky bar in Kensington she had taken a circuitous route on the London Underground, changing trains and lines several times, without any real sense of purpose or direction. A strategy she'd read about in some spy novel to throw off a tail. She was going to go straight home from the club, but when she caught sight of a blue Volvo parked in her street, she had turned back at once to the tube station at a half run.

Overnight at a drab bed and breakfast, where she had paid cash, and whiled away the morning just walking the streets. Now she lingered over a glass of tepid vodka, tracing circles on the tabletop with her finger.

She should call the police. Next to her glass on the table her mobile phone reproached her with its silence. She had a full signal in this place - there was no excuse. And how would she explain herself? Why had she run away? Who was she running from? What did the men want? She shuddered as she recalled the appraising look that the vulture-like one had given her just before he hauled his friend into the car. And the fleeting *'dos vidanye'* that confirmed her fears. This was all connected in some way with her inner life. Poor Gold. Poor, poor Gold. She steeled herself against the onset of tears. Out of the corner of her eye she caught the barman shifting, taking a n interest. She flipped back her hair, lifted her glass to her lips and swallowed the vodka straight down. The man at the fruit machine shot her a secret glance when her chair scraped back. The barman raised his eyebrows.

'Another please. A large vodka. Do you have any that's cold?'

'You want ice?'

'No, not really. It doesn't matter.'

The barman shrugged, hitched up his trousers, and pulled her a large vodka from the optic. She paid and took it back to her table near the door. If not the police, then what? She couldn't stay on the streets. But she couldn't return home either. She had to resolve this whole thing on her own. Whatever it was.

The mobile phone trilled and her stomach turned. She looked at the number in the display. *'Home'*. She pressed the red button to terminate the call. *'Home'* meant Robert. It was one of the things she kept meaning to change. Somehow too painful to do. Like the door key that she hadn't removed from her key ring. It didn't open anything now except old wounds, but she kept it there nonetheless. She waited for the familiar beep that told her that Robert had left a voice message, which he always did.

Gold was dead, she reminded herself. She kept reminding herself at odd intervals, because she felt she owed it to him to keep him alive, at least in her head. To repeat that one horrific fact. *Gold is dead.*

When the phone bleeped she stabbed the voicemail button with her thumb and clamped the phone to her ear.

'You have one new message.' The voice informed her. Then a faint hissing before she heard Robert's voice. 'Kate where the hell are you? The police have been round. What's going on? What kind of trouble are you in? Phone me as soon as you get this message.' There was a pause. Then in a more measured tone: 'Please, Kate. Whatever it is. Phone me. Maybe I can help. They wouldn't tell me anything. Just asked a lot of questions. Phone me.'

She tossed the phone onto the table with a rattle that made the scrawny couple in the corner look at her with a shared frown. She smiled at them and they turned away. Of course the police would want to talk to her. She was a murder witness. She shivered and threw back the vodka. She could only hole up here for so long. With a sneaking realisation she thought the police may also want to talk to her about the takings from the club. She had the moneybag in her sport bag beside her. As she absorbed this, another thought occurred to her: Beside herself who else had seen Gold's attackers? And if the police didn't know about the two men, then who's to say that she hadn't shot Gold herself, to steal the money?

Some half-formulated idea made her pluck up her phone again and called up Manda's number from the memory. Everything pointed to Russia. Her 'false' memory. The man who thought he recognised her on the tube. Gold's killers. The samovar. Her newly reconstructed past. It seemed to ring for an age. Kate was on the point of giving up when there was a click.

A tired voice said: 'Hello.'

'Manda it's Kate.'

'Oh... hi Kate.'

Kate tried to detect anything unusual in her voice, but she sounded as disinterested as ever. 'Manda I'm in trouble.' She tried to keep her voice low. She felt that the whole bar was listening in.

'Why am I not surprised? You only ever call me when you're in trouble.'

'This time it's different. This time it's really bad.' Manda's silence implied a shrug. 'Manda I need you to do something for me.'

'What is it this time?'

'I need you to go to the flat.'

Across the road from the pub, outside the anonymous entrance to the Russian embassy, the visa queue snaked around the block.

Chapter Seventeen

'Amateurs. Fucking amateurs. This isn't the Wild West. What did you think you were doing?' Dmitry was shouting, spittle flying. He picked up a file from his desk and raised it as though to throw it, then seemed to think better of it and slapped it back on the desk in exasperation. 'What were you thinking of?"

'We were picking the girl up. Like you told us,' said Petrov. He sat with his legs open wide, slumped in the chair.

'And in the process you shot up the town like some Wild West cowboy and killed some guy.' He pointed two fingers across his desk at Petrov and made a gesture of a gun recoiling. 'Fucking John Wayne. In London!'

'Just some black guy. Look …. with respect, you weren't there.

We had no choice. You should have seen Sasha's face. What he did. An animal. Bigger than a bear.'

'Our all powerful KGB. You must be crazy.' He screwed a finger into his temple in demonstration. Then, 'What did you do with the gun?'

'It's safe. In the river.'

'And the car?'

'Well of course, the plates were fake, but I had someone take care of it. Don't worry.'

'Don't worry, he says after starting a fucking war with Great Britain. What am I going to tell Moscow?'

'I guess you'll tell them we fucked up. Sorry Dima. Sometimes it happens.' Petrov shrugged.

'Don't tell me "Sorry Dima we fucked up" or I'll fuck you up for sure.'

He had been putting off reporting this latest development to the General, but there was no choice. He picked up the phone. Looked at Petrov. 'Still here?'

Petrov stood up. 'I did what anyone would have done.'

'Anyone without a brain. Get out. You make me sick.'

The General answered the phone on the first ring. 'Borilyenko.'

'General, there was an incident.'

'I heard,' Said the General. 'You're speaking to me only now?'

'I wanted a full report. From the officer.'

'I already had a full report. From another source. It's not acceptable.'

'I'm sorry.' The receiver whined, and he wondered if it was tapped. More of a probability than a possibility. A question of *who* was listening, rather than if anybody was listening.

'Yes. Tell me something. When you met with our friend?'

'General?'

'Did she describe anything of her memories. Anything you can think of?'

'She mentioned Simbirsk that's all. Wanted to know what it was.'

'You're sure she didn't mention anything else about... well about our *facilities*?'

'I'm sure.'

'And if she did, you would tell me? At once?'

'Of course, General.'

'Sooner I hope than in the case of this latest incident.'

'I'm sorry General...'

'Yes. It's noted. Tell me something else: when you left town, all those years ago. After you were *reassigned.* Did you have any further contact with, shall we say, former *residents*?'

'It was forbidden.'

'Well yes. It was. But you didn't answer my question.'

'Of course not General. I mean, I didn't have any contact.'

'Good. Keep me closely advised of developments.' The call ended with a click.

Dikul peeled off the list of names with undisguised relish, with barely a glance at his notebook, and watched Nikolay's eyes widen involuntarily. It served him right. They were messing with the wrong people. Now he would see sense.

'But what were they doing there?'

Dikul indulged himself in a shrug. 'How the fuck should I know? That's who we saw. Right Andrei?' He turned to Chernov for assurance, but Chernov seemed to have discovered an unnatural interest in his fingernails. 'That's who we saw.' He repeated in a reproachful tone. He turned to his notebook and read aloud, 'At nine-forty-five Minister for Justice - Minister for Fucking Justice,' He bracketed unnecessarily, 'Yuri Chaika followed General Borilyenko and,' he paused archly, '*others*, into the building.' He looked up at

Sokolov. 'The Minister for Justice,' he repeated again in wonder. The jangle of the phone startled him out of a kind of reverence. Nikolay snatched up the receiver in annoyance.

'Sokolov.'

Dikul counted the moments and traced the hairline cracks in the walls with his eyes trying to display disinterest.

'Good. I'll send someone over. Yes, yes,' Nikolay was saying, drumming his fingers in frustration, and his eyes darted about the room. Dikul secreted a smile. 'Me? No, I don't need to come. Why should I?' A pause. Sokolov frowned and looked directly at Dikul, but with unseeing eyes. 'For what reason? No, of course you don't. But do you know who? Well, I suppose I could find out.' Dikul flung Chernov a sly look, but Chernov was inscrutable. 'If you're sure. OK – then I'll be there.' Sokolov laid down the receiver thoughtfully.

'I have to go into town,' he said. 'To interview a foreigner.'

Chapter Eighteen

MANDA STEPPED INTO the apartment, thrust the keys into her jacket pocket and pushed the door closed behind her. She stood there for a few seconds absorbing the silence, listening for the slightest disturbance. When she was satisfied, she padded down the passage and put her head around the door of the bedroom. Everything orderly and tidy. A bedraggled teddy bear was perched on the white duvet, looking disconsolate. The curtains were half open and the grey sky weighed against the glass like a threat.

She passed into the sitting room and glanced around. The vacant TV met her gaze from the corner. A stack of fashion magazines lapped over the edge of a coffee table. A pale blue cashmere cardigan lay over the back of the sofa, neatly folded. She knew it would be cashmere because that was Kate.

In the kitchen there was an empty coffee cup in the stainless-steel sink. The window looked out onto the dingy walkway. She knew where to look.

Under the sink, in a plastic bucket filled with a jumble of cleaning products was a folded brown A4 envelope. She felt around inside for the familiar shape of a passport and a thin wad of banknotes. She crammed the folded envelope into her handbag then as an afterthought reached up and opened and closed the cupboards one by one, purely out of curiosity. Nothing there to betray Kate. There was a general absence of personal items, personal touches. Except for the teddy bear. Manda had known Kate for years, but when she tried to call her to mind there was almost nothing she could recall about her at all. She had a daughter. A failed marriage. And now she was in trouble.

Chapter Nineteen

GRIGOR SAT ON his usual stool at the bar with a bottle of vodka and a meaty cigar, drifting in a narcotic trance. A few of the girls arrayed themselves along the bar, lithe and animated with smooth bare limbs, exchanging inanities and smiling at the guys. The guys puffed their chests and sucked on beer bottles, watching the show or trying to catch a girl's eye. The music was loud and the tracks were all the same to Grigor's ears.

A mercurial shape shifted in the spotlight, melting and twisting on the stage. Once he had found it sexually stimulating to watch the girls, but no longer. He had slept with many of them, and his curiosity had waned. He shrank from the sham of the false connection: he had nothing in common with these girls, just a prehistoric desire fulfilled, and then in the morning there came the usual void.

The lights pulsed, throwing shadows on the faces of the grim statues of past Soviet leaders that passed for macabre decoration, lending them expression. The barman picked up Grigor's empty bottle and raised an eyebrow.

'Another one, Boss?'

He nodded, and the barman slid a full bottle of Stolichnaya across the counter.

He didn't see the girl at first. A persistent presence at his side, waiting. When he looked at her she seemed to wipe away a tear, leaving a thin track in her make up. She wore too much make up for Grigor's taste. Lipstick the colour of blood. When she leaned towards him he recognised the perfume, sharp and enervating.

'Can I talk to you, please, Grigor?'

He guessed she was less than 20. She had an alabaster look about her, fragile and pale. Her eyes were liquid, and she had a tiny scar on her chin that was becoming.

'Pull up a chair.'

'Not here,' she said, looking afraid. 'Privately.'

'What is it?'

'It's personal.'

'I don't do personal. The other girls must have told you that. You're new here?'

'Yes. A couple of weeks. But the girls said I could talk to you.'

'They said that?'

'Can I have a drink?'

'Help yourself.' He signalled to the barman who stopped serving a customer to get him another vodka glass. He filled it and she drank it in one. He watched the contraction of her throat and felt a sudden desire.

'They said you understood.'

'I'm surprised they'd say that.' And he was.

'My boyfriend was in Chechnya. In the army.' She had to raise her voice above the music, putting her mouth up against his ear. Her breath was hot and smelled of spices. A girl on the stage bent double, splaying everything. More biological than sexual, he thought.

'So?'

'On Monday he comes home on leave. He's changed.'

'Chechnya changes everything.' He didn't bother to raise his voice so she had to come closer to hear.

'What?'

'Chechnya. It changes people. Everything. It changes

everything.'

'Have you ever been?'

'I was there.'

'He's violent. Hits me. Last time he broke my arm. He did this,' pointing to the tiny scar on her chin, 'with a knife.'

'He's a soldier. Soldiers can be violent.'

'I'm afraid, Grigor. I'm afraid next time he'll kill me.'

'Leave him.'

'I would, believe me. But where would I go? I don't have any money. As it is I pay all the bills. In the daytime I work in retail. His wages he just drinks away. It wasn't always like this.'

'What's your name?'

'I'm so sorry. My name is Lizok.' She offered him a slim white hand but he didn't take it.

'What do you do here, Lizok? Dance or what?'

'Up to now just dancing. But I'll do whatever it takes.'

'What do you want from me, Lizok?'

'I have to leave him. But I need money. To get another place. A deposit. A loan. I can pay it back, I promise.'

'I can't help you Lizok. It's not my policy.'

'I'd do anything Grigor,' tipping her flawed jaw at him. Another tear traced her cheek.

'Anything?'

'I could make you happy.'

'I can't help you.'

'I understand.' She turned away, and as she crossed the room Grigor tried not to look as a man took her arm.

'Hey. What's wrong beautiful?' he heard. Tears are attractive to some men. Her reply was lost in the blare of the music, and soon she was lost too, somewhere in the crowded space. But he didn't forget the man. He had untidy red hair and a tattoo on his arm. A military tattoo of some kind with a dagger. His face was bloated and he had a gut that jutted over his waistband.

Later that same evening Alexei steered the red haired man into Grigor's office. The man was trying to shake off Alexei's hand, but Alexei was strong.

'What is this? What the fuck's going on?'

Grigor leaned against his desk.

'Let him go, Alexei. I'll take it from here. Thanks.'

Alexei left the room shutting the door with care. The man's complexion matched the colour of his hair. He looked hot and dishevelled. He put his hands on his hips.

'What's going on? Who the fuck are you? Is this some kind of shake down?'

'I own this place. And a few others.' He poured a shot of vodka. 'Drink?'

'I'm an American citizen.'

'You don't say,'

'What do you want?'

'You're with a girl.'

'She's not under-age is she?' he looked nervous.

'I doubt it.'

'So what then?'

'Her name is Lizok. I don't care what transaction you agree between you.'

'What do you mean transaction. You mean sex?'

'Yes. Or a private dance. However it turns out.' Grigor took an envelope from the desk. It was open and he flipped through it to show it was full of dollars. He flipped out a hundred dollar bill and held it out to the American. 'This is for you. For your trouble. The rest - there's a thousand dollars here – you're going to give as a tip. To Lizok. You won't mention our cosy chat. You're just a generous guy. And she lucked in. Understood?'

The American looked suspicious but took the hundred dollars and the envelope full of cash. 'Why?'

'Because that's what I want. It's my business. Just give her the money. And believe me I'll know if you don't do exactly as I say.'

'Are you threatening me?' He looked at the envelope. Flipped through the greenbacks. Changed his stance, one leg advanced. 'So what's the catch? You can't fool me. I'm an American. This is some kind of scam, right?'

Grigor regarded most Americans with contempt. Maybe because of the Cold War, even though it seemed like a generation ago. But he hated the synthetic toughness. The naïve self-assurance. 'Go and find your girl,' he said.

Grigor left the night club to look in on a new project: a glossy fronted casino on Odessa Street. There he patrolled the tables for a few hours, watching pallid men exchange their cash for plastic tokens, spoke to a few of the croupiers, and spent an hour looking at the books with the manager, before leaving with a feeling of renewed propriety, and a conviction to find an additional site. He wondered why he hadn't thought of this before. Gambling. With gambling there was no product: only cash flow.

When he got back to Tverskaya Street there were three police cars parked outside his club with their blue lights spinning. It was just after three in the morning, and normally at this time there would still be a small queue of men waiting to enter. His first thought was there had been a fight. It wasn't unheard of.

He drew up in his SUV close to the rear of a police car, almost touching, then barrelled towards the entrance. Nobody on the door he noticed with rising anger. What was going on?

Inside the lights burned bright and the music was silent. People with startled faces milled around, trying to assemble themselves into two orderly lines, one for the men and one for the women. Police officers were taking details at the head of each line.

'Name? ID?'

'Who's in charge here?' Grigor said to one policeman. The policeman pointed with a pen to a Lieutenant standing alone, and Grigor approached him with rising fury. 'Would you mind telling me what the fuck you think you are doing here?'

'Who are you?' the lieutenant was young and his uniform was freshly laundered. He had red cheeks.

'This is my club.'

The lieutenant consulted a notebook. Alexei and Fyodr appeared, looking ashamed.

'Sorry Boss,' said Fyodr. 'They just burst in waving a warrant.'

'Grigor Vassilyich Malenkov?'

'That's right. So what's happening here?'

'We've had a report about illegal prostitution taking place in this night club.'

'This is a respectable place.'

'Well we've had a report, and we have to act on it.'

'Who from?'

'A foreigner.'

Grigor guessed at once. 'An American.'

'Not that it matters - but yes. An American.'

'You can't do this.'

'I need to take some details from you, as the owner,' said the lieutenant.

'I'll give you some fucking details.' Grigor took out his mobile phone and dialled a number from memory.

'What are you doing?'

'I've been raided,' said Grigor into the phone. 'I can't speak to you now because I am too fucking angry. Talk to this person. He wears the uniform of a lieutenant.' And Grigor held out the phone without looking at the policeman. The lieutenant took it and put it to his ear.

'I am Lieutenant Pavel Petrovich Kirov of the Moscow police. Who...' He stopped speaking and listened. Grigor felt a little sorry for this young policeman as he watched his demeanour change. The confidence, what little there had been, drained away. He cupped his hand around the mouthpiece and turned his back on Grigor. 'Yes. But I didn't know. Nobody told me.... Yes of course... but we had a complaint... ' He was silent several moments. 'Yes sir. I understand sir ... Yes, he's right here.' The lieutenant turned again to face Grigor and gave him back the phone. When he put it against his ear the receiver was hot and a little slippery with perspiration.

'Colonel?'

'The misunderstanding has been resolved.'

'It's not over Colonel,' said Grigor.

'I understand. See to it however you see fit.'

Grigor terminated the call without saying goodbye. The lieutenant was waiting for him. 'I am very sorry sir. Nobody told me.'

'Just take out your trash,' he said, meaning the other policemen and regretting his words. But he didn't apologise. 'What are you waiting for?'

'Of course sir. I am very sorry to have disrupted the evening.' He clapped his hands for attention, and shouted. 'Everybody can go back to what they were doing. My officers - meet me outside. I apologise for the inconvenience.' The lines of erstwhile revellers evaporated almost at once. Some men, Grigor noticed, headed straight for the exit.

'You need to be more careful.' Said Grigor. 'You're new around here I think …. Even so there must be some kind of list. Places that are - what? Let's say *regulated* by the FSB.'

'You're right, I'm new. I was assigned here from Uglich. A promotion.' He was ashen faced. The lights darkened. A voice over the PA encouraged everyone to carry on having a good time. There was a surge of people towards the bar.

'No harm done.'

'I don't like to ask.. But there'll be no formal complaint, will there? Only it's my first assignment as a lieutenant and…'

'It's nothing. Not your fault. I just want to get my place back to normal before I lose all of the night's trade.'

'Thank you sir,' and the lieutenant walked over to where some policemen stood in a superfluous group'

Alexei put a hand on Grigor's shoulder.

'Boss - in your office. I'm sorry but I let her wait there.'

And when Grigor entered his office there was Lizok quietly sobbing. She stood up when he walked in. Her eyes glistened. 'Grigor. I don't know what to say. I'm so sorry. And so grateful.'

'What do you mean?'

'I know what you did. I know it came from you.'

He poured himself a vodka. 'I don't know what you're talking about.'

'But I couldn't have sex with that man. Even for money. And he got angry. Still gave me $1,000. He insisted. Told me you'd instructed him to give it to me. But I couldn't … I'm sorry. I know it was him that caused all this. I caused it.' She started crying again. 'You must want your money back…'

'Keep the money. Find an apartment. But don't tell anybody. Nobody, understand? I don't want anyone to think I'm going soft. Go and dance. Make me some money.'

She rushed up to him before he could stop her, and planted a damp kiss on his cheek, then left the room. This was not the right business for her, and he should have told her to go home. But how else does a girl survive on a shop worker's money in Moscow? He had done the sums, and they didn't work.

Chapter Twenty

WRITHING IN HER lumpy seat, she listened to the announcements first in Russian then in accented English, and understanding them both couldn't help but feel a little proud of her new found linguistic skills. The safety information in the seat pocket informed her that she was flying in an Aeroflot Ilyushin 62 jet, which had been substituted after a two hour delay at Heathrow for the modern Boeing 737 was described on her boarding card. It was a full and restless flight.

Throughout the journey it seemed to her that the pilot had been in the habit of turning the engines on and off in mid flight, leading to unpredictable descents and ascents that made her ears hurt. Maybe in an effort to save fuel, she speculated. A wide-bodied man in a sheepskin coat was picking his nose, his elbows planted on a large aluminium briefcase on his lap. Throughout the five hour flight he had drummed on the briefcase with plump fingers, paying her no attention. Now they were drawing to the end of the flight. The crew made languid preparations to land.

She turned her attention to the undulating scenery below, trying to awaken her alternative memory, searching for some vestiges of déjà vu but none came. The plane banked. Below the land was green and wild looking, sprinkled with what looked like ramshackle country houses. They were flying low, and the misty greens and greys sharpened as they hurtled up to greet them. A sudden wave of apprehension swept over her. She wondered, not for the first time, what she expected to find in Moscow. It was as though she was trying to locate questions for a series of answers that she had known all her life. There was an ethereal umbilical cord that attached her to this place, and recent events had given a sharp tug to that cord. Something in her 'false' past had led to this.. *pursuit*. And who was pursing her? It had led to Gold's murder. His *murder* for God's sake. She tried to work up some extra emphasis in an effort to make it real. But it wasn't real. It was like a part of the memories that she had set aside: vivid, and realistic. But not genuine. Lacking *credibility* somehow. She frowned.

The plane landed with a jolt at Shermetyevo 2 airport to a ripple of applause in the cabin and taxied with an undulating roar towards an orange and grey terminal building. The man beside her was oblivious, drumming his fingers. Drumming, drumming, drumming.

She was surprised to find that the airport was a modern building, alight with the gleam of chrome and glass. There were police and guards everywhere. She steeled herself, trying to awaken her false memory, but it seemed to have evaporated altogether. She was Kate Buckingham from England, she reminded herself. She retrieved her single bag and joined a lengthy queue at customs, where she waited in line for almost two hours to be processed. Most of the passengers waited in silence with blank stares. It occurred to her that nobody complained. Everyone seemed remarkably calm, even the customs officials whom she watched as they unpacked each bag with methodical care.

When it was her turn, she began to unfasten her bag. It was then that some intuition made her look up in time to catch a glance, real or imagined, exchanged between the customs official and a man in a brown suit beyond the barrier.

'It's ok. Go. Go.' The Customs man was waving for her to continue.

'You're not going to search me?'

'You may go.'

Bewildered and uneasy, she hauled her bag off the table.

'Welcome to Moscow,' said the officer with a grim stare as she passed him. She looked around for the man in the brown suit, but he was nowhere to be seen. Perhaps she had imagined it after all?

There were people milling everywhere with assorted bags, labouring at the handles of overloaded trolleys. The pavement was punctuated with fossilised gum. She had a strange feeling of abandonment. Just then a man with a bushy grey moustache and shaved head rushed up to her. He was stocky and angular, wearing an olive green military style coat with a red and white kerchief tied around his neck. 'Taxi?' He said in a thick accent. She tried to wave him away, but he produced a handful of creased snapshots and thrust one at her. It was a picture of three toothy children. 'Look.' He said, 'My family.' He was grinning at her, in such an ingratiating way that she paused for long enough for him to snatch up her suitcase and steer her towards the exit by the arm. 'Yes? With family like this I cannot be Mafia, OK? No problem.' He laughed. 'First time in Moscow, yes?' He tapped the side of his nose, talking to her all the time over his shoulder. 'Is good to be careful in these times. OK? OK. No problem.'

He was waving his unencumbered arm around in a placatory manner. She protested at first, but then she reasoned that she needed a taxi after all, and he seemed harmless enough.

'American,' he pronounced with authority as he opened the boot of a battered Lada and threw her case inside.

'English,' she corrected.

He nodded in stern affirmation. 'It's OK. No problem.' He pointed at the passenger door. 'Please..' and she tugged at the door, which opened with an alarming creak. Before getting into the car himself he rummaged in the glove compartment and produced two windscreen wipers, which he attached with intricate care to the front of the car. As if in explanation he looked at the sky. 'It will rain,' he predicted. The car smelt of dogs and gasoline, and she noticed with an uneasy glance over her shoulder that the seats were matted with fur. The driver settled himself on the beaded seat behind the wheel with a deep sigh. 'Thieves everywhere. Where we are going?'

For the first time she realised how ill prepared she was. Maybe she had been hoping that her other set of memories would take over and fill her head with familiar places, but her thoughts were unambiguous. She was simply Kate Buckingham from England after all.

'I ... I don't know. A hotel. Somewhere ... reasonable. Maybe you can recommend somewhere?' she said.

The taxi driver was unperturbed. 'You have dollars.' He said in the irrefutable way he seemed to have.

'Pounds,' she said.

He shrugged as though it was all the same to him. 'Of course. So, you will stay at good tourist hotel. I know such a place. No problem.' The engine fired with an angry rasp and he pulled into the traffic with not even a cursory glance over his shoulder.

And still the memories refused to stir. They drove along wide boulevards choked with traffic, beneath lurid banners advertising cars and casinos, past tall grey apartment blocks with cracked plaster, and incongruous statues and monuments. After they had been travelling for ten minutes the driver shot her a sidelong glance and announced with a grin: 'I am called Leonid.' He gestured with sudden triumph at the windscreen. 'Look.'

'I'm sorry ... what?'

'It rains. No problem,' and as if to emphasise the fact he slapped the windscreen wiper stalk with his hand which fell off at once. This left him delving in the floor-pan to find it with one hand on the wheel, his shaved head bobbing up and down to keep an eye out for the traffic, which did not prevent the car veering erratically. Since every other car on the road seemed to change lane without indication and for no apparent reason, it seemed to make no difference. Sometimes they would weave around a broken-down car in the middle lane.

Along the route Leonid proudly pointed out landmarks, like a tourist guide. 'Tank traps.' He gestured out of the window at a row of angular concrete constructions. 'For stopping of Nazis in Great Patriotic War.' He raised his chin, throwing her a sidelong glance. 'Germans stop here in Great Patriotic War. In tanks. No problem.'

After 40 minutes or so, when she had started to relax, he cut across 3 lanes of snarling traffic and careered to a halt in front of a broad art nouveau facade with a green roof. She gazed up at the rows of windows and counted 8 floors. Leonid gestured down the street as he propelled himself out of the car. 'Red Square there. Not far. OK? No problem.'

While she stepped into the street, Leonid wrested her bag from the boot. 'You have dollars,' he asserted.

'I have roubles ... and ... and pounds.'

'Of course. No problem.' He nodded, and she produced a twenty pound note which seemed to be enough, because Leonid accepted it and secreted it instantly inside his jacket without looking at it. 'No problem. Here..' And he fished inside his coat before thrusting a creased card at her which featured a picture of a limousine and a telephone number. The limousine was a world apart from the asthmatic yellow Lada. 'Please.. if you need car. Call Leonid. No problem,' and he deposited her bag outside the glass doors of the hotel and gave her a cheery wave. 'No problem. No problem.' He said again, in response to her thanks, and he levered himself into the taxi and revved the engine as he pulled away.

She tugged her wheeled case through a revolving glass door and into a galleried atrium lobby. She wondered how much this smart hotel was likely to cost, and made an effort to tot up the afternoon takings of Whites, which she had exchanged for notes in a bank in London, so distracted as the teller had counted them out she had no idea how much money she had.

At the desk a tall darkly dressed man in a pearl grey tie and with what seemed like a perpetual sneer eyed her suspiciously when she told him that she had no credit card. The tariff was listed in dollars on a polished wooden board behind the desk.

'You will pay the full room rate in advance.' He instructed.

'I'm sorry – I don't have US dollars.'

He shrugged. 'We couldn't take them if you had them. It is the law. We accept only Roubles.' He tapped some numbers into a calculator and announced a number in Roubles that sounded like a lot, and she counted out the grubby, unfamiliar notes, disappointed not to feel faintest awakening of her false memory.

After leaving her bag in her room, she took to the streets, seeking a flame that might re-ignite her absent memories. Perhaps she was mistaken after all. Perhaps Moscow was not the city of her past? She had to make a plan anyway. She had to see if Ekaterina Ivanovna was a fiction.

Her 'false' memory drove her to a corner of Gorky Street. Except that when the Cyrillic letters melted into meaning it wasn't Gorky she read, craning up at the sign, but Tverskaya. Her relief tainted with despair, she watched the fleeting traffic on the broad, tree-lined highway and wondered which way to turn. Tverskaya Street wriggled with colour and people. The evening sunshine cast long shadows. Above the growl of the traffic rang the clangour of construction work. This unexpected air of industriousness took her breath away. Everywhere she looked the sky was intersected with gallows like cranes. Scaffolding scarred the facades of once elegant, soon to be again apartment blocks. She sniffed the abrasive, gasoline-tinged air. A thump of rubber made her start. She stumbled out of the path of a wide-bodied BMW mounting the kerb to avoid a pothole out of Gasheka Street. Disorientated, she turned south along Tverskaya Street looking for evidence that this had once been Gorky Street, weaving through a Moscow that seemed all wrong. The bread queues of her memories supplanted with designer boutiques and jewellery shops. Maybe the others had been right all along? Maybe her 'false' memories were nothing more than dreams? She quickened her pace, her heels tapping, as though in flight or pursuit. Which was it? A street trader alongside a barrow dripping with fruit and vegetables devoured her with greedy eyes. Out of habit she smiled and swung her hair behind her. She passed a sushi restaurant, a shoe shop, a café. Every other building she observed was racked out with scaffolding, long chutes disgorging rubble into skips and dust into the air, as though they were busy dismantling the entire city. Further down the street she thought she saw a banner that she recognised: Pizza Hut. She could be in London. This could be yesterday.

Then, just as she was giving up hope, her memories were brought back into focus. Outside the offices of Izvestiya she came to an abrupt halt. A man behind her cursed, almost collided, then shot an angry glance over his shoulder as he passed, muttering something about tourists. Izvestiya. Anonymous, shabby offices with grimy windows.

And just across the street, the rugged, red-brick City Hall building fronted by white pillars that looked like a monstrous portcullis. Above them hung the tricolor of the Russian Federation, no longer the hammer and sickle. She felt vindicated - but there was something odd too. Something about her thoughts. It was as though they had taken on an angular, ill-fitting property. Then, when she glanced above the glittering window of another jewellery shop and read the sign "Tsentr Yuvelir" it came to her with a shock. Her thoughts had slipped into Russian, as naturally as if it were her mother tongue.

This realisation made her stop sharply. She looked all around. At the cafes and shops. At the pastel buildings. No longer grey but golden. No longer grim but garish. The pedestrians wore colourful clothes. She looked up, at the clear sky. Was this where she belonged? In the gentle breeze a red flag swayed above an entrance. She picked out the hammer and sickle and it sent a shudder through her because it was as though her other past had interceded. The sign above the door said 'Red Nights'. She shuddered again and pushed against the heavy glass door stencilled with Stalin's portrait, because it seemed the most natural thing to go inside.

As she stepped through the door she was struck by the acrid hint of disinfectant in the air, with an undertone of stale tobacco. She entered a vast room with parquet floors and spindly tables with chairs scattered all around. At the far end of the room, flanked by two giant concrete statues - one of Lenin, one of Stalin - was a stage with a backdrop of red curtains. Two men sat before the stage smoking cigarettes in a halo of smoke, hanging in the air like gossamer There was a bottle of vodka between them on a table. One of them swore, in a deep down, scathing voice. '*Na Hui!* Fuck you!' He stabbed out his cigarette angrily. 'Show me again.'

A girl on stage crossed to a music console and pressed a button. She had spidery limbs and long dark hair. She was a plain-faced girl with pointy features. When the music began with a resounding blast she leapt into the centre of the stage flashing a big fake grin at the two men, pivoting her long legs around. She was naked.

Kate watched enthralled, like she was watching her own performance from a world apart. She watched the girl perform all the usual stunts, pushing up her butt into the audience and peering from between her legs, laying on her back with her legs splayed. The men watched too, inscrutable and in silence, as she played out her routine. Her act was wooden in spite of her efforts. Stilted. Not like her own smooth motions she reflected, her dipping and kicking.

One of the men turned and saw her standing there. He had a

broad forehead, like a Labrador, and vast shoulders hunched over the table. Smoke obscured his features. Without a word he lifted a thick arm and beckoned to her. The other man turned then too, narrower, smaller. He looked surprised. She began to back away, knocking over a chair. It fell with an alarming clatter. With her heart in her mouth she turned and fled towards the door. She heard the laughter of the two men above the music as she flung herself through the doors into the street. One of them yelled at her: 'Come back. It's OK.' What had she been thinking of?

She hurried down the street - in the direction of Red Square she was certain, because now she seemed to recognise the side roads. Many of the names had changed, she realised, but there remained enough familiar ones to reinforce her memories.

She tried to formulate a plan, more composed now. She would go first to the police. She remembered the taxi driver's card. Leonid he said. She would call him from the hotel.

Chapter Twenty-One

WHEN BRAD SPENCER left his hotel, it was a crisp Moscow morning, but there was an aftertaste of petroleum in the air. His regular driver was not waiting for him outside, and he cursed the lazy Russians. He waited 10 minutes outside the hotel, refusing the approaches of cab drivers in one of his sparse words of Russian 'Nyet.' He didn't know what they said to him in return and he didn't care.

A black Mercedes swept to the kerb, tyres crackling on the icy road. The window was down and the driver was smoking. Brad saw him look over.

'Mr Spencer?'

'That's me.'

'They sent me to pick you up.'

'OK great. You're late, you know?' He crossed to the back door and waited an instant but when nobody made any move to open it for him he hauled it open and got in, swinging his laptop bag onto his knees. The car smelled of leather and stale tobacco. 'Better hurry,' he said, 'Where's the regular guy?'

'He was unavoidably detained,' and the car pulled away with a jerk of sudden power.

Brad watched the busy street without much interest. There were long lines at the bus stops. He wondered how the women all dressed like cat walk models in spiky heels and sometimes calf length boots. Yes sir, the women were more beautiful in Moscow than back home. Then he lost his train of thought, just drifted. 'Where are we?'

'We're taking a different route today.'

It irritated him that the driver was still smoking. The driver's window was open a crack, but it didn't stop the fumes from reaching him. 'Would you mind putting that out?'

The driver didn't answer.

'I said would you mind...?'

The buildings they passed were more like he had expected to see in Russia. Crumbling concrete blocks. The roads were more broken up too. The driver veered around a deep pothole, and it caused him to reach out for the grab handle.

He saw the driver glance in the rear-view mirror and smile. 'Mr Malenkov sends his regards,' he said.

'Who?'

'The owner of the night club that you visited last night.'

Everything tightened up at that moment. Everything concertinaed. There was just this moment in the back of a Mercedes with a belligerent Russian at the wheel. He had heard about heists in Moscow. Everybody had warned him. Why did he phone the police last night? Some stupid false bravado. His stomach churned.

'So where are you taking me now?'

'Mr Malenkov thinks that you need some education.'

The car swung into a bumpy side road between a series of tall apartment buildings. They blocked the sun.

'What kind of education?'

'A Russian education.'

They reached a piece of wasteland. There was a burnt out car, hard to tell what make, and a discarded mattress.

The Mercedes stopped, and the driver turned and grinned at him. Brad pulled at the door catch, but the doors were locked.

'This is where you get out.' He said. 'But before you do, there's something you should consider.'

Brad tasted the saliva in his mouth. He felt sick. 'What?'

'Some people would call Mr Malenkov a gangster. Some people say Mafia,' said the driver. 'And there are gangsters I know personally who would cut your tongue out for what you did last night. There are gangsters that would dump you in the Moskva river and not even give it a thought.' He paused. 'Give me your wallet.' Snapping his fingers.

Brad obeyed without thinking, and the driver put it in his jacket pocket without looking at it.

'So you are very lucky to be dealing with a *civilised* gangster who is not as *insecure* as others might be. In a minute, I'm going to leave you here. Without money and without ID. I warn you, it's not a safe area. And you don't speak Russian, which will make it more interesting.' He pushed open the drivers door and came round to the back, opening Brad's door. 'Get out.'

'Is that it?' He knew he was trembling and bunched his fists to stop himself shaking.

'Maybe,' said the driver. Brad saw now that the driver was a head taller than him, and thick chested. 'Now get going. And if I were you I would fuck off back to America as soon as you can. I respect Mr Malenkov, but sometimes I think he can be too restrained. If it were me, I can tell you I would at the very least break some bones. Do you understand?'

'I understand.'

'One more thing.'

Brad had turned away, and when he turned back he was horrified to see that the man was holding a gun. 'What?'

The driver grinned at him like before. Pointed the gun at his head. A dozen feet separated them. 'Take off the shoes. Maybe I want them as a souvenir.'

Brad took off his shoes.

'Toss them over here.'

He did as he was told.

'That's all. Now fuck off and I never want to see you again.'

Brad limped away, the concrete hard beneath his stockinged feet.

Chapter Twenty-Two

'YOU HAVE COME, let us say, to report a disappearance?' the officer spoke in a tone of unfounded suspicion. He was a man with frosty hair in his fifties wearing what passed for a tweed jacket and a greasy brown tie. His fingernails, Kate noticed, were bitten to the quick. There was a reek of tobacco about him. After several attempts to make headway in English Kate had submitted to Russian and was shocked to find it felt like coming home.

'The disappearance of Ekaterina Ivanovna Borodina.'
He had Kate's passport in his hands and was laboriously reading each page with unmerited concentration. He turned the pages slowly, sometimes turning back as though he had missed something. They were sitting across a desk strewn with documents, mostly hand-written

in cramped Cryllic script. An ashtray was brimful with unfiltered cigarette buts. The police station was chaotic. The phones rang constantly but nobody seemed to answer. Everybody seemed to be in a rush about something but it was hard to see what. Some uniformed officers levered a huge drunk through the doors protesting loudly and hoarsely. A few detectives hurried to assist and lent their shouts to the commotion. The officer in front of her seemed oblivious.

He snapped closed her passport suddenly with the air of someone who had finished reading a book with an unsatisfactory ending.

'You are a foreign national.' He concluded with infuriating logic.

'You know that already.'

'Exactly. I must find an appropriate person to deal with your allegations.'

'I'm not making any allegations. I just want to report a missing person.'

'I must find an appropriate person, all the same,' he said darkly, then stood up and ushered for her to do the same. 'You will kindly follow me.'

He led her through another office, almost identical to the first, then to a corridor that was eerily silent. He opened a door. 'You will wait here.'

It was an austere room with a desk and two plastic bucket chairs. There was a single barred window, high up and almost out of reach.

'Can I have my passport back?' she asked in sudden panic.

The officer grimaced. She suddenly realised that he was no longer holding it, and she wondered what he had done with it.

'Soon,' he said. He gestured to a chair with a stubby, nicotine stained forefinger, then closed the door silently and she was alone. She felt strangely abandoned. Her breathing was laboured. She walked around the perimeter of the room like a caged animal. She tried the door once, and was relieved to find it unlocked. When she put her head out into the corridor it was empty. She ventured out almost on tip-toe, Listening intently to the silence, then returned at once to the relative sanctuary of the room.

In order to see out of the window she had to put a chair up against the wall. The window looked out upon a small courtyard with two identically battered police Zhigulis parked side by side. A row of high windows like her own spanned one wall. The walls were grey. The tiled floor was grey. The metal table was grey. A symphony of grey. The colour of detention.

She looked at her watch, believing that she must have been in this room an hour already, but only ten minutes had passed.

Time sauntered. Sometimes she sat at the table. Sometimes she walked around the room. She supposed she could leave if she wanted to. She wasn't a prisoner. But then she reminded herself they had her passport. She might as well be a prisoner. She listened for a sound in the corridor, but there was nothing to hear except the buzz of the neon light. It was a mistake to come here, she decided. A mistake to come to Russia at all. What had she been thinking? She looked at the white plastic clock on the wall that measured each minute with an irritating buzz and a click and a wavering minute hand that was maddeningly never pointing precisely to the minute markers. It was set to the wrong time, as though time here was meaningless, and checked off the passing of the minutes in somebody else's time zone.

She remained there alone for almost two hours, thirsty and miserable. She was about to brave the corridor again when the door was flung open by a surprisingly elegant man in his thirties. He wore an affable smile, vaguely apologetic. He offered his hand which was smooth and warm, and looked at her with grey eyes that seemed to see beyond her.

'Traffic, I'm afraid.' He excused himself in flawless English. 'I'm sorry you've been detained for so long. I am Captain Nikolay Sokolov. Can I offer you some coffee?'

'Thank you. Yes please.'

He disappeared for a few moments then returned bearing two steaming polystyrene cups, pushing open the door with his knee. 'No milk I'm afraid.' He shook his head despairingly. 'You don't want to know what they have in that fridge.' He set both cups on the table making puddles around the bases.

'Now,' He laid her passport carefully between them like a peace offering. 'I'm told that you wish to report a disappearance?' He had switched to Russian and she barely noticed. She was getting used to this, she thought with a rush of dismay.

'As I told the officer. Of Ekaterina Ivanovna Borodina.'

Sokolov had produced a form from somewhere and was examining it as though working out which parts needed to be completed. 'And she is what? A friend? A relative?'

Kate hesitated. 'A relative I suppose?'

'You suppose?'

'Of the family.' She completed hurriedly. 'I myself have never met her.'

'The officer was right about one thing.' Said Sokolov with a strange note. 'Your Russian is impeccable. May I ask where you learnt?'

'In school.' She lied. The coffee was thick and black and scalded the roof of her mouth.

'Remarkable.' He shook his head again, this time in apparent wonderment, and studied the form closely, then produced an expensive looking pen from inside his jacket. 'First, some formalities. Your full name please.' He had reverted to English again.

She watched him closely as he filled out the form with meticulous care.

'And you last heard from Ekaterina Ivanovna when?'

'I didn't ... I mean I haven't. She disappeared some time in 1966,' she finished hopelessly, suddenly feeling rather foolish.

Sokolov lay down his pen and pushed back his chair. He looked tired. 'A lot of Russians disappeared around that time. Maybe you know something of our history?' he said after a long pause. She had a sinking feeling. 'It would be impossible to investigate every disappearance. Even if we had the resources. Which we don't.'

'So you won't do anything ?'

He sighed and held up the form. 'I will fill out a report if you want me to. It won't do any good.'

'I'm sorry to have wasted your time,' she said with bitterness.

He tapped his pen thoughtfully. It was obvious that he wasn't finished with her. 'Why did you come to Moscow, Miss

Buckingham?'

'To find Ekaterina.'

'No other reason?'

'No.'

'Have you heard of the FSB?'

'No.'

'The KGB, of course?'

'Of course.' *Komiter Gosudarstvennoi Bezopasnosti* the words strung themselves together in her head involuntarily, and she tried to suppress a shudder, which she thought he couldn't have failed to notice.

'The FSB is the same thing. The new face of the KGB – there have been many faces.. NKVD, MGB, Cheka.. take your pick.' He sighed. 'Have you any idea why the FSB might have an interest in you?' He was watching her attentively. She felt an ominous tingling sensation.

'In me…? But they can't have. Why would they...?'

'Why indeed?' He pursed his lips. 'You think it could have anything to do with this person you are looking for?'

'But why?'

'That's what interests me.' He thought for a moment then seemed to reach a conclusion. 'I'm going to tell you something that I will later deny. I have not been brought halfway across Moscow just to investigate your disappearance report. It's a hangover from Soviet times. When a Westerner of your ... profile comes to the attention of the authorities.' He caught her puzzled frown. 'Your excellent Russian, for example...' He waved a hand. '—it's thought you must either be a spy. Or if not, then perhaps you could be induced to spy for us. So, we are informed of course. And we send someone. More for the sake of form than anything else. A waste of everybody's valuable time.' He coughed into his hand and then laughed, almost to himself. 'As I said—a hangover from Soviet times.' There was a pause. 'But this time I came personally because I'm informed by the police that you were followed here by agents of the FSB. The police are not stupid. Not always anyway. We often make the mistake of assuming they are. If they say you are being followed by FSB then it is certainly true. It's unusual, to say the least. Foreign nationals are the responsibility of my department, you see.'

She felt a queasiness in her stomach, a quivering in her bones which she was not sure was visible. Was it possible that the men in London had something to do with the FSB? She dismissed the thought out of hand, but not without a lingering doubt. Poor Gold.. Had she imagined the man at passport control who had seemed to be observing her? He was observing her closely. She crossed her legs and gripped herself tightly with her arms around her torso in an effort to ease the shivering. She willed her other set of memories to admit her, but all she could remember was the here and now and an ordinary childhood in Tring, Hertfordshire. She was all deserted and alone in Moscow, she reminded herself, but the city harboured no more connotations than an encyclopaedia entry. Solokov's expression was sympathetic, and somehow sorrowful.

'Is there anything ... anything at all that you wish to tell me? Anything you *can* tell me, I mean? That might shed some light on why you are being followed?' he ventured.

What could she tell him? That she was being *haunted* by another person's memories? In vain she looked inside for something that she could confide, something that would help. But there was nothing. She felt empty. She said: 'I think I may have been born here in Russia. I can't explain it...'

He picked through the pages of her passport and referenced the place of birth without saying anything for what seemed to be a long time. The hands of the clock on the wall fizzed and clicked, paused endlessly, buzzed and clicked, with a fateful resonance. Finally he said: ' They're waiting out there. A blue Volga across the street. You're not in any danger. At least, not as far as I can tell, not as far as you've *told* me.' He held up the open passport. Frowned. 'What do you mean when you say you think you were born in Russia?'

She flashed him a doleful smile. Her back ached. She felt very weary. She felt a need to unburden herself to somebody. 'A man I've known as my father all my life told me two days ago that I'm an orphan, smuggled across the border from Russia as a baby. Into Turkey.' As if that wasn't enough to convince him she added: 'I've always felt—different.' She couldn't quite bring herself to talk about the memories.

He tapped the edge of her passport on the desk thoughtfully. 'And Ekaterina Ivanovna? What's she to you? Who is she?'

'I honestly am not sure. I think she might be.. might be an aunt. Or something. I don't know. She might know the answers. That's what I'm hoping..'

He looked at her as if from a long way away. 'And what are the questions to which you seek answers?' She picked at her fingernails nervously. Captain Sokolov sat back in his chair and sighed. 'I'm going to try to help you, Kate Buckingham. I'll make some enquiries. Nothing guaranteed. I'm curious. But there's something you are not telling me. I hope perhaps you'll learn to trust me.'

Outside the sun was low in the sky, and as she pushed through the doors, she looked around for Leonid without much prospect. But there he was languishing against his cab in his thick parka as though she had been away only minutes. The evening traffic snaked past. Leonid looked anxious.

'It's OK? No problem?'

'No problem.' She said, glancing across the broad street at a blue Volga with its nearside wheels on the pavement. The occupants were looking straight ahead out of the windscreen and not at her. So it was true.

Petrov stood in the doorway with his legs slightly apart and his hands deep in the pockets of a short leather jacket. He nodded. 'Dmitry.'

'What do you want?' He looked out into the corridor, left and right. Petrov shifted a little.

'Are you going to invite me in?'

'You shouldn't be here. What if you were followed.'

'I wasn't followed.'

'I can't believe you would come here.'

'I have my instructions.'

'Instructions? What instructions?'

In a fluid motion Petrov took his hand from his pocket and raised a small gun with a snub double barrel which he pressed hard into Dmitry's forehead. Dmitry took a deep breath. Stepped backwards into the apartment. Petrov followed pulling the door closed behind him. 'Bathroom.'

'Let's talk about this,' Backing down the hallway.

'Nothing to say Dima. I can't talk to you. It's not personal.'

'You work for me, Petrov.'

'We all work for Moscow. This it?' He pointed to a closed door. 'Open it.' The barrel still solid and cold against Dmitry's forehead. He fumbled with the door handle. Tried to un-jumble his head. Evolve some plan. 'Quickly.'

'Please…' Petrov with outstretched arm pushed him into the bathroom. 'You don't need to do this.'

Then the gun discharged with a harsh echo and the blood left an intricate pattern on the white tiles.

The car bumped over a broken section of road, and stuttered to a halt beneath an apartment block that stretched to 20 stories at least. Leonid tugged at the ineffectual handbrake, and the car rolled backwards a few inches when he removed his foot from the brake. Surrounding this block were smaller blocks of 5 storey buildings with precarious looking balconies in serried rows.

'Krushchoyovki.' He muttered through his moustache, half to himself. 'After Kruschev he make them when there were not sufficient house for everyone in Moscow. Now just rot and nobody repairs. What you do here?'

Kate and Leonid had developed a protocol when it came to language. Kate would speak in flawless Russian, but Leonid would continue to struggle with his flawed and heavily accented English. Each time she implored him to please speak Russian, he would tell her it was 'no problem' and would continue undaunted to speak in English.

Kate emerged from the taxi gingerly, and gazed up at the cream and brown building, shading her eyes against the sun. There was an alarming rift across the entire width of the building, over halfway up. The rows of black windows spanned the building like pock marks. She felt a frisson of excitement. This building had the day-worn familiarity of an old pair of shoes. She turned around, and there before her was the patch of scrubland that served as a park, just as she thought she there would be. Some twisted framed children's swings occupied the centre of the park, and a colourless wooden roundabout with slats of wood missing.

'I used to live here.' She said with assertion, pursing her lips in emphasis.

Leonid laughed in the merry, hearty way he had that reminded her of Santa Claus. 'Not live here. Not you. This Kruchchoyovki. *I* live in apartment like this. It was good times. You are from USA. Not live in Kruchchoyovki.'

'No, really,' she said, wishing he would speak Russian, 'I lived on the twelfth floor. I feel it.' She pointed in the direction of the building, but Leonid laughed, and opened his arms in a shrug.

'No problem.' He said with a laugh.

She walked across the street, and Leonid followed, protesting. She had a blurred vision in her head of the building without the crack in its plaster, and with fresh paint. Instinctively she knew where to go. It was the identical feeling she had had when she returned to her parents' home in Tring after so long.

A chocolate brown painted steel door led onto a stairwell. To the left of the door was an entry-phone and keypad, but it was broken and the door hung open. There was an elevator of course with room enough for two slim people, but a handwritten sign taped to the door said simply 'Broken.' Apologies were unnecessary. 12 floors to climb, then.

Leonid said in surprise: 'You go up?'

She glanced back. ' Thanks, Leonid. Can you you wait down here?' He looked relieved.

'It is not so dangerous.' He pondered. 'No problem.' And he turned to the car, quickly before she could change her mind.

She focussed her mind, looking up at the unevenly cast steps with cracked and pitted plaster. Suddenly she was a child. A child with a vision of a golden samovar in her mind. The destination. The objective. A cramped room with a samovar, up 12 flights of steps. 306 steps! She remembered with an unconscious smile of delight. She remembered that she counted them once. Who counted them? She frowned, interrupting the dialogue building in her head, and the memory dissolved at once. She was standing on a flight of broken concrete steps with the odour of cabbage and urine and rotten plaster ripe in the air. She was still Kate Buckingham after all.

Up the steps. Twice she encountered women struggling down the stairwell. There were no nodded greetings, just hostile, incurious stares. She wondered why they would not be in the least bit curious.

Each landing was scattered with cigarette ends, and cracked windows hung awry from their frames overlooking a bleak concrete landscape.

When at last she reached the 11th floor she found it sealed off with scaffold poles across the steel door and a sign that said 'DANGER NO ENTRY'. Her heart leapt as she remembered the fissure across the width of the building.

She ran rather than walked the next flight of stairs, panting for breath, her heart thumping. But when she reached the 12th floor to her dismay it was the same. Rusty scaffolding was wedged across the doorway. She felt sick. The taste of blood mingled with her saliva. On each floor the stairway was exposed to the outside, and she looked out across suburban Moscow with a sliver of recognition. She turned back to the door and pulled at the scaffolding pole, without much hope. It was firmly seated, and anyway the door was padlocked. There was no alternative but to descend.

As she reconciled herself sadly to another wasted journey and began to make her way down the steps, she thought she heard a rustle from the steps behind her. She turned around to see an old lady in long black skirts negotiating the stairway with stoicism. The old woman looked at her in a strange way, then stopped, several steps above Kate.

'What brings you here?' she said, without a flicker of

friendliness.

'Do you ... Do you remember me?' she ventured.

The old woman continued her descent. Screwed up her face. 'She lived here. Your mother. Not you.' Kate took a step down, keeping pace. 'That floor's been shut for years. And the one downstairs. An earthquake, they said.' Kate took another two steps down and wondered how long it took for the old lady to get to the ground. 'Your father lived there too. Drank too much,' she added.

For some reason it had never occurred to her that Ekaterina had a father. 'My father?' she said.

The old woman paused in her descent and looked at her for a moment. Her eyes were bloodshot. 'Grandfather.' She corrected. 'Worked at the University I think. Didn't have much to do with the likes of me.'

Kate slipped further down the steps. 'So where did she go? My mother?'

'Where did any of them go? How should I know? Maybe they moved them to a better apartment. Maybe *something else*,' she said, darkly. 'I'm not told. I don't ask. I'm still here.'

'But you knew her?'

The old woman could have been any age between fifty and

eighty. She had an uncompromising look about her. The air of someone who had experienced continual despair, and had determined to plough on in spite of everything. When she came within a few steps of Kate she could smell stale linen tempered with the scent of lavender. It somehow called up an apparition of the samovar again, distinct and real this time. A real memory, not a false one.

'I lived on the 12th floor until they moved us. Too dangerous they said. Now I live on the 14th floor and the elevator works less often than it doesn't work. I'm too old for these steps. Your mother lived a few doors away. She wouldn't remember me.'

'So why do you remember her?'

'She was the *scientist*. We all knew about the *scientist*.'

'What kind of scientist?'

The old woman leaned against the wall with her hand, pausing between steps. She looked at Kate. 'How should I know? If I knew that maybe *I* would have been a scientist too.'

Moving down the steps again, Kate tried to console the old lady. 'What else can you tell me?'

The old woman was getting back into her stride now arching her back and steadying herself against the wall as she negotiated each step. 'Nothing. I can tell you nothing. Your mother lived here. Not for long.

And then she went away.' Lean. Step. 'It wasn't a sociable time. Paid to mind your own business.' Lean. Step. 'Why would you come here?' Lean. Step.

'I'm trying to find out what happened to her. That's all.'

'Dangerous to know things in those days.' Lean. Step. 'You didn't want to know too much. Just leave it I say. Don't ask. I never knew anything about anything. I survived.' Lean. Step. 'Keep myself to myself. That's what respectable comrades do.' Lean. Step.

'Would anyone else remember her?' Asked Kate with a flicker of hope.

Lean. Step. Lean. Step. The old woman paused to catch her breath. 'All gone.' She said weakly. 'They've all left. Why would they stay?'

'And do you.. Do you keep in touch maybe?' Attempting for a foolish moment to apply Western standards.

'When they go, they're gone.' Observed the old woman with bleak determination. 'Wherever they go. Me, I keep myself to myself.' Lean. Step. Lean. Step. Her feet echoed in the stairwell.

Chapter Twenty-Three

GRIGOR WEDGED HIS bulky frame into the passenger seat of the Volga and scratched his beard. 'You're late.' He observed, hauling the car door shut with a tinny bang. He had a fearsome headache, and he worried that he might try to take it out on someone soon.

'Affairs of state,' answered the driver with an ironic smile, looking straight ahead.

The car felt claustrophobic.

'I heard about Yugorsky bank.'

'News travels fast.'

'In Moscow it does.' Grigor reached inside his leather jacket and produced a thick envelope. 'Anything to do with your people? Yugorsky Bank I mean?'

'I would conclude it was intended as a message to those that don't pay their dues. A man of Ivan Bokovsky's stature should have invested more in his health, I think.' Lisakov accepted the package. 'It's a sad business.'

Grigor grunted. 'It's the second banker in less than a week.'

'You should be careful to trust your money to the right banks.'

'How is anyone to know which are the right banks?' Grigor complained bitterly.

Lisakov glanced at him. 'Be guided,' he said. 'There are criminals everywhere in Russia today. Criminals everywhere.' He patted the pocket into which he had secreted the envelope.

Grigor craned to look over his shoulder. The rugged grille of a Range Rover filled the rear window, and he felt comforted to see Oleg with his forearms hanging over the steering wheel. The perpetual lines of traffic swept past in the yellow dawn. He turned back to the windscreen and shook his head slowly. 'You're all just a bunch of gangsters.'

'Speaking of which..' Lisakov fumbled inside his coat and took out the envelope Grigor had given him, appraising it for the first time and weighing it in his hand. 'How is business?'

'We get by.' Grigor felt a swell of anger and clenched a fist, unseen.

'Sometimes it's hard to tell who the gangsters are and who the businessmen.'

'And the policemen,' added Grigor.

Lisakov settled himself back in his seat, with a supremely dignified air. 'That too,' he agreed.

'And what if I were a legitimate businessman? What then?'

Lisakov sighed. 'We do our best. But we don't have the resources. Sooner or later the mafia would launder money through you, or sign an agreement with you that you wouldn't be able to refuse. You know how it is. That's capitalism I'm afraid.. What's to be done?'
Grigor pressed himself into the seat to make more room for his knees. He said 'I think I'm paying for too much protection.' Keeping a wary eye on Lisakov's reaction.

'You can never have too much protection. You of all people should know that.'

'Now there's Olensky feeding at the trough.'

'I'm sure you can deal with him.'

'Isn't that what I am paying you for?' Said Grigor, bitterly.

'I like to think of our relationship more as patronage than protection.'

Grigor laughed out loud. 'What the fuck does that mean?'

Lisakov flashed him a dangerous look. 'Whatever I want it to mean.'

Grigor returned his look, calculating just how easy it would be to snap Lisakov's neck. It would take no more than a movement. A strategically directed elbow. What he was trained to do. Over in a second. Then he would be closeted in the Range Rover in the whiff of leather and wood, and whisked away . It would be a popular murder. Instead he reached for the door handle.

'I'll deal with it then. But I don't want any trouble.'

'*That* is what you pay me for.' Lisakov smirked.

Chapter Twenty-Four

KATE HAD SPREAD her money over the bedspread, a rainbow of banknotes, Pounds mixed with Roubles, Queen Elizabeth rubbing shoulders with Peter the Great, fretting over how she could stretch her resources.

For the past few days she had pored over maps and telephone directories. Borodina was a common name. She had made countless abortive phone calls. Leonid had dragged her on pointless excursions through the altered streets of the outer reaches of her memories, to dingy, broken stairwells of half familiar apartment blocks, spoken with harried, frightened people that proved to have no connection with Ekaterina Ivanovna at all. She had phoned Nikolay Sokolov half a dozen times, but he had no news for her, and when she left messages he never returned her calls. She wondered if he even made the slightest enquiry. Why should he, after all? What was she to him?

And everywhere she went, there followed in her wake a Volga or a Lada with blue official license plates, not even trying to conceal their presence. Sometimes they parked immediately behind Leonid's taxi. Always there were two of them, reading newspapers, chain-smoking while they waited, resting their elbows on the open windows and shedding cigarette butts into the street.

The city was only half remembered. The same shape, but the parts had different functions, different names. Sometimes she would follow a promising trail, delighted with a flood of recollections, breathless with anticipation, only to find the building she remembered so vividly had been demolished, or had been refurbished, changed purpose beyond recognition.

As she sat in her hotel room counting banknotes, she wondered if she should go home. She had an open ticket to London. Then she remembered Gold's murder. She remembered the vulture like man and the struggle. Nothing could put that right. It was a mess that was waiting for her return. She wasn't safe in London. She wasn't safe in Moscow – but in Moscow was the answer. In Moscow she could find out why this was happening to her. In some ways the men that were following her were a comfort. They were proof that something existed to be discovered. Nikolay had told her she was not at risk. So she felt she could turn their presence almost into a positive. Maybe they were seeking the same answers? Maybe they were watching and waiting for her to show the way, to shine a light?

She had to play the hand out, and Moscow was where all the cards were to be found. The trouble was, she was running out of money. She couldn't sustain herself for more than another 2 nights at the Tverskaya Marriott.

And now she thought the memories were just beginning to assert themselves, to sharpen. They were seeping into her dreams just as her dreams used to seep into her memories. Everything all mixed up. She remembered a white pole with what looked like twisted orange and white ribbons wound loosely around it, as high as a tree. Like a huge maypole. Next to it was a long, wide sign in Cyrillic. She was trying to decipher it in her head, but it was jumbled up with other signs. It began with an 'O' she was sure. Or an 'S'. She knew it was a gateway to something… to somewhere. It had been important to her once. Or at least, important to this other someone that inhabited her memories when they lost their focus.

She went to the window and yanked back the net curtain. All

along Tverskaya Street the boutiques and cafes were shaking off the shadows, letting in the light. The stream of traffic crawled at its usual pace. An official car, or an Oligarch's car, raced down the middle lane with a blue light flashing. People marched single-mindedly towards their private destinations, with as much or as little hope as any city dweller in the world. As she strained to see further down the street, in the direction of Red Square, she caught sight of a limp red flag above a doorway. Then she had an idea.

Chapter Twenty-Five

'IT'S CLEAR THAT this group needs to take positive action to prevent the traitor Viktor Chernomyrdin from attempting to succeed the President.'

The room was silent for some moments. A bluebottle was clearly audible, buzzing at the window, tapping against the glass.

'When you say positive action..' ventured the Duma deputy. Borilyenko silenced him with a savage glance.

'It's unthinkable that this illegal regime should be perpetuated through the second millennium. Gentlemen, it is left to us to prevent this proud nation from being *destroyed* though the cynical and corrupt offices of its leadership. The Feliks Group is a voice in the wilderness that needs to swiftly demonstrate that it is in fact the voice of the people.' Borilyenko was tapping the table with the heel of his clenched fist in a restrained but powerful gesture. 'It's time we made plans. Time we made the way clear for a new leader.'

Vassillov observed Borilyenko , and thought that he looked somehow re-invigorated. A spark that had been missing had returned. 'You mean we should plan for the assassination of the President?' said Vassillov slowly, vocalising the dreadful course of action that was festering in the minds of all of them. The room was hushed. Even the bluebottle had gone silent.

'I mean we should prepare the way. Remove the .. *obstacles*. In a short time the president will step down. I am sure of this. But there are many *pretenders*. Many that the President has been grooming to assume his mantle. It is this that we must prevent. We need to escalate the activities of the Feliks Group. We need to prepare. We need to take action now.' He looked around the stern faces. 'Are we agreed, gentlemen? Are we *united*?'

There were mumbled approvals, and each man knew that they were sanctioning murder. The murder of the prime minister. And others. Maybe Lebed. It was a renewal of a kind. A communal feeling of renewal. The chairs scraped back. The usual toasts.

After the meeting Borilyenko phoned a number at the Lubyanka and

Lisakov answered. 'What news of the girl?' he said with suppressed anticipation.

'She's an assiduous tourist,' replied Lisakov. 'She's been driven around to.. to various locations. I have a report. It's difficult to see how these places are connected. It would perhaps help if you could tell me what we're looking for. What's her importance? It would help.'

'It is not for me to tell a KGB officer what to look for.'

'FSB.' Reminded Lisakov with a hint of irony.

'Of course.' Borilyenko paused. 'Let me have your report tonight. If we can't determine the purpose of her visit here, then we need to pick her up. Give it another day.'

'Yes General.'

After Borilyenko had laid down the phone, he thought about Project Simbirsk, and the more he thought about it, the more he thought that it must have been a success after all. Not a complete success.. but one that could be replicated. One that could be harnessed. He would be a custodian. Keeping the faith.

Chapter Twenty-Six

GRIGOR MALENKOV SAT in his office with his boots on the desk in a tobacco trance. There was a poster of Stalin on the wall which someone had defaced with devils horns. Smoke spiralled from a large Havana that festered in an ashtray, and the desk was strewn with documents and scraps of handwritten notes. A handgun doubled as a paperweight. The smoke from the cigar shifted and swirled as the door opened and Oleg leaned in the door frame, grinning in that manic way he had.

'There's a girl out front. The one you frightened off the other day.'

Grigor frowned, then remembered the pretty blonde that had scuttled out of the club when he called out. 'The cute one? What does she want?'

Oleg shrugged. 'Says she wants to audition.'

Grigor plucked his cigar from the ashtray and reflected upon it. 'We're always interested in fresh talent. Has she done it before?'

'In England, she says.'

'England. What the fuck? OK then. Let's take a look' Grigor stood up and pushed the gun into the back of his waistband. He slotted his cigar into a corner of his mouth and followed Oleg down a short corridor and into the club. A stocky woman was washing down the bar, overlooked by a rocky bust of Lenin. Leaning against the stage was the same girl that had ventured into the club a few days before. She had sharp inquisitive features, and an animated look about her. Her blond hair tumbled over her shoulders.

He stopped at the other end of the stage from the girl and smiled. 'Welcome,' he said, his voice sharp and resonant in the empty club. 'I'm Grigor.' He looked around him with a proprietary air. 'What do you think of my collection of memorabilia?'

He watched her perch herself with a balletic leap on the edge of the stage. 'Interesting,' she said, sniffing the air as though catching a hint of something unpleasant. Grigor sauntered over to a statue of an impish man with a pointed beard and a cap tipped back on his head adjacent to the club entrance. He gestured to it with his cigar.

'My favourite,' he said, assessing it as though he were inspecting a soldier on parade. He glanced at her with a raised eyebrow. 'You know who he is?' When she didn't reply he said: 'Allow me to introduce the infamous Felix Edmundovich Dzerzhinsky. *Iron* Felix. The architect of the Cheka. The KGB. Still keeping an eye on us after all these years, aren't you Feliks Edmundovich.' He patted him on his shoulder. 'He was the first. The first of the statues. It was him that gave me the idea ... you know, of a *themed* club. Red Nights. These days there's a lot of.... nostalgia about Soviet days. Misguided of course, but still ... It has its appeal. And then there are the tourists of course.' He turned to the girl and rubbed his hands together. 'So! Oleg tells me you dance? What's your name?'

'Kate. Kate Buckingham.' She smiled a smile that didn't seem to touch her eyes.

'And where are you from, Kate Buckingham?' He felt like a compére on a TV talent show.

'I'm over from England.'

'Oleg – can we arrange some music? Any preference, Kate Buckingham?

'Do you have "Sexual" by Amber?' She said, getting to her feet.

Grigor thought she looked a little fragile. But she was slim and pretty, and seemed to have a way about her. Grigor settled into a chair at the very front of the stage, where the hard-core clients sat.

'Good choice. We have that.' Yelled Oleg from the deck, and as the music begun to play Kate begun her routine, skipping on her toes across the stage, loosening her clothes.

Grigor tapped his foot to the music, and watched Kate writhe to the rhythm, discarding her clothes on the stage. Her skin had a pale sheen, and she swung her long legs high in the air – like a real dancer, Grigor thought. Grigor had a sensation as he watched her of being a voyeur. It was a feeling he hadn't remarked in himself before, and he wondered if he had blocked it out. She performed all the ritual moves, caressed herself, splayed her legs. It was like always, but somehow lacking. Then all at once he knew what was missing. She was lacking *pornography*.

When the music stopped, and she gathered up her clothes, Grigor's slow and stark clap echoed. She was beautiful, there was no doubt. She stood there naked on the stage, trailing her clothes in one hand, head on one side, almost a little gawky without the rigour of her dance routine. He felt a tautness in his stomach.

'So?' She said. 'What do you think?'

'Thank you Kate Buckingham. Please get dressed.' Grigor left his hard-core position at the front of the stage to pour himself a vodka behind the bar, jamming his glass under the optic, and watched Kate as she stepped into her jeans. He raised his glass to her but she didn't notice him at all. Oleg fussed with a pile of CD's at the deck, shuffling the cases. He caught Grigor's eye and gave him a thumbs up.

When Kate was dressed she looked around her and Grigor beckoned. 'Over here,' he pronounced loudly. 'Drink?'

'A vodka please.' Kate propelled herself from the stage and crossed the room, wriggling onto a bar stool. 'Did I pass?' she enquired with her lifeless smile.

Grigor considered for a minute, pouring himself another shot. He passed a hand over his beard. He'd decided for no particular reason that he did not want her on his stage. He was a man of impulse, and he refused in his head to justify his attitude. He pushed a glass of vodka across the bar, and the glass scraped on the tiles.

'You're talented.'

'Thank you.' She tipped the glass in his direction with irony. '*Davai!*'

'*Davai!*' He returned, and drained the glass. He slammed the glass on the bar. 'But it's not quite the dance for "Red Nights". I am sorry.'

'Not the right dance,' she repeated.

'Not for our audience, no.' He ran a hand though his shaggy mane. 'But I have something else that you could do for us...'

She looked nervous. 'I don't do sex. Not for money.'

Grigor laughed. 'That would be unusual here. Another reason why it wouldn't work out for you at "Red Nights". But it's not what I had in mind.' He ruminated on the ways he could keep her to himself. 'I think that you could do some other work for us. Some *courier* work. As a Westerner you're almost beyond suspicion these days. And you're unmistakably a Westerner. A Russian girl as pretty as you would be far more.. chic.' He saw her injured expression and let out a sudden guffaw, touching her knee in a conciliatory gesture. 'Nothing personal. But your clothes are chain-store not designer.'

'What do you want me to do, exactly?'

'Oleg!' He summoned with a bark that made the girl start.

Chapter Twenty-Seven

'IT'S ABOUT A girl.' Nikolay ventured, sitting opposite General Artur Blodnieks. The General had bloodshot eyes and a heavy jowl. Nikolay had been summoned to review the progress of the investigation into General Borilyenko. He felt empty as a shell crater.

'Isn't it always?'

'From the archives...' Nikolay produced a black and white photograph of an attractive girl standing on a bridge. He slid it across the desk. Then he produced another photograph in colour of the same girl, this time walking down a busy shopping street. 'Recent surveillance.'

The General looked at both photographs without much curiosity and sniffed. 'Pretty.' He commented.

'These photographs were taken at least 20 years apart.'

The General looked at him without a flicker of interest. 'Nikolay, are you going to get to the point sometime soon?' He gestured to a pile of buff folders. 'As you can see, I am busy.'

'The point is that Borilyenko is having this girl tailed. This one,' he continued, tapping on the black and white print, 'disappeared around 20 years ago.'

The General leaned to inspect the two photographs, squinting his eyes. 'Are they not the same girl?'

'The similarity is remarkable, I agree. The first is Ekaterina Ivanovna Borodina. She was a microbiologist. Her file is—incomplete. She was engaged in some classified project before her disappearance. The other girl is from London. Kate Buckingham. She came here asking questions about Ekaterina Ivanovna. Our investigations have revealed that the surveillance of this Kate Buckingham was ordered by Borilyenko himself. Why the special interest?'

'You think she might be working in any intelligence capacity?'

Nikolay shrugged. 'She seems to be only interested in finding out about Ekaterina Ivanovna.'

The General grunted and pushed aside the prints. 'All very

fascinating, I'm sure – but I think there are more important matters when it comes to Borilyenko. What of his involvement with the Feliks Group? Is there evidence?'

'It's difficult.'

The General rubbed the back of his neck with his hand as if in an effort to relieve some tension. 'You don't say. It shouldn't be for us to pursue this type of enquiry. We've become embroiled in some political manoeuvrings, and I don't like it at all.'

'You don't have to tell me.'

'That Borilyenko should position himself as a presidential candidate...'

'Unthinkable.'

'Some believe so.' There was a lengthy pause. The General looked at Nikolay.

'General, I also believe that the FSB is in some way responsible for the recent murders of bankers. In particular, the Uvyerenny Bank. Colonel Lisakov was at the scene, and I had the distinct impression that his men were there to tidy up.'

Hotel Rossiya, she knew, was the largest hotel in the world. Splayed along the banks of the Moskva River and overshadowing the Kremlin to the rear, it covered over 30 acres of the once important, historical district of Zaryadye. The hotel reminded her of the base layer of a huge mouldering wedding cake. Inside, she clicked through the murmuring marble lobby with its gambling machines that blinked and tumbled, avoiding the stares, and caught a lift to the eleventh floor. The attaché case hung at her side. It was heavy, and she wondered what was in it. Whatever it was, Grigor was paying her $150 to deliver.

At the end of the corridor the *babushka* sitting on a wooden chair glared at her. The whites of her eyes were marbled and her lips had the in-grained pucker of a chain smoker. Kate ignored her and walked along the corridor where she paused at the door of room 1127, listening to the rumbling of voices and laughter from within. She glanced back and tried to gulp away the dryness of her throat. When she tapped on the door the room fell silent, and she wondered if it was in her imagination that she heard the kind of metallic click that signalled the loading of automatic weapons in the movies. But that was in the movies.

When the door opened the acrid smell of stale tobacco stung the air. Traces of smoke drifted from the room. A man in an Adidas track suit held open the door, looked her up and down. Shorter than her, but barrel-chested, he stood with his legs apart as though preparing for a gun-fight. He had crimson, hangover-rimmed eyes.

'Grigor sent me.' She told him as instructed, trying not to catch his eye.

'Of course.' He made as if to execute a stiff bow and stepped aside.

It was a large room with a bay window with crimson drapes that were swept aside to reveal a view of St Basil's Cathedral. Everyone was smoking. There were five men in the room lounging on beds and couches. A bald man was sprawled on one of the twin beds nursing an empty bottle on his chest and dribbling into his stained shirt. Empty vodka bottles and stub-filled ashtrays littered the tables and the floor. A TV babbled unregarded. American football. The door to the bathroom was open and there were towels on the floor. She felt all eyes upon her as she stood in the centre of the room. The man behind her snatched the attaché case.

'I'm Olensky,' he said. 'This—' he announced to the room with a gesture towards her '—is mine. Apparently.' and she felt the heat rise in her face. A man with rusty hair and bad teeth got up and came up to her with a grin. He stopped, and examined her with clinical curiosity, like the men at the club would do when they thought she wasn't watching. But this man didn't care that she was watching. He seemed to be making his mind up about her. She took a step backwards. Without warning he made a grab for her and his hand slipped inside her skirt and clenched her buttocks with sharp fingernails. An involuntary yelp escaped her in a single breath. From behind her she head the click of the attaché case. Then she rammed her knee as hard as she could between her assailant's legs. The hand on her buttocks froze, but the man didn't move. He didn't double up. Just inches from her face the reek of vodka on his breath was nauseating. She remembered the Russians had a word for this smell: '*peregar*.' All colour had drained from the man's rocky features. A sickly grin formed. She felt more terrified than she had ever been in her life. She pulled at his arm. It was unshakeable. Opened her mouth to say something. Then there was a shout that caused the man to retrieve his hand and straighten up.

'What the fuck is this?' Olensky was ranting. He thrust a handful of banknotes at her. 'Who does he think we are?' Kate noticed only then that he was brandishing a heavy looking pistol. He pointed it at her and she flinched as he pulled the trigger. There was a hollow click. She tasted bile. Somebody laughed. Olensky turned to him, a long faced man with a thin beard. 'Don't you laugh!' He shouted, pointing the gun with a straight arm. 'Don't you *ever* fucking laugh at me!' The man shifted backwards in his seat, and she saw he was afraid.

'Sorry, Boss.'

Olensky swung the barrel round at each man in turn. 'Anyone else see anything funny?' Then he cursed and tugged out the magazine. Kate was horrified to see that it was full of bullets. A misfire. She could be dead. She backed away as he slapped the magazine back into the gun with his palm. He pointed the gun, but she saw his anger had subsided. 'It's disrespectful, that's what it is. Nobody disrespects me. Tell Grigor that. Tell him our business is in dollars not roubles,' he began, 'and tell him that I'll keep his fucking roubles as a forfeit.' He thrust the gun at her forehead. 'Not in payment. As a forfeit. I should send his messenger back in a box to insult me with this monopoly money. But I won't. Not this time. You're lucky.,.' He tucked the gun into his trousers in a swift gesture that made her flinch. His eyes were misty. 'Tell him that I want the money by noon tomorrow at the latest. Or there'll be a fucking war. Now piss off before I change my mind.'

As she was leaving the room he stopped her. 'And bring it yourself. Tell Grigor we want *you* to bring it.' He winked at the rusty haired man. 'Let's call it a condition. I think Rubletsy here has taken a liking to you.'

As she hurried down the corridor, under the suspicious stare of the old woman, the tears were welling in her eyes, and she was sniffling and shivering all at the same time. All she could think about was the click as some mechanical fluke had saved her life. The hotel was a blur. In the lift a wave of claustrophobia came over her and she almost stopped at the next floor. When the doors parted she pushed through two waiting guests and crossed the lobby.

When she emerged from the hotel she found herself gasping for air. It was cold and the cars droned along the broad Varvaka Street with its scaffolding clad monuments. Her eyes were watering either from the cold or from fear, she wasn't sure. She looked around her, and set out with her head down in the direction of the Kremlin.

The Hotel Rossiya seemed to occupy the whole of the street. When she reached a corner she glanced towards the banks of the Moskva River to her left and then up at the hotel, seeking out the eleventh floor, wondering if they were watching. She hated Grigor. She would never go back to Red Nights.

And then the eleventh floor of the Rossiya Hotel threw up over the shabby street in a stream of glass and rubble, with a bang that resounded like two cars colliding. She almost slipped on the pavement in front of a dark windowed Mercedes, craning her neck. At least three rooms were eviscerated. A tangle of metal and blackened, ragged brickwork. The sky revolved above her. People in the street were looking up. She could hear an urgent rasping sound. Then she realised that someone was calling her.

'Kate! Get in! Hurry!' The passenger door of the Mercedes was open and a man was leaning over from the driving seat, beckoning. 'Get in the car, fuck your mother!'

She dipped into the car. Sat down. The man reached past her pulling the door closed. The traffic noise deadened.

'Vanya.' He introduced himself. 'Don't worry. Grigor sent me. Let's go.'

A muted roar and they pulled away with a sharp jolt. Jumbled pieces in her mind assembled themselves, as though the bomb in the hotel had ripped her thoughts apart and they were settling back into place. She looked at Vanya. He smirked.

'Did I—? Did I have anything to do with that?'

The driver's smirk spread wider, but he didn't answer.

'Of course I did. Oh my God..' Rain stippled the windscreen. A fire engine with its horns wailing passed them at speed in the opposite direction, splashing the windows with rain that the wipers swept away. 'I killed them. I killed those men didn't I?'

'Grigor will be happy.'

She shrank into the leather seat, feeling child-like. She had murdered those men. And who else? Who was in the other rooms? Two police cars and another fire engine flailed past, bathing them in blue light for an instant. Inside the warm car it was like watching a movie. 'One of those men almost killed me.' Her voice was quivering, and she realised that her whole body was trembling.

'Scum like that.'

'What about the other rooms?'

He shrugged. 'Similar.' He said. 'They have rooms in that hotel permanently blocked out. For... meetings.'

The leather creaked as she twisted to look out of the rear window. They had passed out of sight of the hotel. 'Who were they?' There was a tremor in her voice that she found impossible to control.

'Mafia.'

'And Grigor.. is he Mafia too?'

'You could say that,' he admitted. 'But not like Olensky.'

'Why not? Why not like Olensky.'

He turned to her with a big grin that exposed a gold tooth, and his eyes crinkled up so she couldn't see into them at all. 'Because we're the *good* guys.'

They sped through the afternoon traffic in silence while she absorbed this, keeping her mind away from the bomb. The good guys. She recognised the broad sweep of Tverskaya Street. They swung right into Kozitsky Lane with a lurch, and stopped. The driver leaned on the horn. They waited. In a moment an iron shutter ground open on their left. The engine growled and as the tyres thudded over the threshold, they were engulfed in darkness. She glanced over her shoulder at the descending shutter. Yellow lights flickered on, and Vanya thrust open his door ushering in a smell of rubber and petrol and spent exhaust. They were in an underground garage with room enough for four cars. Parked next to them was a mean looking Range Rover with gleaming chrome and dark windows. Inches from the three-pointed star on the bonnet was a set of iron steps where a wiry man in a leather bomber jacket languished, hand poised over a bank of light switches. He was grinning. She could hear strains of Russian folk music from somewhere. Through the windscreen she saw him put up his hand. 'Welcome back.'

A gentle touch at her elbow prompted her to get out of the car. She was finding it hard to perform simple functions. She tugged a few times at the door catch before she could make it work. When she stumbled out of the car she allowed herself to be directed up the steps, feet clanging on metal. They ascended a staircase with greasy walls.

'Where are we going?'

'I'm Fyodr.' Said the man at the stairs, as if in answer to her question. He had a voice without edge. 'Like Dostoevsky.' He added with mock pride. At the top of the stairs Vanya flung open a wide door and the music crashed and echoed off the walls. She followed him in a daze into the brightly lit Red Nights bar, and a ripple of applause broke out. Grigor was there. He shouldered his way towards her, a vodka bottle hanging from his arm, and stopped after a few steps, looked at her, his broad forehead angled down in earnest appraisal. Intent. Then without a word he crushed her in his arms, lifting her from her feet, so that all her breath escaped in a grunt. She wriggled, trying to touch the floor with her toes, and he released her.

'We'll be celebrating thanks to you.'

'I don't understand. What was it for? What did I do? Why me? The money ... the bomb. How could you…?'

'Protection money. Only as it turns out it wasn't us that needed protection,' he laughed, guided her to the bar. She blinked at the faces all around her and it was an all male cast. It hardly occurred to her that it was unusual that many of the men were carrying guns. Grigor himself, she noticed had a large pistol tucked into his waistband.

'Drink?' Without waiting Grigor edged behind the bar and took a stubby glass from a shelf, splashed vodka into it and offered it to her. She took it with both hands because she was still trembling. Threw back her head, letting the spirit course down her throat. It seemed to make her feel less shaky. Holding out the glass Grigor filled it again.

Nodding at Grigor's gun before she took another gulp she said: 'Everybody has guns.'

'That's right.' He pulled the pistol from his belt and waved it with pride. 'This is a Browning .380. You can't imagine the damage this can do.' He inspected it with reverence. 'You can't imagine,' he repeated, half to himself.

'But why?'

Grigor eased the gun back into his belt and looked solemn. 'Possible repercussions. Just a precaution, but who knows? They'll regroup. Have to. A new leader I expect. And then they'll come after us.'

The atmosphere in the bar was taut. The music was merry and the vodka was flowing, but there the faces were steely, and men sprawled at tables without talking. At either side of the empty stage the statues of Lenin and Stalin presided. Lenin had a yellow streamer hanging from his ear. The red flags hung above them like becalmed sails. She felt sick.

'Why would you send me to do something like this? Horrible. It was horrible.' She was shaking again.

Then she heard a thumping at the door. A rattle of weapons being readied. Somebody turned off the music. She backed towards the stage and crouched at Stalin's granite feet. Her throat felt knotted.

Somebody banged again. There was a muffled shout. Grigor nodded to Fyodr and another man who lifted the bar from the doors, and when they tugged open the doors they stood well back.

A silver-haired man in a long fur-trimmed coat strolled into the club with his hands deep in his pockets, his heels squeaking on the parquet. He paused and looked around him until he caught Grigor's eye. He nodded. Fyodr and the other man peered into the street behind him, then pulled the doors shut and barred them again. Most of the men in the club had lowered their weapons, but Kate could tell he was not a welcome visitor.

'Well, Grigor. A successful day for you?' His sharp tone resonated in the big room. Grigor leaned on the bar. He shrugged.

'Not especially.'

'That's not what I heard. I came straight here, of course.'

'Vodka?' but the silver haired man ignored him and paced in

Kate's direction. He stopped. looked up at Stalin's bust and gave an ironic salute. Then for a fleeting second he caught her eye, and she thought she imagined a glimmer of recognition. He seemed to lose his composure, but then he turned and paced back to Grigor. Drank the vodka.

'What are you talking about?' said Grigor.

'I need a few minutes of your time, Grigor Vassilyich.' The man headed towards Grigor's office. Grigor said:

'I'll be right back.'

Kate watched the office door close behind them.

'Who's that?' She asked a haggard looking man with an AK47 propped over his shoulder.

'KGB.'

'So who's the girl?' Said Lisakov when they were alone.

'The girl?' Said Grigor with surprise. 'Just a girl.'

'Trust me,' said Lisakov narrowing his eyes. 'that girl is not *just* a girl. There's more to her. If I were you, I would be careful when it comes to that girl.'

Grigor was taken aback. What would Lisakov know about some scrawny tourist from London? Did he suspect that he had used her to deliver the bomb?

'She's just a girl,' repeated Grigor, watchfully.

'Anyhow. The bomb.'

'The bomb?'

'It was a bit public.'

Grigor shrugged. 'He was well protected. Anyway the Rossiya could do with a little *renovation*.'

'It may be expensive.'

'It's always expensive.'

'I will ensure there are no loose ends.'

'All I can ask.'

Lisakov stood up, brushing off imaginary dust from his trousers. 'I'll head over to the Rossiya to supervise. It's important that we find out who is responsible for this outrage. Round up the usual suspects, as they say in the movies.'

'Do you have a preference?' said Grigor, without getting up.

Lisakov smiled. 'We'll see.'

Boris Yeltsin mopped his neck with a towel as he limped from the tennis court, racket hanging from his left hand. Borilyenko's eyes were drawn to the two missing fingers no matter how much he tried not to notice. An accident with a grenade they said. Not heroism but a boyhood stunt.

Yeltsin landed next to him on the bench with a grunt.

'Not bad for an old man.' He punched Borilyenko in the arm and it hurt. 'We old men can still give the youngsters a run.' His shirt was sticking to him, a gluey mess, and his chest heaved. The sweatband around his head made Borilyenko think of a coronet.

The youngster he had given a run today was a rugged man in his 40's who saluted with his racket as he left the court. Yeltsin leaned and buried his head in the towel whilst he steadied his breathing. Droplets of the president's sweat made dark patches on the concrete floor.

'All that running around,' he muttered between his knees. 'Even five years ago, it would have been nothing. I'm an athlete.' He looked up at Borilyenko with rheumy eyes. His face was strained. '*Was* an athlete. Did you know that? Takes a younger man, Yuri Ivanovich. This game. Tennis. More importantly this—this high office. The thing about getting old ... I used to make things happen, now things just happen to me.' He made a wide gesture, voice thin, raspy, but still resonating amongst the courts. He leaned in. 'You're an old man too, Yuri Ivanovich. But not sick, like me.' Then like a disclaimer, 'Sick? That's what the doctors say. Sick and tired more like. Pah!'

'What are you saying, Boris Nikolaevich?'

'All this terrorism. Bombs. It has to stop. I lost money, you know. Uvyerenny Bank. I was an investor,' he continued with a sigh, 'International terrorism. Domestic terrorism. Then Chechnya. Feliks Group. It's all around. Needs a strong man with a belly for violence. I say we need to come down hard.' He slammed the handle of his tennis racket on the wooden floor. 'Put a stop to it. But what I always say is: you can build a throne from bayonets, but you can't sit on it for long.' A stale expression that Borilyenko had heard before. Yeltsin swivelled his eyes. 'I'm not the man for this task. Used to be. Not anymore. Not now. When I was an athlete..' He grimaced. 'Maybe you could build that throne, Yuri Ivanovich? Think you could?'

'I'm at your service.'

Yeltsin coloured. 'It's not about *my* service you idiot. No about one man. Just like it wasn't about the Party before. The Communist Party ... that was just an idea. Pie in the sky. I told them that. Saw through it at once. You people ... those people.. It's about the State. About Mother Russia. Take hold!' Exasperated he made a fist of the hand with the missing fingers. 'Somebody needs to... somebody.' Then seemed to falter. 'You know, Yuri Ivanovich, if you want it, it's yours. I can make it happen. But you have to really want it.' He looked dismal.

'Are you offering me the presidency?'

'It's the heart you see. People - I don't care what they say - people think it's the vodka. But it's the heart. And these drugs they give me. You know this to be true, Yuri Nioklaevich. I swear.' He seemed to drift. 'Somebody needs to take hold.' a mantra, repeated to himself. 'If not me then who?'

'I thought Chermonyerdin?'

'Yes, yes. Everybody thinks that.' Dismissive. He thought for a moment, eyes narrowing, watching tennis balls thrashed around. He nodded at the courts. 'How long do you think Viktor Stepanovich would last out there, on the tennis court? Chermonyerdin - he's got seven years on me. Man's senile. Dribbles in his kasha. No, no no. Not him. For God's sake, not him.'

'If not Chermonyrdin, then..?'

Borilyenko thought he heard Yeltsin mutter 'Speak of the devil' as he rose suddenly to his feet. Borilyenko stood up as a taut, compact man with a bald head approached wearing immaculate tennis whites. His expression reminded Borilyenko of a picture of a fox in a children's story book. Yeltsin shouldered past Borilyenko so that he had to step aside, and embraced the man. 'Vladimir Vladimirovich.

Welcome.'

'Thank you, Boris Nikolaevich. I flew in from Petersburg this morning and came straight from the hotel.'

'Good. Good of you too come. Let's play a couple of sets, then go to my office. Maybe I have a proposition for you.' He gave a wave in the direction of Borilyenko. 'Take care of it. The Feliks Group. I want it stopped, and I'm relying on you, Yuri Nioklaevich,' and he realised that he was dismissed as the two men headed for the courts, Yeltsin with a paternal hand on the other's shoulder, or maybe for support. Borilyenko felt abandoned. Who was the stranger from St Petersburg, he wondered? And what to do about Feliks?

Chapter Twenty-Eight

THE EARNEST MAN with neat brown hair leaned across the coffee table with his hands clasped together. Robert eyed him warily. It was odd, but if he turned away even for a moment, he could not recall a single feature about the man in front of him, except the colour and length of his hair. He had already established that he was not a policeman. He had met various types of policemen over the past few days, asking about Kate.

'Your wife..'

'Ex-wife,' reminded Robert.

The man began again, with just the hint of a foreign accent that was almost indiscernible. 'Your *ex*-wife. Do you have any idea where she is?'

'As I've already told the police, I've no idea. Who are you anyway? You didn't say...'

'I can tell you where she is. Your wife. Your ex-wife.'

Robert was taken aback. 'What is this? What's going on?'

'Kate is in Moscow.'

Moscow? Why in the world would Kate go to Moscow? His Kate? 'I don't understand.' His brow furrowed and he leaned towards the man, mirroring his posture. Two men hunched over a coffee table.

'She's quite safe. For now,' he added.

'But what is she doing there?'

'That's what we're trying to find out.' The man reached inside his plain, dark jacket, brushing aside a plain dark tie, and produced an identity card with a bland photograph, surmounted with a gold crest surrounding a blue globe. He laid it open on the table. The letters looked like Greek. Or Russian. Definitely Russian, he thought. 'This won't mean much to you, I'm afraid,' he said. 'I work for the Russian security services, and I'm hoping that you can help us to help your wife.'

'So you're what—KGB?' He hazarded in a whirl.

The man smiled, showing a perfect row of white teeth. 'That particular acronym is behind us now, thankfully.'

Robert swallowed. He felt as though he had been swept away on some wild excursion. This was not his life – this was like something from a movie. He was an observer. 'What about the police? They want to interview Kate. Will you tell them where she is? Can you put me in touch with her?'

'Let's treat this as our secret for now. I don't suggest that you or I communicate with the British police until we have done some detective work of our own. We want to help. Do we have a criminal at large in Moscow... or something else?'

'A criminal? Kate? What can I do?'

'All you can do is to give me some background. Tell me about Kate. Anything you like. Anything you know. We're looking for something in her background. A connection. We don't know what ... but we think Kate may be in danger. We know of course about the *incident*. We know about the unfortunate death…' He paused. 'It's most probably connected with her visit to Moscow.' He smiled as he said: 'We are—how do you say it? Trying to join up the dots.' He smiled over Robert's shoulder. 'And who is this lady?'

Robert turned to see Becki standing in the doorway with a curious expression.

'Please go and play,' he said, gently.

'You can call me Pavel.' Remarked the visitor, producing an A4 notebook and a pen from his bag as Becki scurried down the hall. 'Now, let's … let's begin at the very beginning. Where was Kate born? Who were her parents? Was there anything unusual about her? He glanced up as Robert sat there in silence. 'It's background. If we're to help Kate, there's nothing that's too trivial.'

Something trivial. Without thinking, Robert said with a sinking feeling, 'She used to have these dreams.'

Chapter Twenty-Nine

'YOU'RE LYING TO US, old woman.'

Emila Alliluyeva sat very still with her hands in her lap and her eyes averted.

'What do you want me to say, sir?' She said with a cracked voice.

The officer stood up, towering over her, and grimaced. 'We want you to tell us the truth, of course.'

She looked up at him with pleading eyes. 'Just tell me what truth you want to hear. Tell me and I will say it for you.'

A man in a long dark overcoat had just entered the interview room and he paused in the doorway. The interrogator glanced at him and nodded.

'You did not leave your post?' he said to Emila, 'Not even for a moment?'

'Never.' She hesitated and looked for inspiration. 'At least I don't think so. Please just tell me what you want.' Her interrogator's face was blank.

'I think you saw nothing,' he said. 'You made up the girl to hide the fact that you neglected your post.'

'I saw nobody. There was no girl,' she said.

'Wait.' Interjected the newcomer. 'Wait just a moment.'

Emila looked from her interrogator to this man, wondering where she should place her faith. This new man looked to be senior. Important. He swept over to her in his outdoor clothes, as though from another realm and spoke kindly. He had intelligent eyes.

'Please describe to me the girl you saw,' the man said.

She glanced at her interrogator who had stepped back to accommodate the superior officer. The officer was tall and well groomed, with silver hair like a doctor. Or a fox. 'There was no girl,' she mumbled at last, looking at the floor. 'I left my post. I will be punished.'

The man knelt down beside her. 'You will not be punished. Trust me.'

Emila looked at him. Could she trust him? She saw no threat in his expression, only empathy. She bit her lip. 'I think I may have seen a girl in the corridor. She may have entered room 1127.' There, it was out. She shrank back a little as if expecting a rebuke.

'Good. Good. Now please describe her,' said the man.

'A foreigner. A Westerner.' A Westerner—to her it was almost a curse. She didn't approve of the new ways. She didn't approve of Westerners here in Moscow, treating the place as their own. Everything was better before. Life was easier then. 'She was tall, with long blonde hair. Pretty, I expect, to a certain type of man. Carrying a big briefcase. She looked wrong. Like a prostitute, but not. I see these girls come and go in my line of work.' She shook her head. 'Not a prostitute, this one. Something else.'

The man seemed to consider for a moment. 'Please think hard. When the girl came out of the room, did she still have the briefcase.' Emila responded in an instant, anxious to please now. 'No. I thought it was strange. In a hurry, she was. And upset.'

Lisakov rose stiffly to his feet, and Emila looked up at him, but he headed towards the door. 'Thank you for your cooperation,' he said amicably. He nodded to her interrogator as he opened the door, and it was then that she noticed a fraction of a shake of the head. A brief communication passed between her interrogator and the other man, and she had an eerie feeling that her fate had been sealed in that tiny gesture. She felt breathless. She started as if to get up, but didn't seem to have the energy, the will.

'Wait!' She called, but the door had clicked shut. The room was silent. Her interrogator was looking at her with an irritated expression, his hands planted on his hips. She looked at the dusty floor and steeled herself for what was to come.

'This girl you have an interest in. She seems to have got herself mixed up in something.' A stark voice at the end of the line. Borilyenko raised an eyebrow.

'What kind of something?'

'She is ... well she appears to be involved with a criminal gang.'

'Mafia you mean?'

'Yes.' There was a pause. Borilyenko waited. This was a completely unexpected development. 'She's—well, it looks like she carried out an execution.' There was a cough at the end of the line.

'A what!?'

'There's no doubt I am afraid. She delivered an explosive device to a rival gang. It was successfully detonated, probably remotely. Six fatalities.' The voice was impartial. Factual. Why would she do that?

How would she get involved in something like this? Borilyenko hunted for possibilities where none existed. There was nothing in the girl's background that would lead her to this…

'I don't understand. It doesn't make sense. Let me think about this—how has it been presented?'

'My people were on the scene. We don't want panic. It was made to appear like an unfortunate incident. A gas explosion.'

'Were there witnesses? To the girl's involvement I mean?'

'There was one. The *dezhurnaya*- the corridor matron.'

'They still have those?' said Borilyenko perversely, his mind still turning circles. In Soviet times every hotel had a woman on each floor that monitored the comings and goings, collecting and dispensing keys. These were the *dezhurnaya,* but it was a practise long since discontinued in most hotels.

'In the Rossiya, yes. They've been useful to us in the past. Sadly, on this occasion the witness suffered a heart attack on the way to the police station. She was not able to throw any light on the identity of the perpetrator before she died. It's a pity.'

'A pity. Yes.' Borilyenko reached a conclusion. 'I think we may need to abandon our surveillance plan and bring her under our control. Her safety is paramount. She is of vital importance to National

Security.'

'National Security,' repeated Lisakov. 'Of course, General.'

Chapter Thirty

IT WAS A fine day. Ekaterina paused outside the glass door of the facility, framed in the rugged concrete lintels of the porch, enjoying the silence and the warmth of the sun on her face. She gazed at the orange and gold and green shrubs that spilled over the brick wall of a square, decorative bed in front of the entrance. It wasn't much of an effort, she thought, but at least someone had tried to brighten the place up. She crossed to the bed and stooped to tug some scrawny weeds from the crumbling dry earth. Not much of an effort, but something. The moss and weeds between the slabs that formed the quadrangle were entrenched. A losing battle. She kicked at some of it and the moss lifted and smeared the grey concrete with a deep green.

Her appointment with the doctor was at 11:00am and so she took her time, walking along the cracked pavement towards the apartment blocks: nine identical buildings, etched with rows of windows, in the centre of a patch of scrubland surrounded by a few wilting trees. Some rickety picnic tables had been placed there for optimistic lunches. She looked up, calculating where her apartment was, halfway up the second building from the left, at the front. Everywhere was still and silent. Everybody working. Or sick, she reminded herself. Half of Sorsk was sick like her with influenza. If it was influenza.

The other side of the apartment block there stretched for several hundred metres a single storey block with shuttered steel windows on one side of the road. The State Research Centre for Applied Microbiology. Even with her clearance she was not admitted to that block, but she knew the nature of the research carried out there. She knew what happened behind those shutters that the sunlight could not penetrate. Everybody did, but you didn't talk about it out loud. Those that worked there were regarded with a little distaste by those engaged in more acceptable projects. And was her own project acceptable? Did it satisfy her own peculiar moral criteria?

Across the road was Building Six, a drab concrete and glass structure five stories high surrounded by an electrified fence. Some of the windows were cracked or broken. The entrance was guarded by two bored looking uniformed KGB officers. They watched her pass without much interest. She could hear the electric fence humming.

When she reached Keldysh Street she turned right and entered an anonymous building with a scrappily painted grey door. She passed through a corridor with scuffed walls and encountered a grim faced woman glaring over a reception desk.

'I have an appointment with Dr Korolyov.'

'Name?' The receptionist spun a rolodex with authority. Ekaterina cursed her. She knew very well who she was. There were not so many residents in Sorsk that each of the patients could not be recognised.

'But you know who I am. And I know who you are, Comrade Lebeda.'

'Name.'

'OK, OK. Ekaterina Ivanovna Borodina.'

Comrade Lebeda plucked a card from the rolodex and squinted at it. Then she picked up the phone. 'You're early.'

When she was directed to the Doctor's office, she made her way along another corridor, her footsteps resounding in the passage. She knocked at the door and waited, but there was no answer. She knocked again, louder this time. For some reason, she felt a rising panic.

Something was gripping her tightly inside. She was hot and flustered. She knocked again. Her forehead was damp and sticky to the touch. She began to bang on the door with the palm of her hand.

Bang. Bang. Bang.

Still no answer. Her breathing was shallow. She gulped. Raised her hand to the door..

When she awoke she was in a hotel room and somebody was banging on the door. She looked around, bewildered and confused. Her clothes were draped over a chair. She was naked and cold. The air-conditioning was fierce.

Bang. Bang. Bang.

Sorsk slipped into its allotted place in her memories. She looked at her watch. Two am.

Somebody banged again on the door and called her name, but she couldn't tell who it was. She grabbed a bathrobe from the foot of the bed and wrapped herself in it before rushing to the door, where she paused. 'Who is it? There was no answer. More banging. She made a decision and pulled open the door.

Grigor filled the frame of the doorway. His broad head was more pronounced than ever. His beard, she noticed, was flecked with grey. He leaned on the frame, clearly drunk. In the corridor a door opened a crack, then clicked shut again.

'It's late,' he said. 'Sorry to wake you.'

Still trying to extract herself from her dream, Kate at first stood firm at the threshold, and folded her arms. 'What do you want?'

His eyes were bleary. 'Do you have a drink?'

She ought to feel afraid but she didn't. She made an effort to rationalise her lack of fear. There was a gangster at her door at two am. She stepped aside and he brushed past, sucking in his stomach, headed straight for the mini-bar in a heavy footed stride that seemed to make the room tremor. He pulled out several bottles from the mini-bar, examining then discarding each one. Finally he held up a miniature bottle of champagne 'Want one of these?'

'What do you want?'

Grigor flipped out the cork with plop, and poured a glass for her with an unsteady hand. It splashed her hand when the took it. Then he twisted the cap from one of the bottles and emptied it into a glass. 'Sorry it's so late.' He repeated, and thrust himself into the single armchair in the corner.

'It's two in the morning.'

'Is it?'

'What do you want?' Trying to feel angry. 'I'm so angry with you.'

Grigor shook his head. 'I don't know. To apologise. To help. But first of all, to apologise. I was wrong to get you to deliver the bomb. It was a kind of joke.'

'A joke?' She knew she had tears in her eyes now. 'I killed those men.' It was the first time she had vocalised it, and it made it real.

'Not exactly a joke. A test. *Like* a joke I suppose ... a bit of a prank amongst men. Not that you're a man, of course. More like a test.' He let out a deep sigh. 'I don't know. Like lots of things it seemed like a good idea at the time.' He looked at her. 'I can't explain. I can only say I'm sorry.'

'People died. How many people died?'

'People always die. Story of my life. In my business ... well anyway, let's look at the people who died, shall we? Worthless people. You need to know this. Gangsters, all of them. I don't know how many were there, but each one of them deserved to die that way. Vermin. In fact it was a good thing that you did, whether you believe it or not. Anyway, I apologise all the same. It's different here. From what you're used to, I mean. You come from a place where policeman don't carry guns.'

'But you - you're a gangster as well. Just like them.'

'Not like them.' He shook his head, looking at the floor. 'I don't think of myself that way. A businessman, yes. I want to make you understand...' He ventured. 'In Russia today, it's not like anywhere in the world. Not even like the Russia where I grew up. The Wild East, they call it. Anything can happen. You just have to get through each day. Who's guilty? Who's innocent? Who the fuck cares? I like to think we're the good guys,' he said, echoing what the driver had said in the car outside the Hotel Rossiya. He pressed the small, empty bottle against his brow and rolled it from side to side to cool his forehead. Kate thought he looked like a man undergoing something that wrenched him. He sat up again, aimed the bottle, and it rattled against the sides of the waste bin. 'Maybe you don't care—I wouldn't blame you—but I came here to try to make you understand.

Not too long ago, I was a soldier. Like my father. I come from a military family. Then I wasn't a gangster like you call me - I was a Major. A Major…' he repeated. 'Not just a Major in any old army, but Spetsnaz. Alfa. That's Special Forces, like your English SAS. The sent me to all the worst places. They sent Alpha first. Afghanistan. Chechnya.. wherever. Dropped us behind the lines. Look.' He fumbled with the buttons of his shirt to reveal an angry furrow that spanned his chest. 'I was wounded many times. I believed in what we were doing.

They told us we were liberators. Told us we were peace-keeping. Told us so much shit. Of course I saw a lot of people die. Good men mostly. On both sides good and bad men dying all the time. You didn't try to get close to anyone because they could be gone the next day. Killing was as commonplace as emptying the latrines. Unpleasant. But part of our routine. I don't take it seriously any more. Death. Some lives are not even worth thinking about. There are men from the Mujahedeen that I'd rate way above the filth I see on the streets in Moscow.'

'But you kill people.' Kate steeled herself to remember every so often that she was here, sitting opposite this big, sad angry man in a hotel room in Moscow. She missed her home, she realised. She wanted to be back in London. She remembered the Champagne and gulped at it in wistful, unshared celebration of occasions not yet met, or those that had foundered untoasted in one memory or another.

'It's true. And they called me a hero for it. But listen, when I left the army I expected a hero's welcome. I was entitled, wasn't I? After everything. All the terror. All the people I killed. They gave me medals to prove it.' He nodded at the window. 'And all this? The way Russia is today? The funny thing—I blame myself. No, really. Not solely of course, but I bear responsibility. Back in '91 I was with Alfa under Karpukhin, and they ordered us to storm the White House. To murder

Yeltsin and the others. Well. I don't have much time for that drunken bastard. Sorry.' A brief smile. 'But we decided, all of us that day, to disobey. We rebelled. Karpukhin too. It was the first time for me that I ever disobeyed an order. Things could have turned out differently. Karpuhkin was a hero too then. All heroes together making history. Yeltsin on that fucking tank.' He laughed. 'Tank 110 it was. Afterwards they rounded up all those criminals who tried to make it happen and put another bunch of criminals in charge. All for nothing. Here's to fucking heroes.' He took another bottle of spirits and tilted it at her and said again. 'Here's to heroes.' He threw his head back.

'When I came out, joined the civilians and of course there wasn't any hero's welcome. None of us realised just how unpopular our wars were, back home. We were too busy defending the motherland to appreciate that nobody thought it needed defending. Not by people like us. We were pariahs. So, these days the bars are full of vets telling their tales, showing off their collections of medals. Their wounds.' He patted his chest, where the scar was. 'But nobody gives a shit. They're tired of hearing about it. We're left with the medals and the scars and there's no work for war veterans. Not anywhere. We find other work to do. You know - I employ girls in my clubs to take their clothes off for tourists … one of them is a physician! One an engineer! There should be more respect.

'And so everybody does what they can.' He shook his head. There was a distant look in his eyes. 'Me? I take what I feel should have been given. I'm not a bad man.. Not in the regular sense. Do you think I'm a bad man, Kate Buckingham?'

'Why are you telling me all this? I don't understand.'

Grigor looked at her. 'I don't know. I like you. I wanted you to understand. I was thinking and thinking. Thinking.' He kneaded his forehead with the heel of his hand. 'Then I decided to come here. I don't know why it matters. Or even *if* it matters. It seemed to matter at the time.' He planted two meaty hands on his thighs and rubbed them. 'So, am I forgiven?'

'Of course not. How could I forget what you made me do.' The debris pattering on the pavement beneath the hotel. The moment of realisation.

'No not forgotten. Nothing's forgotten. We all have our *memories*.' He grinned at her. 'I've paid off your bill at the hotel. Stay as long as you like. It's taken care of.'

'Why would you do that?'

'Why wouldn't I? It's a big thing you did.'

She was a murderer, she thought. 'And the police? What about the police? Surely there'll be an investigation.'

'You don't need to worry.' He stroked his beard. 'Now,' he said, 'is there something else I can do for you?'

'What do you mean?'

'Everything's not what it seems with you, Kate Buckingham.' He shot her a sly look. 'You did know that you're being followed? By the FSB?'

Nikolay spent a loveless, sexless night with 2 hookers in a downtown nightclub. It wasn't sex he wanted, and it wasn't sex they wanted. He just craved the company of two pretty girls that were fun and intelligent and undemanding. He paid a premium price for the vodka, and they helped him to consume it without making him feel guilty.

Two 'o' clock in the morning. Too late to go to sleep. Too late to be awake. The music pounded and smoke hung in gossamer layers. The club had a Soviet theme, pandering to the Western businessman's image of Russia. Reclaimed statues lined the walls, of once notorious Soviet officials. He recognised Krushchev and Brezhnev with their heavy jowls scowling at him, and he raised a glass to them.

Nadya, who told him she was a law student by day, was toasting the health of the president, her irony not lost on anyone. A freckled girl with an angular jaw that made her every expression emphatic in some way. Everyone followed her toast because old habits die hard in Russia. '*Davai!*'

Nikolay's head was swimming, but he wanted to preserve this state of half sensibility indefinitely. To his left sat Irina. She was dark and sincere, and made all the usual small talk. The shadow of her breasts reached low into her silk top, and he had to check himself more than once when his eyes strayed too deeply, trying to stretch the shadow to its source. Irina wanted to make small talk about his family, and raised her voice above the pulsating music, leaning into his ear. Her nicotine breath lingered in the air. Since Nikolay had no family other than an elderly aunt in Volgograd, he was happy to invent one for her, just as his training had taught him. And as the inane conversation washed around him, and as he half-heartedly fended off the attentions of Irina and Nadya, his mind turned once more to the English girl, and the connection with Borilyenko.

On stage, a long-limbed girl in a KGB peaked cap was making swift, angular movements in time to the music. Her milky, naked limbs gleamed where they were caught by the spotlight. Nadya tugged his sleeve and asked him if he thought the girl was sexy. He flashed her a grin.

The report from London had done nothing to reveal any possible connection. Except for the odd dreams of course, which were fascinating but hardly relevant. Then there was the Russian scientist with the classified file. Why would a stripper from London flee to Moscow in search of a dead scientist, pursued by the FSB? Why would the head of the FSB be interested? It made no sense.

Nadya asked him in her emphatic way for a private dance, and he shook his head.

'What is it you do, when you're not dancing?' He asked her.

She smiled. Everybody asks. They also ask what she is doing working in a place like this. He knew the answers already. She was a medical student or a law student. Maybe even a doctor. Or she was an engineer.. mostly it was the truth. Here in today's Russia the professions barely generated enough Roubles to pay for a miserable apartment in a shabby Moscow suburb. The girls came here and places like it for as long as their beauty and youth endured, to supplement their incomes. To get by.

'I'm a micro-biologist,' she said.

A microbiologist. Like Ekaterina Ivanovna, he thought. He looked at her faintly freckled face, and saw that she was older than he had first noticed. Thin lines were discernible through the make-up. It was quite feasible that she might really be a microbiologist.

'Interesting,' he said, and Nadya pouted. 'No, really.. That's really interesting.' Although he didn't understand why. 'Where are you working?'

'I'm doing a research project just now. At Moscow State University.'

Nikolay considered for a moment, twirling his empty glass in his fingers. A question too ludicrous to vocalise was on the tip of his tongue. She was looking at him through half-closed lids. 'You are a microbiologist,' he intoned with infinite care, the way that drunks pronounce unfamiliar words. 'And what is your specialist area?'

'Genetics.' She said without any hesitation, throwing back another vodka.

It was too late now. The question had crystallised in his head. There was nothing else he could say. 'Have you heard of a woman called Ekaterina Ivanovna Borodina?'

Music played. People danced and drank. A short-lived flurry as someone was ejected from the club. Nothing out of the ordinary happened at all. It was a simple question, after all. Irina thought for a minute, wrinkling her nose. 'I think so...' she said at length, pushing her hair back. 'The name's familiar. I think I've seen a paper... Who is she?'

Nikolay felt as though he had been roused from a deep sleep. He straightened up. Nadya looked startled.

'What was the subject, do you remember? This paper, what was it about?'

Nadya had shuffled sideways on the bench. 'Does it matter?'

'I'm sorry. I think I'm very drunk. Do you remember anything? About this paper?'

She flashed him a broad smile, and took up his hand between her soft warm palms, leaning inwards so that his eyes were drawn to the shadow of her breasts. Her scent was heady and intoxicating and his nostrils flared. 'Let's forget about genetics.' she said, and wriggled back towards him, cosying herself against his arm. Irina looked away, bored. She was chewing gum.

'There's an English girl in Moscow. Called Kate. She's looking for Ekaterina Borodina.'

She released his hand, and the mood had changed again. Her smile had vanished. 'Kate,' she repeated. 'What's your interest in her?' Nikolay's eyes were leaden. The music resonated inside his head. He felt like he was underwater. 'I don't know.' He shrugged. 'Maybe nothing.' He pulled at his glass, knowing that he shouldn't drink any more.

Suspicious, she said: 'Are you Cheka?' Then she thought for an instant, and seemed to make up her mind about something. 'Wait.' She stood up, grasping her purse. ' I will be only a moment.'

'It's OK.' Avoiding eye contact Nikolay watched the dancers, as they weaved around the bar, whispering heated confidences and touching the arms of the men, tugging a sleeve. Nadya sashayed to the other side of the bar where she was lost in the shadows and the throng. The music wailed. 'Iron' Felix Dzherzhinsy glared down from his perch with disapproval. Nikolay glanced at Irina, but she had lost interest and she nursed her sickly cocktail, seeking out a new man to signal her with his eyes.

After a while he felt a light touch on his shoulder, and Nadya stood like a shimmering phantom at his side. She beckoned with her chin. 'Get up. You need to meet somebody.' And without waiting for him to struggle to his feet she swept away. He found he was unsteady on his feet and put it down to cramp. She led him to a heavy door. 'He's expecting you.' She said, and turned to walk away. Over her shoulder she said 'Good night, Nikolay.'

He took a deep breath, and was on the point of knocking, but instead pushed open the door. Through a haze of cigar smoke a gruff voice said: 'I hear you're looking for a friend of mine?'

A giant of a man raised himself from behind a desk, and pointed to a chair. Nikolay noted the Makharov PM pistol on the desk. He glanced around at the heavy wooden furniture, the leather sofas stationed around a glass topped coffee table that seemed to be fashioned out of a huge shell casing. The smoke irritated Nikolay's eyes.

'Drink.' The man wiggled a bottle of Stolichnaya at him as he sank back into his seat. It sounded like an order rather than an invitation.

'Why not?'

The man grunted and splashed vodka into two glasses, leaning to push one across the desk. 'I am Grigor Vassiyivich Malenkov, proprietor of this fucking dump.'

'Pleased to meet you, I guess.'

'And whom do I have the pleasure of addressing?'

'I'm Nikolay.' He stretched a hand towards Grigor, who grasped it briefly and firmly. 'Nikolay Sergeyevich Sokolov.'

'And who exactly is Niokolay Sergeyevich?'

Nikolay shrugged, feeling the weight of the man even from where he was sitting. 'I'm nobody.'

'You here on official business? Or would you say you're just another punter?' Grigor swung around in the chair and rose to his full height, pouring himself another drink as he did so. He did not offer Nikolay another.

'Official?'

Grigor sniffed. 'You smell like a Chekist to me.'

'No. I'm not a Chekist.'

'You were asking about the English girl. In there.'

'I mentioned her.'

'Funny. Everybody's mentioning her lately.'

'What's she to you?'

Grigor shot him a look. 'She works for me. I'm a caring employer. If she's in trouble I'd like to know about it.'

Nikolay made an effort to focus. He could hear the thump of the music outside, but it was as if from another world. He felt shipwrecked here in this office.

'Maybe we're both looking out for her.' He said at length.

'And in what capacity would you be dong that?' And when Nikolay remained silent Grigor laid a heavy hand on his shoulder. 'I could have you searched. I could even beat it out of you.' he said, but it was with a casual humour. 'If you're not a Chekist - then maybe you don't know—those guys have an interest in her.' He said, leaning on the desk.

'I know.'

'So what's to be done? If we're both looking out for her, then maybe we should lay some cards on the table. What do you think?'

Nikolay said: 'Sounds like a plan.'

'So maybe you can start by telling me who you are?'

'I'm with the security services. Not FSB but something else. All I can tell you.'

'I knew you were a fucking Chekist. What's your interest in this girl?'

'She was brought to my attention when she entered the country. She came here to look for somebody. A scientist from Soviet times. Some kind of expert in genetics. All I know is the scientist was engaged in something so secret that there's no access to the files. She says that this person is a relative. I'm not so sure it's the truth. I said I'd help to find her... But of course, you know. It's an almost impossible task to find out what happened.'

'I was with Kate just a few hours ago. At her hotel. We talked.' He made a vague gesture with his arm, and Nikolay realised that he too was drunk. 'I like her,' he said, and grunted. 'Anyway, for some reason the FSB is very interested in her. They're tailing her everywhere. She's no idea why. She seems ordinary enough. Maybe to do with this scientist. Her work?' He paused. 'You're some kind of policeman?' Looking up from his chest.

Nikolay shrugged. 'Not really. But it seems that's what they want me to be right now.'

Chapter Thirty-One

BEFORE THE EXPLOSION that ripped through the house on Privett Avenue, Ralph had spent a lot of time standing at the front window and not sitting in his usual armchair. He chewed the stem of his pipe, but rarely lit it. When Hayley entered the room he had remarked on seeing strangers in the street.

'He seems in a hurry,' or 'They don't look quite right as a couple, d'you think?' She had given it little thought, appeasing him now and then with a word of consensus.

There was something awkward and ill-fitting about the days, and he had a feeling of foreboding that he put down to a kind of resurgence of his training from the old days, like dementia in reverse. He found himself looking for small signs in the street that something was out of place. In particular, there was a blue Volvo he had noticed more than once, one morning idling at the kerb for almost two hours across the street and some way down, almost out of sight. Two male occupants.

He'd been thinking a lot about the Job, and about Kate. Disappointing how it had all worked out. He had such high hopes in the early days, such optimism. Kate would have gone to University of course: she would come to visit at the weekends, sometimes with a new boyfriend. Eventually with grandchildren. A good job: something in medicine, he always imagined, even when it looked like she was never going to be an academic. And she would never know about her past. About the secrets that would expire with him in accordance with the terms of the Official Secrets Act. A minor diplomat. Hayley knew the truth about the Job but nobody else. It was the Job that had brought them Kate, ultimately.

Apart from Kate, he couldn't claim to have done anything of significance in his career. A secret intermediary was all it amounted to. Passing secrets from one party to another, never truly being in the know. Never possessing the knowledge that he so freely shared. But they taught him to observe. The importance of covering one's tracks. He had thought all that was behind him, a long time forgotten, but as it happened they'd programmed into him some residual instinct that something had awakened now.

Hayley hovered behind him on one occasion as though searching for some common thread. It was easy to slip out of the habit of conversation, and not so easy to resurrect. Kate was the unspoken subject of all of their communication, carefully set aside as a topic that they had plenty of time to consider over dinner or at breakfast. But somehow they brooded in silence and picked at their food instead, suffering Kate's absence.

'What do you see out there?' she had asked.

'I'm not sure.'

'All this time, looking out of the window. You ought to know what you're looking at by now.'

'Not looking at. Looking for.'

'So, what're you looking for?'

He didn't answer. There was a number for Kris that he'd never used up to now, and when he tried it the number was unobtainable. Well, and why not, after all this time? What would he say anyway? He wondered if Kate had been to visit. Considered making the journey himself, but reluctant to shake the shadows. He didn't like to use the phone - another precaution they'd instilled in him, a mistrust of telephones - but even so he phoned Kate every day with no reply.

They said it was a gas explosion, those who knew about these things. The elderly couple that once lived in the prim cottage keeping themselves to themselves were both killed in the blast. Recorded in the local newspaper with a picture of the carcass of a bedroom, but never made the nationals. There was a daughter, the papers said. Police still trying to trace her.

The banging and creaking of the pipes kept her awake for most of the night. The pipes seemed to make an unnecessary amount of noise about performing their function, and yet delivered precious little as a result in the way of heat. She tugged the bedclothes around her tightly and stared up at the cracks in the plaster. Dmitry was sleeping on his back with his mouth open, and his throat cracked softly when he breathed. Sometimes she thought she despised him, like now. But there were so few people she could talk to, and even fewer men that were remotely attractive. Dmitry was remotely attractive, she thought. It was the best that could be said of him – the best she could do here in Sorsk. So when Olga was away in Moscow, which she was frequently these days, she and the political officer engaged in acts of sordid gratification that made her feel empty in the morning, like a husk.

She pulled herself onto her elbows, but the blankets slipped away and it was bitterly cold in the sparse bedroom, so she shuffled back beneath them and lay there on her back What kind of life was this? It was all about her work, she supposed. But what did her work represent? Was it morally justifiable? Who was she to play at being God? It was a dilemma she had turned over and over in her mind, ever since she had confirmed that she was pregnant.

They knew so little about the science. It was more about physical mechanics than science. They were working in the dark. For instance, they had no idea what elements, what *characteristics* of the cell donor would be replicated from the cloned cell. *Her* cell, in this case, she reminded herself with a grimace. What is the container of the soul, if there is such a thing? The container of the soul.' She turned the words over in her head, pleased with this new turn of phrase. Should they be meddling in such things at all?

Dmitry stirred, and she hoped he wouldn't wake. His breath stuttered, and she held her own breath for an instant until she heard that familiar rhythmic patter of his breathing resume. She wondered, not for the first time, if she was Dmitry's *assignment*. Was Dmitry assigned to keep a watch over her. Who would trust a political officer?

Even if she accepted they were lovers in the conventional sense, she would still have to be wary about confiding certain of her innermost thoughts. Olga's convenient absences were almost too convenient, allowing them to pursue their clandestine relationship with impunity. She frowned. Something was wrong. Something was *missing*. She reached out to touch Dmitry's warm body but the bed was empty.

She sat up with a start, her eyes darting around the empty room, restoring things to their proper places in her head.

Hard to judge precisely when her dream had morphed into a memory. Hard to judge precisely how long she'd been awake. Boundaries between her false memories and her here and now were slipping away. Was she dreaming still? She clutched her temples, wanting to banish the other memories that flooded her head. Was she going mad? With a wrung out feeling she remembered Grigor late last night. Was that a dream too? A memory? If so, whose memory was it? It was all mixed up in her head - the real, the imaginary, the quasi-real. Why would the Russian security services be interested in her? The Major she had met before - he had said the same thing. Maybe this was what triggered her dream. Her brow was damp with perspiration. An irrational fear had taken hold of her. A feeling she was under observation. It was KGB no matter what label they put on it. She shuddered. Dmitry was

KGB. A blast from her other set of memories.

She had tried not to notice that if she concentrated really hard she could slip into her other set of memories at will. Sometimes she couldn't help herself, and achieved this level of concentration in spite of her fears, like prodding at a bad tooth with her tongue. The memories were still fragmented, and she couldn't control at exactly what point she would arrive because she had no bearings, few reference points: but as each memory hardened into reality, the reference points accumulated, and she was beginning to find new and unexpected depths to her memories. Once inside her other self, she found that she could direct her thoughts forwards or backwards, which alarmed her at first.

The phone beside the bed startled her. She glanced at her watch as she fumbled to pick up the receiver. Nine a.m. 'Yes?'

'I've been thinking some more,' said the gravelly voice in flawed English without preamble. For some reason she felt flustered. Did Grigor come to her room last night or was that a dream too? Perhaps this whole KGB story was a dream too?

'And drinking?' she ventured.

He laughed. 'You think I was drunk?' He sounded offended. 'You never saw me drunk.' He muttered. There was an awkward pause, before he went on in a conciliatory tone. 'I'm sorry. Last night.. I hope you didn't mind..?'

That settled one thing. 'I didn't mind. But now..?'

'I need to talk to you. I want to help. Believe it or not.'

She remembered that Grigor had settled her hotel bill. The bomb... 'You've helped me enough.'

'Not with money. I'm worried for your safety. These men... I know them. They wouldn't waste time with somebody like you unless there was a good reason. There must be something.... '

'I'll meet you at the club.' She said at once, surprising herself.

'In an hour.'

'OK.' She rang off, and almost immediately the phone rang again. She lifted the receiver warily.

'Kate?' said a familiar voice 'Kate, is that you?'

'Robert?' She swung around and sat rigidly on the side of the bed. Part of her was horrified, and part of her happy. 'How did you find me?' The line wavered and clicked.

'Kate, what's going on?' he said anxiously. 'The police..' He stopped, and began again. 'The police have been around. Asking questions about the doorman at the club. The murder. It was in the papers. Then you were gone and...'

'How did you find me?'

'Somebody else came. A Russian.'

'What? A Russian? Who?'

'Said he was from the Security Services. Showed me his badge. Could have been anything I suppose... he said he wanted to help. The police.. they don't know. I haven't told anybody anything. Are you all right?'

'I'm OK. This Russian—what did he want?'

'He knew where you were. The hotel and everything. He said you were being watched. That you were in danger... but he wasn't sure why.'

'How's Becky?' She interrupted. It would be mid-day in England. She would be at playgroup.

'Becky's fine. She's fine, really. I'm worried about what you've got yourself into... I'm really worried Kate. Russia. Why are you in Russia? What's going on?'

She glanced at her watch. 'It's difficult. I don't really know myself what's happening at the moment. But you don't need to worry.. if anything, this trip is helping me to come to terms with some things.. you know, with my *past*.'

Robert knew that when she mentioned her past in this emphatic way, it wasn't her past that she meant, but the other past that he had found so difficult to believe in. 'I see.'

'But you don't see,' she said flatly. 'You've never seen. Nobody has. Nobody *can*. You don't understand how *real* all that is to me—' she trailed off. There was a pressure behind her eyes. She wiped away a tear. 'It's *real* Robert. This person inside my head she's real. She died, I think. But she was real. I know that now. That's why I'm here. That's what I'm trying to find out.. what happened to her.. what it all means.'

'What about the Club? What happened there? The doorman.'

'I have to go.'

'Please come home,' pleaded Robert. Kate laid down the received, pulling her hand away like it was electrified, and when the phone rang again she let it ring for a long time before Robert must have finally given up. She pictured him alone in the house, sitting amidst the stage set of another stream of memories, worrying about her. Wondering about her. He wasn't to blame. He probably thought she was crazy. He'd even tried to get her to see a doctor. A *head* doctor. But she wasn't insane. Her memories were real. She was convinced more than ever. Somehow this Ekaterina Ivanovna was living inside her head. She was as real as Kate Buckingham ever had been.

The phone rang again several times while Kate showered and dressed, and she steeled herself to ignore the shrill bleating. It was still ringing as she glanced around the hotel room one more time, checking for her key before clicking the door to.

She was quietly fretting about Becky and Robert when she took the lift to the ground floor, and as she weaved her way through the tourists milling in the lobby, a familiar face appeared at her side. Nikolay Sokolov shunted her with his shoulder and apologised, touching her gently on her shoulder – the good-looking officer who had interviewed her at the police station and promised to help. In English he said hurriedly:

'Why don't you answer your phone?' Then he brushed past, saying fleetingly out of the corner of his mouth, 'Follow me. And don't make it obvious.' Instead of heading directly across the marble lobby, he weaved through the armchairs and coffee tables.

A glance around the lobby, and she was just in time to spot a badly dressed man with a florid complexion catch her eye then avert his gaze. She thought he wasn't trying too hard. Nikolay pushed his way through the revolving doors, and after waiting a few moments she followed, keeping a furtive watch on her tail in a shabby grey track suit, lounging in a corner seat with one striped Adidas trainer propped

314

on his knee. He uncrossed his leg and leaned stiffly forward in his seat in preparation to rise and follow her from the hotel.

Out in Tverskaya Street where the traffic boomed relentlessly, Nikolay had already hailed a taxi, a bright yellow Volga with a missing wing mirror and a cavernous dent in the rear door. He was stooping over the driver's door and straightened up as she emerged from the hotel.

'I'm sorry.' He said with an open handed gesture. 'If you're looking for a cab, you're welcome to take mine.'

She thanked him, playing along, and ducked into the back seat, propping her handbag on her knee. The damaged door creaked. No sooner was she in her seat than the driver rammed the column mounted gear leaver into gear and edged the car into the stream of traffic without a word. Then suddenly he careered across the road, turned sharply into a small side street, tyres squealing, and made two more swift turns that sent Kate scuttling across the plastic seat, reaching out for the seat in front. Afterwards he drove for two blocks in silence as though nothing had happened, then pulled into a narrow street where he wedged the stocky Volga between two abandoned SUV's.

'What now?' She said hesitantly.

The man shrugged. 'We wait.'

315

'Are you a real taxi driver?'

He glared at her. 'Of course.' He said without seeming to care if she believed him or not.

Out of the rear window she watched the traffic crawl past on the main road. After fifteen minutes or so a red Volkswagen turned into the street, and she saw Nikolay mount the kerb and leave the car without locking it. He slipped into the back seat of the taxi behind her.

'Amateurs.' He said, in an almost injured tone. 'I could never have gotten away with that in the old days.' He gestured out of the window. 'He's not following now.' He glanced at the driver meaningfully, who sighed and levered himself out of the car into the street, where he lingered, leaning against the bonnet and lit a cigarette. 'We spoke with your husband in London.'

When Lebed arrived at the offices of the Russian Democratic Union Party offices on Arbat Street flanked by two beefy bodyguards, a tall, silver haired man in a long coat was presiding over the breaking open of a row of steel filing cabinets. Colourful campaign posters of Lebed in army uniform adorned the walls. The bodyguards looked at Lebed for the lead.

'Stop. It now,' he commanded, with a calm inflection that

suggested he was used to being obeyed. The intruders faltered, appearing uncertain. They hadn't expected he would show up in person. Their leader was unfazed, abandoned the filing cabinet, and approached with an affable smile, snapping open his ID with its twin headed eagle.

'Good morning, sir,' he said breezily. 'I am Colonel Lisakov of the Federal Security Services. We have orders, I'm afraid.' One of Lisakov's men was engaged in levering open a cabinet, and it made a retching sound like someone clearing his throat loudly as the metal buckled. Lebed barely glanced at the ID. He assessed the situation unhurriedly, like the General that he once was, running scenarios and outcomes through his head. Three FSB men and this Colonel. The FSB men looked unprofessional, thuggish. Not much of a match for his own men, if it came to it. Then he said:

'Please instruct your officers to stop what they are doing.'

Lisakov shrugged. 'I'm sorry sir. Orders…'

'I'm not without influence you know, Colonel.' Lisakov looked a little uncomfortable. Lebed put back his head and laughed. Lisakov started. 'I know your kind Colonel—what is it—Lisakov? You think you have some useful patronage, some mandate. But you don't. You don't have anything. Borilyenko would drop you like a hot potato if you caused him the least embarrassment... ' He paused, and glowered at Lisakov from beneath dark forbidding eyebrows. 'Whereas I could have you transferred in a moment to some god-forsaken outpost of Russia to work with some hick militia outfit in the snow...' Lebed snapped his fingers. 'In an instant.' He said, regarding Lisakov with his intent poker stare.

Lisakov gestured to his men. 'Wait,' he said.

The windows in the taxi were already steamed up. Kate made a porthole with her glove. The traffic rolled past, giant trucks with throaty growls, tantalisingly close to the parked cars.

'Robert,' she said.

Sokololov smiled. 'He was of no help to us. I thought you should know. But he's very worried about you.' He paused. 'He told us about the.... Incident in which you were involved. Before you left. To come to Moscow.'

'So it was your people that told him where to find me?'

Sokolov coughed into his hand in a small gesture of discomfort. 'I didn't see the harm... But if it was me I would have played things differently.'

She threw him a sidelong glance. He looked somehow forlorn,

with a far away look in his grey eyes, and a strange empathy stirred within her. The collar of his blue suit was turned up, like a small act of rebellion.

'I have a meeting,' she said. 'What do you want?'

'So.. I've been doing some research, Miss Buckingham. Like I promised I would.'

'You found her?' she started.

'I really don't think that will be possible,' he sighed. 'The person you are looking for disappeared in, well... what I guess were predictable circumstances for the times.' He glanced at her. 'But I have found out something about her.'

'So, she's alive?'

Sokolov shook his head. 'No, no. Doubtful I think.'

A silence ensued. She listened to the traffic. Sometimes the car would rock in the wake of a heavy vehicle passing, its exhaust spluttering.

'Ekaterina Ivanovna Borodina.' He paused, and for a moment Kate thought he was addressing her by this name. It felt reminiscent of something. 'She was a scientist. And so far as I can tell she was well regarded in all of the right places. By which I mean the Party. She distinguished herself at University. And went on to specialise in genetics. Then... she is lost to us.'

'Lost?'

'Miss Buckingham, (can I call you Kate?) in my position I have a long reach. I can access many things that to others would be inaccessible. But in the case of Ekaterina Ivanovna.. I've drawn a blank. Which means that whatever work she was engaged in was not for for the usual consumption. Highly secret.' As if for emphasis he repeated, as if with some relish, 'Classified.'

She frowned. 'So what are you telling me?'

He grinned unexpectedly - a wry, boyish grin. 'I was rather hoping you could do the telling. Is there anything you can tell me about Ekaterina Ivanovna? For instance, why do you come here looking for a scientist who most probably died a long time ago, and whose background is a mystery?'

'Ok ... So I told you before she's a relative. An aunt most probably.' She lied 'I wanted to find out what happened to her.'

'An aunt. Most probably.' He sighed, and wound down the window to summon the driver. 'Can we drop you somewhere?'

A rainy day in November. Warm for the time of year. They walked to the Registry office, not hand in hand but with a joint determination.

Kate was 8 months pregnant. He wore his long overcoat, a suit but no tie. She looked beautiful with her long hair in ringlets and her sweeping red silk dress with the plunging neckline.

He remembered the swift professional execution of the service. The exchange of rings. The desultory walk back to the cold apartment. It was a day that he had longed for. It was a day that he had dreaded. It was a day that passed like every other in a series of gestures and images of happiness and despair, culminating in a night that was curtailed too soon by a bleak insipid dawn. Their wedding day.

He watched the clouds skim past the cabin window. The plane was on its descent into Shermetyevo 2 and the passengers were restless, packing away their books and magazines. The chime of the seatbelt warning sounded and a sultry voice made a lengthy announcement in Russian.

He felt a chill pass through him. Flipped through his passport to where the newly appended visa filled up a whole page. Wondered again why he was here.

Chapter Thirty-Two

LAYERS OF TOBACCO smoke hung wispy in the air like angel hair, half-remembered from the Christmas tree when she was a girl. It lent a dreamy feel to the cavernous nightclub with its empty chairs and tables and the open jaw of the stage, where a row of empty Baltika beer bottles stood at the edge like green teeth.

The door banged behind her. From their perches in the wings the sentinels of Soviet history acknowledged her with stony grace. The statue of Iron Feliks glowered. She ventured forward, feeling like Alice lost in some strange and vaguely threatening world. She heard her voice resonate. 'Anyone here? Grigor?' It seemed harsh and uneven and didn't sound like it came from her. When her thigh bumped against a table the sound made her start. The air was tinged with disinfectant and stale sweat. When Grigor appeared at the office door she was relieved at first, but at the same time felt a frisson of apprehension.

Grigor had a way of occupying space, even large spaces. His sound and size and energy eclipsed his surroundings. And yet somehow he made her feel at ease, with his bluster and bulk.

'Welcome,' he said in English, and beckoned to the open door of his office. 'You're late of course - but I knew you'd be here.'

She allowed herself to be steered into Grigor's office, his large paw in the crook of her back like he was leading her to the dance floor. Then he pulled out a chair for her, and seated himself behind a broad, heavily carved, mahogany desk. A large gun rested on a sheaf of envelopes and paper on the desk. Two empty bottle of Stolichnaya were upended In the wastepaper bin. He looked at the bottles and snorted.

'Yesterdays' empties.' Then he sat behind the desk and scrutinised her. She held his stare until he said. 'Tell me everything. Tell me what is so fucked up in your life that you end up here in a strip joint in Moscow, with a KGB tail.'

She felt a sudden impulse that made her want to unburden herself. Here with Grigor she experienced a perverse feeling of security.. She longed to air her other past in front of somebody that might believe her.

'Everything?' she said, instead.

'OK. Let's start with why you're here. In Moscow, I mean.'

She shook her head. 'That's a hard one. Difficult to explain. I'm not sure you'd believe me anyway.'

Grigor made an inviting gesture with his hands and sat back in his chair with a creak of old leather, like he was preparing for a vigil. He moved his legs as if to rest them on the desk, and then seemed to think better of it. 'Let's try. Because there are guys out there,' he nodded towards the door, 'who seem to have an unnatural interest in you. For whatever reason. And now you've brought them to *my* door - which considering my business activities isn't particularly welcome either. I'd like to find out why they think you're so important. From what I see you're pretty ordinary. If that's not insulting.'

'It's not insulting,' she said, feeling slighted all the same. Where to begin? 'I think I'd give anything to be just ordinary. It's going to sound weird, but bear with me: you see, for as long as I can remember I've had these... dreams.' She began. 'No, not dreams exactly - because they come to me when I'm awake as well. The first one I remember was a dream I kept having about a samovar. I didn't even know what a samovar was. I dreamed I was looking up at my reflection in this big urn thing, and an old lady wearing a long dress was walking around. Busy.' She frowned. 'There were lots of other dreams. What you might call ordinary dreams, most of them. But the samovar dream was different. It was *real*. It was in my dreams, but it felt like a part of my past. Then there were daydreams that were more like memories than dreams. Mum used to call it... misremembering. I misremember places I've never been to. People I've never met.' She glanced up, flustered. 'See? I told you it was weird.' She said.

'Keep going. Let's hear it.'

'So it turned out it was more than that. More than misremembering. You know…' She paused, took a breath. '..nobody *taught* me to speak Russian. I just… well I speak it like I speak English. Seems like I always have.' She wondered what he must be thinking, but he said nothing. 'And then there's maths. Science. I know things about biology and disease that had my GP reaching for his text book. I've known the periodic tables all my life. Nobody taught me them. Nobody *could* have taught me these things - except, I remember learning them. I misremember learning them I mean. I misremember schools I've never been to. Teachers I've never known. Books I've never read - stuff from Dostoevsky, Turgenev, Pushkin,

Lermentov. I can even quote you lines of verse.' She was on the borderline - almost in tears. She recounted more from instinct than memory:

"I have outlasted all desire,

My dreams and I have grown apart;

My grief alone is left entire,

The gleamings of an empty heart."

'You think I'm crazy don't you? Everybody does. It's very beautiful - but I don't even know what it is. If I thought about it maybe I could remember…'

'It's Pushkin,' said Grigor. 'Yes, I like this poem. But I remember only:

"I live in lonely desolation,

And wonder when my end will come."

From the same verse. Beautiful. So you must have learnt it somewhere. Where did you go to school? Not in England but in this other world of yours. This alternative past, if that's what you think it is.'

She answered without thinking. 'School 66.' And a vision of the iron gates came to her at once. Waiting in a snowstorm for them to open, pounding the packed snow with her heels.

'Could be,' he said. 'But only if you were a lot older.'

'But I didn't. I didn't go to that school at all. I went to St Andrew's junior school. In England - and then to The Highfield School. Not a school with a number. But I *definitely* remember it, School 66. Every detail. There used to be a crack in the wall a few inches wide above the entrance, maybe five feet long. It scared us and we used to be afraid it would collapse. That's why we were always in a hurry to get through the doors. The teachers thought we were keen, in a hurry to get into class….' She stopped. 'You see? Even small details. And I wasn't even aware of that detail until this very moment. It came to me just now.'

'So where do you think they come from? How do you come to have these dreams? Something you read? Somebody you know?'

'I don't know. It's like being haunted. Possessed. I've never read anything about Russia. Never known any Russians. It's like there's another person in my head. I think I even know her name.'

'What name?'

'I met someone recently. Somebody real - but someone I seemed to know already from my misrememberings. He works at the Russian Embassy in London. Some kind of diplomat. And he mistook me for this person - this person that lives in my head. He called her - he called *me* - Ekaterina Ivanovna. *Katya*, he said first. And I knew her. I *felt* her   if that makes sense. Like she was part of me. That's when I realised these memories must be real. I *understood* him. That's what I still can't get over. He spoke Russian and I knew what he was saying. And after that, things started to happen. People following me. Sorry. I don't know why I'm telling you all this.'

'Never mind. It's getting interesting.'

'It made me look at myself. Look at my past. I discovered my English past is every bit as much of a fiction as my misremberings. I'm not who I thought I was - at least, it turns out I was adopted. As a baby. I don't know how they could have kept it from me for so long. Those hypocrites.'

'So who are your real parents?'

She shook her head. 'I don't know. But I know one thing - I'm from here. From Russia. I was smuggled out of the country as a baby.'

'Why would they do that?'

'That's what I was trying to find out. Before they killed Gold.'

'Gold?'

'Somebody who tried to help me when they…' she sniffed away the panic that had gripped her at the though of Gold. 'When they came for me. When they tried to take me away.'

'Slow down. Who tried to take you away?'

'No idea. Russians. And they shot Gold.'

'Some Russians killed him? And they shot him for helping you?'

'He tried to stop them taking me.' Gold, thrown backwards and left bleeding on the wet pavement. 'He tried. Poor Gold. I felt so… he was…' She faltered. Thought about the son she never knew he had. What was to become of him? 'Anyway, I ran away and somehow managed to escape - but I just knew they'd be back - That's why I decided the only thing to do was to find out why they were after me. Find out what it was all about. It led me here, to Russia. But it's different here. Not like the Russia I remember. The Moscow in my dreams. Even the street names. I'm no further forward. Not really. And people are still after me. You said so yourself . Those men outside.' She checked Grigor's face for signs of disbelief.

'Maybe you need to tell me more about this Ekaterina Ivanovna. Her work, for instance.'

'I was a scientist,' she said at once, before correcting herself. 'She, I mean. She was a scientist. In Sorsk Gorod. That's where she worked. And lived.' And as she said this she realised that this was a brand new recollection, something that she had uncovered like wiping away a layer of snow on a tombstone.

'Sorsk?' He said. 'I never heard of it.'

She lifted her chin, as though straining her neck to see over a barrier as she said 'It was a ZATO. A secret city. We were involved in secret work. Nobody even with a foreign passport was allowed to go there. It wasn't...' She checked his face to see that he wasn't laughing at her. 'It wasn't on maps.' She paused. Felt awkward. 'I'm not making this up. I don't think so anyway.'

'I know about ZATO's. *Zakritye administrativno-territorialnye obrazovaniia*. There were lots of them in Soviet times. You needed a permit to enter. And to leave. And you're right - they're not on maps. Usually they're known just by a postcode.'

'That's right! The postcode. It was: Veliky Novgorod-120.' With sudden certainty, her misrememberings, having acquired a fresh vigour.

'It means,' he said, 'that it was probably 120 km from Veliky Novgorod. I say probably, because sometimes they changed it. For EXTRA camouflage.' He laughed. 'So tell me about this secret work?'

'It was...' she began, 'I was...' But the source had died up. She concentrated hard. Closed her eyes. She was wearing a white coat, like a doctor. She was working. Working...' Her mind drifted. 'It's too difficult.' She shrugged. 'Sometimes it's like they just dry up. The memories. They stop coming.'

Grigor hefted himself out of his chair and stood for a while, just thinking. She watched him, angry at herself for revealing so much in the vague hope of some miracle. Finally he said:

'I can't explain any of this. The only thing I know for sure is that there are some serious government people who are interested in you, and it can only have to do with what you've told me.' He paused. 'If you were smuggled out of the Soviet Union as a baby, there's got to be a reason. Maybe…' he said, 'maybe they were experimenting on *you*. Seems like science fiction I guess, but maybe, I don't know, *thought implants* or something. They did crazy things in those days from what I know. Especially in those ZATO's. Nobody was accountable for the damage they did.'

'So what do you think I should do?'

He thought for a few moments. 'I think we should go and find Sorsk.'

It was cold in the apartment. The fire in the grate barely reached out to touch the chill of the room. She looked at her reflection in the bulbous metal and inclined her head, watching her left cheek inflate, and pulled a wide grin.'

'Keep away from the samovar Katya. I've told you before. It's very hot,' said a kind voice.

'It's funny'

The long skirts whisked past her, and she felt a firm hand on her shoulder. 'You won't think it's so funny if you are scalded Katya darling. Come with me and I will make you some supper.'

'I'm cold. It's warm here.'

'I will put another log on the fire.'

'Why is my face backwards?'

From above came a rippling laugh that made Katya feel warm inside and diminished the cold of the room.

'You're looking into the mirror world Katya. The samovar is like a window on the mirror world. Everything there is topsy turvy.'

'Can I go there?'

'To the mirror world?'

'Yes. Where it's topsy turvy. I think I'd like that mama. Can I go there?'

Then a big laughing moon-like face swept down from above, and Katya's mother was there at her level, pushing away a wisp of hair from her face. Katya thought her mother was very beautiful. 'You can go wherever you want darling. So long as you are safe and happy.'

Katya reflected for a moment and glanced back at the samovar. 'Will you come too mama?'

'I will always be with you darling...' And Katya felt her mother's warm lips pressed against her face, and then she was swept from the ground and carried away...

The sheets were damp and crumpled when she awoke, and she worried that she might be sickening for something. She felt as though she'd been tugged from safety and deposited here in this bleak hotel room. She ached to go back - to lose herself in her dream again in that topsy turvy world of her other life. She looked at the clock on the bedside table. Only 11:45 pm. She sighed and tried to immerse herself in sleep, but conflicting images stumbled and collided in her head. Moscow then. Moscow today. London seemed like a lifetime away.

Chapter Thirty-Three

'WHY WOULD YOU be interested in this girl?'

'She works for me,' said Grigor, tapping the gun on his desk with a pen. The gun was a relic. A souvenir from Afghanistan. He had his feet up as usual on the corner of the desk and a large Coriba smouldered in the ashtray. After Kate had gone he had sat for a long time before phoning Lisakov.

Lisakov laughed down the phone. 'Many girls work for you, Grigor Vassilyich. What's special about this one?'

Chink. Chink. Chink. He tapped the gun. 'I don't know, Comrade Colonel. That's what I'm trying to find out. What *is* special about her? Maybe you can tell me. There must be something—you said so yourself, after Olennsky. At the club.'

'You're asking the wrong man.'

'Then who do you think I should ask?'

'I don't think you should ask anyone. And I've already forgotten that this phone call ever took place.'

'Give me something Colonel. I pay you.' With a playful, cutting edge.

'Not for this you don't.'

'It's not enough?'

'It's never enough Grigor Vassilyich. It will never be enough.'

'You people have been following her since she came to Moscow. Do you deny it?'

'I don't confirm it.'

'She's just some Western bimbo. Not a spy. Not anything at all.' He laughed. 'What can you possibly want with her?'

'Is she pretty?'

'In a Barbie doll kind of way.'

'So I can guess *your* interest at least.'

Grigor grunted. 'Maybe. But what's yours? That's what I'd like to know. That's why I'm phoning.'

A pause. 'Grigor Vassilyich, I'm thinking about this very carefully, and I don't believe this girl is for you. Find another Barbie doll. You have a wide choice at your establishment.'

'You're not going to help me?'

'I don't think I can. But I'll tell you all I know.'

'What does that mean?'

'I mean.. What I know is nothing. I have orders, and I follow them. You remember what that's like? Probably not. I represent other peoples' interests - not my own.'

'Whose orders?'

'Leave it, Grigor Vassilyich.' And the line went dead.

Grigor pulled on his cigar and watched the smoke fold upon itself in the air. Where did the smoke go to, after it disappeared, he asked himself? What happened to a secret city when the secret was out? He checked an ancient rolodex, pulled out a card and picked up the phone again, dialled a number.

'Sergey Ivanovich. It's been a long time.' and after the usual exchanges of old comrades, after enquiries about the expired and the soon to expire, he said, 'Tell me what you know about a ZATO called Sorsk Gorod?'

Robert put his head in his hands. 'I don't know what you want from me.' It seemed like they had been in the airless room for days, playing and replaying the same questions and answers.

'We just need to be sure, that's all. About what she told you,' said the man with a face like a gnarled oak.

He fought against a wall of frustration and anger. 'But she didn't tell me anything. She sometimes had these dreams. I told you everything I know about them. They were just dreams. Like I told the other guy. In London.'

'Other guy? What other guy is this?'

'From Moscow. Asking me all these questions. About Kate. About her dreams. Not KGB he said, but something else.' He tried to remember. 'Just not KGB. Said his name was Pavel.'

'Describe him, please.'

Robert could see that the man was paying close attention. 'I don't know. Not tall. Brown hair. Personable. Excellent English.'

The man waited. Robert floundered, searching for more to give.

'What did you tell him exactly? About the dreams. This is very important.'

'Just what I've told you. What is there to tell?'

The man with the oak face stooped to look into his eyes. He saw his eyes had flecks of yellow. Saw empathy there, but maybe it was only something he projected for his own comfort. Robert's vision faded briefly - there was a blackness around the edges. Tiredness. He wanted to be somewhere warm and he envied the man his thick coat. The man raised himself again to his full height.

'Tell me about *Simbirsk*.'

Robert shook his head. 'I don't know what that is. I told you a hundred times.'

'You're sure she never mentioned it?'

'Never.'

'*Simbirsk* was the birthplace of Lenin. Now Ulkyanovsk. Kerensky was born there too—and what about *Pustinja*? Did you ever hear her mention this?'

'I don't know what that is either.'

'She didn't talk about it?

'No.'

'*Pustinja*,' he repeated. 'You're quite sure? And this other man in London, he never mentioned it?' He said looking hard at him. Robert shook his head.

'No. I never heard her mention that name. What is it?'

'Everybody's worst nightmare. It means "Wilderness"' He turned to one of the guards and said something in Russian. The guard nodded and left the room, banging the steel door behind him. 'At length he said, 'So… when she talked about these dreams - they were always about the same thing?'

'No. Different. Always about different people. Places. Except for some childhood memory. Some ornament. She seemed to have that dream quite often.'

'A samovar, maybe?'

'I don't know. I've never heard that word. What is it?'

'A Russian tea urn.'

Robert shrugged. 'If that's what it was.'

'And you thought these dreams were what? Her imagination?'

'Like I said: She's always had these dreams. Like another memory. Since she was a child.' He remembered the wistful expression that would descend upon her sometimes when she entered that world that he couldn't penetrate.

'What are you thinking?' he would say.

'Nothing. Just misremembering,' she would reply. By then he knew about misremembering.

'So what, exactly?'

'Now? I'm remembering the circus.'

'Circus?'

'Yes. A man fighting with a small bear. The bear was wearing a red neckerchief like a pioneer.'

'A pioneer?

She looked at him like he had caught her out. 'Yes. It just came to me. A pioneer. I don't know - it's natural for a pioneer to wear a red neckerchief, I suppose. Isn't it?'

And these were the conversations they used to have about her dreams. If they were dreams.

'I just played along,' he said, and the self reproach made him look away from the yellow flecked eyes.

The man grunted, thrust his pink hands into his coat. Then the door opened and the guard appeared again, this time accompanied by a vaguely discomfiting man in a crumpled suit, who followed at a respectful distance. When he saw the man in the long coat he acknowledged him with a flutter of his eyelids. The man looked at Robert in what he sensed was a meaningful way. 'You'll have to excuse me,' he said. Robert felt deeply emotional for some reason.

'You're leaving me?'

The man articulated a smile, and left, and then the man in the crumpled suit regarded him with a dutiful expression, assuming responsibility for him. His hair was grey but streaked with silver. His face was grey like concrete, and scoured with thin lines like somebody had skated there before the concrete had set. He had with him a scuffed plastic case - what used to be known as an attaché case, and which he swung onto the table, clicked it open. Robert half expected him to whistle. He strained to see the contents. He wasn't tied down, but he felt as if magnetised to the chair and each time he moved he glanced once at the guards, feeling the pull of invisible restraints.

'Roll up the left sleeve,' said the grey man, and Robert rolled up his sleeve almost without thinking, his whole being shivering. 'It won't take long.' And the man took his arm and pressed a needle into a vein.

Robert had the urge to do something heroic, but he did nothing heroic. He willed himself to struggle and prayed that nobody would judge him later. There was nothing he could have done, he told himself. There was no escape. And Robert sailed blissfully into oblivion with the guilt of somebody leaving their baggage on a train.

Borilyenko walked alone down the corridor. Wilderness. Project Pustinia. Everybody's worst nightmare: that's what he'd told him. His own worst nightmare: he hadn't told him that, although it was implied.

He remembered the weighted muzzle of the mask that chafed and pulled and filled with moisture when he spoke. Yellow flames lapping out of windows. A wall of heat. His skin slippery with perspiration inside the NBC suit that crackled when he moved. The troops looked like mutants with doleful round eyes and long snouts, clad in wax ponchos. It was lunchtime and the canteen building was full. A strident voice through a megaphone was giving orders: 'Stay inside the building. Do not panic! This is a drill.'

A soldier fumbled with his weapon, made intricate by thick gloves, then directed it at the building. Some people hovered at the doors, torn between flight and the concrete security of the building. A child shouted for his mother. A woman sobbed with loud gulps of distress. Above everything he could hear his own hoarse breathing.

Then the rocket ignited blanking out the screams.

Colonel Borilyenko clamped his hands over his ears, ducked his masked head, then looked up through steamy goggles in time to see the roof erupt. Empty windows filled with bright light, white then yellow. The heat was like a slap. He took a step back. The building crumpled and baked and a haze of heat surrounded the concrete like a halo.

The looped red sign above the doorway had turned to black, buckled but still legible: 'Stolovaya'.

And it felt—lke Stalingrad. For the greater good. A city burned and smouldered all around him, like Hades.

A Zil fire tuck drew up behind him and waited with its big diesel idling.

Every last living organism, he told himself. Everything must be exterminated. The alternative too horrific to contemplate. A necessary evil. A necessary contingency. Cleaning up after himself.

And now the general found himself cleaning up again, covering his back.

An officer unlocked a door at the end of the corridor.

Chapter Thirty-Four

THEY DROVE PAST serried blocks of Krushchoyovki apartments, steep barracks with empty eyes and sooty faces. The traffic had thinned out. She settled herself in the deep upholstery and looked down at the other vehicles as their SUV powered past. Grigor steered the car with calm authority, the engine little more than a murmur, rasping now and then when he accelerated past other cars or swung the wheel to weave around a pothole or a broken-down car. Soviet relics with smoking engines. He threw her a glance.

'Soon we'll be out of the city.' He waved a hand at the window. 'See those houses? Meant to be temporary. Five storeys of misery. Freezing in the winter, hot in the summer. I grew up in a place like that. Bathroom down the hall.'

Hard to imagine this rugged bearded man as a child, she thought. 'How long is the drive?'

'Who knows? Maybe two or three hours. Depends on the roads. The trucks. They won't all be like this..' And as if to emphasise the fact, the tyres rumbled where the road had been broken up for resurfacing. A solitary red and white bollard stood in the centre of the road and Grigor flipped the car around it. The wheels thudded when they re-joined the surfaced road. They slowed in the wake of an 18-wheel truck in a brown fog of exhaust, and the undertow of sludge spat at them smearing the windscreen. The truck's engine laboured, changed note. Acrid fumes tainted Kate's tongue. As they passed Kate caught a glimpse of the driver, stolid and oblivious, staring straight ahead, both hands planted on the wheel.

Sorsk. She thought about the name, hoping to awaken some memory, but it just whispered to her, composed itself in her head in Russian characters, *Сорск,* empty of meaning. 'I'm not sure what I'm hoping to find there. Not even sure if it'll be there at all.'

'Maybe you'll find nothing.' He shrugged. 'Maybe everything.'

'I just hope it's not a disappointment. Hope *I'm* not a disappointment.' She said with a sidelong glance. Grigor said nothing.

'You say the location of these places is some big secret?'

He shrugged. 'You had part of the secret already. You knew the name. There are no secrets without the people that keep them.'

'Do you know a lot of secrets?'

'A lot. In this case, I know somebody that knows about these places. Closed cities. He's from my network. Reliable until now. I told you I wasn't a gangster all my life.' he finished the sentence with a clearing of the throat.

A road lined with birch trees. Up ahead a line of girls, teetering on pointed heels and bare-legged in the freezing weather. Snowflakes spiraled. A ragged blonde in thigh length boots gestured as they passed, seemed to shout at them.

'Prostitutes. They're always here. The police try to stop them, but it's no use. Ordinary girls. Shop girls.' He shrugged. 'Sex is better paid than selling beetroots in the supermarket.'

'Where do they come from? There's nothing around here. Not for miles.'

'From the town. *Chornaya Graz*. It means Black Dirt. Describes it perfectly.'

Now there was a line of mournful shopfronts, facias of grimy blues, oranges, yellows, that flapped with paper bills. An ironmonger's wooden porch cluttered with rattletrap lawnmowers and a tired cement mixer. A baker's empty window.

'It's debatable whether there's life beyond the Moscow ring road.'

A hotel with a statue of a golfer and an empty car park, then a timber yard.

'What do you think about those girls back there? And the ones that work for you?'

'For me a lot like places. Some colourful. Fun to stay one night, but that's all. Some places sophisticated. Spend a week there and learn something new every day. Then there're the ones where you live. Familiar. Habitual. I had a wife like that.'

'From your club?'

'Not mine. From another club.'

'What happened?'

'I was always away. When I was a military man. It's rough on the women.'

'Did it have an effect - the work she did before? From the club, I mean?' Drawn to the question.

'Never thought about it. A lesson from the army. Nobody wants to find where the bodies are buried, so we don't dig in those places.'

The interior smelled richly of leather. 'Grigor. You've been so helpful, and I'm grateful. But why? Why are you helping me?' picking up an abandoned conversation.

Eyes glinted in the lights of a passing car. 'Curiosity. About the dreams. About you. Also about the attention you're getting from those guys at the Lubyanka. You need a friend here, whether you know it or not.' He reached and brushed her hand but didn't take it and she felt a tremor so fleeting it could have been imaginary.

'My hero,' she laughed. 'So you want to be my friend?'

'If you want it.'

'Anything else?' It sounded arch. He didn't answer, and she was glad.

She thought hard to dredge up some vestiges of her misremembered past that would prove helpful when they reached Sorsk but her head was empty. 'How does it work for you?' she said. 'Remembering? I mean the mechanics?' Hard to articulate what she meant by the mechanics. Hard to know what she meant. Did people remember things in a different way to her?

He threw her an odd look. 'I just remember. Or sometimes I don't. Maybe choose not to. Vodka helps to carve out some of the worse bits. Each day we add to our memories by taking a cut from the future, like another deck of cards. Also sometime we invent our past to fit our present. Make it fit who we think we've become.' He shrugged. 'My experience, that's all.'

'I like that. Making it fit. For me it's not so easy. The mechanics. I have to really concentrate. It's an effort to recall things. Then sometimes I think so hard about the process of remembering that I forget how to do it. Or not forget, exactly. Just not remember. I'm not making much sense. When it happens it's like breaching a membrane - I get this flood of stuff. New memories - but they're not new. Memories can't be new. That's stupid. They've been with me all my life. Just... misplaced.'

'You're making my head hurt.'

She laughed. Wanted to laugh so much. 'Ordinary people.. I mean other people - they accumulate.. what would you call it? Terms of reference. With waypoints. Then they use the waypoints to locate their memories - that time on holiday in Rome; that time at school. Except for me there aren't any waypoints with my other memories. That's what makes it so difficult to remember.'

They drove on for almost two hours, Kate drifting in and out of a stupor that passed for sleep. Grigor left the highway once, and drove along a straight, single track road. She awoke when the car turned onto a deeply pitted road with alarming ruts that made the SUV dip and buck.

'Is it far?'

'Who knows? I wasn't even sure this road existed. No signs. Sometimes there are roads on maps that were planned but never built. Other times there are roads like this that aren't on any maps. At least the road's here. But Sorsk Gorod? That's not on any map. If it ever existed then we'll find it. Trust me.' And she did.

The road swept around to the left, and afterwards there was an abandoned checkpoint, with rusted red and white poles standing upright and two guard houses with empty windows. Grigor sped through the gates and the road widened into two carriageways again. The surface was surprisingly smooth, although the central reservation was overgrown. Brown tentacles crusted with fresh snow, tumbled over the outside lane.

'Like a highway,' he said in disbelief, accelerating. 'Without any traffic. But some tracks in the snow. Look.' He nodded, and there ahead of them was a single set of tyre-tracks. 'Seems like at least one other car came this way today.'

The snow had begun to assert itself, and seemed to close in around them so it was like travelling in a gauze bubble, landscape a streak of brittle-backed frozen fields and leaden skies, a blur of snowflakes. She shivered, even though it was warm in the car, huddled into the folds of her coat.

'Soon,' he said, turning his head briefly. 'Maybe,' he qualified.

They drove for another hour on the straight road, and Kate dozed again. She awoke with a start when she sensed the motion of the car had stopped. 'Are we there yet?' Like a child's refrain, she thought.

Ahead was a checkpoint, this time occupied. The road had narrowed to a single lane each way and there was a guard house on each lane. Barriers barred the route in both directions. At the side of the road there was a parking area, and a battered Lada with a blue light was parked at an angle taking up two spaces. Above the checkpoint hung a sign pronouncing 'SORSK GOROD'.

'Looks promising,' said Grigor.

They edged forward, snow crunching under the wheels, and a uniformed guard emerged, adjusting his fur cap with one hand and swinging an automatic weapon over his shoulder with the other. In front of the barrier he raised his hand. A crooked yellow sign at the side of the road read 'Contaminated Territory. Access Prohibited'.

'Contaminated?' she said.

With a creak of leather and a burst of cold air, Grigor manoeuvred himself out of the car.

'Wait.'

When Grigor approached him the guard unslung his weapon and pointed the barrel at him, then yelled something Kate couldn't hear. Grigor walked with his palms aside, as though showing he was unarmed; slipped once on the frozen road, and the guard tensed at the unexpected movement. Kate looked around, but there was nothing to be seen except the checkpoint and a line of black and barren trees on either side of the road. The engine ticked as it cooled. She watched Grigor stop a few paces from the guard and thrust his hands into the pockets of his leather jacket. He looked relaxed. Kate tried to put down the window to hear what they were saying, but without the engine running the electrics were off. They mouthed silent words at each other, and appeared to share a joke. The guard hoisted his gun over his shoulder again and gestured a few times in the direction of the town. Grigor turned towards the car. The guard looked. Then Grigor produced a packet of cigarettes and offered one to the guard which he accepted. Grigor pushed the packet on him and the guard first pushed the pack away without much conviction, then accepted. They smoked, standing together in the falling snow, the guard stamping his feet now and then. He seemed friendly enough. Then they shook hands, and Grigor turned back towards the car. The guard threw his cigarette butt into the wind, where it faltered and blew back at him, then swung the barrier up as just as Grigor tugged open the car door again.

'Let's go,' and the instruments beeped and blinked as the engine burst into life.

'What happened? What did he say?'

'Not much. He's been assigned here a year. They don't get visitors, so he's pretty bored sitting in his cabin. Plays chess with himself; drinks plenty of vodka by the smell of him. Lives in a village a couple of hours away. A bitch of a commute, but there are no traffic jams and he gets to stay warm in his cabin. Nobody's lived here for years. He doesn't know how long. The area's contaminated he said, but he's not sure with what. Thinks maybe radioactivity, but he doesn't really know. He says he's not ventured much further than the guardhouse because he's nervous about the contamination. He's got orders to stop anyone from going in. The whole perimeter's fenced off beyond the checkpoint, so this is the only way in or out.'

'Why did he let us through?'

'My natural charm,' he said, baring his teeth in a grin. 'He's just a boy. A conscript. We talked about army shit. I asked him for a favour, one comrade to another. He didn't take much persuading. I told him my girlfriend used to live here when she was a kid, and wanted to see how it looked now. He told me it's your funeral.'

'Girlfriend?'

'That's what I told him.'

'Is it dangerous?'

Grigor gave a wave as they crunched past, and the guard made an ironic military salute, then hauled down the barrier. 'Whatever happened here, it was a long time ago. Even Chernobyl's safe enough now, so they tell us - although you wouldn't want to live there.' They passed three ancient soviet military trucks hunkered down at the roadside with flat tyres and rust flaked paintwork. 'Your funeral, he said to me. Our funerals. We can go back if you want?'

'No.. no. If it's OK with you. Let's go on. We can't go back after coming all this way. Anyway, I 've *got* to see it.'

He shrugged. Then as they drove over the brow of a hill Kate seemed to recognise an imposing white edifice with a faded mural of a rainbow on its cracked white plasterwork, pitted and fragmented with exposed brickwork. The rows of windows were desolate and soot stained. 'I remember that.' She breathed. 'I think I do.' To their right was a series of fossilised shacks, and blackened skeletons of once meaningful structures. Abandoned military vehicles lined the road. Grigor stopped the car.

'A war zone.'

Something was welling up inside her. A queue of memories jostling their way to the forefront. A long grey building. 'Over there. Turn right.'

They passed what had once been a children's play park. A swan's head on a ride-on had been deformed into a monstrosity, and the seat had burned away to reveal only a charred metal chassis. The swings were reduced to blackened chains hanging from a buckled frame. The snow had settled like a thin layer of icing sugar, turning the scene into a black and white print of Armageddon. In a half-hearted attempt at looting or rescue or both somebody had dragged some furniture from an official building with un-timbered doorways and windows, and the charred remains spilled over the stone steps. Some twisted pieces of furniture lay in the road: The bones of an office chair; a twisted metal cabinet with stove in drawers. The mangled letters along the facade of the building showed that this had once been Administrative Headquarters. In front of the building a bronze statue of Lenin gestured to the sky like a fruitless plea, from a fractured concrete plinth. She pointed.

'Borilyenko worked there.'

'Borilyenko? Here? You mean *General* Borilyenko?'

'I don't know. He was in charge. He wasn't a General. At least I don't think so.' A monstrous Zil fire truck with its ladder half extended was mounted on the kerb, scorched grille like an angry grimace. ' I used to come here a lot. He had a big office overlooking a small park at the back. I mean.. *she* used to come here. I think. Have you heard of him?'

'Borilyenko?'

'Yes. Him.'

'General Borilyenko. Of course. He's in charge of the Presidential Security Service. KGB. A big man. Maybe even a presidential candidate on day. He was here, you think? In Sorsk?'

Kate wasn't listening. 'Look! Drive over there.' She pointed to a charred building with a long empty frontage that had once been glass. The road was littered with debris.

'What happened here?' he said steering the car around humps in the snow. A spindly dog was sniffing at the wreckage. It bared its teeth, and was joined by another, which stood and watched them pass. 'This is not like any closed city I've ever seen. More like Chernobyl.' He stopped the car.

'It used to be a biological research centre. Part of Biopreparat.' Half-familiar words assembled themselves in her head. 'There were lots of projects. I was working on…' she thought for a moment and the name came to her in an instant. '*Simbirsk*. I don't know what it means. Does it mean anything to you?'

'Only the city. It's the old name for Ulyanovsk - before they renamed it after Lenin. His real name, Ulyanov. Simbirsk is where he was born. Kerensky was born there too, but of course they named it after Lenin and never changed it back to Simbirsk. Not like Stalingrad or Leningrad.' He shrugged. 'That's all I know.'

'*Project Simbirsk*. That's what I was working on. I mean that's what she was working on. Embryo research. It was called *Simbirsk* because they were planning to make a human clone. From cells taken from Lenin's embalmed remains … They planned to build a clone of Lenin.'

Grigor barked once. A humourless laugh. 'What kind of science fiction is that? What kind of bullshit?'

'It wasn't science fiction. I think it was real. I remember… I feel it was. We were doing stuff with human cloning. Experiments. We'd come a long way, and the next stage - it was the first real implanted embryo. Not Lenin. That was going to be later. Sounds crazy but.. ' She remembered the operating table. Remembered staying awake through the process in wonder at the culmination of her work.

Remembered pale green curtains at the windows of the ward. How she must have felt afterwards with her swollen belly. How she would wrap her arms around the unborn foetus. How she would whisper to her unborn child at nights. She took a deep breath. The memories swam and merged. She felt she was one with them. 'She was my mother." She started, with sudden resolution. "I believe my mother was called Ekaterina Ivanovna. Maybe she cloned herself and produced me. And then somehow - something they never thought about - somehow I've inherited her memories, like they were embedded in her DNA.' She stopped, looked at the shell of the former research centre and remembered the long glass window gleaming in the sunshine, shrubs lining the entrance. 'It explains everything. She shook her head slowly. 'We go through life thinking we're unique and purposeful. But in the end we're just composites. What makes us who we are? Where's our personality, our memory bank, our strengths and weaknesses? Where's all that stuff that we've been cosseting - where's it all kept?' Shattered buildings; foraging dogs; broken paving and silhouettes of trees. Tears began to come, and she buried her face in her hands. Who was she? Kate. What kind of abomination of nature? And she wept for an imagined past that would haunt her forever, a new past that was not hers to own. Who was she? Her dreams, her memories belonged to somebody else.

A weight around her shoulders. Grigor had his thick arm around her. She felt the bristle of his beard touch her forehead.

'It's OK,' he said.

But it wasn't OK and it never had been. This was all that was left. *Sorsk Gorod.* The ravaged shell of a life never lived, but which had lived inside her all her life. She felt cold when he pulled away. Then the door thudded; she heard the squeak and splinter of boots on fresh snow. The engine was still running and when the door closed the warmth was restored at once. The aircon laboured. She looked up, wiping her eyes; saw Grigor through the streaked windscreen stepping through the rubble towards the Embryonic Research Block; saw him pick his way up the stone steps. A dog with sparse fur and pink blotches pricked up its ears; took a few faltering steps towards him, but decided to keep its distance. Grigor disappeared inside the building. She stepped down from the car. It was fiercely cold but the temperature invigorated her and she breathed hard. A dog barked. Should she be afraid of these creatures? The place was familiar to her now, derelict as it was. She followed Grigor's footprints up the steps, seeking the struts of metal that would have supported the wooden handrail she remembered, and finding the buckled metal beneath a thin layer of snow with a perverse feeling of satisfaction. She reached out a hand, as though to place it on the wooden rail, and imagined her mother as she would have stood there over a quarter of a century ago; trailing her hand along the rail, ascending the steps. Now they were slippery and she climbed them with care. At the top, she turned to face the once imposing columns of the Administrative Headquarters, misremembering Dmitry with his bulging attaché case and stern poise standing in the doorway consulting his watch. Not a flashy Western watch like he had now, but a *Chaika* watch, made in *Uglich*.

A guttural snarl made her start. A large brown dog down on its haunches, fur bristling, fixing her with a malevolent stare from a few metres away. She stepped backwards, but the dog edged forward. She felt breathless. Took another step, heart pounding. Scrabbling of claws. A howl. The dog launched itself. Stumbling. Raising her hands. Colours making fast patterns.

An explosion.

The dog landed in the snow in a halo of pink, its body limp and useless. It made no sound, not even a whimper. She bit the back of her hand. For an instant she couldn't understand what had happened.

'I thought you were in the car,' said Grigor from the doorway, a pistol hanging from his right hand. He looked at the lifeless dog.

'These dogs are dangerous. They're wild and starving.' She looked too, wondering what would have happened if it had connected with her.

'Good shot.' Her throat was parched. 'I didn't know you had a gun.'

'I always have a gun.' After the detonation of the gun, everything seemed silent. 'Come and take a look.' Grigor turned back into the building. She trailed after him, keeping a watch behind her, looking for more wild dogs. She felt unsteady, hands trembling. Inside, there was nothing that was recognisable, just a vast expanse like a factory, with no interior walls. The exterior walls were scarred and blackened by fire. Grigor's boots crunched on broken glass, harsh and resonant in the empty building. Where before there had been a reception desk there was only rubble. No carpet, just a vast bare concrete space littered with broken masonry and mangled, rusted metal. When she looked up, the ceiling was gone, and the floor above was exposed. Charred timbers hung from above like a thickly drawn spider's web.

'What do you remember about the layout of this place?' he said.

She closed her eyes, trying to visualise how it had been. Left of the reception the security doors with criss-crossed safety glass. She would have swiped a card for entry, then headed down a corridor. She moved in that direction, picking her way through the wreckage. The labs would have been along here. She heard his heavy boots grinding glass and debris. 'Here. I think.' She stopped. The cold was a deep down numbness in her bones. Grigor was at her side. He stooped to pick up a fossilised relic in a gloved hand, turning it over. It was unidentifiable. He tossed it far into the shell of the building where it bumped and skittered, echoing off the walls.

'If there was one thing you could rescue from a burning building, what would it be?' she said.

'I don't think I have anything that means that much to me.'

'I feel like I'm all washed up. I don't have anything to cling on to. Nothing to rescue.'

'It doesn't look like a regular fire.'

'What do you mean?'

'There's not a single thing. Nothing intact at all.' He gestured back to the entrance. 'And it's not like they didn't try to put out the fire. That fire truck.. I've seen damage like this before. In Afghanistan. And in Chechnya.' He pointed to the open sky. 'Bumblebees. The first thing that happens is they blow the roof off.'

'Bumblebees?'

'Rocket propelled flamethrowers. We used them to clear

occupied buildings. Or to destroy evidence.' He nudged a twisted haft of metal with his boot. 'Creates a hell on earth. 2000 degrees Celsius. We used to call them Devil's Pipes.'

'What evidence would you want to destroy?'

'I'm not proud of it. We followed orders, that's all.'

'I see. But what makes you think they would use something like that here?'

'Maybe I'm wrong. It's the only way I know to incinerate an entire city. That's what they've done here.'

They made their way back to the car, where a mangy dog eyed them with curiosity. Kate avoided it in a wide arc. They drove slowly around the empty city at her direction. Turning into precincts and boulevards, lined with black eyed apartment blocks and windowless shopfronts. She pointed out landmarks to him. Here a school. There a supermarket - well stocked, not like Moscow in those days. More labs. An athletics stadium. All hollow and soot stained. A devastated, post-apocalypse landscape. Wilderness. Some half sketched association made her shudder. They passed a few more Zil fire trucks and many other soviet era vehicles, some burnt out, some atrophied and scoured by the elements.. 'They left a lot of kit here,' Said Grigor. 'Like they were in a hurry.'

May day in Sorsk. Gleeful radiant faces along birch lined Marx Prospekt, crowds flapping red flags. Military bandsmen who smiled into their instruments with pride, and belted out Tchernetsy's Jubilee March. Brightly coloured balloons floating past the pharmacy and the bookstore. Feeling special and privileged. The warmth of the sun, but with an edge that was winter's legacy. Rows of marching soldiers and sailors, tight lipped and severe - but sometimes with a playful wink for a child or a pretty girl who was cold but determined to air her summer dress for the first time since September. Kate's other set of memories flowed.

There were no trees on Marks Prospekt any more, only a few ragged black stumps like crows. The pharmacy and bookstore were not distinguishable from the other empty windowed stores and offices, with soot lined doorways open to the street.

'*Sorsk* was a nice place to live. Believe it or not.'

'These memories? You're remembering now?'

'Yes. I remember this street well. They had parades here. It's like having *real* memory. These are memories like you have memories.'

'Unbelievable.' He frowned. 'So do you think you can remember what happened here?'

'Whatever it was - it must have been after I was born. After I was born I have only one memory. My own memory. If that makes sense.'

'None of it makes sense to me. I'm just a gangster, remember? So you remember everything your mother knew?'

'Well. Not quite. Memory plays tricks. Sometimes we make things up and they get mixed up with the past. And I don't remember everything - just like you don't remember everything. It's improving now. Now I believe in it.'

'So about Borilyenko - it's possible he wants you for something you may remember. Or because you validate his experiments?'

'It's strange. I remember my mother's childhood better than I remember her adulthood.'

'What about Borilyenko?' he pressed, 'What do you remember about him?'

'I didn't have so much to do with him directly. He wasn't a scientist. But he was interested in our work. Other projects took up much more of his time. Project Simbirsk seemed like a bit of a plaything. Not entirely serious.'

'What kind of projects took up his time?

'It was better not to ask.'

'Why?'

'Those days…' she trailed off 'People didn't ask.. and this was a military facility - look. Stop.'

'*Stolovaya*'. The blackened metal sign with buckled loops and curls was still there, edged in snow - almost festive. She stepped down from the car. The building was little more than four scorched walls.

'Like the rest,' she heard him say. 'Like every building here. Worse than Grozny.'

'Beyond belief,' She murmured. Where she had eaten almost every day. A cavernous place alive with the rattle of cutlery and crockery. Long tables and benches she remembered. And Yevgeny.

Yevgeny was a Jew but almost nobody in *Sorsk* cared. It was said his father was in the camps. Yevgeny it was that inserted himself on the bench beside her that time, slamming his loaded tray on the table.

'Everything good?' He said, pushing back strands of hair and looking at her through thick lensed glasses.

'Couldn't be better. How's life on the Hill?' They called it The Hill because it was the highest point in *Sorsk* but it was an ironic label as the hill was no more than an incline.

'The Hill is bracing,' was his invariable reply. 'Actually,' he said, lowering his voice and looking around 'we have some issues up there on the Hill, if I'm honest.'

'Issues?' She didn't know the nature of Yevgeny's work. Never asked. Everything in *Sorsk* was a closely held secret,

'Yes,' he said, spearing a cube of meat with his fork. 'Quite serious.' He raised an eye as though seeking her complicity. 'I've been meaning to talk to you. To *somebody* anyway.'

She watched a vast breasted woman ladling anaemic dumplings onto plates from behind a row of steaming steel dishes. Somebody shouted something unintelligible, and another person laughed.

'Will you take a walk with me, Katya?'

She felt wrong footed. An unexpected invitation. Looked at her watch. 'Now?'

'In a minute.'

'I'm expected. I have some technicians...'

'Just for a short time. OK let's leave now. I'm ready. Come on - you don't want to eat that shit.'

The food was coagulating on her plate. She lay down her cutlery. It couldn't do any harm. After all, she liked Yevgeny, and she was intrigued. 'Five minutes.'

He dabbed at his mouth with a paper napkin and stood up, tossing the napkin on the table. 'Let's go.'

As they emerged into the bright sunshine, Yevgeny leaned into her. 'You know what they say, don't you? About my father?'

'What about him?'

'That he was in the camps.'

She nodded. 'I heard that.' They were going down the steps to the street.

'It's not true.'

'No?'

'Sometimes I wish it was. I know it's a terrible thing to wish for, but it's true. This way.' He guided her to the right at the foot of the steps.

'Where are we going?'

'I wish he'd been in the camps in preference to where he really was. He was a scientist. Like me.' Now he was walking briskly. Not a casual stroll. 'He worked for them. For the Nazis. Of course, they forced him to do it. I can't blame him for that. He was working at a secret underground base. They had a nuclear weapons program - did you know that?'

'I read about it.'

'He was working on developing a nuclear warhead. They already had rockets, you know. It's a blessing that the war ended before they could use them.' They walked in silence for a few moments. Yevgeny had a habit of thrusting his upper body forwards when he walked, as though to give himself extra impetus. They were heading in the direction of The Hill.

'And today,' he continued, 'I find myself working in much the same line of business.' He stopped. He had an earnest expression. 'Do you know? Have you any idea what we do, up there on The Hill?'

He was very close to her. She took a small step backwards. 'No. I … you shouldn't talk about this, I suppose.'

'I have to tell somebody,' he said, walking fast again. 'Even if it's the *wrong* person. I can't live with it anymore. And now we have these *problems*.'

'You said that there were some issues.'

'It's my project you know. *Project Pustinia*. Wilderness. It's a horrible name but it describes the objective perfectly. If we ever get to use this weapon, God forbid, then it will lead to a wilderness. The consequences are too terrible to think about.'

'So are you going to tell me? About these issues?'

'You sure you want to know?'

She wasn't sure. It was forbidden to discuss their work with anybody outside their immediate group. She found that they were standing before a compound with a barbed wire fence. There was a long low building inside with blacked out windows. A dusty military truck was parked outside with a covered loadspace. He held her arm. Glanced around. The street was empty. 'Let's keep walking. Know what that is?' he said.

'An eyesore?'

He didn't laugh. 'It's a hospital.'

'But there's a hospital on Potemkin Street.'

'Not an ordinary hospital. More of an isolation ward.'

'Isolation?'

When he glanced at her she thought she caught a tear in his eye. 'It's out of control, Katya. We thought we could control it but we can't. And there's no cure. People go there to the isolation ward to die. We're manufacturing the mother of all diseases. And now it's killing people. Our people. They take the dead away to be buried in bleach at night. I don't know where they take them. Katya, I don't know what to do.'

She heard Grigor say: 'You OK?'

'I think I might have an idea why *Sorsk* had to burn.' She said, looking at the burnt-out refectory with regret.

Chapter Thirty-Five

"HUMAN CLONING TECHNIQUES

Professor Ekaterina Ivnaovna Borodina

Moscow State University 28 August 1962

Procedures employed in cloning human embryos have much in common with the cloning of animal embryos, with the exception of the zona pellucida. The methodology would require that several sperm cells and mature egg cells are gathered from donors, and combined in a petri dish using in vitro fertilization procedures to form an embryo."

Nikolay had acquired the paper through the Moscow State University Archive. It was a print from a microfiche, and the images of the pages were lop-sided, speckled with background, but legible nonetheless.

"An alternate methodology, provides for pre-produced embryos from volunteer donors that have embryos left over from prior in vitro clients. The embryo would be placed in a petri dish and allowed to develop into a mass of two to eight cells. Next, a chemical solution is added that dissolves the zona pellucida enveloping the embryo. The zona pellucida is a protective protein and polysaccharide membrane that covers the internal contents of the embryo, and provides the necessary nutrients for the first several cell divisions that occur within the embryo."

He sensed a presence at his desk and looked up to find Dikul hovering there, dour faced and petulant.

'What's up?'

'A press release from our famous "intelligence agent" Ivan Ivanov.' He laid a single printed sheet of A4 on top of the microfiche copies. 'Printed in Izvestia. I had it typed up.' A single paragraph:

"From out of the ruins of our once glorious Soviet Empire, a criminal state is evolving the likes of which the world has never experienced. Witness Yevgeny Nikolaievich Kirilov, Chief Executive Officer of the Narodny Mining Corporation. This officer has evidence linking Mr Kirilov with narcotics, racketeering, embezzlement and money laundering. His criminality is blatant and far-reaching, but

even so Kirilov appears to seek election to public office in the Duma? Please be in no doubt, that if the authorities refuse to acknowledge the criminality of this individual and to take action against him, then the Feliks Group will take it upon itself to restore order."

'What does it mean do you think?' Said Nikolay 'Restore order?'

'I guess it means they'll take him out.'

Nikolay sighed. 'I'm not a policeman. This is a case for the police, not an intelligence officer.'

Dikul sniffed and hitched up his trousers. 'Borilyenko. You really think he has his hands in all this?'

'I think that's what we're supposed to find out.' He pushed aside the press release and looked at the microfiche copies again. 'I wonder what interest the General could have in a girl from England who's looking for a scientist from the Soviet days?' He put his hands behind his head and sat back in his chair. 'What do you think about human cloning? Do you think it's possible to make a replica of a human being?'

'Cloning? Replicas? I find it difficult enough to master the photocopier.' He said with a snort. 'What's it about?'

'The general is keeping close tabs on a girl who has travelled from England to find a distant relative. The relative was a soviet scientist who wrote a paper on human cloning whilst at MSU. She has these dreams..' He began

'Dreams? We all have those. I dreamed I would have a posting in some fucking embassy abroad. A warm climate with beaches maybe. Not this ...' He waved his hand to indicate the office and the building generally. 'About making replicas of humans. I don't think it can be done.'

'Why not? We sent men into space before the Americans could make a decent car.'

'They still can't make a decent car. Anyway, if you want my opinion, it's Science fiction. Take it from me. The General has an interest in a girl, why doesn't he just pick her up. Ask her some questions?'

'Why indeed?'

'*Sorsk*! What would they be doing in *Sorsk*?'

'My officers followed them only as far as the gates. They were afraid to risk going inside the perimeter.'

'Risk? What kind of risk?'

'The sign said it's contaminated, they said.'

'That was decades ago. The instructions were to keep her under surveillance. Why did your people not follow?'

'Like I said… but also it would be difficult to keep a watch on her without being noticed. The town is empty after all.'

'I suppose so.' Borilyenko ran through the implications. Another breach. It was becoming as difficult to contain as the disease itself. He pressed the telephone to his ear, as though in an effort to prevent anyone overhearing, although Borilyenko's office was empty. 'And this gangster? What's his connection?'

'Romantic I would guess. I know him well.'

'How well?'

'We do some business from time to time. You know how these things are. He owns a few clubs and bars. A casino on Odessa Street.'

'Who else knows about *Sorsk*?'

'I don't know, General. I doubt Malenkov would have discussed it with anyone, but you never can tell for sure. He's impetuous.'

'Does he have a big network? Of people he might talk to?

'Nobody close. Business associates. He's a vet. Alpha in fact.'

'Alpha. So he should know how to keep his mouth shut.'

'I should say, yes.'

'All the same… this gangster—what's his name again?'

'Grigor Vassilyich Malenkov.'

'Malenkov. He needs to be eliminated. Does it cause you a problem?'

'Not me. It doesn't cause me any problem.'

'As for the girl. It's time I met her. As soon as possible.'

'Yes General.'

'Your people - are they still there?'

'I imagine so. I haven't given them further instructions.'

'Tell them to look for them in *Sorsk*. Deal with the gangster. Bring me the girl alive.'

'Bring her to the Lubyanka?'

'Yes. And another thing. About *Sorsk* - it never existed. There was never a town by that name.'

'That goes without saying, General.'

The General sat a long time after the call. Loose ends. Every time he cut he created another loose end. What to do about Lisakov, now that he knew about *Sorsk*? Something he would hold over him. And the others, Lisakov's people. Where would it end? Cut, cut cut.

In the distance they heard it: the buzz of a car going slowly, the engine whining through the lower gears. It seemed like the only sound in the universe.

'I thought this place was off limits?' said Kate.

'For some people there are no limits.'

They listened, in front of the scorched '*Stolivaya*', for the car to get closer. Sometimes it seemed to get further away. At other times it sounded like it could be in the next street. Then they watched a black Volga with blue license plates turn in at the top of Chukovsky Street, and weave its way down the cratered road. Its headlamps were pale and dim and they lifted and fell as the car negotiated unseen debris, humps in the snow, bouncing hard on its suspension. 50 meters from Grigor's Range Rover it halted and the occupants sat huddled in the car for a few moments. The windows were steamy and there was a jagged smear in the centre of the windscreen where they had tried to clear their view. Two men got out. Both wore long dark coats and fur hats. They stood either side of the car, watching. One man had his arm on the roof.

'So, comrades.' Grigor called. 'Seems like you must be looking for us, since there's nobody else here.'

The men looked at each other, then seemed to make up their minds, and walked towards them. They were both carrying pistols in gloved hands. Kate noticed Grigor tuck his gun into his waistband beneath his coat and leave one hand on its handle. A few paces away they stopped. They looked cold and ragged, and they pointed their weapons without much conviction.

'You both need to come with us.'

'In that fucking thing?' said Dmitry, nodding at the Volga.

'We'll take yours.'

'I wouldn't trust the Cheka with an expensive car like that. So, what if we decide we don't want to come?'

'It's not an option.'

With great care, watching for a reaction all the while, Grigor removed the gun from his waistband and slowly levelled it at the man who had spoken, who glanced with unease at his companion.

'Now we have an impasse.'

The man had a prominent forehead that made it hard to discern the direction of his eyes. It gave him a look of intensity. When he spoke he pronounced his words deliberately, swallowing his 'G's like a Ukrainian. 'What is this place? What happened here?'

'It was a *stolovaya*.' Said Grigor.

'Is it dangerous, do you think?'

'I doubt it. Not anymore.'

'Not much left of it. Not much left of anything.' The man looked around him. He seemed to have forgotten about the stand off entirely, although his gun still pointed in their direction. 'It's the same all over. We drove around for a while, looking for you.'

'Looks like somebody didn't want to leave any clues.'

'Devil's Pipe.'

'That's what I thought. You were in Afghanistan?'

'A few places like that, that I would rather forget about.'

'So what happens next?'

'I have instructions to bring in the girl. As for you...'

'Whose instructions?'

'Does it make a difference?'

'I expect not.'

The man lowered his gun. His face seemed to relax. 'You know...'

The first gunshot made her ears buzz and the second seemed muffled, far away. She clamped her hands to her head. Felt like she was under water. The two men had dropped where they stood. Both were still. Kate took a step back. The snow lent the scene a graininess, like an old photograph. Monochrome. Except for the blood. Silence, except for the ringing in her ears.

'Why did you...?' she began. There was a tremor in her voice.

Dmitry was looking at the two corpses with a clenched jaw. 'It was a signal. When he lowered his gun I saw the other one flip off the safety. It was them or us. Them or me at any rate. I don't think they would have killed you. Not yet. A pity I had to shoot them. This guy did the right thing. Just orders.'

'That's how it is with you people? Just orders?' Kate was angry.

'What else is there? We need to live our lives by one rule or another. There have to be rules. Look at what happens when there are no rules. This place.' He was bending over the body of the first man, rummaging in his pockets. He withdrew a white envelope and opened it.

'Theatre tickets,' he said. 'Moscow Art Theatre. For tomorrow. What a fucking waste.' She didn't know whether he meant the tickets or the life. He bunched them up and tossed them in the snow where they fluttered and fell. He flipped through a cheap leather wallet.

'What are you looking for?'

'Some ID. Would be nice to know who I shot. This guy was careful. A professional. Doesn't carry ID. You don't find many like him anymore. A nice set up. They sat there in the car agreeing the plan. Lowering the gun like that for a distraction. Then: bang. The other one was stupid to have the safety engaged. Could have been a different story.'

'It's a game,' she said, her stomach tight. She was trembling, and not from the cold.

Grigor looked fierce. 'A game of life. I'm just trying to survive it.' He had started on the other corpse. 'This one's not so careful.' He flipped open a booklet, flashed at her the sword and twin headed eagle emblem, then threw it in the direction of the *Stolovaya*. 'No surprises. *Parporshchik* Medvedev. Yegor Ivanovich. A Checkist.'

'But these killings. Don't they mean anything to you? You… you root through their clothes like they're just tailor's dummies.'

'To some people the act of killing is incidental. Others carry their corpses to the grave.'

'Which are you?'

'I have a broad back but I promise you I struggle with my burdens.'

He slipped his hands under the Chekist's armpits, and began to drag him in the direction of the abandoned Volga. The heels of the man's boots carved twin trails in the snow. She felt rigid and frozen inside her coat. Her coat felt as if it had grown in size. Grigor sprung the boot of the car, and hauled the lifeless Chekist over the lip, then he stooped to arrange him inside like baggage. He came back for the first man.

'What are we going to do?' She said.

'I'll move the car. Then we'll head back to Moscow.'

'You mean just leave them?'

'You want to bury them?'

'What if somebody finds them?'

'Go and wait in my car. Switch on the engine. You look frozen.' He reached out and put a hand on her arm. 'Go. It's a long drive and it's late already.'

Grigor parked the Volga in the burnt out shell of a building, and when they drove to the barrier the gatehouse was deserted. He climbed down and swung up the barrier so they could pass though, then padded around the gatehouse leaving crusty bootprints, peering through the windows, before getting back behind the wheel. The Lada was still parked where they saw it earlier, now swathed in a crisp white shroud.

'Nobody at home,' he said. 'Maybe some more tidying up, poor bastard.' Kate felt her eyes widen, but she said nothing. The heater rasped, blasting warm air in her face.

Chapter Thirty-Six

IT WAS THE EARLY hours of the morning by the time they joined the Garden Ring Road and headed towards Tverskaya Street. The traffic was sparse and the Garden Ring was 10 lanes.

'I can't leave you alone tonight,' said Grigor.

'I'll be OK,' said Kate.

'They'll come for you again. It's not over.'

'I know. But I don't know what to do.'

'Go back to London. If they'll let you.'

'You think it's possible?'

'I know somebody in the FSB. A Colonel. Maybe he can help.'

'I'm scared Grigor.'

'Stay at my apartment tonight. They won't expect that. You'll be safe there. At least for now.'

'No. I prefer to stay at my hotel.'

'Then I'll stay with you there.'

'No, really.'

'You're afraid of me?'

'Of course not.'

'Then let me take care of you.'

'I can't'

'I'll take a room next door.'

'You're very sweet.'

'Nobody called me sweet before.' He laughed. 'I'm not the kind of man that makes that kind of description trip off the tongue.' Grigor braked suddenly and they were outside the Marriott. In the lobby were the usual prostitutes, looking bored. They went to the desk.

'I want to take a room next to this lady. She is room 4661.'

The clerk assessed him critically. 'I'll see what I can find.' He tapped something into the computer. Paused. Kate thought his face tightened. 'I can give you three doors down. 4664.'

Grigor handed over his ID and a credit card. The clerk entered it into the computer, then handed him a key and announced with a blank face:

'Room 8001. Presidential suite. You have a free upgrade.'

Grigor slid back the key. 'I don't want it. Just give me the regular room. 4664, you said.'

The clerk shrugged. 'You're the boss.' He tapped at the keyboard. Issued a new key. 'Have a nice stay.'

They travelled up together in the lift to the fourth floor. Outside her room they stopped.

'I don't know how to thank you, Grigor. For everything.'

He took both of her hands. Squeezed gently. She saw his eyes were bloodshot. He leaned in and she let him kiss her. His lips were softer than she expected—had expected firm and parched. She stepped backwards, pulled her hands away.

'No Grigor. Not like this.'

'It's OK. Get some sleep. I'm down the hall. Tomorrow we'll decide what to do.'

An elegant girl with translucent limbs and burnished golden hair played harpsichord and the music rippled through the restaurant. Nikolay thought Mozart, but he was no expert. The walls were lined with leather volumes like a library and the light had a copper hue. He hardly thought that places like this existed in Moscow. He weaved through the tables to a corner where Lebed was standing to greet him, head slightly inclined, holding his napkin in place with one hand while the other was extended in greeting. Nikolay thought he had a politician's smile and it was hard to recall the warrior from before. He felt ashamed of the coarse wool of his suit and his thick soles. This was not a place for thick soled shoes.

'Nikolay Sergeevich. Thank you for giving up your evening.'

They sat, and a waiter in a crisp white apron appeared at their table at once with an improbably large menu.

Nikolay glanced at the businessmen at the next table, and recognised at once they were not businessmen at all but the security detail, a shared bottle of mineral water and a basket of bread on the table between them. They didn't speak to each other.

'Thanks for inviting me, General.'

'Please. It's Pavel Ivanovich here. But what will you have to drink? Some vodka?'

'Just water.'

'I thought it would be more amenable than the office. You know this place?'

'There are too many noughts on the menu for my rank.'

'I like it because they're discreet.'

Nikolay read the menu, looking more at the prices than the food. 'I'll have the Olivier salad, please. And the chicken.'

'Good choice,' said Lebed, and Nikolay had the impression that he would have said the same if he had ordered stale bread. 'As for me I've already ordered.'

When the waiter had gone, Lebed lowered his tone, speaking more to the table linen than to Nikolay.

'The Prime Minister would like to know about progress. What have you found out?'

'I briefed General Blodnieks on some of my findings.'

'Yes of course. Blodnieks. But better to hear it from the horse's mouth I always think.'

'General Blodnieks is my superior.'

'I don't have superiors. I'm as high as it gets, except for Boris Nikolaevich. You understand what I'm saying?'

Nikolay sensed disappointment in Lebed's tone. 'I'm sorry, sir. Look.. this is speculation - but my view is that General Borilyenko is at the heart of some kind of conspiracy. And the people are involved are mostly old communists - at the highest levels. Cronies from the old days. It seems probable that this association is responsible for the Feliks Group communications, and for some of the recent atrocities.'

'Yes, yes,' said Lebed with impatience. 'You have proof?'

'Not yet.'

'We need incontrovertible proof Nikolay. And we need it quickly.'

'We've done our best to keep General Borilyenko under surveillance. But it's not easy. He uses the FSB like his own personal bodyguard. It's my belief that the murder of the banker Bukovsky was carried out by Russian Special Forces on his orders.'

'Spetsnaz you think?'

'There were indications. Like the weapons. The procedure.'

'I see.'

'There's an FSB officer. A Colonel. He's everywhere. He had two of my men intercepted whilst they were in pursuit of Borilyenko's car. He was also at the Bukovsky murder scene.'

'Name?'

'Lisakov.'

'I'll see about him.'

'And this conspiracy—if that's what it is—may involve people like Yuri Chaika. I have to say I feel completely unqualified...'

'You're doing a great job, Nikolay Sergeyevich. An important job.'

'There's something else. Something odd. I don't know if it's important yet.'

'Go on.'

'As I already reported to General Blodnieks, General Borilyenko seems to have taken an interest in a Westerner. A girl. She came here from London some days ago.'

Two waiters brought the first courses and set them on the table. One of them poured some water into Nikolay's glass.

'So, this girl you were telling me about. What kind of interest are we talking about?'

'Not the usual kind. He's having her followed. But she's just ordinary. A nobody. I've been trying to work it out. She came to Moscow to trace somebody. A relative, she said. But I don't believe her.'

'So, what's the connection?'

'I wouldn't even mention it. But the person she's looking for disappeared in Soviet times. Some scientist. A geneticist. Good degree from MSU. She wrote a paper on the viability of human cloning back in the '70's. I found it in the University archive. It's the last mention of her I can find anywhere. Like she dropped off a cliff. I appreciate many people disappeared suddenly in those days.'

'Human cloning?'

'I don't know what the connection could be. But look…' Nikolay produced the same photographs he had shown to General Blodnieks in his office. 'You would think it's the same girl - and yet these pictures were taken 30 years apart.'

Lebed studied the faces. 'Remarkable.' He sat back in his chair. 'What I know is that General Borilyenko headed up a secret biological research facility in the 70's. Not much else is known about it. Almost nothing about the work they did there. All highly classified. I'll try to see if I can find out anything else, but any light you could shed…'

'You think it might be important?'

'We need to know everything about Borilyenko. Anything we can find out could be something we could use against him.' He glanced again at the photographs before returning them to Nikolay. 'Pretty girl.'

'I didn't know who else to call.'

'Then maybe you called the right person,' said Nikolay.

'A lot has happened since we last met.'

'It doesn't surprise me.'

'Can we meet?' said Kate.

'If you want.'

'Maybe there's a library in town? I want to check some things.'

'There are many libraries in Moscow. The biggest is the Russian State Library.'

'I'll meet you there. At 11:00. Where is it?'

'It's not hard to find. It's a landmark. Can't you tell me anything now?'

'Nothing. Except—can you do something for me? See what you can find out about a man named Yevgeny Peshevsky.'

'Peshevsky. Patronymic?'

She strained for the memory but it didn't come. 'I don't know it. Just Yevgeny Peshevsky.'

'Who is he?'

'A scientist. I think he was a colleague of the person I'm looking for. And another name too: Andrei Illyich Sverdlov.'

'I'll see what I can find out. See you at 11:00.'

'One more thing…'

'Yes?'

'They tried to pick me up yesterday. The KGB. FSB. Whatever you call them.'

'What happened?'

'There were two of them.'

'And?'

'They're dead.'

'I'll come for you now.'

'No. I don't want that. I'm safe for now. Let's meet at the library.'

'Kate, you're going to need a lot of help.'

'I know.'

She put down the telephone. Tried to phone Robert's mobile twice but there was no reply. Then she phoned for Leonid who said everything was OK, as he always did, and that he would be there in 20 minutes.

It would take Nikolay half an hour to reach his rendezvous with Kate. That left him with two hours. He called Dikul.

'Find out everything you can about two people. Yevgeny Peshevsky and Andrei Illyich Sverdlov. Drop everything. Both were scientists in Soviet times. Most probably in the seventies.'

Then he called Lebed on the private number he had given him.

'The dissident Sverdlov? I remember something about him. I'll see what my people can dig up.'

'Is there any way we can protect the girl? In the meantime?'

'From the FSB?'

'From Borilyenko.'

'Not a chance.'

'They tried to take her in yesterday.'

'That's good.'

'Good?'

'Something's about to break. What happened?'

'I'm meeting the girl in a couple of hours. I'll know more then. But the FSB agents are dead.'

'Dead?'

'That's what she said.' After he put the phone down it rang almost immediately. It was Dikul.

'We think that Yevgeny Peshevsky is Yevgeny Pavlovich Peshevsky, and he has no file.'

'What do you mean, no file?'

'I mean there's no record of him beyond his birth. He was a German Jew. At least, his father was. His father, Pavel Ivanovich Peshevsky was involved in secret work. We don't have much of a file on him either.'

'Is he dead? Alive?'

'There's no record of his death. But there's no active record for him either.'

'And the other one?'

'There we had more success. Andrei Illyich Sverdlov. Born 18/01/19 in Uglich. Also a biologist. Executed 15/06/78 for counter revolutionary activities. Some nonsense about Darwin had him exiled to Siberia. Then he made a name for himself spreading malicious rumours about a doomsday bug developed at some closed city. Details are sketchy. Probably went a bit crazy. He was tried and executed but the file's been removed.'

'On whose authority was the file removed?'

'Nobody's authority. It's just not there.' A pause. 'Don't read anything too much into it. If you spend any time looking at the archives for that period you'll see there are many missing records. More missing than not, in fact. Some of them just misfiled by some drunken clerk. Nothing sinister. And counter revolutionary activities could mean almost anything. Like reading George Orwell.'

'It's no problem,' said Leonid, when she told him to take her to the Russian State Library on Vozdvizhenka Street. 'The Leninka.' He corrected over his shoulder, because people still called it that.

The windows of the taxi were mottled with grime, so that shapes of cars and buildings were ghostly, blocky shadows, but when she put the window down the cold took her breath away. A few flakes of snow wet her face like spittle. She worked the window winder again but it stuck with a centimetre to spare and the air roared through the gap. 'How far is it?'

'Yes. It's no problem,' and she wished he would speak to her in Russian instead of pretending to understand her English. The ride lasted at least 40 minutes, stopping and starting and grinding gears.

Leonid pulled up at last, tugging at the useless handbrake, at the foot of the steps to a long and angular stucco building with square columns and tall windows. The statue of a grim-faced bearded figure sat on a plinth before the entrance. Kate leaned over to pay, while the engine rattled and the exhaust stuttered. 'Dostoevsky, ' said Leonid with a kind of pride, reaching back to take the money. 'The statue. Very great Russian writer of…'

The rear door was tugged open. She shrank. A man reached inside. She felt his grip hard on her arm. Caught sight of a burnished wedding ring as she tried to free herself. He was strong and he hauled her from her seat. Leonid let go of the roubles in a flutter. Stretched out his arm to grab her.

'What the fuck?' he yelled in Russian.

She fought so hard her arms ached, floundering with her fists, but when another man came and held her from behind it was useless. She was powerless when he manoeuvred her towards a black Volga that stood behind the taxi with its engine ticking. Leonid leapt into the road with improbable speed, cutting in front of the Volga. A whirlwind of grimaces and shoulders and prods and pushes. Leonid took one of the men by the shoulders and tried to pull him away while Kate kicked out blindly. Now she was being wedged into the Volga. Her assailant turned his back, made a swift movement with his right arm. A shot. Leonid buckled. Kneeled on the tarmac. Free now, the other man came around the car, kicking Leonid aside and threw himself onto the back seat next to her. The seat creaked. She screamed, but the man forced his hand over her mouth. 'Shhh.' Tried to bite but his grip was firm.

Straining to see what had happened to Leonid she felt the car jolt and pull out onto the road. A horn sounded and the driver made a gesture. The engine rasped as they accelerated into the traffic, leaving a puff of black smoke in their wake, and Leonid lying half on the pavement.

'No need for struggle,' said one of the men in fractured English, breathing heavily, so close to her that she could smell pickles and alcohol on his breath. He looked over his shoulder and said in Russian, 'Somebody's following.'

'Call Igor,' said the other man.

'She'll scream if I let her go.' He looked at her. Shrugged. Took his hand away and raised a warning finger. She turned in her seat and didn't scream. The kidney shaped grille of a silver BMW. She thought it was Fyodr, driving close. The man fumbled in his leather jacket and took out a Nokia.

'The girl's with us. Some asshole following. Maybe the gangster's men. What do you want us to do?' He looked at Kate while he listened to the phone. The whites of his eyes were yellow. 'OK... Not long.'

She looked back again at the BMW, willing it to catch up, but a red Lada slotted in front and they fell back. Then she saw a Volga pull into the middle lane with a blue light flashing, and she knew they would cut off Fyodr before he could reach them. She wondered if Leonid was alive.

The cigarette smoke inside the car was stifling and it stung her eyes. She wanted to explain her tears to the men. That it was the tobacco. She felt the need to persuade them she was strong. Not some tearful girl. But her cheeks were wet with tears all the same.

'OK, OK. Seems like he's gone.'

As though picking up an earlier conversation the driver said, 'The BMW is faster than the Mercedes in a straight line. It was an M750i.'

'You're right. But the Mercedes - it's better engineered. Turn left here to avoid the jam on Petrovka. I prefer the Mercedes.'

'Doesn't matter how fast your car is in Moscow. You still have these fucking queues.'

'Better to be comfortable then. I think the Mercedes is more comfortable. Maybe it's a better choice for Moscow roads.' Talking like she wasn't there at all.

'Who are you?' She said, trying to control the shake in her voice.

'No need to worry,' said the driver over his shoulder. 'We're official.' He laughed. 'Hear that, Stefan? Us, official? That's what we are.' Then he shouted at the windscreen 'Fuck you!' and rammed his hand on the horn. 'Out of the way fuck your mother!' A small hatchback pulled out of their path. 'Sorry,' he said under his breath as an afterthought. 'Sorry for my language.'

Chapter Thirty-Seven

'EXCUSE ME BOSS.'

'I'm busy.' Fyodr still languished in the door frame with a wry grin. It wasn't a humorous grin. 'We got some trouble.'

'What kind of trouble?' said Grigor.

'You need to come to the cellar. We had a delivery this morning.'

'What the fuck? Now you want me to supervise deliveries? What's going on in your head, Fyodr?'

'Andrei thinks he can defuse it. I hope he can.'

'Defuse it?'

'Instead of beer they delivered around 500 kilos of RDX. If Andrei can't defuse it then we won't be opening for business today. Or maybe at all.'

'Jesus, Fyodr. Why didn't you tell me? Let's get everybody out!'

'I've got a lot of confidence in Andrei. It's on a timer he says. Quite primitive. Set to go off an hour from now. So, we have an hour. At least.'

Grigor leapt to his feet and reached instinctively for the ancient Makharov pistol. *If there was one thing you could rescue from a burning building, what would it be?* He remembered her saying.

'No need to panic Boss. I think Andrei is a good guy.' Grigor pushed past Fyodr, who followed him. 'It's nobody we know. Nobody we know would use RDX in these quantities.'

'It's sure as Hell *somebody* we know.' Grigor led the way down a narrow passage past the toilets, to a private door which he pushed open. 'Who took the delivery? Was it the regular people?'

'Arkady let them in. He didn't say if it was the usual people.'

'We should be more careful.' They hurried down a flight of stone steps. Grigor ducked his head beneath a steel beam. The yellow lights gave them a jaundiced cast and illuminated a long low room with a line of steel barrels and plastic pipes. There were crates of beer and mixers still shrouded in plastic packaging, and piles of boxes. At the end of the cellar, Andrei was crouched over a wooden pallet loaded with oblong white bricks like wax.

'Igor saw it first,' Andrei said without looking up. 'Ripped open the packaging to check. Lucky that he did. It was just the bottom case. The rest was beer. I fucking hate Baltica.' He had a small electrical screwdriver in his hand and a bright flashlight in the other. 'It's not very clever. Not booby trapped as far as I can tell. We weren't meant to notice. Laziness I call it,' he said with the scorn of a professional. Andrei shared the scars of the Soviet campaign in Afghanistan.

Feeling superfluous standing over Andrei with the heavy gun hanging from his arm, Grigor said 'Who d'you think might have done this?'

Andrei sat back from the pallet, admiring his own handiwork. The bare wires of an LCD timer connected to a detonator in an aluminium sleeve lay twisted and exposed. 'It's safe,' he said with a weary sigh. 'A lot of explosive. Enough to take out the club and a few places each side. Somebody wanted to be sure. Hate to say this, but smells to me like Cheka.' He, turned his head to look up at Grigor. 'Unprofessional too. I would have booby trapped it. Schoolboy stuff.'

'Good job. What are we going to do with it?'

'Here's as good a place as any. It's very stable. We can dispose of it when we want. Maybe we can use it for something…?'

But Grigor wasn't listening. He headed straight back to his office and phoned Lisakov.

'Everyone is still alive.'

'Should I be surprised?'

'Your outfit filled my cellar with RDX today and I want to know why.'

'Why would we do that?'

'That's what I'd like to know.' There was a long pause. Grigor wondered if Lisakov was consulting with somebody.

'I can send some people. To check,' said Lisakov at length.

'To check what?'

'Forensics people. Maybe I can help find out where it came from.'

'I have my own people to do that.'

'I suppose you do.'

'It was KGB. There's no question. Which points to you.' Another long pause. 'Are you still there?'

'Yes, yes. I'll come to your club. Let's see what can be done.'

'When?'

'An hour or two.'

'Come alone.'

'Of course.'

Grigor laid down the phone. 'Fucking snake.' He crossed the room and opened the door. 'Fyodr! Get in here.' He needed to make some plans.

An old and craggy man with a very straight back walked in, followed by two men in blue-grey uniforms. A door banged somewhere far away, followed by an angry interchange. She couldn't make out the words.

The old man smiled at her, and she hoped he didn't notice when she brushed away an involuntary tear. He was wearing a bulky black overcoat over a squarely cut grey suit, and a red tie. He clasped his hands together in front of him and they were red and gnarled, then he greeted her softly in Russian.

'Hello Miss Buckingham. I'm sorry that you were brought here this way. We'll try to make you as comfortable as we can. I'm sure you'll soon be going back to England. If that's what you want.'

She felt reassured by the mention of England. 'Who are you?'

He seemed to consider for a moment, gimlet eyes taking in the room. 'You can call me Vladimir,' he said at last, pulling up the chair opposite her in a leisurely way.

'Is that your name?' she said with suspicion.

The man simply smiled. The two men in uniform had placed themselves behind her, one either side, their faces inscrutable when she craned her neck to see. The room was empty except for a cheap laminated table and two hard chairs streaked with the grime of past occupants. 'Can I order some refreshment for you? Some Tea? Coffee?'

'What am I doing here?' Her voice echoed off the blank walls.

'Vladimir' shifted uncomfortably on the chair. He pulled his overcoat around him and thrust his hands into his pockets. It was cold in the room and her breath formed a fleeting mist in the air. 'You don't have to worry,' he said. Another uniformed officer came swiftly into the room without acknowledging anyone, deposited a pile of notebooks and some pencils on the table, turned on his heel and left. His boots squeaked on the tiled floor. 'You're in safe hands here.'

'They shot that man,' she blurted. 'My driver. Leonid.' The emotions swelled up in her. She was trembling.

'That was unfortunate.' He said, nodding, without emphasis. 'I wish I could change that, but I can't. I understand he was trying to be—gallant. One of my officers was overzealous. These things happen from time to time. Nothing to be done about it.'

'Is he dead?'

The old man shrugged without interest, and from his coat pocket he produced a miniature tape recorder. He held it up for Kate to see, raising an eyebrow. 'Do you mind?'

'Why should I mind? I've got nothing to hide. But Leonid... is he alive?'

He placed the recorder delicately on the table and pushed a button, waiting for the red light to flash. 'There.' He said with a smile. 'Now...' he continued, settling himself into his coat, 'Forget about the taxi driver. I'm sure he'll be taken care of. I want to ask you what you know about Project *Simbirsk*.'

Since her visit to *Sorsk*, the name had haunted her. *Simbirsk* - a city on the Volga now known as Ulyanovsk, notorious for being the birthplace of Lenin. Project *Simbirsk* – perhaps the rebirth of Lenin. She looked at the old man again, and recognition stirred: another misplaced jigsaw piece from that other set of memories slotted into place.

She couldn't help herself from saying out loud 'Comrade Borilyenko!'

His eyes widened a fraction. Then he shook his head in wonder. 'Do you know me, my dear?'

The sombre, spacious office with its twin portraits of Lenin and

Stalin. The smell of new carpet. Borilyenko with hands folded on the table. Smooth skinned. Eyes so sharp they could make incisions. A leisurely dignity. Unmistakably the same person ... cracked at the edges now, and forlorn, like a sepia portrait, but the same man.

'I seem to remember...'

Borilyenko leaned forward in his seat, his eyes flashing. 'This is remarkable! You—*remember me* you say?' he said. 'So unexpected.' Kate watched him, thinking that he didn't look surprised at all. Then he seemed to sharpen up. 'What else do you *remember* Kate? - You don't mind if I call you that? - What else can you recall from those days?'

She bit her lip. What else? How much should she tell him? How much did she know? She frowned and concentrated. 'Why are you keeping me here?' Was all she could manage. 'Why have you brought me here?'

Borilyenko looked around him as though noticing the bare room for the first time. 'Here? It was just convenient. My office is upstairs.' He pointed upwards as though to the heavens. 'It's safe. But I'm sure if required we can transfer you to somewhere more comfortable for a full debriefing. Would that help?' He smiled with that benign look that he always used to have.

'What do you mean by a full debriefing?'

'Well of course you hold the key to a lot of state secrets, if these memories of yours are to be trusted. In many ways you're state property.' He smiled as though to soften the implication. To take away the bad taste.

'Is that what you think I am?'

'Of course not. A joke. In bad taste.'

A thought occurred to her. 'What happened to her? My mother?'

He looked at the tiles and rubbed his hands. 'Your mother. Yes. So she was, I believe. So she was, my dear. Well, those were difficult times Kate. For us. For our country.' He looked sincere. Sad.

'She was definitely my mother? Ekaterina Ivanovna?'

He looked up. 'I should think so, yes. The resemblance is… quite remarkable. It might be her sitting here.'

'In some ways it is, isn't it?' Something shifting in her stomach.

He nodded slowly, appraising her with a kind of fascination. 'Yes. Yes that's right. I suppose it is.' He sat up. 'So… you remember me. Does that mean you remember other things about your mother's life?'

'What happened to her?'

'I'm afraid to say she did some foolish things. Towards the end.

It was taken out of my hands. Those were dangerous times ... but your memories—are they what you might call detailed? I mean, eating kasha for breakfast—those kind of memories?'

She shifted in her chair. The cold was inside her, gripping her with icy fingers. 'They're not always clear. Maybe sometimes they get confused with dreams. Or present day things.'

'At what point do the memories stop?'

'Older memories are clearer than more recent ones. But my last memory of those times—the most recent memory—that would be in the lab. It would be when I biopsied my skin cells for use in some experiments. I remember because it was a big dilemma for me at the time. Cloning my own DNA. HER own DNA, I should say—' she trailed off.

'And after that?'

'Nothing. Just my own memories. At that point it's like a kind of separation.'

A silence. She heard one of the guards stir behind her. A sniff. A shuffle of boots.

'What about your earliest memory? Think carefully Kate.'

'That's much clearer. A samovar. Looking at my reflection. I've always been kind of distracted by my reflection. I think it's because of that memory. I used to like to watch my reflection in the samovar. An old lady is always there telling me to keep away. It was dangerous because of the hot water, she said. An old lady.. My mother.' Then, 'Grandmother. *Her* mother.' She corrected. She remembered the face vividly, close up. A powdered face with grey, kindly eyes. High cheekbones. Smiling. Always smiling.

'No, that's not your memory Kate.' Like a slap. 'Try to focus on your own memories. Your mother. What do you remember about your mother?'

'Not much to be honest. Not much at all. She must have sent me away very young.'

'Any tiny thing that you can think of would be helpful. Her appearance, for example.'

'Her appearance?'

'Yes, yes. Was she fat? Thin? Dark haired? Light haired?'

'We're identical in every way.'

'How can you be certain? Maybe she was ill. Or pregnant.'

'Pregnant?'

'A bad example. Like I say, any tiny thing you can remember about her may be enormously helpful. Any condition. Conditions are things you wouldn't share would you?'

She felt empty and forlorn. She tried to imagine her mother - tried to imagine herself fatter or with different hair. Or pregnant.

'There's nothing.'

Borilyenko seemed pleased. He lay his hands on his stomach and leaned back in his chair. 'I'm interested in what you can remember about Project *Simbirsk*. The experiments. The processes. Can you remember any of that?'

'I remember,' she said. 'I remember the objective. To manufacture a clone of Lenin from the DNA of his embalmed remains.'

The old man leaned over, his eyes glinting. 'And what do you remember about the success of those experiments?'

'We validated all of our findings with practical experiments. On rats. Everything in line with expectations. The final step was to clone a human being. It had never been done, even in the US. Let alone working with DNA samples that were over 50 years old. That was the ultimate plan, of course. We were ready to take the first step, I remember.' She looked at the old man and saw a fierce intensity. It took her back to Borilyenko's office in *Sorsk*.

'Why wait?' she remembered asking. We're ready. We just need a donor.'

'Some ethical concerns have been voiced. At a high level. We just need to satisfy all of those concerns before we can proceed.'

'What kind of concerns?' She had been protective of her project. Prickled at any hint of criticism or doubt.

'There's no need to concern yourself, comrade. In a matter of days, we'll get the mandate we need, and we will find you a donor.'

But it hadn't been a matter of days. Weeks passed without word. Lab technicians played chess and card games. Morale melted away.

'And so, your mother took matters into her own hands, and you are the result. Quite incredible. She was an exceptional scientist. One of life's pioneers.'

'That's how it seems to me.'

'But we could never have imagined that memories were somehow embedded in the DNA. What else? The soul? If there is such a thing.'

'We couldn't exactly interrogate the rats.' Her head was tight. She was making an effort now to block out her own memories, pushing away the here and now. To live inside the head of her mother. It gave her a head ache.

'So far as anyone knows you are the only clone of a human being in existence.' There was something of a challenge in his voice that caused her to wonder what he meant.

'So, is that what I am? A clone? A copy. Not a person in my own right? Property of the State.'

'You're much more than that, Kate. You are TWO people. Now Katya, think carefully. This is very important. Do you remember hearing about Project *Pustinja*? Project Wilderness?'

'I heard about it. I don't know what it was.'

'Yevgeny Peshevsky? Does that name mean anything?'

She felt like she had been connected with electricity - like she read the KGB might do for interrogation purposes. She tried not to register her shock. *A walk to the infirmary. Have you any idea what we do, up there on the hill?* She frowned. 'I'm not exactly sure,' she said.

'Think about it. Write it down—write everything down that you can remember. It wasn't part of your work, of course—I mean, your mother's work. But it helps to build a picture. Of those times.'

She looked at the scratched surface of the table. Borilyenko was thinking. At length he said: 'I apologise for the way you have been treated. The way you were brought here. Your driver. That's unfortunate. We'll make contact with his family. Some compensation, perhaps. And this—' He made a wide gesture, '—cell. You're not a

413

prisoner. Not exactly. But we'd like you to stay a while. To debrief. To rebuild what we know about your mother's research. And other things you might remember. Wilderness in particular.' He raised himself to his feet, placing a frail hand on the table. 'We'll move you to somewhere more comfortable soon. I'll see to it. We'll prepare somewhere you can work. In the meantime,' he nodded at the notebooks, 'it would help us a lot if you could begin to write down what you remember. About the project. About the science. About Wilderness.'

'Compensation? For Leonid?'

'If it's appropriate. The least we can do. A tragic accident.' He stood over her, waiting.

Leonid. *It's no problem*, she remembered with a stab of guilt. But it turned out to be a problem, after all. 'Surely you have your own records? Of my mother's work?'

'Sadly not.' He shook his head. 'Everything was burned. A long time ago. Nothing remains at all from those days. All destroyed. You saw yourself the state of that place. A terrible thing.' He waved a hand at her as he moved to the door. 'I'll see you tomorrow. Tell the guards if you need anything. Anything at all. Then we'll get you installed somewhere more pleasant.'

'You said pregnant.'

'I'm sorry?' He paused at the door.

'You said to tell you if I remember my mother being pregnant. Why did you say that?'

'I also said fat.'

'There's another one, isn't there? Another clone.'

He stood up.

'You are quite unique, Kate, I assure you of that. Please write down whatever you can remember. We'll talk again in the morning.'

And he left the room like a phantom.

Chapter Thirty-Eight

'I WARNED YOU about the girl, my friend,' said Lisakov, easing into a chair in Grigor's office. He looked relaxed.

'So it's about her? About Kate?' Grigor was leaning over his desk. The radiators clicked and muttered. 'Why the fuck would the KGB be interested in some girl from a village?'

'It's not my business to know that. Knowledge is a dangerous thing. This… situation is evidence of that,' said Lisakov. 'Anyway, she's out of reach. Yours and mine.'

'What does that mean?'

'Take it from me, you don't want to be mixed up in this.' He paused. 'She's in the Lubyanka.'

'She's where?' Grigor hadn't made up his mind how he felt about the English girl, but suddenly he was enraged and alert and he felt something churn deep inside.

'In the hands of the FSB. But more than that: she's been taken by General Borilyenko. Anyway, never mind about her now. We have our own situation. You and I.'

'Borilyenko? Jesus. And the bomb - I take it that was yours?'

'I'm sorry about that. Really. I could lie to you, of course. I could tell you we'll hunt down the perpetrators. We will anyway, if you report it. But you were a soldier. A practical man. You understand we can't question orders. Otherwise there'd be chaos. And I had instructions.'

'To kill me.'

'Not just you.'

'Who then?'

'Everybody. Your associates. No survivors.'

'And now what?'

'Yes, what now…? That's rather the question, isn't it? What happened in that place? *Sorsk*? I sent some people, who never came back.'

'We met them.'

'Lozik in particular was a good man.' Lisakov looked wistful.

'That was his name? The Ukrainian?'

Grigor plucked the Makharov from the desk, weighed it in his hand and pointed it at Lisakov, looking down the barrel and flipping off the safety with his thumb. Lisakov was still and unfazed. Grigor held the gun there for a few seconds, then lay it down again.

'I didn't know. That he was Ukrainian,' said Lisakov.

'So what do you suggest? Now?'

'Well.. We could have a war.'

'You brought some help?'

'Outside, of course.' He changed the subject. 'So what did you see on your excursion?'

'Not much. Burned buildings. Nothing I haven't seen before.'

'*Sorsk* was a closed town.'

'I know.'

'I've been trying to find out what happened there.'

'I thought that too much knowledge was dangerous?'

'The problem is, as your girlfriend is finding out, you can't *unknow* something. And I'm beginning to worry I already know too much. It was made very clear to me that I should forget everything I know about *Sorsk*. But like I said, we can't very well unknow things. So I've had a hunt through the archives. Top secret archives. I have clearance at the very highest levels. And I've drawn a blank. There's no file. No such place.'

'Looked to me like there was a thorough clean up.'

'Yes. But who did the cleaning up? There's no record of any operation like that.' He took up the previous conversation. 'So, we could have a war. I'm sure you're prepared too. That you've taken sensible precautions.'

'Just as you'd expect.'

'I think that's the outcome the General is expecting from this meeting.'

'Or?'

'Or we could cooperate.'

Not a prisoner... Borilyenko had assured her. But confined to a cell all the same. Finding it impossible to sleep on the iron bedstead with the thin mattress, she lay on her back, avoiding the prospect of the inevitable use of the bucket in the corner for her toilet. The light built into the wall just above the bed could not be extinguished. They had left her with a ceramic jug of water and cup on the shelf beside her, and the pad of paper and pencils.

She thought about Yevgeny, earnest and riven. She now knew how much courage he had needed to tell her about Project Pustinja. She remembered how many times he had come to her seeming to be on the brink of something.

'Katya. It's a pleasure. Not with Dima this evening?'

'Called to Moscow.'

Yevgeny seemed relieved. 'It's a good party.' Sipping his vodka like a fine wine and seeking something of interest to point out in the small crowded apartment. Shostakovich played in muted tones. 'Everybody's here.' But in reality there were notable absences, fearful of association with Sverdlov, who was marking his departure from *Sorsk* with a small celebration. 'Comrade Sverdlov is a good man,' he said.

'Do you think so?' she said, wary of entrapment.

'Of course. I've followed his work for a long time. I'm an admirer.'

'Comrade Sverdlov should be less outspoken, don't you think?'

'You mean about that Darwin nonsense? I thought after Stalin we were supposed to be more enlightened. Surely the modern view is more progressive? He expressed his view of religion in the context of Darwinism. So what? In fact there are people that say that Darwin purposefully left the door open for a religious interpretation.'

Katya drew away from Yevgeny. Did people openly express these views? Even whilst Comrade Sverdlov was discredited?

'But you think I'm reckless.'

'No, just… It can be unpopular to express support—'

'—for poor Comrade Sverdlov, you mean?' Yevgeny laughed. 'I'm sure in time the Party will recognise him for the genius he is. And if we can't engage in some harmless scientific dialectics, then what was the revolution about?'

Katya willed him to lower his voice. Instead he helped himself to another glass of vodka from a bottle on a coffee table, excusing himself as he reached past other guests. 'It's time we acknowledged that Stalin is dead.' He said in a voice that seemed to silence the room. In reality, faces didn't turn and conversations didn't falter. The world continued on its regular course around the sun.

'Please don't ever talk like this when Dima's here.'

'Sometimes I think you're a dangerous lady.' Yevgeny's voice was tainted with disappointment. 'Your association with Dmitry for example… our resident Party thug. As for me I always say what I think,' he said. 'There's nothing they could do to me. I wanted to talk to you about something… But maybe now's the wrong time. I'm tired,

Katya.'

'Dima's no thug,' was all she could bring herself to say. Then Sverdlov joined them. A tall, rugged man with a high, broad forehead. He was beaming and his cheeks were pink. 'Well my friends. Thank you for your support.' He put an arm around Yevgeny's shoulders and pulled him tight. Yevgeny was a head shorter than Sverdlov and it made him look like a child. 'Good of you to come, Yevgeny.'

She tried to sleep on her side, but she could still feel the ridges of the steel skeleton of the bed beneath the mattress. Poor Yevgeny - he thought his work made him invulnerable. He could say anything. But in the final reckoning it was his work that destroyed him. And her work? Did she even have a view?

'You're a geneticist. You must have a view,' said Yevgeny that night.

'I take the Party view,' she had said.

'Even the Party can't really decide. Hitler decided of course. He at least had a definitive view. About Darwinism.'

Sverdlov recognised the direction of the conversation and became fidgety. He had a very deep voice, full of self assurance normally, but she caught a waver in his tone as he said 'Let's keep the evening light.' Then he walked away, a little unsteady on his feet.

Yevgeny, the tragic Jew, driven like his father to develop more and more destructive weapons to support a system that they both doubted.

What more could Borilyenko want from her? She could see where his questioning might lead, and everything led to Yevgeny and the Wilderness Project. Pustinja. But she knew so little. Nobody knew anything. At least, nobody alive. So what would happen, after she told him everything she knew?

She picked up a pencil and knew that she had only to concentrate and the memories would come thick and fast. Withdrawing memories like files from the archives. She began to write. Ponderously at first, and then with a fury in cyrillic loops and curls that she had never learned to make, but that struck her as ornate and satisfying.

'*I was transferred from Moscow to the closed town of Sorsk to administer a scientific project, codenamed Simbirsk. Simbirsk was the town where Lenin was born, before it was renamed Ulyanovsk in his honour. The objective of the project was to create a successful clone of a human from the cells of Lenin's embalmed remains.*'

'Do you think it's even possible?' she remembered Colonel

Borilyenko asking. It was her first day in *Sorsk*. She had been allocated a comfortable two room apartment in *Karl Marksa* Street, and had left her bags unopened inside the door while Dmitry waited outside with the engine running to take her to the headquarters building.

'I wrote a paper on the subject, Comrade Colonel.'

'And I read it, Ekaterina Ivanovna. It was most interesting - but only theoretical. Do you think it's really possible to recreate a human being from the cells of another?'

'I certainly believe so.'

'And then there are other challenges that we theorists tend to disregard, if you don't mind me saying. Nobody has even begun to think, for example about the consequences. There may be moral questions. What do you think about moral questions?'

'I don't think about moral questions, Comrade Colonel. I leave such things to the Party.'

'And so you should. But even so, there are interesting dilemmas. Where is the repository of the so-called soul? Is it contained in a single cell? Can we, *should* we recreate dead souls? Can we influence the personality, the biological make up of a cloned human?'

There was a series of framed certificates and photographs on the wall of the office, and she saw that Borilyenko had a degree in physics from Moscow State University. She saw also that he had been made a Hero of the Soviet Union, and wondered what he had done to distinguish himself.

'You'll have every resource at your disposal. Anything you need, you only have to ask.' He leaned across the desk at her. She thought he looked evangelic 'You're about to make history, Ekaterina Ivanovna. How does that feel? More than that... you are going to *recreate* history. Just think of it: to bring back Lenin from the dead. A new Lenin. What do you think of that?'

'I think it's exciting work Comrade Colonel and I thank you for this opportunity.' She meant it, but it sounded trite. He didn't seem to notice.

'You'll find there are many scientific projects here at *Sorsk*. Most of them are much more mundane than your own work - but equally secret. You've met Comrade Dmitry Andreyevich of course. He 's probably explained already that he's the Commissar here - he does so at the first opportunity with any new visitor,' said with a forbearing smile. 'He'll be giving you the usual security briefing. This facility is top secret. I hope you'll find the community of *Sorsk* to be interesting and stimulating, but you mustn't on any account discuss the nature of your work outside of your immediate colleagues. Is that understood?'

'I understand, Comrade Colonel.'

'Good. Then your first task is to start to build your department. Anybody you need to work with you from outside - any specialists or technicians - just give me a list. We have a laboratory for you but it's a shell. You're the expert - you decide how it evolves. Make a list of everything that you'll require. I'll see to it personally.'

'Thank you, comrade Colonel.'

Afterwards, alone in the spartan apartment that smelled of wood shavings and mothballs, she stared out of the window at the empty street lined with spiky saplings and indulged herself in daydreams. She was so proud to be here. So proud to be chosen. And for such a project...

'*The principles of the research were at first firmly established in rats. After 2 years research we had successfully cloned sustainable living rats from skin cells.*' They named the first ones Gagarin and Titov, she recalled. Pioneers, like the cosmonauts. Unlike their namesakes however they were sadly short lived and had died within the week.

'*But the project had stalled because sanction was withheld for experiments with human DNA. We went nowhere with the project for weeks. There was resistance to the project from somewhere, but I wasn't told where.'* She wrote, and writing she learned, because it seemed that the memories flowed directly to her pen bypassing conscious deliberation. *'We had progressed to the point in our work where the only logical next step was to experiment with humans, I was frustrated because I knew that we were ready. That's when I decided I would be the donor, and that I would continue with my work in secret.'*

The nocturnal visit to the laboratory. Alone in the cavernous room with laminate faced work benches and rows of petri dishes, and a tiled floor that magnified every footfall. It was cold there at night and the harsh neon lights threw distinct shadows she had never noticed in the day. She must have paced the laboratory for hours, busying herself with minor tasks, fighting off the moment of decision. And then, preparations complete, she laid out the instruments on a sterile tray. The iris scissors, suture, needle, punch biopsy instrument... all set out in a neat row. Then the anaesthetic. The jolt of pain as she inserted the needle.

After that moment she remembered nothing at all. She had reached the buffer zone.

A key scraped in the lock and she guessed it must be morning. Her eyes were sticky but she felt an electric alertness. She put down the pencil and sat on the bed with her feet on the floor. A guard opened the door and stepped aside for Borilyenko to enter. He seemed more familiar to her than ever now, a memory ignited and burning bright.

'Good morning, Ekaterina Ivanovna.'

'I'd rather you didn't call me that. It's not my name.'

He was sympathetic. 'No. It's not. I apologise.' He seemed at a loss for a moment. 'Please follow me, Miss Buckingham.' And he turned and walked out. She followed him into the corridor, and they walked past a row of cells. The guard followed. 'I'm sorry you had to stay here overnight. Later we'll...' but he didn't complete the sentence. Instead, he opened a door and ushered her inside. 'Please,' and she recognised the room where he had questioned her the previous day.

She sat down at the scored table where she had sat before. 'I'm hungry,' she said.

'I'm so sorry. It's very thoughtless of me. I just wanted to get on. I was forgetting...' he turned to the guard and ordered him to arrange some food. He left at once, without saying anything.

Borilyernko was reading her notes, and she wondered how it was that she hadn't noticed him pick them up. There were several pages of closely covered cyrillic, and she was surprised at how much she had managed to write. He shuffled the papers and then lay them on the table.

'This is quite incredible,' he said. 'Your recollections are much more detailed than I would have ever imagined. And your Russian is… did you ever have lessons? I mean in England?'

'Just French. At school. And I don't remember much of that.'

'Quite incredible. I would never have expected…' He leaned forwards, his elbows on the table. He seemed to drift for a few moments. His skin was sallow in the artificial light, and there were folds in the skin of his face, like valleys. 'Even the grammar is perfect…' he mused. 'And after this you remember nothing.'

'After the laboratory that night. After the biopsy. There's just me. Kate. The other memories seem to just cut off, no matter how much I try.'

'I see.'

'When can I leave?'

'It's because those memories—your Russian memories—must have been contained in the DNA sample that your mother took. Your memories - your mother's memories in fact - were replicated, just like everything else. You're a complete clone of your mother, including her memories. Quite extraordinary.'

'You didn't really say, what happened to her. I'd like to know.'

'What I'd like to know - what I'd like to talk some more about - is whatever you can remember about Project Wilderness. It's very important, Kate.'

'I need to know what happened to her.'

Borilyenko got to his feet. He placed himself with his back against the wall, opposite Kate.

'I was sorry about your mother. But she brought everything upon herself. Her unauthorised experiment. But then to bundle off the result of her experiment to the West. Well you must understand that we couldn't allow that. When I say the result of her experiment - well that means you, Kate. Ultimately.'

She felt sick. The result of an experiment. What she was. 'So, what did you do?'

'Not me, Kate. First Dmitry. He was Commissar. We needed to find out how she had got the baby out of *Sorsk*. The route. The identities of the collaborators. But Dmitry of course was conflicted. In fact we reassigned him shortly afterwards. So, we had to send her here, to the Lubyanka. The KGB were given the task - to question her.'

'And then?'

'Sad to say, many records are incomplete of those sent here for questioning in those days.'

'But you must know what happened to her?'

'Many people do not survive the rigours of questioning.'

'They killed her? *You* killed her.'

She stood up. Gulped down a silent scream. Ekaterina Ivanovna.

'You must appreciate the position she put us in.'

Once in Trubanya Square there was a Palace, where now there is a vast, gloomy derelict house with sunken window frames and snowdrifts that hunker up to the walls. A moment's grizzled speculation and a glance over his shoulder and then Grigor kicked aside the timber doors and he led his men into a vast hallway. A spartan chandelier, empty of jewels, hung high above them. As their boots resounded through the empty rooms Grigor wrinkled his nose at the stench of urine and looked at the rubble and burst and abandoned mattresses all around. Vague shadows in military fatigues, weighed down with bulky sports bags followed.

'That room,' growled Grigor at last and he pointed the way through a broken doorway into what may have once been a library.

Splintered panelling and a network of empty slatted shelves lined the walls. The stone floor was littered with rubbish. They dispersed and drifted around the room watching their feet, no talking, looking for signs. Then in a corner of the room Grigor found what he was looking for.

'Here.'

One of the men set to work on a slab of flooring with a tyre lever, and soon it scraped aside releasing a foul breath.

'I'll go first.' Each man produced a mining helmet from his pack, and began to fasten battery packs for the lamps to their waists. All of this was carried out in silence. Grigor illuminated his lamp and descended into the hole, shifting his bag to his back. Vassily Gronsky had told Grigor that he had discovered this tunnel years ago through studying some archaeological books and making some deductions. There was a story that the master of the palace had built a subterranean passage to the Kremlin where he had carried on an affair with Tzarevna Sofia.

It seemed that as soon as his head disappeared below the surface his lungs contracted. The steps were steep and narrow and slippery beneath his boots so that he had to descend them as he would a ladder, face down, clinging to the wet stone as he felt below for the next foothold. His breathing became laboured. Above him he heard the echo of his comrades' boots and the rush of their breath. As he climbed he tried to direct his thoughts to Kate. What was she feeling now? Had she lost all hope?

For five minutes he climbed downwards. It felt as though he was entering an ice compartment. His clothes felt clammy. He shifted his bag with a shrug and a clang of metal.

Suddenly a voice rang out. 'Welcome Grigor Vassilyich!'

Grigor looked down and strained to fix the beam of yellow light in the direction of the voice. He caught a glimpse of a shadowy figure, then solid rock some metre or so below. He jumped the remaining distance, stumbling with a clatter on the greasy surface, but quickly regained his balance. The beam followed the movement of his head, skirting around what appeared to be a bell shaped cave with a high ceiling. Then it lighted on his friend, Vassily Gronsky. He was tall and wiry and wore a shabby Red Army greatcoat two sizes too big from The Great Patriotic War. On his head he wore a fur hat with earmuffs sticking out absurdly like rabbit's ears. A wreath of rope was slung over one shoulder. Over the other hung an AK47 secured by a length of string.

'You look like a *zek*,' said Grigor. A *zek* was what they called the prisoners of the Gulags. He embraced him tightly. At his back he heard the others leap to the ground one after another. The cave reverberated with the sounds of their boots and their breath, spiralling endlessly, turning upon themselves in the darkness beyond. There was steam on their breath that was thick and grey in the lamplight.

'We don't have much need for your western fashions down here,' said Vassily, not without bitterness Grigor thought. There was a hint of madness in Vassily's expression that may have been a trick of the light, but it made Grigor wonder for the first time whether Vassily might lose them in the labyrinth that he knew they were about to enter.

Grigor looked all about him, lighting up the entrances to passageways that seemed to head in all directions. Obviously the system had expanded since that single lover's pathway. 'Which way?'

'We'll head out first for the Neglinka River.' Said Vassily with confidence. He produced a wooden shaft with a lantern on top like peasants once carried. As he lit it, only then did it occur to Grigor that Vassily had been waiting down here for them alone in complete darkness. He fixed the shaft into an empty holster in his belt. 'Let's go.'

They followed him towards the mouth of a tunnel that redefined itself as the light played upon the shadows. Then for some 250 meters they proceeded sideways, crab-like, because the tunnel was so narrow, although it was at least four meters high so they were able to hoist their equipment onto their heads. Grigor felt the coarseness of the rock rubbing against his clothes, and when he looked down the lamp revealed that his tunic had acquired a slimy sheen. He tried not to think about the popular legend of rat-mutants in the caves below Moscow. Instead he tried to focus upon the plan. He tried to focus on Kate.

The slime on the walls down here was a peculiar yellow. Sometimes scraps of it fell upon them from above, disturbed by who knows what. Grigor picked a length of it from his shoulder and it felt like a length of soapy hair. He heard the others cursing behind him in low murmurs that had a harsh resonance, as they scraped through the tunnel until finally they emerged at another cavernous junction. This time there were other sounds, and other lanterns, and grotesque shadows flickered on the walls. Grigor looked around in bewilderment. It was a strange underground community. Vassily appeared not to notice them at all.

'We need to head over that way.' He said pointing. 'We'll pass under the Maly Theatre. Over there is where the tunnel joins with Metro-2.'

'Metro-2?'

Vassily glanced over his shoulder. 'Built in Soviet times. A secret metro system that connects to Vnukovo-2 airport, amongst other places.'

'I heard about it. Thought it was a myth.'

'The trains still run from time to time. You can hear them.'

'Who uses it?'

'Whoever needs to.'

'What about these people down here? Who are they?' A cackle rang out from somewhere, and a shout.

Vassily shrugged. 'Illegals. Dispossessed. Who cares?' Then he grinned, and Grigor caught a glint of madness again. 'Sometimes the militia do a sweep. But they've never come this far. My private quarters are not far from here.'

They passed odd people carrying out mysterious acts that they carried on in oblivion. Grigor noticed a woman stretched out naked upon a table, surrounded by black robed figures like jackdaws, muttering vague obscenities. The woman wore a black mask, and there were black candles burning around her.

'Satanists.' Vassily said in casual explanation over his shoulder. 'Sometimes I've known them bring children down here for sacrifice.' At the entrance to another wider tunnel, a bearded man with long greasy hair sat idly nursing a pistol. They passed him without comment. The caves seemed to whisper urgently all around them. Grigor glanced uneasily behind him. 'Wait.' He called, unhooking his bag and heaving it to the ground. The shuffling behind him stopped abruptly. Vassily looked back, waiting. Grigor stooped to unzip his bag and removed the weapon which he strung around his shoulder.

'Afraid, Comrade Major?' asked Vassily.

'Not afraid. Careful.' His men followed his lead and began to arm themselves. He heard the rattle of cartridges being inserted, checked. 'How far now?'

Vassily shrugged. 'Not too far.' He turned, holding his lantern aloft like a tourist guide. *This way for the Lubyanka tour.*

They proceeded in silence for about twenty minutes, tramping along the glistening tunnel. Grigor fixed his eyes on the ground, watching his step. Finally, brandishing his lantern before a huge door with a rusted lock Vassily stopped the column at last. He glanced at Grigor, as if in affirmation of something, then kicked at the door which submitted at once.

Further ahead the way had once been bricked up, but now there was a crumbling arch and lumps of masonry. Vassily picked his way through the rubble with exaggerated care, then trailed his hand along white stone as they walked, looking for a breach.

'Here!' He stopped abruptly and hauled off a broken section of the wall. Then another, a cloud of dust swirling in the light of the lanterns. Behind it was a rugged steel door, stippled with rust. 'This door will not have been opened for a hundred years at least.' He traced his fingers down the door as though admiring some artefact. 'We can have a go at the lock. Or we can just blow it away.' He looked at Grigor with his mad eyes.

There was restless scuffling behind him, the creak of leather harnesses of automatic weapons. 'Let's try the lock first. Yegor!' He called over his shoulder.

'Here boss.' The whisper was close to his ear and made him start.

'See what you can do with this,' ordered Grigor, pointing to the lock.

It took just a few moments for Yegor to release the lock, scrabbling with steel and complex instruments like a dentist. Then he twisted the handle, but the door wouldn't budge. He stood, put his shoulder to it, and finally it burst open sending guttural reverberations through the tunnels behind. 'We're in, boss.' Grigor sensed a collective intake of breath.

They emerged into a dimly lit pale green corridor with chipped masonry. At intervals there were wooden doors with square grilles. Their boots echoed starkly in the tiled passage.

'We're on the lowest level. There are 8 floors below ground. She's on six,' said Grigor, leading. 'This floor is unused.' They came to a sturdy pock marked door with two locks. Above it was an ancient Soviet made security camera. Grigor took the handle and paused. 'Now we'll find out if Lisakov can be trusted.' He opened the door. The hall was deserted. There were two steel elevator doors and doors that he knew led to the stairwell. Another camera watched them from the ceiling.

'What about these cameras?' Said Fyodr.

'I was told not to worry about them.'

'You have some pretty good sources, Boss.'

Chapter Thirty-Nine

HE WAS IN A dismal bar in Serafimovicha Street when Dikul called him on his mobile.

'What have you got for me?' said Nikolay.

'Sverdlov. There was an administrative error,' said Dikul.

'What kind of error.'

'He wasn't executed.'

'So he's alive?'

'Transferred.'

'Where is he now?'

'He was sent to Perm. Then in 1986 there was the General Pardon.'

'He was pardoned?'

'That's what it looks like.'

'So what happened to him?'

'He lives in Moscow,' replied Dikul.

After the call Nikolay slapped his glass on the bar and shrugged into his coat as he pushed through the doors into the street. He followed his own tracks in the snow back to his car, which had acquired a phantom like property beneath a thin, translucent layer of snow. He wrenched open the door with an alarming crack, had already half frozen shut. In the car, his breath steaming, he called Lebed and told him the news.

'Get to him. Make sure he's safe.'

'I'm on my way there now, sir.'

From the glove compartment he pulled out a map, and it took him almost ten minutes to find Borisova Street. It was hard to focus after half a litre. He closed one eye as he drove across town in a hurry, randomly changing lanes.

If Sverdlov had spent time in Perm he was likely to be a shell of a man. And how old now? Would he in fact be any use at all?

Borisova Street was a collection of grey blocks on the edge of town with precarious balconies some of which had been enclosed with windows. A deserted play park was situated in an open space in front of Sverdlov's block. Icicles hung from the swings. Only a handful of vehicles were parked along the street, and there was single set of tyre tracks passing by the building. He stopped right outside the entrance.

When he pressed the intercom there was no reply, so he stabbed at the buttons for other apartments until somebody simply buzzed him in without bothering to answer. In the damp concrete lobby he saw there was a row of tin postboxes and one was marked 'A I Sverdlov'. Somebody had sprayed a line through each mailbox, and a meaningless circle on the wall in blue paint. The paint was old and nobody had made an attempt to remove it. He tried to reach inside the flap of the mailbox but it was too deep. He pressed the button for the lift, and it made agonising progress. The doors rattled when they opened and he stepped inside, pressed the button for the fifth floor.

The door of apartment 512 had a brown fake leather fascia studded with buttons. He pressed the bell, then after a few moments banged on the door with the heel of his hand. He heard bolts pulled aside on the other side of the door, and then it opened to reveal a tall, emaciated old man.

'Andrei Illyich Sverdlov?'

The man squinted at him. 'Who are you?'

Nikolai held out his ID, and Sverdlov looked at it without much interest. 'A Chekist.'

'Something like that.'

'You're drunk,' admonished Sverdlov as he held open the door and Nikolay slipped inside. The interior was gloomy and had a raw metallic smell. There was no carpet and the sound of his shoes on the boards sounded vaguely intrusive. Balls of fluff moved in the draught. 'You want to see my papers?'

'No. Nothing like that.'

'What then? What do you want?'

Nikolay was ushered without enthusiasm into a small bare room containing two armchairs and a TV on the floor. One of the armchairs was worn and shabby. The other looked almost unused. He chose the unused armchair and sat down.

'It's about *Sorsk*.' It was very cold in the apartment – as cold as the lobby. Nikolay thrust his hands deep into his coat.

'*Sorsk*.' Sverdlov said without emphasis or recognition.

'You were a scientist.'

'I've been many things. Lately I was in geology. I broke rocks. Where was it you said?'

'*Sorsk*. A ZATO. A closed town.'

'A closed town. I wouldn't know anything about a closed town, would I?'

'It doesn't matter anymore.'

'If I knew about this place – what did you call it?' He leaned forward as though to hear him better.

'*Sorsk*.'

'If I knew about a place like that I might find myself back in Perm.'

'Perm is closed permanently.'

'Some other place then. They're all the same.'

'You have my personal guarantee...'

'The guarantee of a drink sodden Chekist? That's comforting. What use is that when I'm digging trenches with my bare hands?'

'I mean there are people at the highest levels...'

'They change like the wind. What did you say your name was?' Sverdlov stood up and went to the samovar on a primitive veneer cabinet. He put his hand to the side of the samovar and grimaced. Then he stooped and produced a half full bottle of Stolichnaya from the cupboard underneath. Nikolay was sure the gesture with the samovar was an act. It was tarnished and looked like it was rarely used. Sverdlov found a glass and slopped vodka into it without offering Nikolay a drink.

'You know this room is bugged?' he said, after drinking.

Nikolay looked around, feeling it was an unlikely prospect. 'Bugged?'

'Of course. You people. Now you're trying to trap me.'

'Nobody's trying to trap you.'

'I wasn't born yesterday. You're here to take me back, aren't you?'

'To where?'

'To Perm. Once a zek always a zek, eh?'

'Perm is closed.'

'My suitcase is packed. I always have it ready.' He had sunken eyes but they glinted with intelligence.

'Alexei Illyich, I'm not here to arrest you. Perm is gone. So are all those places. Since Gorbachev's time,' although he wasn't sure that was true. The labels changed but the confectionary tasted just the same.

'I'm not afraid.'

'There's nothing to be afraid of. I need your help. With *Sorsk*.'

'Never heard of it.' He poured himself another vodka. Lifted the glass in Nikolay's direction. 'Catching up.'

'Andrei Illyich, we know you worked there.'

'Show me your id again.'

Nikolai produced his ID and this time the old man squinted at it, holding it close to his eyes. Seconds later he handed it back.

'Impressive, Major. And not KGB. Different letters.' A bark to indicate irony, but without humour.

'The KGB was disbanded.'

'Not gone. Just hiding. Different badges. Different acronyms.'

'If you believe that, then you really must help me. Because you're right.'

Sverdlov put a finger to his lips and indicated the small room with a frantic gesture. Pointed at the door and rose from his seat.

'I think you should go now,' he said.

Nikolay went to the door and Sverdlov accompanied him outside. He locked the door with particular care, and they went down in the lift.

Out in the open Sverdlov walked fast with a wide, urgent gait, and Nikolay struggled at first to keep up.

'Where are we going?'

'For a walk. Away from prying ears.' They passed a row of run down shops. In the window of one was posted a picture of a line of leggy girls displaying the winning numbers for the latest Goslotto draw. There was a wooden kiosk up ahead and Sverdlov stopped and bought a half litre of Stolchnaya and some cigarettes. Nikolay stamped his feet to keep warm while he waited and hoped Sverdlov was the sharing kind. He needn't have worried as Sverlow took a deep tug at the bottle and passed it to him. The spirit slipped easily down, and it felt like kindling, lighting up his stomach. He reminded himself that he hadn't eaten. Sverdlov resumed his pace with a sidelong glance at Nikolay.

'Not discreet, are you Mr chekist? The question is, are you here to bury or to praise Caesar?'

'Not to bury,' said Nikolay, thinking that Sverdlov was an unlikely Caesar.

'I don't want to go back to the camps. If you're here to trick me, then you should question your humanity.'

'I'm not here for that either.'

There was a bench at the side of the deserted street, and Svedlov sat down. On the other side of the road a few spindly black trees stood out against the white landscape.

'Tell me exactly why you've come, Nikolay Sergeevich. No bullshit.'

'I need to find out about *Sorsk*. What happened there. Why they would burn it to the ground.'

'Is that what happened?' Sverlov passed him the bottle. It was half empty already. Sverdlov had eyes like oysters. 'I'm not surprised. It would have been the only way.'

'The only way?'

'I worked with Peshevsky on a biological warfare project known as Wilderness. Our task was to take the naturally occurring Ebola and Marburg viruses, and to genetically modify them. They're haemorrhagic fevers with no known cure, leading to internal and external bleeding and vomiting. With ebola death occurs in six to 16 days. It's a painful death. The disease is transmitted through bodily fluids, and this was not ideal for our purposes.'

'Didn't we sign up to the Biological Weapons Convention?'

'Of course we did. We signed up to anything to get hard currency. But we paid lip service. There were Military compounds all over the Soviet Union working on biological weapons programmes. Look at Biopreparat - this was a completely open, public agency for biological warfare! Military compounds produced hundreds of tons of Anthrax. Who the fuck cared about the Weapons Convention? Our task at Sorsk was to weaponise Ebola and Marburg. We were trying to genetically alter the virus so it was capable of airborne delivery. And the particular function of my department was to develop a vaccine.' He shook his head sadly, looking at the ground. 'I'm sorry to say I failed. But we had some minor breakthroughs. Ebola is a particularly virulent virus. Then I was transferred to Moscow. Which proved to be a euphemism.'

'So what happened? With the virus?'

'I don't know. Yevgeny's work was gathering momentum. But without a vaccine I thought it was a hazardous strategy. Made the mistake of saying so. So did Yevgeny, but you didn't question orders. And Colonel Borilyenko was an ambitious man.' He threw Nikolay a twisted grin. 'So they burned it? The City? Is that it?'

'I understand so.'

'Then I would suggest that maybe the project got out of hand. It would be the only way to eradicate the disease. To burn it. Once it was airborne... wilderness.'

'I think you should go and get that bag you packed,' and when he saw the sudden panic in Sverdlov's face he rushed to reassure him. 'There's nothing to worry about. Nobody's arresting you. But I think it may not be safe for you to stay alone in your apartment for a few days. You were right about Borilyenko. He was ambitious. Still is. Have you any idea what he's doing now?'

'I read the newspapers, Comrade.'

There was a scrabbling at the door. Not like keys but something else. Kate swung her feet onto the floor and waited, feeling sick. Her back ached and it was cold in the cell. Somebody pushed open the door and it slammed against the wall. She started. A bulky man in military fatigues filled the doorframe. He wore a gas mask, and a heavy automatic weapon hung by a leather strap from his shoulder. He threw something brown and ragged into the room, and Grigor's voice, suppressed but recognisable said:

'Put it on.'

'How did you…?' she picked up the ragged object and unravelled a gas mask.

'That will be the first thing they try. Gas. We would use Kolokol-1. I don't know what they'll use in here. Time to go Kate. Hurry.'

She pulled the mask onto her head, fumbled with the straps, and an eery isolation imposed itself. Grigor reached out to her, and she looked back once at the iron bed before being led out into the corridor. There was a huddle of men in the corridor wearing camouflage and masks like hers. Every movement resonated. Nobody paid her any attention. Guns spiked in all directions.

'That way.' She wondered how they knew. How did they get here? How would they get out? She allowed herself to be pulled along. 'Did they give you anything? Drugs?' She shook her head.

Far ahead she heard the sound of a pneumatic drill. Except she knew it wasn't that. A downward pressure on her shoulder propelled her to the floor. Her wrists stemmed her fall. They hurt.

'It's started.'

When she looked up she saw through the twin portholes of her mask a body in a pale blue uniform curled like a foetus at her level. The sawing sound she heard was the panting of her breath. Some people were shouting. A single gunshot was followed by another burst from an automatic weapon. There was a sour smell in the air that reminded her of bonfire night as a child. Boots thudded past her head, and she saw two men running up ahead, crouching. They reached the turn in the passage, stood with their backs against the wall. One of them threw something blindly around the corner. An explosion. More shouting. The men launched themselves around the corner and there were more bursts of gunfire. She tried to press herself into the cold tiles but found herself plucked to her feet like a package.

'Come on.'

A voice she didn't recognise said: 'We need to reach the stairs.

You need to run fast, OK?'

There seemed like many people surrounding her, but she thought that after all there were less than 10. Kit jangled and rattled. The edges of her goggles were steamed up, and threw her periphery vision out of focus.

'Everything will be OK.' Grigor's disembodied voice. Echoes of Leonid's reassurances. She tried to believe it. Her lips were trembling. He gripped her arm and they pressed forward.

They reached a door. Somebody kicked it open and sprayed shells into a hall. It was empty. There were elevators there. Grigor bundled her through the door, directing his weapon, suspended from its sling, with the other hand. He fired at the surveillance camera which shattered into fragments which clattered on the floor. Her hair was sticking to her brow.

'Can we go back to the tunnel? Or do we need to find another way?' somebody said.

'That's the best route. But we'll need to fight our way down the stairwell. Now's the time, before they bring in reinforcements. It's unlikely that they will use gas on the stairs. Let's do it.'

Two men were already pushing open the doors, tentatively. One of them threw something onto the stairs, where it skittered and bounced. Then silence. She watched them advance through the doors, one with his weapon pointed upwards, the other downwards. Nothing happened.

'I think it's safe for now Grigor.'

She felt herself thrust towards the doors. 'Come on,' said Grigor. 'Looks like Lisakov came good for once in his life. By now this area should be swarming with Chekists. Quick. Down here.'

She almost lost her footing once or twice as they hustled her down two flights of stairs, scuffing against the walls, heavy tramp of boots, clap of hands on gun shafts as they changed the direction of their aim. She was tall, but felt dwarfed by the men.

They crashed through the doors on the lowest level, and emerged into a passageway with black and white chequered tiles and rows of wooden doors with heavy iron locks. The fluorescent lights flickered. Then a single shot rang out. The returning fire was a deafening cacophony. A door was pushed open and she was pushed into a cell. The others backed in after her. Another series of shots rang out. Then silence. The cell felt stifling.

'What now boss?' She thought she recognised Fyodr's voice.

A hoarse voice said: 'Next they'll use gas.'

'We wait.' Said Grigor. 'We'll be hard to dislodge from here.

We're not in Grozny now. This is the centre of Moscow.'

'How will we get out?' she said.

'I'm hoping that there'll be an intervention,' said Grigor, 'but first we're going to have to defend our position for a while. I don't know for how long.'

'An intervention from who?'

'Your friend Nikolay.'

'We understand,' said Lebed at the other end of the line, 'that you have a situation at your offices.'

'I see.' Borilyenko was at his desk. 'And where would you have acquired this information?'

'Our sources are impeccable.'

'There's no situation here.'

'My sources tell me the Lubyanka is under siege.'

Borilyenko laughed. 'A siege, you say? I'd hardly call it that,' he said. 'A few militants managed to break though our security. Everything's under control.'

'A rescue party we're told.'

'I don't know where you get your information from. Who would they be rescuing?' the fresh implications were running thorough

Borilyenko's head. The leader of the opposition party in Russia had somehow found out about a misguided assault on the Lubyanka. That was bad enough. But what did he know about the girl? What could he infer about Sorsk? 'There are no princesses to rescue in the Lubyanka.'

'An English girl, I'm told.'

'An English girl?' how much did Lebed know? How much had leaked beyond the corridors of the Lubyanka?

'I think we should meet, General. Before this causes a diplomatic incident.' Said Lebed.

After an hour that seemed like a day, the lights went out.

'No torches. Use infra-red.' said Grigor. 'We'll see them coming if they use lights.

Kate felt claustrophobic inside her mask and with no light at all.

Fyodr heard it first. A soft hissing sound in the corridor.

'Here it comes,' he said. 'Gas. Like I said.'

Grigor whispered in her ear. 'Don't panic. I know it's easy to say. Trust that your mask will protect you. The darkness is to scare us. We have lights if we need them, and we have infra-red.'

'They'll give it 10 minutes for the gas to do its work, then they'll come.'

In the blackness her mind drifted. She worried about Becki. Where was she? Would she see her again? Why did Robert not answer his phone? What about Gold's son? Death was life's punctuation. Gave it its rhythm. Pauses. Questions. But never a full stop. She could die here today, she and her mother, and life would go on. But she wasn't her mother, even though she was grown from her cells. She knew it. For her mother she was no more than a memory store. Ekaterina Ivanovna didn't share her pain or her aspirations. Her life was over, but she had left a record in her daughter's genes. She knew she wasn't her because all she felt right now was her own raw fear, and not anybody else's. She dreaded her own loss but it was her loss, unique and strident. She was alone in the darkness.

Grigor? She wondered. What did he dread?

'You OK?' He said, as if awakened by her thoughts.

'When will it end?'

A scuffling in the corridor then. Occasional tiny sounds. A muffled footfall. A brush of clothing.

She didn't see the movement but she felt a disturbance in the air.

Then an explosion. The bomb in the hotel Rossiya. Like that. And white flashes. A sustained burst of detonations. Ringing in her ears. Tinnitus. Curses. A scream, rising and falling, like a banshee. Movement all around. Darkness, pressing in on her, amplifying the sounds. She pressed her back against the wall and it felt cold and hard through her clothes. More gunfire, the sound bouncing off the walls. A crash. An urgent shout. It seemed to last no time at all. Then silence and blackness, like a shroud descending. Becki. Her gappy smile. Her assertive manner. Where was she? Gold. The gunshot that brought down such a big man in a fraction of a second. She was tense against the wall. Then a hand touched her arm. The rumble of Grigor's voice.

'Now we wait again. Be brave Kate.'

Little was said in the pitch black cell. She felt afraid to be alone with her thoughts and tried not to think at all. But she kept seeing Yevgeny, the last time she saw him. He was waiting for her outside her apartment.

'Hi Katya. Do you have a few minutes?'

She was surprised to see him there. Surprised he even knew where to find her.

'I'm on my way to the lab.'

'Mind if I walk with you?'

'Of course not.' But she felt somehow cautious.

It was a bright day and she felt the pleasant warmth of the sun on her bare arms. Yevgeny was wearing a short sleeved shirt and Western blue jeans. She wondered where he bought them.

'My work is going well.'

'That's good to hear.'

'Too well.'

'That's bad,' she wanted to tell him to go away. She wanted to surround herself with ignorance. She wanted to unknow what he had told her that last time they took a walk on The Hill.

'The virus is airborne. We're trying to contain it. Experiments take place in an airtight environment. We're very, very careful.'

'Yevgeny… you shouldn't be telling me,' she felt an irrational anger at him.

'But still,' he went on, 'Sasha was put into the isolation ward yesterday. He has influenza symptoms. That's how it starts. Sasha's a technician. A friend of mine. Do you know him?'

'I don't think so.' She walked quickly, and he kept pace.

'Katya..'

'Yevgeny, what do you want me to do? This isn't my area. It's not my responsibility. I shouldn't even *know* about it.'

'A few years ago I ran an experiment. On the Moscow Metro.

458

We released an influenza virus.'

She stopped walking.

'On the Metro?'

'We wanted to see how quickly an airborne virus would spread. Just a harmless virus.'

'Somebody told me. A friend. Everybody seemed to have a cold one year. It was you?'

'We calculated that 87% of the population contracted the virus within 7 days.'

'Yevgeny…'

'Imagine if it was ebola and not influenza. Imagine if it was *my* virus. In London. New York. Here in fucking *Sorsk*, Katya!'

'You have to control it.'

'We're trying. And a vaccine - that's my number one priority. Sverdlov was doing good work on that. It was a catastrophe to lose him when we did. He was a genius.'

The memories were clear, but lacked definition around the edges. Some of the detail was absent. The colours. The sounds. Dreams had more depth.

Then the lights came on.

There were measured footsteps in the corridor. Figures around her came to life, cradling weapons, standing, kneeling. A voice from outside.

'Don't shoot. I'm here to talk.'

From Grigor 'Lisakov?'

'Who else?' the voice was calm. Self-assured. But muffled all the same, and Kate guessed he must be wearing a gas mask.

Grigor pulled one of his men away from the door and stepped out into the corridor. He had a large pistol in his hand, but she noticed he wasn't carrying his automatic weapon. She heard them talking.

'Is this your idea of cooperation?'

'I can't supervise every activity of the FSB.'

'They used gas.'

'You have masks.'

'So what are you doing here?'

'A negotiating team has arrived. Upstairs.'

'Who?'

'Lebed is here.'

'The politician? What the fuck has he got to do with this? What do you suggest we do?'

'I think you should leave the way you came. Fight your way back.'

'Fight?'

'I'll do what I can to ease your passage. But so long as Borilyenko is still in charge, I can't guarantee what will happen. You need to be prepared for anything. I'm here to formally request your surrender. I'll take the message back that you're considering our proposal. My men will be stationed beyond the doors. It means you can reach the tunnel without opposition, in all probability.'

'In all probability. Thanks for that assurance.'

'The best I can give you.'

When Grigor shouldered through the door he stood for a moment. Kate thought the mask gave him a look of melancholy.

'Let's get out of here.'

Hunched men straightened up in readiness. Equipment passed from hand to hand. Nobody said anything as they pressed through the doorway. Somebody placed a hand on Kate's back and urged her forward. She knocked her shoulder against the doorframe and felt a dull pain. Faster now, they moved down the corridor until they came to the door to the tunnel. Grigor hauled open the heavy door which scraped on the floor, then stood aside and motioned for each of his men to enter. Kate was last, and she felt him grasp her arm. He peered at her through the grotesque eyeholes.

'You know—' he began. She felt his grip tighten.

Then a sharp reverberation; Grigor's head whipped back. She reached to keep him upright, but he was too heavy, and he sagged to the ground. She tugged at his clothes. Another shot. Two more. She was trembling, eyes stinging. She heard her breath, shallow and sibilant. The smell of cordite seared her throat. Another shot, and she backed into the tunnel - saw Grigor's hand twitch on the tiles. Somebody was yelling from behind but she couldn't make out the words. Her face was wet inside the mask. She felt hands grappling with her, then pulled backwards. A bulky shape pushed past her and levelled a gun around the door. A deafening volley. She caught the swift movement of an arm, and there was a loud explosion in the corridor, followed by the patter of falling plaster. She backed deeper into the tunnel, and found herself propelled in the path of dancing flashlights into the darkness, her head full of Grigor, slipping out of her reach. From the corridor she heard a drawn out moaning, like a Muslim call to prayer. She recognised Fyodr's disembodied voice.

'Katya, we have to go. The Boss is dead.'

Chapter Forty

A PROCESSION OF glossy black vehicles stopped at right angles outside the main entrance of the Lubyanka. Nikolay hung back as Lebed, flanked by assistants and security men, converged upon the teak double doors, his coat tails flapping. Nikolay thought it looked like the arrival of a delegation from Washington.

The guards were expecting them but still made a show of examining papers.

'Don't you recognise me? Do we need to go through this charade? You must have seen me on TV,' said Lebed. The guard just handed him back his papers in silence and nodded towards the interior. When Nikolay passed through he exchanged a secretive smile with the guard that had held up the Great Man, and he barely glanced at

Nikolay's ID.

Their shoes stomped in the marble reception hall and their voices boomed. A single uniformed FSB officer greeted them at once, and directed them up an ornate staircase to the third floor offices.

They were shown into a wood panelled ante-room with chairs around the wall. A secretary sat at a desk to one side of a double door. She had sharp birdlike features and her fingers pecked at a keyboard, ignoring them.

The FSB officer accompanying them stood in front of her desk and waited. She sighed. Looked up.

'General Borilyenko is expecting…'

'Two men,' she said. 'Not this pack.'

'They're together.'

'Not in the General's office they're not. They'll have to wait there.' Still not acknowledging Lebed and his entourage, she stood up. She was tall and slim and Nikolay noticed that her nails were perfectly manicured. 'I'll tell the General they're here,' she said to the FSB officer, and opened both doors to enter the General's office, offering Nikolay a brief glimpse of a rugged mahogany desk and a hammer and sickle flag. The doors closed behind her. Lebed was fidgety. He looked at him.

'She better be quick.' But without much assurance.

Three uniformed officers entered the ante-room. Two of them took their places at either side of General Borilyenko's office and the other remained just inside the entrance door. Their faces were impassive and they avoided looking at anyone. Nikolay thought they were not regular guards: They were wide shouldered and poker straight and had a combative air about them. One had a purple discolouration over half his face. He recognised a red and silver ribbon representing the medal For Distinction in Military Service. A war hero.

The doors to Borilyenko's office opened again and the secretary emerged, followed by an FSB Colonel. The secretary resumed her duties.

'I am Colonel Kvitinsky.' He did not extend his hand, but stiffened just enough to acknowledge Lebed's rank. 'Please follow me - just General Lebed and Major Sokolov. Everybody else can make themselves comfortable here.'

'These men are with me,' said Lebed

'They'll wait for you then,' said Kvitinsky, turning back to the office.

'A town of 150,000 inhabitants,' said Lebed with incredulity. Outside the window the sound of the traffic undulated. 'Just wiped out.'

'Necessary casualties. The disease had to be contained at all costs. *At all costs*. I did what I had to do for the sake of the Soviet Union.'

'You did it to protect yourself General. Why was nobody else informed? Nobody in government. This was your dirty secret.'

'The KGB was a state within a state in those days. We looked after our own.'

'Even Comrade Andropov - the head of the KGB at the time. Did he know what was going on?'

'Not precisely. Comrade Andropov would not involve himself with day to day matters.'

'Day to day matter? A doomsday scenario?'

'It was contained. There were many incidents, in those days.'

'About the clean up operation,' said Sokolov. 'there's no record of such an operation at all.'

'It was of course classified. As many things were.'

'So far as we can tell it was not even known about by the Politburo. Not by Comrade Andropov himself. Nobody.'

'It would have been unthinkable to implicate the Party in such a thing. And I had everything under control.'

'So, what happened to the men that implemented your clean up solution?'

'After the operation they were redeployed.'

'Redeployed to where?'

'Oh look. It was a time of mass migration throughout the USSR. It was common for specialist troops to be deployed throughout the Union. Wherever they were needed.'

'But these particular troops? Where were they deployed?

'It was no more than a Company. Perhaps 200 men at most.'

'So what happened to them?'

'They were sent to assist our colleagues in the DDR. At Wismut.'

'The uranium mines?'

'Their expertise was invaluable there I'm informed.'

'How many survived.'

'It's not recorded.'

'So you were responsible for the deaths of 150,000 residents of Sorsk and perhaps the deaths of a company of specialist government troops?'

'Less than that. Much less.'

'How many people died in Sorsk?'

'It's not recorded.'

'Not recorded,' repeated Nikolay.

'It is also not recorded how many people would have died an agonising death if I had not implemented the necessary containment strategy. Throughout the USSR. Throughout the world perhaps. Not to mention the negative impact of the exposure of a mishap in our biological weapons programme.'

'A mishap?'

'An unfortunate set of circumstances.' He looked up at his interlocutors. 'Let's not forget this could have been a global environmental disaster with implications for all humankind. The outcome of not taking appropriate action cannot be exaggerated.'

'And *Project Simbirsk*?'

Borilyenko laughed. 'A naïve aberration. A pet project of mine, I have to admit. Soviet advances in DNA and genetic manipulation led the world. In secret of course. But the application of human cloning was unorthodox at that time. My idea to clone Lenin. Something of a personal crusade. Well. It could have been done. I've been proven right.'

'Because now you have your human clone.' Said Sokolov.

'That crazy bitch.' Said Borilyenko.

'Were there others? Other human clones?'

'It's not recorded.'

'It seems that for a scientific research centre not much of anything was recorded.'

'It's the nature of the kind of secret work that we carried out.'

'Tell us about *Project Pustinja*. What was the nature of the work exactly?'

'I can't tell you about that. It was classified.'

'We've talked about *Sorsk*. There'll be an investigation. It's my belief that you were criminally negligent.'

'Think what you want. You're too young to understand the imperatives of those days. The sense of duty. And what is there to investigate? A few charred buildings. The evidence of the daughter of a dissident? Will anyone believe this cloned memory fabrication?'

'I believe her.'

'But who are you? A war hero, I concede. But outside the army you're just some mouthpiece in an expensive suit. Maybe you made the most of your popularity. It's not the same as power. You're just a flawed legend.'

'Whereas you?'

'Whereas I'm still in charge here. Whatever it may look like.'

'And what about your connection to the *Feliks Group*?'

Borilyenko laughed. A cracked and mirthless laugh that left barely a trace on his features.

'A myth. Invented by dissenters and enemies of the state. My department has fully investigated this non-existent cabal.'

'Colonel Lisakov?'

'Amongst others.'

'He'll testify to the contrary.'

'I doubt that.'

Nikolay suddenly realised that Borilyenko was a sad and lonely old man, increasingly isolated.

'The real criminals,' he pointed to the floor, 'are down there.' I need to resolve our security issues in this building. So, if you'll forgive me…'

'Tidying up some more loose ends you mean?'

'I've heard enough.' Borilyenko pressed a buzzer and looked at the door, but nobody came. They waited and Borilyenko buzzed again.

'As I said. Lisakov will testify. I think he wants your job,' said Lebed.

'Lisakov. Who does he think he is?'

'In addition to the testimony of...' Nikolay hesitated, unsure how to refer to her, and felt awkward when he settled on: 'the former Ekaternina Ivanovna Borodina, we've located a reliable witness to the work that was being carried out on *Project Pustinja*, and to the former status of the closed city of *Sorsk*. We've enough evidence for the Prosecutor General to launch an enquiry.' He felt like a policeman, and found himself couching his words in a contrived, legalistic way that was not his own.

'What witness?' said Borilyenko, adding 'The Prosecutor is a good friend.' His tongue flicked out to moisten his lips in a manner that reminded Nikolay of a lizard.

'Andrei Illyich Sverdlov was a scientist engaged in the development of a vaccine for the virus that was being developed at Sorsk. The work on this virus was in breach of the Biological Weapons Convention.'

Lebed watched Borilyenko.

'Sverdlov was executed.'

'I'm afraid not, General.'

'He was a traitor.'

'Some would argue, a patriot,' interceded Lebed.

'It's impossible to condemn all of the judgements of all of the courts back then, just because of a fashionable hostility towards the

Soviet Union. Sverdlov was judged to a be traitor to his country. Do we need to cast doubt on the judgements of murderers also? The rapists? The thieves? You think all of the judges during those years were corrupt or incompetent? The man was a traitor and deserves to have been executed in accordance with the court's sentence. As for me - you think you can hold me accountable for a breach of the Biological Warfare Convention? No more than a Colonel at the time. You think I wasn't just obeying orders?'

'Why don't we let the President decide,' said Lebed. And at that moment the phone on Borilyenko's desk shrilled, making Nikolay start. For several rings the General seemed to ignore it. Then without taking his eyes away from Lebed he lifted the receiver.

'Borilyenko.' He shifted his gaze away at once towards the window. 'Of course Boris Nikolaevich. May I ask the nature…. No, no. I understand. I'll be there at once.' He lay down the receiver with exaggerated care. 'I have been summoned to the Kremlin.'

Lebed laughed without humour. 'And you're going? In the middle of a siege? In the middle of our meeting?'

The General raised himself up. 'The FSB will tidy things up. The President wishes to see me.'

'And what about our meeting?'

'You mean interrogation.'

'If you want to call it that.'

'I've had enough of it for today.' He flapped his hand at them and walked to the door.

Nobody tried to stop the General leaving his office. Nikolay heard a flurry of activity in the ante-room. Some barked instructions.

'That went well,' said Lebed, after the door had closed.

Somebody must have led them back through the tunnels, but she had no idea who. The anaemic light from a flash lamp danced ahead, casting cameos in the darkness. She was surprised to see there were other people down here, huddled in crevices, bulked up in heavy clothing. Muttering unintelligible greetings or imprecations.

Hobbling on the uneven surface, she reached out a hand to steady herself now and again, then pulled back her hand, repelled by slime or debris. She wondered if they resented her for the death of Grigor. It was her fault. When she felt a hand on her back, prompting her, she wondered if it wasn't a shade too unrestrained, betraying more than just impatience. The guilt attached itself to every small thought and gesture. Grigor had come to rescue her, and now he was dead.

Nobody spoke, unless you counted the occasional curse when

toes were stubbed or hands were scraped. Sometimes metal jarred or scraped against the walls, and she thought that it was their weapons that did this, whenever the passage narrowed. They pressed forwards.

She was glad to be rid of the gas mask. Even the foetid air down here was fresh compared to the mustiness of the mask. It was very cold - her fingers throbbed but when she thrust her hands into the pockets of her jacket she felt unsteady. And when they emerged from the tunnel, what then? It wasn't over. No final resolution. And her misrememberings, no longer misremembered, were with her forever. A life pre-lived that wasn't in her power to dismiss. Her mother's life. The gleam of the bowl of the samovar.

Two of the men fell back at intervals, nervous about an assault from behind, then rejoined them in a rustle and jangle of equipment and heavy footfalls, flash lamps playing erratic patterns on the stone walls. She imagined once that she heard the rumble of a train.

What time would it be now, out there in the real world? What time in England? She wished she wore a watch. She couldn't return to the hotel, like nothing had happened. Would they be waiting for her? Her feet ached.

The man in front stopped, and held up a hand. Somebody shined a light on him and she saw he had a ragged grey moustache and a washed out monochrome face. Unlike the others he wore a mangy fur hat with a red star, and a long coat. She had never seen him before. Everybody listened to the silence, broken only by the sounds of breathing and the faint scrabbling of a small animal. She shuddered at the thought of rats down here. There must be rats out there in the darkness, beyond the range of their torches. Somebody trained a light in the direction they had come, and it revealed an empty void. Then they moved on.

When they finally hauled her from a hole in the ground, like Alice she thought, the world was so stark and white and loud she had to blink. The sun was hot on her face, and light bounced off the snow banks along the walls. A toothless, bearded old man wrapped in a plastic sheet sat propped in a corner on a pile of snow watched them without displaying much interest. He was nursing an empty vodka bottle. The faces of her companions had acquired a new vibrance, brought into sharp relief in the sunshine.

'No reception party,' said one.

'What did you expect? Nobody knows about this place. If they come for us it'll be through the tunnel. And it's a labyrinth down there.'

The men seemed to mill around, lacking purpose. She started to say: 'Grigor…' and it was Fyodr who looked at her with a blank stare that she didn't know how to return. She thought that the impetus seemed to have drained out of him and all of them, and they stood around the ruined house thoughtful and morose.

'What do we do now?' she said.

A short stocky man with closed cropped hair hoisted a rucksack onto his back. 'We load up the cars and get out of here.'

'And go where?' said another.

'Wherever we go, they'll be waiting for us now.'

'Grigor would know what to do.'

'Fuck Grigor.'

'Yes,' agreed Fyodr. 'Fuck him.' And they observed a respectful stillness for a few moments. Kate thought about Grigor's body in the cellars of the Lubyanka and wondered if they had removed it. Fyodr shouldered his weapon and ran a thumb through the shoulder strap. 'Let's go.' He said, and she followed them to where a short line of SUV's were parked in the road. Somebody began to throw kit into the rear of one of the cars, where it landed with a thud and a clink. The oblivious Moscow traffic buzzed and growled and breathed malevolent fumes into the air. A horn sounded, but not for them. She felt all washed up. A heavy hand on her shoulder, and when she looked it was Fyodr.

'It's not your fault,' he said, speaking to her thoughts.

When she spoke it surprised her that she choked on her words. 'Whose fault is it, then?' Her eyes were moist. Maybe from cold or from the shock. She thought about Grigor.

'We'll wait for them at the Club,' he said, and he helped her to climb into the back of a huge Toyota. 'Everything will be OK,' he said, pushing the door closed. Leonid again. Another life lost.

Chapter Forty-One

A BLACK MERCEDES awaited Borilyenko in the courtyard, issuing two perfect plumes of exhaust from its tailpipes that sailed away in the cold air. A uniformed driver opened a door for him. He wondered how much the President already knew. He wondered how to take care of Lebed. What was the strength of his position? He sat back in the supple leather.

'Let's go,' he said, and wondered what the driver was waiting for. 'The President hates to be kept waiting.' He didn't recognise the driver. He looked at the square shoulders and the shaven neck, and leaned forward to make himself heard. Then the other door opened and somebody slid in beside him, pulling the door to.

"Good afternoon General,' said Lisakov, removing his gloves.

'What are you doing here?'

'Drive,' said Lisakov, and the driver responded at once, pulling forward with a powerful jolt. Lisakov spoke with brisk authority. Borilyenko slumped, feeling the spirit drain out of him. He had waited a long time for this moment, and it was accompanied by what was almost a feeling of relief. 'I regret to inform you General, that you are under arrest.'

'On whose orders?' but he knew already. There was only one man in Russia that could issue orders for his arrest.

'Surprised? Surely not.'

'I'm an old man. There's nothing left to surprise me. Are we going to the Kremlin?'

Lisakov shook his head. 'Lefortovo Prison.'

The very name of Lefortovo struck terror into the hearts of all who were taken there. But not into the heart of Borilyenko. Not today. 'Do I get to meet with the President at least?'

Lisakov's profile, he thought, was not a worker's profile. He had an aristocratic look about him, an association of privilege. He did not have the look of an executioner, but he knew he was a dangerous man.

'Not for me to say,' said Lisakov.

'What *is* for you to say?'

'Only that you will be required to answer questions about certain allegations.'

'About *Sorsk*?'

'I'm sure Sorsk will feature in discussions.'

The Moscow traffic was at a standstill on the inner ring, and stationary vehicles flashed past as they sailed down the middle lane reserved for official cars. In the other direction cars swarmed around a broken down truck, belching black smoke. Their driver had attached a flashing blue lamp to the roof.

'Am I permitted to learn the origins of these allegations?'

'In time. They won't come as a shock to you.'

'Lebed of course.'

'I've been tidying up, General. Just like you. The gangster that was protecting the girl is dead.'

'Good work.'

'As for the girl - I think we'll repatriate her.'

'You think it's wise?'

'It doesn't matter what I think.'

Borilyenko craned his neck to look out of the back window. He felt stiff and lethargic. 'This isn't the way to Lefortovo.'

Lisakov sighed. 'The prisoner, escaped our custody on the way to be interrogated.'

Everything felt strangely detached, as though he were watching events unfold from the sideline. 'You intend to kill me?'

'No, General. That's not my current intention.' He glanced at him. 'The girl will be our insurance policy, of course. And Peshevsky.'

'Insurance against what?'

'Against your return, General. I'm taking you to the airport.'

'What about Lefertovo?'

'My little joke. I hope you'll forgive me. You're fortunate, Comrade General, to have friends in high places. The Government is in a weak position today. It can't afford another scandal. Not of this magnitude. You would be notorious.'

'Notorious?'

'The extermination of an entire population. I would call that notorious.' He thought he detected a hint of humour. 'And then of course there are your other activities.'

'Other activities?'

'The *Feliks Group*.'

The engine of the Mercedes undulated as the automatic gearbox churned up and down. Borilyenko tried to think of something to say. It was useless to deny anything. Everybody talked eventually. Lisakov said: 'We've known about *Feliks* for a long time. Practically since the beginning. And we've been observing with interest.'

'I don't understand.'

'Comrade General, you know the system better than anyone. Everyone spying on everyone else. Lebed thought he'd stumbled on some epic secret that would remove you from whatever succession plans the President may have had. So he commissioned the other team to uncover your links to *Feliks*. But he didn't discover anything new. The President already knew what was going on. The organs are aptly named. They're part of the tissue of the state. It's like a biological system: Every function interdependent. We know almost everything. I can tell you for example about the contents of your Cyprus bank accounts, your property in Barcelona, your links to organised crime. There are no secrets. You think we're amateurs? Not like the KGB of your era, maybe. Different. Maybe better in some ways. Worse in others. Your precious Soviets failed to make the collective farms work, but they discovered collective policing, and it's acquired a life. A life of its own. When they founded the police state they made spies of all of us. But the *Sorsk* business. That was a surprise. You kept that a secret for a long time. I commend you, General.'

'So if you knew about Feliks why didn't somebody stop us?'

'It suited everyone to have a bogeyman. It was useful. The oligarchs are out of control. They need to be reined in - and not by the Government, which can't be seen to trample on the free market. You did a good job, and we tried to support you whenever we could. Cleaning up after you, as it were.'

'Why does *Sorsk* make any difference. Such a long time ago. All such a long time ago.' He ruminated.

'I'm no politician, General. I have no ambitions in that direction. But I understand how *Sorsk* might have an *international* flavour to it. How would it look to the Americans, for example - the nature of your work back then? What if it became known that you'd murdered an entire community in a cover up? Sadly the American view has become increasingly important to us. So, you'll understand that the President could not allow you to occupy public office - especially with political pretensions.'

'What now?' the car was already drawing up at the airport terminal. Muffled up families tugged wheeled luggage to and from the taxi rank, bent against the cold wind.

'We understand you have a delightful villa in Barcelona.' He withdrew an envelope from his pocket. 'We've taken the liberty of booking you onto the next Aeroflot flight. One way. Your ticket's here.

Your passport is also in the envelope. Just a word of warning: you'll have company out there. Nice assignment for somebody in our business, don't you think? Just to watch over you. Think of them as a security detachment, looking after your welfare.' The driver opened Borilyeno's door. Lisakov leaned across the seat as he got out. 'Boris Nikolaevich sends his regards, and wishes you to enjoy your retirement in the sunshine.'

He wondered for a moment about *Project Simbirsk*. That should have been the true legacy of *Sorsk*. He was about to lean back into the car to ask, but the Mercedes was pulling away. He could see the back of Lisakov's head. He didn't even merit a glance backwards. His coat thrashed in the wind and his cheeks were numb. A freezing snowflake slipped down his collar and Moscow wished him a chill-breathed farewell as he turned towards the glass doors, contemplating the nature of memories.

She left a pink imprint on a paper cup as she sipped at a scalding latte, taking care to keep her bag close, and with one eye on the departures boards. Her flight was delayed of course. They were playing Gangsta's Paradise in the background, above the rattle of the baristas' jugs and spoons. Sheremetovo was a cosmopolitan compound and Moscow stopped at the perimeter with its exhaust tainted breath.

The copy of Pravda she'd been reading reported the departure of Borilyenko from his role as head of the Presidential Security Service to enjoy a 'well deserved' retirement. The President acknowledged the 'breadth and competence' of the General, and thanked him for his years of service. The appointment of an unknown and recently promoted General Lisakov barely merited a line at the tail end of the article.

The chair opposite was hauled back and she looked up.

'Hello, Kate,' said Nikolay, and the pull of Moscow gave her a jolt.

'They said I was free to leave,' she said, putting the newspaper aside.

'Free? Of course you're free,' he said, before understanding. 'Oh, I see. You think I'm here for you?'

'Aren't you?'

He sat down, folding his coat and laying it on a vacant chair. 'No. Nothing like that. I've been posted to Barcelona. At my request. A position has become unexpectedly available. My good fortune.' He placed a polystyrene cup on the table. 'If that's what it was,' he added. 'I'm really pleased to see you. You don't mind if I join you?'

'It's your country.'

'Yes, it is, isn't it? And I can't help feeling ashamed of it sometimes. At other times… well, I'm a Russian after all.'

She turned her face away. She didn't know what to say to him. Without Nikolay things could have ended differently, she supposed.

'They gave you a hard time?'

'Not especially. In the end it wasn't about me. It was about Wilderness. I'm sorry, but I'm not allowed to say—they made me sign.'

'Of course they did.' He dipped his head and drank some coffee. 'So what now?'

'I'll see my daughter at last. She's been with her grandparents, all this time. Since … anyway she's in bits. She loved her father. I'll miss him too.'

'I'm sorry, of course. About your husband.' And she didn't bother to correct him. 'So difficult to know what to say. Without knowing him. What will you do? When you get back?'

'They've been generous. The Russian government. On condition that I don't talk about… well about anything.'

'That's good.'

'I don't understand how they could let him get away it. Robert was a good man. So many people... There was Grigor too. Even him— he was a good man too. In his way—' but she welled up and found she couldn't talk any more without betraying herself. A wide hipped waitress in a stained white apron clattered crockery as she loaded a tray of empty cups and debris at the next table. She added: 'I suppose I should thank you.'

'If you think so.'

She fixed her attention on the monitor displaying columns of constantly refreshing flights. 'I don't feel like I'm anyone any more. I feel like I'm in somebody else's body.'

'That must be... strange.'

'What's strange is feeling like I'm not a real person. Like somebody invented me. Like Frankenstein's monster. Property of the State. That's what Borilyenko called me.' And as her eyes became blurred with the onset of tears she caught a man and a woman watching her too closely in the reflection of a mirror. It hardly surprised her. She would never be alone again, in her head or on the street. 'Property of the State,' she repeated.

'I guess it's something you'll have to learn to live with. I don't know how that must feel. I guess that nobody does.'

'He said something else too. Something I've been thinking about it a lot. He wanted to know if I remembered my mother being pregnant.'

'Pregnant?'

'Yes. A strange thing to say.' She felt swollen with frustration and emotion all at once.

'What do you think it could mean?'

'I think there's another one. I think they used the work my mother did, and they went through with it. They made a clone of Lenin.'

He laughed. Then, 'Your flight…' he said, with a gesture towards the departure board.

She saw in the reflection of the mirror the man and woman gathering their coats and bags and checking their boarding passes and knew she would never be truly alone again.

Epilogue

HE MISSED NADEZHDA. To other people he knew it would seem odd to miss a person he'd never met, but for him it was normal. Nadezhda, the spouse of his benefactor. Beautiful a long time before the sickness ravaged her, but even the bulging neck and swollen eyes which were the hallmarks of Graves disease were dear to him now if not attractive. He thought he needed her practical, forthright nature to make him whole. He longed to ask for her advice. The wife of Lenin.

He liked to walk beside the lake, in summer and in winter. They'd rented a rambling place for him outside Zurich with a small mooring and a broken-down boathouse. A half-immersed dinghy floundered at the end of a rusty chain, like a mournful mongrel. In summer he would swim off the jetty for hours, and his security detail would watch him through binoculars when they could be bothered. He was embarrassed by them when he went into town. They were boorish Slavs who wore army boots and had shaven scalps that marked them out as soldiers or policemen amongst the quiet suited bankers and the designer set. He was grateful they didn't sit at his table in the cafes, but took a table to themselves where they grumbled in Russian and ordered their vodka and zakuski and no longer needed to explain to the waiters what that meant. They watched him eat with disinterest. He ate alone. There was no space in his life for companions. Instead he read about love and friendship, and that would have to do.

Sometimes, tantalised, he lingered in Spiegelgasse and took a turn past number 14, close to the now rotting Cabaret Voltaire that the record said he had never visited - although he alone knew that Lenin was a Dadaist. Could anyone seriously doubt that his hand was behind the Dada Manifesto, that most nihilist of anti-artistic pronouncements?

A simple plaque recorded that Lenin had lived in the apartment at number 14 from February 1916 to April 1917. Above a butcher's shop, now gone, so that if he had lived here today he would not have had to keep the windows closed during the day because of the smell of carcasses.

The General promised him one day he would go home. There would be street parties and banners, and statues would be erected in his image. But Zurich was his home, not Moscow, and he could live without the statues. There had been enough poor effigies of him created to last an eternity.

It was his destiny to lead Russia again, the General had told him, but he didn't think much of destiny. He'd read all the speeches that he dimly recalled writing, and they left him feeling anxious and morose. He didn't want to destroy state or society – or indeed anything. He preferred Pushkin to Marx.

The General behaved like a father to him, like Pinnochio's Gepetto. He sensed he was ashamed, but like Pinnochio he couldn't help his true nature. Perhaps he was the man that Vladimir Illyich never had the courage to be. Now that the General was in exile in Europe he feared he would be a more frequent visitor, embroiling him in his conspiracies, preparing him for an office to which he had never aspired.

It began to rain, and he turned up his collar. The lake rippled with rainfall, disrupting reflections of black boned trees, trees that shed heavy tears into the water, but not for him. He was not Lenin, even though he shared his head with Lenin's memories, and he was happy

with who he was. Vladimir Tupovsky. No need for patronymics. After
all, he had never had a father.

Printed in Great Britain
by Amazon